NATIVE

MANIFEST DESTINY, BOOK 1

NATIVE

MIKE J. SPARROW

FIVE STAR
A part of Gale, a Cengage Company

Farmington Hills, Mich • San Francisco • New York • Waterville, Maine
Meriden, Conn • Mason, Ohio • Chicago

This novel is a work of fiction. Names, characters, places, and incidents are either the product of the author's imagination, or, if real, used fictitiously.

LIBRARY OF CONGRESS CATALOGING-IN-PUBLICATION DATA

Names: Sparrow, Mike (Mike J.), author.
Title: Native : Manifest Destiny, Book one / Mike Sparrow.
Other titles: Manifest destiny, Book one
Description: First edition. | Waterville, Maine : Five Star Publishing, a part of Cengage Learning, Inc., 2017.
Identifiers: LCCN 2017018158 (print) | LCCN 2017029960 (ebook) | ISBN 9781432835729 (ebook) | ISBN 1432835726 (ebook) | ISBN 9781432835675 (ebook) | ISBN 143283567X (ebook) | ISBN 9781432835903 (hardcover) | ISBN 1432835904 (hardcover)
Subjects: LCSH: Lakota Indians—Fiction. | Indians of North America—Fiction. | Whites—West (U.S.)—Relations with Indians—Fiction. | Indians of North America—West (U.S.)—Government relations—Fiction. | Manifest Destiny—Fiction. | Political corruption—Fiction. | Frontier and pioneer life—West (U.S.)—Fiction. | GSAFD: Western stories.
Classification: LCC PR6119.P375 (ebook) | LCC PR6119.P375 N38 2017 (print) | DDC 823/.92—dc23
LC record available at https://lccn.loc.gov/2017018158

First Edition. First Printing: October 2017
Find us on Facebook–https://www.facebook.com/FiveStarCengage
Visit our website–http://www.gale.cengage.com/fivestar/
Contact Five Star™ Publishing at FiveStar@cengage.com

Printed in the United States of America
1 2 3 4 5 6 7 21 20 19 18 17

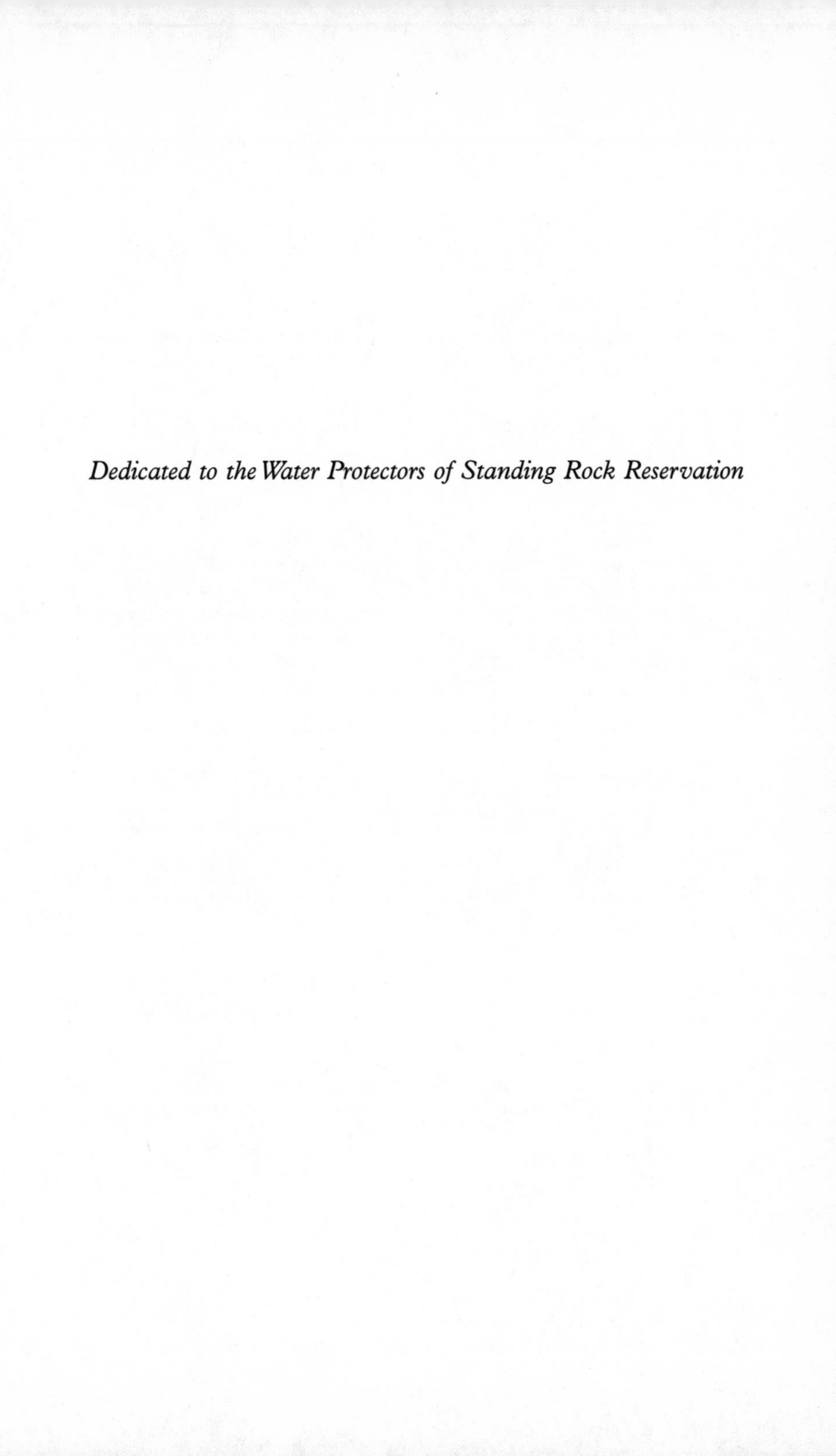

Dedicated to the Water Protectors of Standing Rock Reservation

ACKNOWLEDGMENTS

The author would like to extend particular thanks for the advice and guidance provided by Larry Swallow of Pine Ridge Reservation in contributing to a deeper understanding of Lakota culture, history, and traditions. My thanks also to Larry's wife, family, and friends for their welcome and love. Blessings to all.

PREFACE

The story of the indigenous peoples of North America is fraught with tragedy, and reflective of much of humankind's intolerance, greed, and destructive influence. Sadly, much of tribal history and culture is undocumented and, sustained by word of mouth over past centuries, is threatened with passing beyond the memories of those who remain today. However, in a world where the growth of human population and associated industrialization presents unprecedented challenges to the preservation of biodiversity and our natural environment, there is much that the ancient traditions and beliefs could teach us about how to care for our "Mother Earth."

Part of raising awareness of the value and wisdom of native teachings is to tell their story, and to tell it in a way that engages the reader, through colorful, authentic characters and relevant historical context.

Native is centered upon the Lakota, whose battle to save their ancestral lands and preserve their cultural heritage and traditional way of life is often represented in depictions of conflicts like the Battle of Little Bighorn or the Massacre at Wounded Knee. However, although important events in their own right, the systematic persecution of the Lakota, among many other tribes, should not be simplified or trivialized by individual events. It is without doubt that the rights and obligations enshrined in the Fort Laramie Treaty of 1868 have been, and continue to be, disregarded. Today, residents of American

Indian reservations suffer the consequences of discrimination, poverty, and social deprivation inflicted by near extermination of the plains buffalo, relocation to reservations, and a devastating enforced boarding school's system.

The three-part series, Manifest Destiny, of which *Native* is the first book, is set in a representative historical context, although the timing and detail of events has been adapted to fit the storyline. The characters are fictional and are not intended to depict real people.

It is the author's hope that *Native,* and the Manifest Destiny series, will entertain but also provoke readers to cultivate a greater awareness, empathy, and respect for indigenous tribes. All proceeds from *Native* are donated to furthering the future welfare of Lakota youth.

Chapter 1

September 1864, along the Greybull River, Dakota Territory

The animal's ears rotated back and forth in agitated frustration. He sensed the presence of the hunter, holding his head high and pausing with increasing frequency to listen. His antlers stretched a full twelve feet from the ground to the tip of the highest tine, and the bulge of his shoulder and girth of his neck were swollen in preparation for the impending rut. Copious quantities of fluid seeped from his preorbital glands and ran down his face in a sticky slick, whilst the exposed whites of his eyes lent him a wild and haunted appearance. But the majesty of his stature was enough to take the breath away.

In keeping with tradition, the hunter had risen to greet the Morning Star, which heralds the coming of the sun and the start of each new day. He had thought of his father, who had spoken to him of his father before him, explaining the story of the creation of the world and the sacrifice of the four-legged beasts, who agreed to give their lives so that the two-legged could have strength and prosper upon the earth.

He had paid homage to the Creator and sung a song passed down through the generations:

> Kola le miye cha, He wau welo, Anpo wiki etan,
> He wau welo.

(Friend, this is me and I am going there, I am from the Morning Star, and one day I will be returning there.)
Ate, Wau welo he Wociciya kin kta cha wau welo he, Wamiyanka yo, Wau welo he yo.
(Father, give me a special kind of wisdom. As I mix my blood with Creation, I will be going there.)

As he had sung, the image of a successful hunt had formed in his mind, and he had felt gratitude in his heart for the blessing of food for his family and the other members of his band.

His prayers and observance of the tribe's time-honored ritual had ensured that he felt thoroughly prepared when he left the village to embark upon the hunt. He would be patient and thoughtful, diligently employing the skills he had acquired over years of training and the knowledge passed down to him through the memories of his ancestors.

He had glimpsed the bull elk at the first light of dawn, grazing at the fringe of the dense forest of ramrod-straight lodgepole pine that shrouded the mountain range his people called "Never Know Summer" because of the year-round snow that capped its thirteen-thousand-foot peak.

As the sun's rays had filtered across the eastern ridge of the valley, the outline of the bull had sharpened, and his immense size had become clear. His shoulder was the height of a man's head, emphasizing the depth of his chest, and he moved with casual indifference, exuding the power of an animal in the prime of its life, certain of his own strength and dominance.

Careful to remain concealed, the hunter watched the bull drop his head and lurch, a profuse stream of urine shooting across his stomach and spraying between his front legs, drenching the long dark hair that accented the underside of his neck.

Then, the animal fell to his knees and writhed in a dusty hollow.

Each year, as summer merged into early autumn, the hunter witnessed with awe the intense physiological changes that prepared the bull elk for the rut. A mature male could add three hundred pounds in weight, and once his new antlers had grown to their full span, they would shed their velvet to reveal the pure white of the massive calcified beams, cups, and tines.

Pawing the ground with his front hooves, the elk would form a wallow in which to transfer the secretions from his eyes to the mane around his neck and shoulders, combining it with the musky ammonia of stale urine to create the potent essence that helped him attract and build his harem. It was this display that the hunter had witnessed.

The elk had been on the opposite side of the valley, and as wisps of wind flicked gently against the back of his head, the hunter had realized that his scent would easily carry to his quarry, unless he retraced his steps and crossed over to the treeline downwind of his original position.

He moved slowly at first, careful not to break cover until he was nearly half a mile from the elk, where he could traverse the open ground of the valley floor without being seen. With the wind in his face, he moved soundlessly and with surprising speed, the early-morning sun on his left hand as he jogged south hugging the treeline.

The forest floor was dry and littered with a detritus of pine needles, branches, and brittle grass, scorched by the intense sun of the sweltering summer. For most people, the clutter of dry undergrowth would have rendered silent movement an impossibility, but the hunter's people had named him O'hiniya he Mani, Walks on Air, following a life-threatening chase, during which he had succeeded in evading the determined pursuit of a column of infantry intent upon his capture, assisted by three

Pawnee scouts. He had led the scouts in circles for hours, employing his incomparable ability to traverse the land without leaving any sign of his passing, in order to confound his pursuers and spirit himself to safety.

An equivalent skill could not be attributed to his companions. The two boys were his sons. The elder, nearly sixteen years of age, studied his father's movements with fierce concentration, determined to emulate the expert hunter's prowess. A year younger, the second son trailed his sibling in preoccupied thought. His passion was the captivating beauty of the bountiful flora and fauna of the Rockies. He understood the need to hunt but wrestled with the tragedy of the kill and could not help marveling at the magnificence of the huge bull they were pursuing.

"Hush, Takoda!" His father had pulled up ahead. He spoke in Lakota and hissed at his son under his breath, glaring at him with a look of fury. "He will hear us, and we will never catch up with him. You must follow in my steps. Only place your feet where I place mine. Concentrate, or the hexaka will be gone like the day turns to night."

His father had pushed them hard all morning and the hexaka, as the tribe called the great elk, had confounded them. Whether it had sensed their presence or merely set off up the mountain with the coming of day, the hunter could not tell, but by the time they had reached the wallow where they had observed it rubbing itself earlier in the morning, it was nowhere to be seen.

Walks on Air had carefully examined the ground along the forest edge, until he was certain that he had interpreted the spoor correctly. At that point he had plunged with purpose into the shade of the trees.

The elk had followed a small but well-used animal trail, weaving its way among the towering pines until it had reached a clearing nestled in a sheltered valley set at the foot of three snow-capped peaks. There, a creek cascaded down the mountainside in a tumultuous series of waterfalls and settled in a shimmering blue oval-shaped lake, reflecting the sapphire tones of the clear midmorning sky.

Had the hunters not been absorbed in their task, they would have been content to sit and marvel at the splendor of the landscape, which described in graphic form the turbulent birth of the Rockies; sheer cliffs of jagged rock driven out of the ground by the rending force of the earth's mighty tectonic plates, dominant and imposing, a striking reminder of the power of creation. But, for now, they could not afford the distraction of admiring the wonder of Mother Earth's mystery.

It was nearly four hours since the pursuit had begun, and it had taken more than a quarter of that time for the trio to work their way around to the far side of the lake, where they had spied the elk grazing peacefully at the edge of a patchwork of verdant grass, its lush mat flowing across the clearing like green lava.

The hunter and his sons had crept stealthily to a position that remained shaded by the surrounding forest, but was close enough to the elk that the elder of the boys could have cast a well-aimed stone and struck the animal cleanly on the head. The range was easily within the kill zone of the arrow knocked to the hunter's bow, but he knew that he had to exercise care. A bull elk is a ferocious adversary, and even a small error in one's aim could prove fatal. The huge animal would not hesitate to launch an attack if the arrow strayed from its precise target.

Walks on Air was assiduous in avoiding any sudden movement that might betray his presence. Very slowly, he drew the bowstring, the muscles in his forearms and shoulders illustrating the intense strain of stretching the bow to its full power. He steadied his breathing to suppress the slight tremor in his left hand, and the feather flight of his arrow brushed gently against his upper cheek.

The elk turned its head to scan the forest, its penetrating gaze drilling into the shadows, searching for any flicker of movement that might reveal the threat it sensed with deep intuitive intensity. A chest muscle twitched in anticipation of imminent conflict.

The hunter sighted the arrowhead slightly behind the foreleg, focused on ensuring that his deadly barb pierced the animal's heart. His bicep burned from maintaining the tension in the bow and he took a deep breath, mentally paying homage to Mother Earth for delivering the magnificent elk into his hands for the benefit of his people.

Being in great awe of his father's wrath, the youngest boy had focused diligently on the hunt since his earlier reprimand, and now that they were upon the elk he could barely restrain his fascination with the impending kill.

He leaned forward, studying the flight of his father's arrow, stretching to his tiptoes to place a hand against the trunk of the nearest tree, his fingers seeking out a good purchase on the rough bark to steady himself. Excited, he grasped the small stub of a broken branch, affording sufficient grip to enable him to reach forward a little further. His mouth was dry as sand, and his skin tingled.

The events that ensued were a blur. The stubby branch snapped with a rending crack and the boy slipped, colliding with his father's elbow at the instant that the hunter released his arrow. The elk responded to the sound with lightning reflexes, spinning to face the danger, dropping its head and charging headlong at the hunter and his sons in one fluid movement.

The arrow's flight deflected slightly, compromised by the boy's collision, striking the bull high in the withers. Although the shaft penetrated deep into the muscle and shattered the elk's shoulder blade, the shot was far from deadly. The pain enraged the bull, and he drove into the forest using all the power of his quarters, his rack of razor-sharp tines scything through the thick undergrowth as he sought to destroy the source of his agony.

The hunter had insufficient time to unleash a second arrow, and his first thought was to lure the bull away from his sons. Swiftly, he stepped out of the cover, so that the elk could see him clearly, and sprung to his left, drawing his hunting knife as he ran.

But the bull was upon him before he had taken five paces, and gripped by a murderous red mist of rage, it thrust its antlers into the impact, the long tines slicing through the hunter's torso like butter, penetrating his abdomen and puncturing his right lung, so that frothy pink blood burst instantly from the wounds.

The bull charged onward, flailing the hunter against the trees like a rag doll, until it tossed him high into the air, where he became ensnared in the branches. O'hiniya he Mani's broken and twisted body dangled from one of the pines, weary eyes fixed upon the shocked faces of his sons as they stood gaping up at him from their refuge. A great weight filled his limbs and a creeping darkness enveloped his sight. His forefathers called.

Chapter 2

Minneapolis, Minnesota

"Show Mr. Stevens into the study when he arrives, Miss Jane," Senator Theodore Winthrop instructed as he turned on his heel in the hall and strode off toward a small anteroom at the rear of the house. "Please be hospitable and offer him a brandy, but not my finest. I suspect that he is not a man who would appreciate the quality of a refined liquor, so it would grieve me to squander it upon him," he projected over his shoulder in a theatrical tone.

The corridor that led to the back of the house was dark, but light from an oil lamp glowed faintly through the glazed portion of the door into the room beyond. Through the frosted glass, Winthrop could distinguish the hazy outline of two men, and his pulse raced in anticipation of the encounter.

Entering the room, he closed the door softly and pulled a curtain across the opaque window. Casting the tails of his long jacket aside, he thrust his hands into the pockets of his pants and turned to scrutinize a short man dressed in a crumpled gray suit.

Winthrop's eyes were dark and penetrating, framed by thick, long salt-and-pepper eyebrows and set under a deep forehead. His jaw was square and strong, sporting a meticulously cropped beard, and he exuded such an innate aura of authority and power that the visitor immediately removed his cloth hat, rolling it nervously in his hands as the senator observed him critically.

To Winthrop's right, a tall thick-set man in his early forties melted into the shadows, his attentive eyes shaded under the broad brim of a black felt hat. The vigilant attendant's jacket was cut wide in the chest, but failed to fully conceal his Remington Army revolver with its eight-inch octagonal barrel.

"I trust you've not failed me?" the senator enquired of the shorter man, his voice a gravelly whisper.

"No, sir. I got wha' you wan'ed." The visitor stooped, squinting up at the senator, his expression irritatingly sycophantic. He pulled an envelope from the inside pocket of his jacket eagerly and handed it to Winthrop. "Hyad to stup in Ch'cago a week to git thiys," he whispered in a conspiratorial tone.

Winthrop said nothing, but took the envelope and turned away to open it, careful to avoid betraying his reaction. He extracted two sheets of papers and unfolded them with assiduous care, placing his eyeglasses purposefully on the end of his nose and bending close to the lamp to examine the text, which was written in an elegant flowing script.

He displayed no emotion, reading both documents meticulously to ensure that he had correctly interpreted their significance. Lifting his head, he gazed thoughtfully into the corner of the room as he refolded each piece of correspondence and slid them back into the envelope. They were love letters, written in extravagant language by a man who sought to express his most intimate feelings and abiding commitment to the woman to whom they were addressed.

"Is this all, Mr. Hart?" Winthrop's tone sounded derisive.

"No, sir. There be mowre."

"Tell me."

"Well, sir. There be a kiyd. A boay. 'Bout four year ole."

Winthrop turned slowly and appraised Hart, seeking to assess the authenticity of his information. "Is the boy his?"

"Guess so. Boay calls 'im Pa, and they looks rait family

min'ed when they t'gether, an all."

Winthrop studied Hart judiciously. The man had no reason to lie, and the evidence he had assembled could easily be corroborated. His work had been more than satisfactory. He had followed instructions and unearthed a scandal that would serve the senator's purpose well.

"What's the woman's name?"

"Miys Mary-Aine Forr'ster, sir. She rait pritty. Ain well t' do I'd saiy." He wrung the cap in his hands as he stumbled to convey his findings to the senator. "Got reel naice hass on Nor' Forty-Second Stree'. Rait fancy, wiy picket feynce outsiy, ain gar'n full o' flowz. Housemai' and gar'ner an' all." Giving a conceited smirk, he thrust his hand into another pocket. "You'll laik thiys, sir!" Hart let out a high-pitched snigger as he handed the senator a slim square package, bound in a square of light linen. "Knew you'd aisk, so ah took th' 'nishtive."

Intrigued, Winthrop accepted the article and turned away again, pensively peeling away the cloth wrapping to reveal a picture frame encasing a formal daguerreotype of a stunning woman with long, dark, curly hair, attired in an elegant dress that accentuated her shapely figure. She looked to be in her mid-twenties, and she beamed with unrestrained delight as she stood with her arm entwined with that of a portly gentleman in his mid-fifties, who wore an expensively tailored three-piece suit. A small boy nestled against the couple, his round face bearing the apprehensive expression of someone for whom photography harbored a dark mystery, as he reached up to grasp the man's hand in a gesture that sought reassurance. It was a family photograph like any other, except that the man and woman were not husband and wife.

The senator suppressed a smile of satisfaction. The quality of the photography was unusually fine for the mid-nineteenth century. Only the wealthiest of people had access to photographers capable of producing a picture of such clarity. It was the kind of evidence that was irrefutable.

"You've done well. Who knows about this?" Winthrop asked casually.

"Laik you sayd, sir. Jus' 'tween you an' me. Confidential laik. Ain't no one knows, 'ceptin' you."

The senator turned to Hart and stared intently into his eyes, concerned to verify his honesty, and the investigator squirmed uncomfortably until Winthrop was satisfied that he was conjuring no attempt at deceit.

"Good. That's excellent. You are a man of your word, Mr. Hart, and you will be lauded for your contribution to the cause of unifying our great country." The senator spoke with the slow purposeful tones of an accomplished orator, pausing for emphasis and employing intonation to reinforce the significance of his words. "The very achievement of our Manifest Destiny resides in the hands of a few men of vision. I am one of those men, Mr. Hart, and you have done me an invaluable service. These are momentous times, and great sacrifice is required to ensure that we secure that providence. Harnessing the hearts and minds of those who must be persuaded to contribute to the cause is my purpose, and you have served that purpose today, Mr. Hart."

Winthrop stepped sideways to set the letters and the photograph on a table beside the door to the corridor, causing the investigator to be positioned directly between himself and the third man in the room. Hart turned to face the senator, fascinated by the inference of his flowery language, hopeful that Winthrop might offer a bonus payment or even commission some additional work, since the senator was clearly pleased with the output of his assignment.

Hart had agreed to a fee of fifty dollars plus expenses for the last job, with half paid as a cash advance. It was a tidy wage for a man like Hart, and he was optimistic that the senator might have further use for his services.

Winthrop smiled, placing his templed fingers against his lips as he inclined his head, gazing thoughtfully into Hart's eyes, his brow furrowed in an intense frown. "But secrecy is paramount in certain circumstances, Mr. Hart. And this is one of those occasions." Winthrop paused, wagging his head almost imperceptibly. "We need heroes, Mr. Hart, and heroes are obliged to make sacrifices for the cause."

The senator lifted his head slightly and nodded to the man behind Hart, who stepped swiftly out of the shadows. A brief expression of confusion crossed Hart's face, followed by a gasp of alarm as he registered the blur of a slim cord whipping over his head. His hands flew up to his neck and his eyes flashed wide as the garrotte was pulled savagely tight, a burly elbow being shoved painfully between his shoulders to provide enough leverage to throttle his breath.

Hart tried to scream in panic, but any sound was extinguished by the searing pressure constricting his throat. Wrestling and thrashing, he made a futile attempt to escape, but the vise-like grip was immovable. His face burned as if on fire, his neck and cheeks bulged, and his skull felt as though it might explode.

Confusion and terror melded into a surreal experience. The hoarse rasping breath of his assailant wheezed against his ear as the senator gazed upon him with a benevolent countenance. Hart could see Winthrop's mouth moving and faintly registered his oratory, although the sound appeared as if uttered from a distant podium.

"You are a hero, Mr. Hart. And your sacrifice for the cause will not be forgotten. We will triumph in the honorable quest of Manifest Destiny. We will build this great country so that its borders kiss the oceans to the east and to the west. One nation, united before the face of god. And you, Mr. Hart, have played your part in ensuring that immense ambition becomes a reality. The lord praise you, Mr. Hart."

Darkness closed about the extremity of Hart's vision, the senator's face centered in a tunnel of fading light, distant and hazy. But Winthrop continued his rhetoric, lifting his eyes to the ceiling while Hart fought with all his remaining strength, clawing at his own neck and tearing at his attacker's hands.

However, his efforts were to no avail, and his frantic entreaties remained unheeded. He danced like a marionette in the hands of a puppeteer, his feet barely touching the floor and his limbs thrashing in erratic uncoordinated twitches, until, abruptly, the struggling ceased. Darkness fell upon him, and a silent stillness enveloped the small room.

The senator touched the top of Hart's head gently and offered a blessing. "Lord, we pray for the soul of this, your servant, who has done his duty. We commit him to your care. May he rest in peace. Amen." He paused to examine Hart's face with the curiosity of one who is intrigued by the mystery of death and expects to elicit some clue as to the life ever after. He pursed his lips briefly and, once content that there was nothing further to be gained, he addressed the man who wielded the garrotte still drawn tightly around Hart's neck.

"Cleanly done, Mr. Stone." He shot an approving smile of acknowledgment. "The streets of Minneapolis can be a dangerous place at night. I imagine it would be unsurprising if Mr. Hart was found to have met an untimely end in one of the dark alleys around the whorehouses and saloons of the East Side."

Stone had performed the senator's bidding for nearly twenty years, gathering information, delivering intimidation, coercing allegiance where required, and at times dispatching those who might threaten or obstruct Winthrop's rise to power. He was well paid for his services and loyal to the man who had rescued his family from destitution when the depression of the late

1830s had ruined so many lives.

"Yes, sir. I know a suitable place."

"Make it look authentic, and check his pockets and his house for anything that might prompt unwanted questions."

Stone nodded his confirmation and let Hart's inert body slump to the floor. Winthrop picked up the letters and the small photograph, placed them carefully in the inside pockets of his jacket, and left the anteroom, closing the door behind him with a delicate touch before striding briskly up the corridor to the hall.

His housekeeper greeted him as he emerged into the brighter light cast by multiple oil lamps. "Mr. Stevens has arrived. He's in your study, sir. I've offered him a brandy like you said," she proffered with a deferential half-curtsy.

"Why, thank you, Miss Jane. But I feel cause to celebrate." Winthrop clasped his hands behind his back and peered at the rotund little lady with a mischievous smile. "I think this calls for my finest brandy after all, and perhaps you have some of those exquisite cakes of yours." He raised his chin and gazed contemplatively at the frescos that adorned the hall. "Yes. I feel a passion for your cakes, Miss Jane. Unaccountably, I have a sudden hunger that will be satisfied only by the excellence of your baking, god bless you!" Shooting a lopsided grin, he turned on his heel and marched off to his study, leaving the housekeeper to wonder what had infused him with such unexpected ebullience.

Winthrop threw the door open and breezed into the room to find a stout dapper man standing alongside one of his bookcases, reviewing the titles with an awkward air of apprehension. His face was a puffy red, suggesting an overindulgence in the pleasure of good liquor, and his waist paid testament to an equal enthusiasm for a hearty plate. A fob watch was tucked into the waistcoat pocket of his elegant gray suit, the timepiece attached to an expensive gold chain, lending the impression of a man for whom precision was important.

"Henry! What a delight to see you. Your work is building our nation, may the Lord grant you fortitude and perseverance! Now, tell me, how is that railroad progressing?" The senator boomed enthusiastically.

Henry Stevens was perplexed at the senator's jovial familiarity, a man whom he barely knew, although as President of the Northern Pacific Railroad Company, he often attended functions where dignitaries and politicians were present, and he had encountered Winthrop on more than one occasion.

"I wish I could say that the railroad was progressing to plan, senator, but, to be honest, we are confounded by almost impossible hurdles at every turn."

"Call me Theodore, please," Winthrop entreated. "And, please take a seat. We have so much to talk about."

Stevens lowered himself hesitantly into one of a pair of wing-backed leather chairs facing the fire, and Winthrop dropped nonchalantly into the other. "Thank you for your invitation, Theodore, but I'm a little perplexed. What can I do for you?"

Winthrop threw his head back and laughed extravagantly. "Henry, you and I are men of the same mold. We are men of purpose, men who hold within our very grasp the means to shape our country. I am a man of vision, and you are a man of action. We are two essential cogs in the machinery of progress. Now, tell me, you like cake? Miss Jane keeps house for me here, but she bakes the finest cake in all of Minnesota."

Stevens nodded his head in acquiescence, musing about the senator's purpose but struck by the eccentricity of his manner. "Yes, cake would be fine, thank you."

"Excellent, but I do believe that your glass is contaminated with brandy barely fit for cooking, and that we cannot have!" Winthrop sprang up and bellowed through the open door, "Miss

Jane! My finest brandy, if you please! What does a man have to do to get a decent drink in this house?"

The housekeeper came bustling hastily across the hall, carrying a silver tray set with an ornate decanter and two enormous brandy bowls. "I'm sorry, sir. I'm here now. Would you like me to pour?" she enquired as she placed the tray on a low table between the two leather chairs.

"No, Miss Jane, thank you. I'll lend my hand to that task. But the cakes, Miss Jane! We are in urgent need of your fine bakery." The senator shooed her away playfully, dispensed a generous measure of aromatic brandy into the two ostentacious glasses, and removed the offending beverage from Stevens's grasp.

"Now, how is that enchanting wife of yours, Sarah, I believe? And your children? Joshua. He'll be twelve now, I assume? And the two young ladies? They must be a delight to you, Henry."

Stevens was astonished that the senator was acquainted with the details of his family. It was a mystery to him how or why Winthrop should possess such information, and he was immediately suspicious of the politician's intent, but the senator's demeanor seemed entirely relaxed and there appeared to be nothing more than a well-informed interest to his manner.

"They're in fine health, thank you, Theodore." He replied haltingly.

Winthrop was amused at the man's unease and revelled in his discomfort. Possession of a comprehensive knowledge of Stevens's personal circumstances would serve to stimulate the railwayman's anxiety about the extent of the senator's knowledge of his affairs and make him more malleable.

"Indulge me, Henry. Enlighten me about these impossible hurdles that obstruct your progress." Winthrop snipped off the tip of a large cigar and rolled it expertly between his fingers to gauge its quality before lighting up and puffing at it contentedly.

Stevens savored a sip of the oily amber liquid in his brandy balloon and the alcoholic fumes warmed his nose and throat, infusing him with a comfortable glow. He relaxed into his chair and considered how to formulate his response, watching as Miss Jane placed a stack of small freshly baked cupcakes on the tray alongside the decanter and retreated from the room.

"The Northern Pacific charter requires us to build a railroad from Carlton in Minnesota through to Washington Territory on the West Coast, and much of the route is well defined in principle. We'll commence construction from Kalama in the West and aim to finish with a final link in Montana Territory, but we need greater clarity about the location of the western terminus. There's no consensus about what's required, and we need certainty so that we can determine where to place maintenance yards and other strategic facilities.

"Additionally, there's the process of defining the detailed route, which is hampered by the security of our surveyors in Dakota Territory, where they're constantly subject to attack from the Sioux. The areas to the east are less troublesome following the Treaty with the Ojibwe, but the Great Plains are difficult and we have little or no protection because the primary focus for military resources is the Oregon Trail.

"But these are both problems that can be overcome. The real impediment is finance. We're struggling to get the charter properly funded, and if we can't resolve that issue, the railroad is going nowhere." Stevens paused and stared wistfully into the bottom of his glass, swirling the liquid around to release its exquisite vapor.

Winthrop considered Stevens's difficulties and leaned forward to pat him on the knee. "Nothing insurmountable in that!" he ventured cheerfully. "You see, the successful completion of the

Northern Pacific Railroad represents one of the most fundamental components in achieving the integration of the States of this great continent. Without your railroad, Manifest Destiny will remain an unfulfilled dream, and we cannot allow that, Henry, can we? It's too important.

"You and I were feted to serve this godly purpose. Without the railroad, trade cannot flourish between east and west. The vast open lands of the west cannot be populated and cultivated. Our country will remain fractured by an uncharted chasm of uncivilized land that severs our nation, precluding us from realizing our potential.

"The antiquated days of wagon trains of weary travelers must be consigned to history. Progress resides in the ability to transport people and products with speed and efficiency from one place to another. The railroad! Commerce depends upon it. Civilization depends upon it. The wealth and power of our nation depends upon it. And, you and I, Henry, can make this happen."

The senator's passion was palpable, but Winthrop's enthusiasm alone would be insufficient to resolve the obstacles thwarting Stevens's progress.

"I understand the importance of the railroad, Theodore, but I seem unable to secure the attention of Congress to consider our application for the allocation of land and grants. Legislators are too absorbed with matters related to the southern states to afford us any attention. The Pacific Railroads Act was passed by President Lincoln for this exact purpose, but you'd think the Act didn't exist for all the response I've managed to solicit. We need government support now or it will be too late."

Winthrop was entertained by Stevens's frustration, but he maintained an affected expression. He had worked hard to ensure that none of the appeals for funding received from the Northern Pacific Railroad had elicited a response, making it clear to the secretariat that as Chair of the Senate Committee for Foreign Relations, he should be the only recipient of requests for allocation of land in the West, the Territories not having been assimilated into the Union of States as yet and their native peoples being deemed in many quarters to be resident foreign nations.

"Ha! Politics. That's my world, Henry. The shady motives of the corridors of Congress." Winthrop's eyes gleamed at the thought of the heady narcotic of influence that wielded the instruments of policy and power.

"But I don't think the financial resources are available. Washington's saddled with debt now that the war's over."

"Oh, don't despair, Henry. Money is a transient thing. We often purchase today with money we don't have, in the expectation of being able to afford the cost tomorrow."

"I don't understand."

"Money isn't the issue, Henry. Motivation is the issue!" Winthrop chortled enthusiastically. "Manifest Destiny is a policy supported by Congress, Henry. There is unanimity upon that objective, and the President is determined to do whatever is required to realize that goal. Everyone knows that the railroads are the key. Lack of money is a temporary condition, and completion of the transcontinental railroads can only serve to generate wealth for the nation. Land is free to the government, Henry, so finance shouldn't be an impediment. And, money can take the form of government bonds. We simply require support from the right people, and a little motivation. We all need a little motivation, don't we?

"We'll get the funding you need, Henry. My estimate is that you'd be entitled to about sixty million acres of land along the route, plus approximately nineteen thousand dollars per mile of completed tracked grade, allowing for premium-rate funding for crossing the Rockies. The land will be yours to sell to settlers.

Land for towns and for industry. You shall have your money, Henry, and we shall have our railroad."

"But much of the land belongs to the Indians."

"Nonsense, Henry! Those prairie rats own nothing. They wander the wilderness with no purpose other than survival. Their possessions wouldn't fill so much as one of your boxcars, and their children play in the dirt like a pack of nomadic dogs. The Indians have no use for the land, and they make no use of it. The Great Plains are the Union Government's for the taking, and take them we must!" Winthrop bristled with vehement indignation.

"That's easier said than done! The Indians won't respect our title to land they believe to be their birth right. They'll fight to the death and we'll never get our surveys done. Our construction teams will be massacred," Stevens complained.

"You leave security to me, Henry. One step at a time. Let's procure our funding first." Winthrop paused until Stevens was looking directly at him. "Do you believe that the men who forge nations should be rewarded for their endeavor, Henry?"

Stevens was perplexed by the question. "I'm not sure what you mean, Theodore."

"Oh, come now, Henry. We are both men of the world. You are a businessman and business revolves around the notion of profit. Success deserves reward, does it not?" The corner of the senator's mouth curled in a meaningful smirk. "The success of the Union is in our hands, and we should prosper from that enterprise, Henry." He reached for a cake and closed his eyes as he savored its light fluffy sponge. "Excellent cake. You really should try one, Henry. Miss Jane is without doubt the best baker in Minneapolis."

It dawned upon Stevens that, rather than the senator's motives representing an altruistic act in pursuit of his Congressional obligations, he was proposing payment in return for assistance. The man wanted to negotiate some form of deal. "What do you have in mind, Senator?" he addressed Winthrop brusquely.

"There you go, Henry. I knew you were a man of reason. The Northern Pacific needs funding and security and I can assist in resolving both of those requirements. In the absence of our bold initiative, the Union's vision will fail. Therefore, I think a small recognition of our contribution would be in order, don't you? I'll be direct, Henry. Together we will assure the construction of this railroad, and I will resolve your financing. In return, you will appropriate three hundred and twenty acres of prime land at each of three strategic locations that will be registered in my title. The first will be where the railroad crosses the Missouri, and the second where it intersects the Yellowstone. The third site is Bozeman, which is increasingly becoming the supply center for the Virginia City goldfields." Winthrop beamed, settling into his wing-backed chair like a reclining cat and sipping appreciatively at his brandy.

Stevens was outraged by the brazen affront. He snapped to his feet and placed his brandy bowl on the tray beside him. "How dare you, sir. You're inviting me to defraud the Union government and my own company! I am no petty criminal. I will have no part in this. I think our business is concluded."

Winthrop remained unruffled and continued to beam as Stevens hurried toward the door. "Now, now, Henry. Calm yourself. I'm sure we have a common interest in this matter."

"It seems we have nothing in common, Senator. I'll see myself out."

"Oh, come, Henry. I'm sure we both have an interest in the lovely Miss Forrester?" Winthrop's voice dropped to a conspiratorial whisper.

Stevens was struck dumb and stood transfixed, his hand poised to lift the latch of the door to the study. Turning, he watched Winthrop lean forward and place a slim, square object on the table to the side of the silver tray, whereupon the senator reclined and drew a deep contented pull on his cigar.

"A good-looking family photograph, I'd say. I wonder what Sarah would make of it? You write a fine letter too. Touching terms of affection," he purred as he dropped the two love letters onto the table beside the photograph.

"You bastard! You wouldn't dare!" Stevens spat as recognition of the intimate picture and his fluid handwriting registered on his troubled face.

"Oh, that would be a rash assumption on your part, Henry," Winthrop crooned. "I am a man of resolve. But we have no need for unpleasantness. I understand that a man can have abundant desires that are not necessarily adequately satisfied by one woman."

Stevens returned to his chair and slumped down, his eyes cast to his feet. The prospect of discovery had haunted him for years. Of course, Mary-Anne knew of Sarah and his other children, and had developed a grudging acceptance of the lifestyle she shared with Henry. He made provision for her and their son, ensuring that they were able to live in comfort in a respectable area of Chicago. Henry visited regularly when travelling on business and stayed for weeks at a time, so many aspects of family life were as normal as she might have reason to expect.

But Sarah was blissfully unaware of Henry's second family. She was the daughter of a wealthy New York banker and had met her husband when he worked for the New York and Hudson River Railroad before he had been recruited to run the Northern Pacific. She busied herself with raising three children and organizing the social functions required of a business leader in the burgeoning township of Minneapolis, while her husband threw himself into the onerous task of orchestrating the endless problems of running a railroad company. She was a loyal and loving partner, and her world would be shattered by the discovery of her husband's adultery.

The senator was pleased with himself. He swirled his brandy around the big balloon glass as Stevens fixed him with a contemptuous snarl. "If you tell my wife, I'll kill you," he growled.

Winthrop crossed his legs casually, reinforcing his indifference to Stevens's threat. "I can see that you feel a little unsettled by all this, but give it a few days and I'm sure you'll come around to the idea. You have nothing to fear from me, Henry. I've made a career out of discretion. I'm sure we'll make a formidable team. All I need is your motivation."

The senator turned to Stevens and his expression hardened, the steel of his character revealed in dark eyes devoid of emotion. "You are motivated, aren't you, Henry?" He paused to assess Stevens's reaction, picking up the letters and photograph and replacing them carefully into his jacket pockets. "Now, you look tired, Henry. It's been a pleasure, but I feel I should permit you an early evening. I look forward to a successful and profitable partnership. I'll be in touch."

Stevens had been dismissed, and the senator rose to open the door as the railroad man struggled clumsily to his feet.

Chapter 3

Autumn 1864, New York to Kansas railroad

Hans Kopp sat in an uncomfortable silence beside his wife and children in the oppressive heat of a dark and stuffy railroad boxcar as it rattled along the tortuous route to Kansas.

Two weeks earlier the Kopp family had arrived at Ellis Island, New York, having left their home in the Ukraine to endure the long and arduous voyage across the Atlantic Ocean, bound for the bright future promised in the New World.

Hans's father, Johannes, had emigrated from the famine-ravaged fields of Germany to the Black Sea region of the Ukraine in the 1820s when conscription, political and religious intolerance, and successive years of crop failure caused by extreme weather had left rural German families disenchanted, destitute, and starving.

Alexander I, grandson of Catherine the Great, Czar of Russia, had offered emigrant farmers free land and liberty to pursue their own religious convictions as incentive to encourage German and Polish families to relocate to the Ukraine, with the objective of stimulating cultivation of great swathes of the hitherto uncolonized Steppes.

Johannes had traveled for weeks with his wife and small baby, their worldly possessions bundled onto a small cart drawn by their remaining ox as they stole out of Germany at night to avoid the brutal clutches of the military, mobilized by the German Emperor to prevent depopulation of his ravaged country.

Hundreds of families had emigrated and the conditions were harsh. Many of the travelers were country peasants ill-equipped for such a journey and half-starved before they set out. Their poor underlying health, combined with virulent outbreaks of typhus and dysentery, condemned many of the old and very young to almost certain death.

Johannes's wife, Marianne, succumbed to the typhus during a period of enforced quarantine, and her baby survived for less than a week after she died. But Johannes was committed to the journey and could see no merit in returning to his homeland. His only option being to persevere, he trudged on, driven by the prospect of a better life in the barren lands proffered by the Russians.

Relationships of convenience became a necessity, and it was not long before Johannes met Matilde, whose husband had also perished from the typhus. They agreed that it would be expedient to marry when they reached the Ukraine and shared the chores and hard work necessary to survive on their allotted farmstead.

They built a primitive home from scavenged timber, sods of turf, and thickly woven branches. But food was meager, so they ate the simple diet of the local Russian peasants, millet gruel and cabbage soup, and they gathered anything capable of being burned to fend off the bone-chilling conditions of the first winter.

As the months turned to years, their relentless fight for survival began to produce a more sustainable life. Crops flourished, and as they progressively extended their German-inspired irrigation systems across the land, their enterprise expanded from alfalfa and vegetables to include the production of cereals. They planted trees and grew flowers and started raising a few of the sought-after Ukrainian Grey Steppe cattle.

Life was hard and unforgiving, and their marriage was

functional, devoid of love or happiness. A successful harvest was not met with joy, but grudging appreciation that its bounty would secure their survival for another year.

Born into this brittle relationship were Hans and his older brother Matheis, not for the pleasure of children, but for the purpose of succession and the practicality of providing extra hands to undertake the work.

Hans and his brother were condemned to grow up in a home that offered little opportunity to develop any sense of family values, and their father soon came to resent the young boys' dependence, their needs absorbing any spare cash and distracting Matilde from her normal chores. Hans soon realized that it was essential to stay out of his father's way, to avoid the flash of his temper and the lash of his belt.

By his mid-teens Hans was often staying out late with friends as a means of extracting himself from the turmoil of his home life, and before long he was fraternizing with the local scoundrels. He and his comrades would roam the town at night stealing whatever they could get their hands on and buying flagons of vodka with their ill-gotten gains.

At age seventeen Hans met Elena Maas, a lanky but attractive girl who lived in an orphanage on the outskirts of town. She and the other orphan girls threw themselves at potential suitors, content to sacrifice their modesty in return for the prospect of securing a husband.

Elena was enchanted by the roguish good looks of the young farmer and reveled in the excitement and danger of Hans's illicit activities. Determined to ingratiate, she threw herself at him and he welcomed her promiscuity, enjoying the ease with which he was able to manipulate her.

At heart Hans was lazy, and although he could have chased other girls, Elena was constantly prepared to run errands for him. She was born to a German father and an English mother, both of whom had died from tuberculosis when she was ten. Her features were typically Germanic, with high cheekbones and a haughty tilt to her chin that led people to believe that she was of wealthy lineage.

Her blue eyes glittered with energy and guile, and her full lips were set in a provocative pout that Hans found irresistible. But, most notably, despite her tall slim frame, a reminder of the bitter frugality of her early years, she was blessed with the kind of seductive curves that no man could ignore.

Appreciating her obvious attractions and recognizing the benefit of an extra pair of hands to help on the farm, Johannes warmed to the young Elena, and Matilde encouraged the relationship enthusiastically. A further advantage to Hans was that Elena's presence provoked Johannes to direct his temper toward Matheis, who was harangued for failing to find a suitable bride.

Hans was delighted at becoming the favored son, and in a short time he and Elena were married. The farm prospered, and the Kopp family was able to hire laborers to help with the sowing and harvesting of crops. On the surface, married life appeared good, but Hans could not resist sneaking away to socialize with his old friends, regularly returning to the farm in the early hours of the morning stinking of alcohol and stumbling into the bedroom incapable of undressing himself.

Occasionally, hard-earned and much-needed money was lost in a card game, saddling Hans with debt for months. When this happened, Elena bore the brunt of his frustration, and although she pretended to be asleep when he returned drunk, she often felt the kiss of his right hand as he vented his anger, the vacuum of emotion from his childhood fueling a self-indulgent desire to exact retribution for his own failures upon his hapless wife.

Despite these dark moments, Elena concluded that her life with Hans was better than the existence most of the other orphan girls had managed to secure, and she focused on the good times. She maintained Hans's attention by satisfying his lust for her body, and it was inevitable that their first child, Johannes junior, was born shortly after they were married. Two years later, a daughter, Carla, was delivered.

The unpredictable excesses of her husband, however, took their toll, and as a means of expressing her anguish, Elena secretly began to cultivate a sinister pleasure in inflicting pain on Johannes junior and the animals on the farm. Small things at first, but slowly more calculated.

Ensuring that no one witnessed her actions, she delighted in stabbing the dogs, horses, and cattle, with a darning needle. While the dogs slept in front of the fire, she took a perverted pleasure in their terrified yelp as she jabbed the needle into their rump, watching them cower by the door as they attempted to escape her abuse. But the horses were most vulnerable when they were in their stalls, where she would stab them repeatedly until they kicked violently against the rails, twisting and turning, and snorting in alarm.

Treating Johannes as a surrogate for the husband, she pinched him viciously until he bawled uncontrollably, telling him that he was evil and that she was compelled to punish him to exorcise his wickedness. And, she threatened him constantly with the prospect of being thrashed with Hans's belt, causing him to quail every time he saw his father.

She reveled in the surge of pleasure she derived from the distress she inflicted upon others, which compensated for her own suffering. Then, inexplicably, her warped persona crumbled and she would feel utterly repentant, feeding the dogs delicious tit-bits of food, stuffing the horses' nosebags with oats, and smothering Johannes with her embrace. Her quiet sufferance at the hands of her husband poisoned her mind and fostered a malicious and devious vindictiveness.

Nevertheless, despite their tumultuous private lives, the Kopps' farm grew in stature in the local community and prospects appeared good. As the years passed, they earned enough money to build a farmhouse in the traditional style of a German Hallenhaus, with an open flett for the kitchen, three large bedrooms at the back, and space for animal stalls at the front. The walls were formed from a lattice of timber in-filled with brick, and the reed-thatched roof swept down to shoulder height at the eaves. It was a graphic symbol of the family's achievement in breaking the land, progressively developing a richly cultivated tapestry of diverse crops.

However, as Hans reached his mid-thirties, everything changed. The newfound prosperity of the industrious German settlers provoked a sense of resentment among the Russian authorities, who coveted their productive pastures. The government passed laws designed to marginalize the settlers, imposed exclusive use of the Russian language in their formerly German-speaking schools, retracted the right of self-government previously permitted by Tsar Alexander, and introduced conscription to the Russian army, which was constantly at war with its neighbors.

To Hans, the choice was obvious. Stay and have your rights progressively eroded, your lands taken from you, and risk being sent to an almost certain death in one of Russia's brutal military campaigns, or flee.

The Kopp family argued vigorously about their prospects for the future, Hans's father refusing to concede the land that he had tamed with his own blood and sweat. He was adamant that he had worked too hard to relinquish his home, and he steadfastly declined to leave.

Hans read that in America land was virtually being given away to migrants who would consider settling in the frontier territories. The incentives were huge and the country was reputed to be rich and fertile, promising a better and more secure life. Furthermore, the United States government welcomed all nationalities and boasted of a land of freedom, where individuals could practice their own religious and cultural beliefs without criticism or discrimination.

So it was that the journey Hans and Elena were embarked upon had started. They had turned away from their Black Sea home with a heavy heart and set off with a cart laden with the barest of possessions, accompanied by their two teenage children. They carried food for the first part of the route across Europe to the English Channel, clothing, and a few personal effects, including Hans's father's writing desk made of walnut with twisted legs and ornate filigree, typical of the Russian style, a gift intended to remind him to correspond.

They stowed prudently sized sacks of seed to sow in the new lands, and gifts were exchanged. Johannes parted with a prized Cossack knife, which he had acquired during the first year he had settled in the Ukraine. Its razor-sharp blade was wickedly curved, and the carved bone handle, studded with extravagant dark red and green gemstones, was worn smooth from long years of use. It was Johannes's means of symbolizing Hans's heritage and an ineffective attempt to provide a memento that might encourage him to return home to assure continuity of the farm in the future.

Matilde gave Elena clothing that she had made for the children and two large iron cooking pots scorched from long use over the farmhouse fire. As a final gift she quietly handed Elena a pouch of gold pieces, which she had secretly accumulated over the years. Matilde was a mother who knew her son well, and although she wanted to ensure that the young family had the means to make their journey, she was pragmatic about the prospect of Hans's having access to money that he might squander. Elena was given strict instructions to hide the gold pieces at all costs, saving them until they could be used to secure the family's future.

The journey across the Ukraine and Poland, and on to the seaport of Hamburg, was onerous, draining the Kopps of both food and resolve. But the bustle of the port soon reignited their hope, with endless hordes of people speculating enthusiastically about the riches to be found in the New World.

They boarded a large sailing barge equipped with supplementary steam engines for the tortuous six-week trip across the Atlantic, and all but the wealthiest of the emigrants found themselves in the cramped conditions of steerage, where the close confines sparked regular fights among the irritable travelers.

Unfortunately for Elena, the principle entertainment for the men was gambling and drinking, so it was not long before Hans was absent for long periods and she was left on her own to occupy the restless children.

Within a fortnight Hans had lost all the money he carried and had drunk himself into a stupor. He reappeared at the family's bunk reeking of alcohol and collapsed into a deep sleep, snoring like a hog for nearly two days.

When he awoke, he was contrite with remorse for his foolishness and racked with concern about how they would acquire the resources to make a fresh start when they arrived in America.

Elena wrestled with the dilemma of telling Hans about the gold pieces his mother had entrusted to her, but she worried that he might lose his self-control later in the voyage and squander their only remaining money. It was a difficult decision because, although she knew that her silence could prove essential to her family's survival at a later date, it was inevitable that she would ultimately pay a heavy price for the lack of trust that she placed in her husband. But the welfare of her children depended upon her courage and for once she acted in their best interests.

Carla occupied herself with ease. She was fourteen years old and a bright, self-confident child. She bustled with energy and was adept at finding a cause in which to immerse herself. It was apparent that many of the passengers struggled with sea sickness and the close confines below decks were a recipe for transmitting illness, so Carla became a self-appointed nurse, ensuring that sick passengers were provided with water and were made as comfortable as possible. She tirelessly roamed the ship, helping where she could and garnering the reverent title Kleine Engel, "Little Angel."

Elena worried that Carla would lose her way aboard the huge vessel or become stricken by the contagious bouts of illness, but nothing seemed to faze the young girl and she confidently navigated her way around, becoming acquainted with the crew and many of the passengers.

By contrast, Johannes was less flexible, cursing the monotony of the voyage and resenting the close proximity of so many people he regarded as inferior. He could not abide the sight of the few passengers who were able to afford one of the six staterooms, which provided privacy from the squalor in which most migrants were compelled to travel.

He had become conditioned to the superior character of the Kopp farmhouse, which had been larger and more extravagant than most of the homesteads in the area where he had grown up, so the ignominy of rubbing shoulders with the masses grated on his pride, kindling the embers of what would become a relentless craving for wealth and power.

Fortunately, the prevailing wind was benign and, unlike many Atlantic crossings of the day, the Kopps' barge made good headway, dropping anchor off Ellis Island on schedule. There, the ship was held in quarantine so that the health of the passengers could be assessed by the immigration authorities, those with fever being moved to the port sanatorium, while the rest of the travelers were provided with fresh food and water.

Following a week of delay, the processing of the immigrants began. The Kopps, complete with their personal belongings, boarded a small tug together with an excited group of fellow passengers and pottered slowly across the bay to the tip of Manhattan Island, bound for the huge circular sandstone edifice of Castle Garden immigration center.

The reception the families received was warm and helpful, and the immigration center was well organized and efficient. Everyone was subjected to a thorough medical examination to confirm that they were free from any illness that might infect the local New York community, and the Kopps were all given a clean bill of health.

Afterward, they were ushered into the central rotunda. The building was stunning, fully circular and forty feet from floor to ceiling, with an airy glazed central cupola accenting the domed roof. An elaborate balcony was set against two-thirds of the inner wall of the rotunda, supported by large round columns that stretched up to the roof, where they splayed into ornate plaster-cast floral fronds. New arrivals lined the balustrade, eagerly surveying the throngs of humanity that bustled between the agents' desks on the ground floor.

The reception area was subdivided into distinct zones, organized to facilitate the efficient processing of the new arrivals. The Kopps proceeded to registration where their names, nationality, and place of origin were formally recorded by a clerk in one of the numerous booths set around the outside wall of the huge vestibule. Elena's English heritage enabled her to converse easily with the clerk, and their forms were completed swiftly without event.

From there, they were passed to the land agents, who

explained in flamboyant terms the boundless riches awaiting discovery on the plains of the western frontier and extolled the virtues of countless sections of land available for occupation. Emigrants were offered the opportunity to acquire 160 acres of their own land for $1.50 an acre, payable in arrears, if after five years they could demonstrate that they had cultivated the land. The Kopps could sign up with the New York land agents and complete the papers necessary to register their land title at the local land office when they arrived at their final destination.

Hans relished the simplicity of the transaction and promptly set aside the practical issue of paying for the land. It was a problem for the future. There was no requirement for immediate payment, and he was certain that he could break the land as his father had done in the Ukraine. The land agents offered an opportunity to obtain title for a second section of land at no cost on the condition that Hans planted it with trees, and he signed up with alacrity.

Within the space of an hour the Kopps had entered the United States and become owners of 320 acres of prime land in the western part of Montana Territory. The scale of their property eclipsed the farmstead that Hans's father had managed to secure in the Ukraine, and he bristled with renewed enthusiasm and confidence. They had arrived in the New World and the future appeared prosperous.

Elated, they moved on, ushered to a desk attended by an agent for the railway company. Here, they were invited to make arrangements for travel out west to St. Joseph, which would be the jumping-off point for their wagon train to traverse the Great Plains.

But, having lost all his money playing cards, Hans's newfound assurance evaporated in a stroke. The agent offered no credit and was unimpressed by Hans's promise to sell his writing desk to raise sufficient funds to procure their tickets. All seemed lost.

Hans fidgeted, rubbing his palms up and down his thighs in an animated gesture of agitation, glaring alternately at the agent and his wife.

"Tell him I'll pay the railroad three times the cost of the fare when we harvest our first crops," he ordered his wife in strident German. "Tell him that we ran the best farm in our village in Ukraine. Tell him we're good for the money."

The clerk eyed Elena quizzically as her husband's voice rose in frustration. She patted Hans's leg, attempting to subdue his fury as other immigrants began to turn and stare at the commotion. "I'll tell him, Hans. Don't shout, Hans, please. All the people are watching us."

"I don't care! We won't be stopped now, having come so far. Tell him. Tell him now!" Hans rose to his feet and leaned threateningly across the table at the alarmed official.

"Sit down, Hans, please! I'll tell him. I'll sort it out, I promise," Elena pleaded.

She wrestled to restrain her husband, noticing that their noisy altercation was drawing the attention of the soldiers standing guard at the main doors. She babbled hurriedly at the clerk in accented English. "I im sorry of my husband. We hiv hard woyage. He is tired. I im pay for our tickets. I hiv money, but he must not know dis. I vill pay you. Please. Let him show his table, unt I vill pay ven he is gone."

The clerk raised his eyebrows in surprise. He tried to avoid eye contact with Hans, whose face was puce with rage, his eyes wide and his mouth frothing with spittle. It was obvious that he would lose his self-control if an accommodation was not reached soon.

"I'd be obliged if you'd tell your husband to sit down, Mrs. Kopp. Do you really have the money to pay?"

"Ya, I hiv ze money, but my husband, he must not know dis. Please, look unt zee his table. I vill pay you."

Hans recognized that the clerk and his wife seemed to be working out an agreement, and he cursed his inability to understand what they were saying, resolving that he would insist that Elena begin teaching him English as soon as possible. Emitting a sigh of resignation, he slumped back into his chair.

Simultaneously, a soldier appeared at the clerk's side to enquire whether he was in need of assistance, and the agent paused momentarily, looking thoughtfully at Elena. He placed his hands together, elbows on his desk, and rested his chin on his knuckles.

"No. I guess we're all good," he advised the soldier. "I reckon we've got this figured out. But keep yerself handy, case Mr. Kopp here needs to be shown some decent manners."

He leaned back in his chair and, peering over the top of his eyeglasses, fixed Elena with a level gaze. "All right, Mrs. Kopp, let's play it your way. You get yer husband to haul out his table and I'll send a runner to take a good look. Mind, I don't want him bringin' the darned thing in here. I can't have no other folks thinkin' they can trade goods with the railroad."

"Oh, sank you! I im promise zat I kin pay. Jus please not tell my husban' zis." Elena turned to Hans and smiled, grasping his face between her hands and gazing into his eyes as she spoke hurriedly to him in German. "Hans. Don't worry, Hans. We can sort this out. Hans, the railroad will look at your table. Go and get the table, Hans, and the railroad will send a man to look at it. Take Johannes with you to help."

Hans looked slowly from Elena to the clerk, who raised an eyebrow and nodded encouragingly. "You're sure?" He searched Elena's face for signs of deceit. It didn't seem possible that the clerk could have conceded his intransigence with such apparent ease. "Why? Why does he say this now? It's a trick to get rid of us."

"No, Hans. No. It's all right. He wants to help us. Show your table to his assistant. I'll stay here and keep our place. Show him your table. He'll help."

Hans placed his hands on the desk and pushed himself to his feet, casting Elena and the clerk a suspicious scowl. Something did not make sense, but he had no option. "Johannes. Come," he growled over his shoulder as he turned away, starting for the doors at the far side of the rotunda.

Elena sank back into her chair, her shoulders sagging with relief as she looked up at the clerk. "Pliz, understand, he is good man, but is no good viz money."

The clerk placed his elbows on the desk and leaned toward Elena. "Mrs. Kopp, I don't reckon we got much time before your husband comes right on back. The New York Central Railroad can take y'all as far as Buffalo. There, you'll have to change to the Buffalo and State Line Railroad through to Chicago. The fare for your family and belongings is $15. But, whatever you may think, the railroad ain't gonna take no table as payment."

Elena was galvanized into action. She reached down to open the drawstring to her bag and thrust her hand to the bottom. "Do you hiv a knife?" She looked up hopefully at the clerk.

"I got a paper knife," he answered quizzically, pushing it across the table at her.

Hurriedly, she picked up the blade and worked it into a seam, worrying apart some rudimentary stitching so that she could extract four coins, which she rubbed briskly on her skirt, sighing as she straightened up and placed them purposefully on the table between the clerk's elbows. She beamed optimistically, but the clerk's face was a picture of astonishment as he stared at the four solid-gold Napoleon coins.

"What in tarnation? Mrs. Kopp, are these gold?"

"Ya. Is gold!"

"I'm gonna have to get these checked out, Mrs. Kopp. I ain't seen nothin' like this before. You'd best come with me." The clerk pushed back his chair and beckoned Elena to follow. She swept up her bags and hustled Carla along, the young girl looking incredulous at her mother's duplicity.

Navigating a circuitous route across the rotunda, the clerk arrived at a small banking booth where the cashier studied the coins and confirmed their authenticity. To Elena's relief, he declared that he would exchange them for $43, and once she had paid the railroad fare of $15 she tucked the balance of cash to the bottom of her bag.

"Don't tell daddy about the money, darling," she whispered, bending slightly to look Carla in the eye. "He mustn't know. This must be our secret. Only you and I must know. Our secret. Will you do this for me, darling? We don't want to make daddy angry, do we?"

Carla nodded. "You don't want daddy to take the money, do you? Are you worried he'll lose it?" She had heard her parents' arguments many times, when her father had returned home drunk and destitute.

Elena was stunned. She stared at her daughter, her mouth gaping, realizing how naive it was to assume that her children were oblivious to the turbulent strain of her relationship with their father. "You're too clever for your own good, madam," she cooed, smiling at Carla. "We need to help daddy look after the money for our farm. Will you help me do that?"

Carla nodded again, grinning. "We can buy cows with the money. A good farm needs cows and horses." She looked triumphant.

Elena laughed and shook Carla gently. "That's right. We'll buy cows! And horses!" She sprang upright and turned to the clerk. "I tell my husband zat ze railroad is like ze table. I say zat ze railroad vill hold a debt against ze table in return vor ze tickets. I tell him zat if he is not pay ze railroad in von year, zen he is have to give ze table. I sign ze paper, but he is not know what is saying. He is not read or speak English."

The clerk wagged his head and raised his hands in submission. "Mrs. Kopp, you can sign whatever paper you want. The railroad don't care, so long as you gone an' paid your fare."

The clerk pulled a sheet of New York and Central Railroad headed paper across from the cashier and wrote out a short paragraph proposing that the Kopps owed the railroad $15, due for repayment in a year. Both he and Elena signed at the bottom of the page, and she gave the clerk a satisfied grin before they turned to fight their way back across the crowded rotunda to the agent's booth.

Hans was prowling at the desk, looking like he might explode. He was furious that the runner sent to meet him had displayed complete disinterest in his desk, and their exchange had been brief when it had become apparent that the young man spoke no German.

To make matters worse, Elena, Carla, and the clerk were nowhere to be seen when Hans and Johannes had returned, and no one appeared able to explain their disappearance. Hans's agitation had once again attracted the attention of the soldier who was at the point of soliciting assistance to eject the burly farmer from the building.

Desperate to avoid an altercation, Elena shouted over the heads of the throng of migrants, waving the railroad paper vigorously in the air. "Hans. Hans, we've got the tickets! We've got the tickets, Hans!"

The big Ukrainian spotted his family and shoved his way through the crowd, provoking angry protests. "Where have you been!" he bellowed.

Elena waved the paper in his face. "I'm sorry, Hans. We had to go and sign a paper. I'm sorry. The railroad has given us tickets, Hans. They liked your desk, Hans. They will take it as security for the tickets."

Hans grabbed the document proffered by his wife and stared at it intently. "What does it say?" he growled.

"It says that if we haven't paid for the tickets within a year the railroad will come and get your table, Hans. It's good, Hans. We have our land, and now we have our train tickets. We can go to our farm, Hans."

Hans narrowed his eyes, peering dubiously at the paper and scrutinizing his wife with barely concealed suspicion. The clerk hurried around his desk and hastily issued Elena with four railroad tickets, hoping that the documents would placate the aggressive Ukrainian and encourage him to leave with his family.

Receiving the tickets settled Hans's agitation as he realized that his wife really had succeeded in negotiating their passage. And, despite failing to understand how she had resolved their inability to pay, he felt it wise to depart before the clerk changed his mind. In his own time he would discover the truth about how Elena had acquired the tickets.

Two days later, packed into an uncomfortable boxcar, pungent with the stale reek of the cattle that it had transported on the trains' journey east, accompanied by two other families and their belongings, the Kopps started their journey rattling and bumping their way across the American continent.

Chapter 4

Near the Greybull River, Dakota Territory

The boys were rigid with shock. The youngest shielded his face with his arms in an attempt to erase the image of his father being flailed against the trees, the elk continuing to utter an agonized series of barks and thrashing its head, snapping its antlers and tearing open its own hide on the sharp barbs of the branches it had broken in its delirium. The rank smell of the bull filled the air, and the rasp of its breathing punctuated by the piercing scream of its bugle assaulted his senses.

His brother stood motionless at his side, not to avoid attracting the elk's wrath, but immobilized by the horror of what he had witnessed. He felt no fear. He felt empty and useless. At first, his father's contorted form had twitched intensely, but now the warrior's body hung limply, the stream of blood that had run down his arm and dripped to the ground from an outstretched finger now reduced to a series of sticky droplets.

Abruptly, the elk stilled, eyes glazed and head held low, its chest heaving and falling in strained effort. It struggled to remain upright, its front left-hand quarter crumpled uselessly where the hunter's arrow had shattered the bone. The exertion had drained its reserves of strength and it staggered out of the forest to the open glade, where it stumbled and collapsed, its neck twisted awkwardly, nostrils flared and pumping like a set of bellows as it clung to its fragile life.

The older boy, Howahkan, stirred. He strode purposefully

toward his father and knelt to pick up the hunting knife that had dropped to the forest floor. The leather handle felt snug in the palm of his hand, and he immediately turned and walked to where the elk had fallen.

He stood facing the stricken animal so that he could look into its eyes. Howahkan did not feel bitter or vengeful for the death of his father. The bull had simply been defending itself, and his father had died the death of a hunter. The macabre dance of the hunt had gone horribly wrong, and the clean kill had failed.

Three years previously, Howahkan had been introduced to the Wiwayang Wacipi, the Sundance ceremony, commencing when his voice had broken, and as he stared at the hexaka the ritualistic training seemed more poignant than ever. Although he had not completed his four years of preparation to become a man, the task of manhood now fell to him.

He remembered the teachings of the Wakiyan Oyate, the Lightning People, whom the sacred lore credited with creating purpose upon the earth. Those doctrines, deeply embedded in his people's culture, required that he treat with reverence and gratitude the great beast before him, which had given its life so that he and his people might have food to eat and clothes to wear.

For a moment longer he locked eyes with the elk. He observed the spark of life draining away and lifted his head to the west as he recalled the words of prayer he had been taught, which gave thanks for all things that live upon the earth. In one flowing motion, he bent forward and reached behind the elk's jaw, drawing the hunting knife smoothly across the underside of its neck and severing the carotid artery as he spoke quietly to his four-legged brother of its courage and strength.

Immediately, warm sticky blood spurted across his hand and pumped onto the ground. The elk heaved as if attempting to raise itself then slumped, its head rolling listlessly to the side. He had told the elk that its spirit would live on in a "drum" that would be known throughout the land, and that its name would be Hekaka Ho Wakan, "Sacred Elks' Whistle." Its sacrifice would not be forgotten.

Howahkan knelt and bowed his head, overwhelmed by his father's death. He felt that he should pray to Wakan Tanka for the peace of his father's spirit, but he did not know what to say. He reeled, confused by the concoction of emotions that swirled through his mind—misery, anger, and hopelessness—and he sat in bewildered turmoil. He had to take control. It was the only way he could cope.

Summoning his resolve, he stood and returned to his brother, who remained transfixed, squatting in the undergrowth beneath the trees. He cleaned the hunting knife on the grass and slid it into a leather thong at his waist.

"Takoda. We must move," he whispered, bending down to speak to his sibling. "Takoda, please look at me. We can't stay here. We must go to the ponies and return to the village."

The younger boy raised his head and gazed at his brother, his eyes wide with shock. "Father. What happened to Father?"

Howahkan put a hand on his shoulder and looked directly at him, composing himself to ensure that his voice did not falter. "Father has gone. He is with the Great Spirit. Come. We must go now." He reached down and pulled Takoda to his feet.

"But we can't leave him here," Takoda whispered. "We must help him."

"Father is beyond this world now. His body hangs in the tree and I can't reach to lift him down. We must go to the village and get help." Howahkan faced his brother and held his shoulders. He looked deep into Takoda's eyes and shook him gently. "Listen. You must do as I say, now. Do you understand? We must go."

Takoda nodded and, without wasting further time, Howahkan turned to retrieve his father's bow, which lay in the brush a few feet away alongside the scattered arrows that had fallen from their upturned quiver. Swiftly, he collected the arrows and placed them in the quiver, handing it to Takoda to carry, as much to give him something to do as to ease his own burden.

Gently, he steered Takoda by the elbow and they walked to where their father's body hung in the tree. The crumpled clothing and distorted flesh possessed a surreal quality that rendered it inanimate and unidentifiable. Nevertheless, Howahkan stretched up and touched his father's hand, muttering a few barely audible words of honor and squeezing the wrist as though expecting the gesture to be acknowledged.

To Takoda the corpse seemed unreal, and he stood silently trying to rationalize its association with his father. "Can we go now?" he muttered.

The boy's words shook Howahkan from his introspection. "Yes, follow me. But we must be careful. The bears may smell the kill and come this way."

Descending to the valley proved considerably faster than the ascent. The boys moved at speed, unconstrained by the need to minimize noise or conceal their scent, and within an hour they arrived at the sheltered location where they had hobbled the ponies, three sturdy mustangs whose blood line ran back to horses imported by early Spanish settlers.

Takoda's leopard-spotted mare greeted them with a gentle whinny of recognition, tossing her head enthusiastically as they approached. Despite their urgency Takoda took time to fuss over the pony, blowing gently into her nostrils and scratching behind her ears. He ran his hands along her heavily dappled neck, dark black spots scattered across a shiny white coat, and she rested her head over his shoulder in affectionate and companionable response.

Aware of the boy's unusual bond with the little mare, Howahkan allowed the brief welcome as he removed the ponies' hobbles. Then, he cupped his hands to help Takoda mount. It was an unnecessary gesture, but Takoda placed his left foot into his brother's hands and grasped a clump of the pony's mane to swing onto her back.

The boys used no saddles and sat comfortably on their ponies' bare backs. Howahkan strung the bow across his shoulder and gathered up his reins, leading his father's horse. Takoda took a twist of his pony's mane in one hand and they set off, the younger boy having no need for bridle or reins, easily controlling the speed and direction of his pony by deft leg movements and subtle changes in balance or a soft touch to the neck.

They eased out of the trees onto the wide floor of the valley and turned north to trace the course of the river back to their village. Howahkan pushed the ponies into a brisk lope, and the afternoon sun burned hot on their backs as they sped across the long grass. A clear cerulean sky stretched from horizon to horizon, unblemished by the light clouds that had shrouded the mountains earlier in the day, and the tranquillity and beauty of the land stood in sharp contrast to the tragic events that had beset the boys and their father.

The Indian village was situated eight miles north of the location where the hunters had found the elk, set alongside a deep horseshoe bend in the river on the southern fringe of a steep forested escarpment. The band had chosen the location because it caught the sun for most of the day, and the inner bank of the river provided a shallow area of slower-flowing water for the women to wash and the children to play. There was plenty of wood for fuel, and the sheer mountain face to the north protected the village against the unexpected approach of strangers, yet provided a treacherous path that enabled a precipitous single-file escape to the ridge in the event of a threat appearing from the south.

The tipis were organized in a circle set back from the river, with one particularly large tipi situated slightly apart, used as a ceremonial sweat lodge. Despite their circular formation, the flaps of each tipi pointed to the east, so that their entrance greeted the morning sun, and wisps of smoke rose in ethereal spirals from the vents at their peak.

The village was bustling with activity, a group of women gathered in the center cleaning and stretching hides accumulated from a recent buffalo hunt, and a gaggle of noisy children playing by the river, supervised by two of the older girls. Alongside a central fire, more women sat tending a steaming cooking pot and slicing raw meat into thin strips, which they hung on a wooden frame to dry.

The Itancan, the leader elected by the band's matriarchs, sat cross-legged in front of his tipi immersed in discussion with a circle of four of the older members of the Council, each listening courteously while another spoke and affording considered thought to what had been said before responding.

The boys hurtled past two of the Akichitas conducting their outer defensive patrol of the village, who set off in pursuit anxiously demanding an explanation for the headlong charge. But the brothers did not break pace as they came within sight of the village, their ponies sweating and heaving from their wild gallop as they hurtled toward the far bank of the bend in the river.

Howahkan yelled as soon as he could see the tipis and urged his pony on faster. "Hau! Hau!" he bellowed as loud as his lungs could muster. "Mother! Mother!"

The children playing in the river were the first to hear his calls and notice the three ponies pounding toward them, pursued by the Akichitas. They broke from their game and ran to meet the oncoming boys, excited to discover what was happening.

Howahkan thought only of the urgent need to inform his mother and the Itancan of his father's death and, instead of swinging away toward the shallow ford, he struck a direct line for the village, aiming for the steep undercut outer bank of the curve in the river, where its waters ran deep and fast and wide. The children squealed with excitement and the women stopped their work, rising hastily to their feet with quizzical expressions.

A young woman with an unusually round face, her delicate features contorted into a mask of concern, ran to meet the boys accompanied by two of the Tokala, the men who were fathers or husbands, responsible for the inner defense of the camp. The woman's long ponytail of raven black hair swung wildly back and forth as she ran, waving her arms and yelling back at the boys.

Howahkan and Takoda reached the far side of the river at a full gallop and launched off the bank, four feet above the water. Their momentum appeared to suspend momentarily, as the trio of ponies stretched out across the river and Howahkan recognized the grim folly of his unrestrained flight.

Takoda trailed his brother out of blind loyalty, but instantly realized that their leap would fail to span the deep water. Instinctively, he leaned back and pulled on his pony's mane, causing the mare to lift her head and lower her haunches.

All three ponies plummeted into the river in an ungainly avalanche of horse flesh, Takoda's mare landing on her chest and driving her hind legs to the bed of the river, cushioning her impact so that her head remained clear of the water and the young Lakota ended up wrapped around her neck.

Howahkan was not so fortunate. Though he was a competent rider, his awareness of his pony's movement was less intuitive, and he threw his weight forward in the direction of their trajectory, hoping to extend his mount's reach. Instead, the pony's neck dipped and it drove into the river headfirst, causing its hind quarters to somersault, catapulting Howahkan off its back so that he slammed into the water and tumbled end over end until he disappeared beneath the surface.

The villagers on the far bank froze, stunned. The women clasped their hands to their faces, shocked at the boys' lunacy, while some of the younger children danced and shrieked with delight at what they assumed to be a marvellously daring game.

Howahkan gasped for breath as his head broke the surface, the resolve that had sustained him on his rush for home evaporating as he thrashed wildly to stay afloat in the river's swirling current.

"Howahkan! What are you doing? You crazy fool. Are you mad?" The raven-haired woman ran into the shallows screaming at him in Lakota, relieved to see Takoda gather his pony and drive it forward until its hooves touched the river bed and it surged out of the water.

"Mother!" he panted.

"Takoda, what are you doing? Have you both lost your senses? Your brother has nearly killed himself," the woman shrieked in exasperation.

Prompted by his mother's distress, Takoda glanced over his shoulder to find his brother struggling in the fast-flowing torrent. Aghast, he spun his pony downstream, pushing her along the bank until he overtook Howahkan, whereupon he drove her back into the river to intercept his brother, who was being washed rapidly downstream. The mare responded without hesitation and Howahkan collided with her withers as he was dragged under water for a second time, but Takoda reached out and grabbed hold of his tunic, the older boy lunging wildly to grasp the pony's mane.

But as Howahkan secured his grip, the little mare stepped out of her depth and all three plunged beneath the surface, the turbulent river swirling around them, and its powerful current threatening to draw them tumbling into the deeper water.

Realizing their perilous danger, several of the band ran along the riverbank parallel to the boys shouting futile instructions. Their mother screamed at them to swim for the bank, and more men came running from the Itancan's tipi to offer their help.

Takoda's pony rolled sideways, struggling to force its head above water, driving Howahkan further under in the process. He wrestled to hold onto the pony's mane, but oxygen starvation, combined with the pain of his impact with the river, left him floundering. His muscles screamed with fatigue and every impulse urged him to release his grasp, but instinct cautioned him that clinging to the mare presented his best chance of escaping the churning river alive, so he clutched at her mane with every ounce of remaining strength.

The pony surged, kicking powerfully to regain its balance and forcing itself into the shallower water, Takoda holding on grimly, his head thrust just clear of the river. He gulped hungrily, attempting to fill his lungs with air, but choked as the horse dipped below the surface again, gathering itself for a further lunge. Its hooves scraped the rocks on the riverbed as it scrambled to gain purchase, thrashing frantically until it sensed firmer footing, whereupon it lurched forward, dragging the boys in its wake.

The pony's foreleg punched through the water and, as Howahkan swung from its neck, the hoof struck him squarely in the chest, driving the remaining air from his lungs and causing him to release the final strands of mane twisted around his fingers. Takoda's weary grip on his brother failed, and Howahkan whirled away as the pony heaved into the shallows.

For a moment it appeared that he might be washed back into

the deeper water, but the little mare had achieved enough, and he was thrust toward the shallows instead, where two of the Tokala plunged into the river and dragged him to safety.

The older boy emerged onto the bank, his eyes rolling and his body limp, and the men lowered him onto his side, heaving down on his ribs in one fluid movement. Almost instantly, Howahkan's head snapped back and he pulled his knees up to his chest, coughing wildly and vomiting water. His eyes sprang open and he gasped desperately, pumping up more water and sucking in a lungful of fresh air.

Takoda's mother seized his pony as it surged out of the river, where it snorted loudly and shook violently, covering her in a shower of spray as it came to an abrupt halt on the grassy bank. Her youngest son slid from its back and crumpled to his knees at her feet, his chest heaving as he wrestled to regain his breath, supporting himself on his knuckles as he fought to speak.

"Father's dead!" he mouthed unintelligibly. "Father's dead!" he wheezed.

Makawee stoked the fire in her tipi. Assisted by her aunt and two of the grandmothers, the elder matriarchs of the band, they stripped the boys of their wet clothes and rubbed them briskly with dry skins to relieve the cold.

Once they were warm, she filled a deerskin-lined cooking hollow with water and used several hot stones from the fire to heat the liquid, provoking violent hissing and a billowing cloud of steam.

In addition to being the boys' mother, Makawee was Medicine Woman to the small band of Lakota. Her tipi was set next to the Itancan's, reflecting her importance to the tribe but also the status of her husband.

She was numb from the traumatic news that Takoda had imparted, but her first priority was the well-being of her sons, so she worked diligently to set out her herbs and other medicines. Once they had donned dry clothes and were sitting beside the fire, she poured each boy a cup of steaming water infused with calming lemon grass, following which she made a poultice from the crushed bark and leaves of witch hazel to relieve the swelling evident on Howahkan's chest.

The poultice would soothe the bruised tissues, and the astringency of the witch hazel would act as a form of antiseptic to prevent infection where the skin had been broken. For additional relief, she added pounded arnica to Howahkan's infusion. Administered promptly, this helped to reduce the inflammation and edema caused by the pony's kick.

The skills of the medicine man had been passed down through generations of Makawee's male ancestors, culminating in her father, who had schooled her in the mysteries of the spirit world and the use of plants and herbs since she had been a small child. While she was not the most senior of the Lakota shaman, she was responsible for the health of her band of Sioux and was much respected for her knowledge and ability, particularly since, as a woman, it was believed that she benefitted from a uniquely profound communion with the spirits.

The band was one of several small groups composing the Teton Lakota division of the tribe, whose traditional hunting grounds encompassed the prairies bordered by the Missouri River and the Bighorn Mountains. Unusually, they had migrated to the plains to the extreme west, bordered by the dramatic Rocky Mountains, adjacent to the smoldering cauldron of geothermal pots and geysers surrounding the head of the Yellowstone River, where they had been dispatched by the Lakota elders to foster alliance with the neighboring Northern Cheyenne.

The lifestyle of Makawee's tribe had evolved significantly over the previous century, encouraged by the advent of the horse as a means of locomotion. Where once the Sioux had employed their accomplished farming skills to survive, the horse had revolutionized transportation, enabling the tribe to shadow the buffalo herds as they roamed the prairies, their enhanced mobility facilitating a readily available and prolific source of food and clothing.

The laborious and time-consuming undertaking of utilizing packs of dogs to carry their belongings was consigned to history. Tipis were constructed so that they could be broken down easily and loaded onto horses, which were capable of bearing the bulky burden over long distances, leading to a nomadic existence symbiotic with that of the buffalo.

Consequently, the buffalo was revered by the Lakota and held a spiritual significance to the tribe, who thrived because of their ability to accumulate a plentiful supply of meat throughout the summer months, sufficient to sustain them through the harsh North American winter.

Having communed successfully with the Cheyenne, the band had followed a herd of several thousand buffalo as they had drifted slowly upstream alongside the Greybull River, meandering toward its source in the Absaroka Mountains, on the fringe of the Rockies.

They had engaged in a productive hunt, and the village was busy ensuring that every part of the beasts they had killed was put to good use. The meat would be dried on racks, smoked and stored, or ground and blended with buffalo tallow and berries to make pemmican, a highly nutritious food that could be packed into deerskin pouches and kept for a year or more, providing essential sustenance during the long winter months. The skins were being de-haired, cured, and rubbed with boiled brain as a softening agent, following which the treated hides would be used to make clothing or stitched together to form the waterproof cover for a tipi. Buffalo hooves could be melted down to produce an effective glue, bones would be fashioned into tools, and in a few instances skulls would be retained for ceremonial use. Nothing went to waste.

The Sioux philosophy centered upon living in harmony with nature, taking only what was needed to provide food, shelter, tools, or weapons. They considered it important that the riches of nature were not squandered and that the tribe should take no more than was essential to assure their survival. Mother Earth provided all that they required, and it was their solemn responsibility to preserve the abundance of her bounty for generations to come.

There was a gentle tap on the flap of Makawee's tipi announcing the arrival of the Itancan, who requested permission to enter. She looked up from the poultice she was preparing and beckoned to him. "Please, Father, come in," she said, casting him a haunted expression.

Her husband was the Itancan's son, and following the death of her own father he had adopted the role of surrogate parent. O'hiniya he Mani's death had hit him hard, although, as the band's head man, he was obliged to refrain from exhibiting his grief. As a respected elder it was expected that he would demonstrate great fortitude and bear his personal anguish with dignified stoicism.

He entered the tipi on the right as was custom for men and sat down on the opposite side of the fire to Makawee and her sons, who were now wrapped in warm buffalo hides, sipping reflectively at their mother's infusion. He had been informed of his son's death by one of the Tokala, and sat with a grave face studying his older grandson.

"Howahkan, tell me now, what has befallen your father?"

Howahkan met his grandfather's gaze briefly and cast his head down. His eyes burned with emotion, but he knew that he must respond factually, steadying his voice to be respectful to his father's memory and maintain the honor of his family. He balled his fingers into a fist and squeezed his nails into his palm, using the pain to focus himself as he felt his voice beginning to crack.

"Father was killed by a great elk, Grandfather," he began. "His arrow hit the hexaka's shoulder and it attacked us. Father stepped in front of it to protect me and Takoda." His voice dropped to a whisper but his tone was firm and proud as he looked up, meeting his grandfather's eyes. "Father faced the hexaka and stood tall. He showed no fear. He did not cry out."

Takoda could not restrain himself. "Grandfather, it was my fault!" he blurted. "I stumbled against father as he was about to shoot the hexaka," he wailed, tears running down his cheeks. "Father wouldn't have missed. He's dead because of me." His voice trailed away as he sobbed.

Makawee put her arms around Takoda and held him to her chest. The agony of her husband's death was almost unbearable, and she wrestled to keep her emotions in check in the presence of the Itancan. But the knowledge that her sons had seen the elk kill their father was too awful to contemplate. No child should have to witness such a thing. She yearned to hug them both, but she restrained herself, her heart aching with pride as she watched Howahkan fighting to suppress his tears and demonstrate his courage to the leader of his band.

The Itancan turned sharply to acknowledge Takoda. Anger flared in his heavily lidded eyes, irritated at the young boy's uninvited intervention, but he composed himself swiftly and his feelings became shrouded by a mask of detachment that settled across his wrinkled face. He glanced away, focusing on the flickering flames of the fire, his features relaxing as if summoning a sense of peace. When he looked back at Takoda his eyes were soft and sympathetic.

"Wakan Tanka has spoken. He has summoned O'hiniya he Mani to be with him. There is nothing that you did, or could have done, that has caused your father's death. It was the will of the Great Spirit. You must be strong now, to honor your father's life. Stand tall before your people. You and your brother must honor his name by displaying your strength and courage." His voice was slow, deep, and purposeful, the words spoken with the surety of many years of leadership entrusted to him by the matriarchs. Though his head was bowed, reflecting his age, his back was straight and strong, and he sat motionless in a state of practiced self-control.

The Itancan addressed Howahkan once more. "Your father was a brave warrior. It was his first duty to protect his family. But why did you not return with his body? Why did you leave him to the wolves and the bears?" His question was practical, bearing no hint of accusation.

"Grandfather, I could not reach him. His body was thrown high into the trees, so I killed the hexaka and we came back to the village as fast as we could."

"You killed the hexaka? Tell me how you did this." The Itancan's dispassionate expression almost cracked.

"After the great hexaka killed father, it eventually fell to the ground." Howahkan's voice trembled, recalling the macabre scene, but he squeezed his nails into his palm again and continued. "I picked up father's hunting knife and went to where the hexaka had fallen. I looked him in the eye so that he knew me, and then I cut his throat."

Makawee flinched at the brutality of the statement, her maternal instincts bristling with both pride and horror. "Howahkan, you could have been killed! What would you have done if the hexaka had attacked you?"

"You did well, my grandson." The Itancan ignored Makawee's rebuke. "You must take us to your father. We must bring his body back to the village."

"He can't do that, Father!" Makawee was astonished. "Howahkan was nearly drowned, and I think he has a broken rib." She turned to face her son, placing a reassuring hand on his knee. "Can you tell us where this happened? Can you tell us where to find your father?"

The Itancan did not permit a response. "Howahkan, you can ride?" He peered intently at the boy, and it was evident that the question was not intended to have an optional response.

The ways of the Lakota were complex, and the Itancan was now forced to carefully balance a number of factors. It was entirely reasonable that the boy's mother should be concerned about his welfare, and her protective instinct was laudable, but there were other matters at stake.

Walks on Air had been a senior member of the tribe. He had been a "Shirt Wearer" appointed by the Wichasa Ithanchan, the group of tribal elders elected by the Naca Ominicia, the political leaders of the tribe. As a Shirt Wearer, Walks on Air ranked as one of the most influential members of the tribe. He had been selected for the role because he was regarded as an individual who demonstrated all of the virtues that the tribe valued. He had been a leader in the Akichitas who organized the training of warriors and enforced the moral disciplines of the tribe. He had consistently shown his courage in battle and endurance in the face of adversity, so that many stories were told about his exploits, consolidating the respect he commanded across all divisions of the tribe. He had married a gifted young medicine woman and they had given generously of everything that they possessed: food, skins, tools, and ponies. They both worked tirelessly for the benefit of the tribe and had a reputation for providing sound advice whenever required.

In time, it was anticipated that Walks on Air would become a tribal leader and that his sons would follow in his footsteps.

Consequently, it was now important that the tribe witnessed the elder son's fortitude. The band had to see that he could bear the anguish of his loss and rise above the agony of his battered body, to do what was necessary. Such a display of courage and endurance would earn respect within the tribe. Stories of his bravery would be told, which would honor his father's memory and cultivate his reputation. The Itancan had to coerce the boy into this public display of determination for his own sake. His mother understood the ways of the tribe, and although she would not wish to see her son suffer, she would not stand in his way.

Howahkan grimaced as he struggled to his feet, the pallid color of his face betraying his discomfort. His lip quivered as he strained to stand erect, but he had made his decision; he would go to retrieve his father's body even if he had to drag himself. The Itancan scrutinized the boy carefully and nodded in silent appreciation. This was a remarkable young man.

Many of the band's warriors had been sent to scout for buffalo, so a rider was dispatched to recall them, while a small party of the Tokala, guided by Howahkan, set off to retrieve Walks on Air's body, anxious to make good use of the remaining daylight. The Itancan stayed in the village, turning his mind to the demoralizing task of planning the funeral arrangements for his son. The fires would burn brightly long into the night, and few people would sleep.

The messenger found the warriors trailing the buffalo as they grazed along the Greybull River. The herd was peaceful and the Indians had enjoyed watching the calves, born earlier in the season, cavorting in frenzied circles as the cows swung rhythmically to and fro, cropping the lush grass with a lazy efficiency.

The sight of the buffalo in such large numbers warmed the hearts of the young warriors, and they immersed themselves in the harmonious tranquillity of the herd. There would be a day for a hunt, and they would thank Mother Earth for the blessing of their bovine brothers, but for now they were content to watch the ponderous progress of the migration, the intermittent puff of dust as an animal writhed in a patch of dry earth to shed itself of ticks and lice, and the occasional skirmish of the young bulls as they locked horns in mock battle.

But the comfortable serenity of the day was shattered when they received the news that O'hiniya he Mani had been killed. The warriors were shocked, all of them holding Howahkan and Takoda's father in great esteem, and they immediately abandoned their vigil to return to the village.

It was late and the sun had set over the mountains to the west by the time Howahkan and the small party of Tokala returned. They had found Walks on Air's body with ease, hanging in the tree, but retrieving the corpse had proven more difficult than expected.

As they approached, it became apparent that the fallen elk had attracted attention. They drew to a halt and watched the erratic behavior of a squabbling congregation of crows as they flitted from rock to rock, rushing in to peck hurriedly at the body before darting away again, their presence indicating that the beast's hide had been torn open.

Incongruously, the whole carcass shuddered, the huge rack of antlers twisting as though the animal had returned to life. The ominous shaggy brown mound of a grizzly bear's shoulders heaved into view as it wrestled to tear flesh from a rent in the elk's belly. A confrontation with a grizzly was not a desirable prospect, and attempting to kill the bear presented an unpalatable risk.

The little group convened to consider their options, eventually acceding to the experience of an old warrior called Mahpee who suggested a technique for encouraging the bear to withdraw. The old man was lean and sinewy, his wiry body cloaked in an ankle-length coat of skins that drooped from his bony shoulders, and his face was puckered by a mass of weathered wrinkles, the large crow's feet at the corner of each eye describing his long years of squinting against the elements. He was an experienced hunter and known to be most accustomed to the ways of bears, so his advice was regarded as sound.

Under Mahpee's direction, two of the party laid out the travois they had brought to transport Howahkan's father back to the village, and the other warriors set about accumulating a large pile of material to build a fire, which they positioned upwind of the bear. Howahkan was assigned the task of keeping watch in case the bear abandoned the carcass unexpectedly, with instructions to remain vigilant to the potential of more bears appearing, and the rest of the party went to work.

Once the pyre was assembled, Mahpee opened a leather pouch on his waistband and removed a flint and stone, using a small nest of tinder to light a fire at the base of the mound of dry sticks and pine needles. He allowed the flames to take hold, then heaped green leaves and grass onto the fire, causing clouds of billowing gray smoke, which blew steadily up the glade carried by a brisk southerly breeze.

The elk's carcass was soon shrouded in the choking smoke, and the Indians eased closer, creating as much noise as possible by beating sticks against the trees and shouting. It was a simple plan, but effective. The commotion alone would not have been sufficient to encourage the bear to retreat from the elk, and he may well have attacked the Indians, considering them a threat to his meal, but combined with the acrid smoke, the sound was enough to persuade him to move.

The big grizzly lumbered away, leaving the warriors free to

approach the Shirt Wearer's body safely. But they knew that they would have to work expediciously. The deterrent effect of the smoke would not last for long, and the bear's hunger would soon drive him to return to his kill.

Howahkan continued to feed the fire, while the rest of the party hastily undertook the more dangerous task of advancing to recover his father's body.

The youngest member of the party, a warrior called Hotah, who had broken his leg badly in a fall from his horse during a skirmish with a band of Crow, climbed the tree to reach the disfigured corpse. The disability in his leg was compensated by the power of his arms, which he had worked to strengthen during a long period of convalescence, and he hauled himself into the branches with ease, trailing a length of Dogbane rope.

Once in position, Hotah looped the rope over a branch overhead and reached down to secure the cord around O'hiniya he Mani's waist. The warriors on the ground pulled in the slack and took the strain, as Hotah worked gently to disentangle the crumpled body from the broken branches that penetrated its flesh, pinning it in a grotesque thorny snare.

The task was intricate and time-consuming. Hotah wanted to avoid mutilating the body further, but removing the impaled branches threatened to suck out the inner organs on more than one occasion, and he was obliged to insert his hand into the wounds to release stubby protuberances that had snapped off within the torso to avoid inadvertently disemboweling the corpse.

By the time his father's body was lowered to the ground, Howahkan was struggling to keep the fire going. Its initial intense heat had waned, the damp grass largely smothering the flames and leaving him searching the glade anxiously, squinting to penetrate the dissipating haze in an effort to detect the bear's return. But there was no sign of its presence.

The warriors laid the body gently onto a bed of soft hides and wrapped it tightly. The bleeding had stopped long ago, but Mahpee took care to conceal the gruesome wounds so that Howahkan might be spared further distress. The travois was then hitched to one of the ponies, and the body secured for the return journey.

Howahkan watched with morbid fascination as the party worked carefully to secure his father's body, appreciating the reverence with which they handled the corpse. It seemed a surreal experience, and he felt numb and detached from what he was witnessing, so he allowed his mind to wander back to events earlier in the day. Preoccupied, he was slow to react to a furtive movement at the periphery of his vision, but a subconscious urgency prompted him to regain focus and he wrestled his attention back to his task. Horrified, he discerned the huge bulk of the grizzly loping down the hill, the other Indians engrossed in their preparations to depart and oblivious to its approach.

The bear carried its head low as it accelerated, aiming purposefully for the elk. His sheer size and the power in his shoulders indicated that he was a boar in the prime of life, bulked with the huge volume of food he had gorged to sustain him through his winter hibernation.

"Bear!" Howahkan screamed, his broken rib sending a searing pain shooting through his chest as he attempted to make himself heard.

Simultaneously, the ponies sensed the bear's approach and stamped nervously, galvanizing the warriors into action, Mahpee urging them to move off as he handed Hotah the lead rope for the pony pulling the travois.

"Go, Hotah. Through the trees, not in the open! Go! Go now!"

Immediately, the bear detected the movement and slackened its pace to assess the potential threat. He was in no mood to share his meal and swerved to intercept the party of Indians, roaring a ferocious challenge and baring huge teeth in a threatening snarl as he bounded closer.

The warriors attempted to weave through the trees as Howahkan looked on helplessly, certain that they would not manage to evade the bear, when to his astonishment, one of the Indians separated from the group and started back to intercept the grizzly.

Wisps of chalky smoke continued to eddy in the air, forming an eerie mist, its ethereal haze penetrated by shafts of afternoon sunlight as a ghostly figure strode out of the trees to meet the bear's charge. Howahkan recognized the craggy features of the old man, Mahpee. He bore no weapons, and the wrinkled features of his face appeared calm. Stepping clear of the trees, he paused, and Howahkan stood transfixed, convinced that he would be torn to pieces by the bear, but an extraordinary transformation occured. The old hunter grew in stature, his shadowy image doubling in size. Then, he rushed at the bear.

It took a few agonizing moments for the bizarre vision to resolve. Eventually, Howahkan could see that the old man had opened up his huge cloak, and thrust his arms upward and outward to enhance his size, before running to challenge the bear.

Ominously, it appeared that the deception would transpire to be a fatal folly, but the unexpected confrontation caused the bear to hesitate, and at the last moment it veered away in a bluff charge, swinging around to stand facing Mahpee, huffing its annoyance in rasping grunts.

The bear stopped between Mahpee and the dead elk, the old hunter having been careful to ensure that he positioned himself to avoid posing a threat to the animal's feast. He stood motionless, his huge cloak hanging to the ground from his outstretched limbs. He remained silent and offered no further challenge as the bear rocked from side to side, shifting weight on its huge front paws and scraping the ground with claws long enough to eviscerate a man with a single swipe. He continued to huff and sniffed the air in confused irritation while the unlikely opponents stood a few paces apart, poised in an obstinate war of wills.

The group of warriors pulled up, mesmerized by Mahpee's apparent lunacy, and held their breath as they watched the astonishing encounter unfold. Howahkan stood awestruck by the old man's selfless bravery, admiring the unflinching composure he displayed in confronting an animal that could have ripped him to shreds in seconds.

The grizzly threw itself onto its hind legs and reared upright in front of the old man, raising its front paws and throwing its head back to let out a rending roar. The apprehensive observers gasped as it seemed certain that the bear would drop down and kill Mahpee, but incredibly the old hunter remained unmoved, gazing directly up at the bear, which stood more than twice his height.

The bear teetered and swiped at the air, weaving its head from side to side, then abruptly dropped to all fours, shook its shaggy shoulders, huffed, and let out a throaty growl as it turned away and ambled back to settle on the elk's carcass.

The old man stood quietly, allowing the bear to immerse itself in its meal, before slowly lowering his arms and backing away to the trees.

Howahkan was speechless. He had never seen such a feat of bravery, or witnessed the confidence of a hunter who was so totally at one with the force of nature. He understood now, more than ever, the meaning of the values that he had been taught since birth and appreciated for the first time the magnitude of the journey that he must take to find a position of respect among his tribe.

CHAPTER 5

Camp of a Sioux band, headwaters of the Greybull River

When Howahkan's party returned to the village, his father's body was carried reverently to Makawee's tipi, causing the women to wail at the sight of the shrouded corpse and prompting the men to congregate around the fire in the center of the village to dance and sing about the exploits of their fallen brother. Makawee, the boys, and the Itancan knelt in quiet solitude in the tipi and paid homage over the inert body, until the Itancan was obliged to absent himself to finalize arrangements for the following day.

Dawn prompted a state of quiet industry. The dancing and singing had continued long into the night, and many stories had been told about the valiant Shirt Wearer, but funeral plans had been made and tasks assigned.

The elders had decided that, since there was no recognized burial ground within many miles of the village, Walks on Air's body would be taken to a place high up on the ridge above the camp, where he would be closer to the Great Spirit.

In preparation, an advance party had been dispatched to fell enough young lodgepoles to build the framework for a scaffold upon which to rest the body, leaving everyone else to follow in procession at midday.

The band was largely interrelated, comprised of an extended family unit as was the norm for small bands of Lakota.

Therefore, the death of Walks on Air represented more than the loss of a senior member of the tribe, since he was also a closely related family member. As such, everyone rallied to help and contribute to the arrangements for his funeral.

Makawee's aunt, a friendly woman with a gaunt face, dark soulful eyes, and long gray hair tied back in a neat ponytail, squatted to assist her in laying out her husband's body and dress him in his finest clothes. They were good friends and worked in companionable silence.

They pulled on leggings, which they attached to a waist belt at each hip. The soft buckskin was decorated with meticulously detailed colored pictures depicting important events in the history of the tribe, and each leg was adorned with long tassels stitched into the outer seam. A square elk skin breechcloth was tucked over the waistband to both front and rear, embellished with an embroidered apron panel ornamented with colorful beads that had been traded with the Blackfoot Indians, all sewn with great skill to portray the head of a buffalo and an image of a swooping eagle, its wings held high and its talons stretched out as if snatching at its prey. Long moccasins were laced at the front, the tops dressed with colorful ermine fur and the sides stitched with simple lines of blue- and red-colored porcupine quill.

Makawee strained to maneuver the ceremonial Shirt Wearer's tunic over her husband's head to cover his torso, but the unsightly wounds inflicted by the elk's enormous antlers caused her to stop and sob uncontrollably.

In the privacy of the tipi her aunt embraced her as the tears ran down her cheeks, and she vented the emotion she had fought so hard to contain. Her heart ached from her loss, and although she struggled to resist indulging in self-pity, her thoughts were overwhelmed by memories of the love and tenderness she had shared with her husband, a blessed intimacy so much at odds with the powerfully muscular and assertive warrior that the rest of the tribe knew.

"Nothing can take the love from your heart or the memories from your head, Makawee," her aunt whispered perceptively. "You must honor his memory to ease the pain."

Makawee leaned back and rubbed the tears from her cheeks; her eyes were red and swollen, and her mouth trembled as she breathed deeply, trying to regain her equanimity. Embarrassed, she glanced awkwardly at the kind-hearted woman, who held her hands gently.

"I'm sorry," her voice quavered as she fought for control. "I want to be strong for him, and for the boys. I don't want to dishonor his memory, but I'm afraid my strength will fail in front of the others."

"Place his fist in your heart so that you may draw upon his strength. You will be true to his name and people will sing of your courage," her aunt smiled encouragingly. "Come, we must finish our work." She gave Makawee no chance to respond and bent down to wrestle the shirt over the broken torso.

Makawee sniffed back her tears and rubbed her face again, but set to the task and helped to straighten the colorful shirt. The top half was dyed red, representing the sun and the bottom half was green, denoting the earth, lines of hair being stitched down both sides of the shirt, each hair representing a member of the tribe, reminding the wearer of his responsibility for their welfare.

Once they had adjusted the tunic, obscuring the gruesome injuries, Makawee felt more composed and was able to proceed with renewed conviction, ensuring that her husband's body was prepared flawlessly.

As a final act of respect, they crowned his head with a sacred buffalo headdress, the privilege of wearing the unique headpiece being a rare distinction, won through many feats of courage in battle. It was crafted from buffalo hide adorned with long shaggy buffalo hair, mounted with a gleaming pair of buffalo horns, their luster achieved through the tireless polishing ascribed to a highly valued artifact. Ermine skins and eagle feathers hung from the sides, and a full buffalo tail was attached to the back. The headdress symbolized the magnitude of his achievements and the veneration of his tribe.

As the midday sun reached its zenith the village assembled, forming a funeral cortege to accompany the body, which was placed upon a thick mattress of furs laid on a travois drawn by the warrior's favorite pony. Once prepared, the party moved slowly out of the village and embarked upon their ascent of the precipitous path that navigated the steep face of the mountain to the north.

The Itancan led the way, clad in ceremonial robes and a long trailer headdress of double-lined eagle feathers that stretched down to the ground behind him, and the whole party conjoined in a soft ululating chant as they advanced in slow procession up the tortuous slope.

Surmounting the crest of the escarpment two hours later, the band reached a point close to the eastern end of a narrow plateau that extended for more than a mile along the length of its ridge. Despite the time of year, the sun was brutally hot, and the climb had been long and difficult, with the travois threatening to slide off the treacherous path on several occasions, so the entire band was drained of energy and many of the children had reached the limit of their endurance. Acknowledging their need to recuperate, the Itancan allowed the party to sit in a reflective circle and refresh themselves from their water skins, while he went to inspect the scaffold built by the young warriors he had dispatched earlier in the day.

The dais was positioned at the extreme eastern end of the plateau, adjacent to its northern edge, overlooking the barren upper slopes of the neighboring valley. Its platform was a robust structure, mounted above head height and lashed firmly to four large lodgepole trunks, which had been felled, trimmed, and planted vertically at each corner. The elevated dais, constructed from elder branches woven alternately in a perpendicular lattice, would be the final resting place for O'hiniya he Mani, placed so that he faced the twinkling images of the spirits described by the constellations, and located as close to Wakan Tanka as was possible.

The Itancan inspected the structure and was pleased with the quality of the young men's work. A wide set of steps was positioned to one side of the platform, enabling the Shirt Wearer's body to be lifted into place easily, but designed so that they could be dismantled to prevent animals from reaching and disturbing the corpse.

The Naca Ominicia, the tribal elders of the band, had decided upon the detailed aspects of the way that the funeral ceremony would be conducted and allocated responsibilities, enabling the formalities to commence without further instruction once the band had rested. Each member of the tribe regarded it as a solemn personal obligation that they should fulfill their ascribed task without fault.

The band assembled in a semi-circle, commencing a soft doleful song as six Akichitas conveyed O'hiniya he Mani's body toward the funeral scaffold with reverential deference, followed in procession by the Itancan, Makawee, and the two boys.

Makawee had plaited her long dark hair into a single ponytail, which she cut off and placed on her husband's chest as a symbol of her enduring love, once the body had been laid upon the dais. The two boys arranged some of their father's prized possessions at his side; a ceremonial tomahawk, his favored bow and a quiver of arrows, and his hunting knife. Next, members of the band contributed food to sustain him on his journey through the spirit world and blankets for the cold nights, so that he was furnished with all that he needed to return to the Creator.

His favorite horse stood quietly beside the scaffold, an exquisitely dappled Appaloosa with roan markings along his back and a speckle of white across his face and center line, reminiscent of a light morning frost. The animal required no hobble, and his intelligent eyes observed the proceedings with somber interest.

Eventually, the Itancan stood before the band and raised his hands to the sky as he commended his son to the Great Spirit. "A man's life is like the seasons. He is brought forth from Mother Earth in the miracle of birth, and he flourishes in the early rains of spring. He grows strong as the sun rises in the sky and shines down upon the summer of his prime. Sometimes the seasons are long, and sometimes they are short. Winter may come with a gradual shortening of the days, or sometimes it may come with savage thunder and storms, unwelcome and unexpected. So it is with man, and so it is with O'hiniya he Mani. Although it is fitting that Makawee should mourn for one year for the loss of her husband, we should not be sad. O'hiniya he Mani was a great man. He was a true leader and a fearsome warrior. He fought with honor and with courage. He led his warriors with the cunning of the fox and the wisdom of the great owl. He served his people as a Shirt Wearer and gave of himself generously. He was true to his wife and a devoted father to his children. The Great Spirit has called him and, like all people of any nation, he must obey. The Great Mystery will be revealed to him, so do not grieve for long. The Great Spirit will take the most courageous and the best of his children out of season to be near him. This adversity does not befall only us, in our lives, but hardship falls everywhere. We are no different. Tonight we will mourn, but tomorrow we will gather our children and we will tell them to be happy, because although a dark sky has fallen upon us all, when the children laugh, when they play in the river and dance around the fire, the clouds will roll back and the sun will shine again. Then the summer of our lives shall blossom once more, and the cycle of life will continue. O'hiniya he Mani will look upon us and he will smile at what he sees. He will laugh at our confusion and innocence, but he will place his hand upon our shoulder and guide us upon our way."

Makawee approached the dais and cut a lock of her husband's long dark hair, which she placed in a sacred buckskin pouch, tying it securely with a thin leather thong. She would keep the hair to fulfill the Nagi Gluhapi rite, the Keeping of the Soul, a ceremony that would be conducted later the same day.

She descended the steps slowly and stood before the assembled band, who chanted in tempo with the rhythmic beat of drums played by two of the Akichitas. Standing proudly, she stared intently at the ground before removing a small knife from her waistband and drawing the blade twice across each of her limbs in a fluid motion, the incisions deep enough to open the flesh but avoid damaging any major blood vessels. The lacerations drew blood instantly, which ran freely down her legs and forearms, pooling at her feet and dripping from her fingers. The scars would be a reminder of her loss and a sign of her eternal suffering. She made no sound and demonstrated no indication of pain, as was befitting of the wife of a man of honor, and of the band's medicine woman.

The Itancan turned to face the scaffold and was joined by two of the elders. They raised their arms and gyrated to the beat of the drums, the entire band observing their lead and swaying in synchronization as they sung to the spirits. Their harmonious voices blended as one and their bodies rocked as if morphed into a single being, mesmerized by a hypnotic state, oblivious to their surroundings.

The singing built to a crescendo, at which point a young warrior moved to the Appaloosa and tied its tail to one of the vertical scaffold posts. The Itancan raised his voice above the singing, and his powerful tones carried across the gathered throng. "Great Spirit, we thank you for the brother you sent amongst us, who begins his journey to return to your breast. Guide him to your side so that he might know you." With this declaration, the warrior swept his tomahawk down onto the horse's neck, severing its spinal column so that it collapsed instantly to the ground, the light from its intelligent eyes draining as the blood washed down its neck and pooled in the dust where it had fallen. The spirit of the favored horse would speed O'hiniya he Mani across the constellations to reach Wakan Tanka.

With the ceremony concluded, the party descended to the valley, where a large fire was built at the center of the village. As darkness fell, the keeper of the pipe, one of the revered elders of the band, assembled a small pyre of burning sweetgrass and stood before the entire village as he called Makawee forward. She handed him the buckskin pouch containing the lock of her husband's hair, and the elder held it up in the air.

"Oh, Wakan Tanka, behold us!" he began. "We will keep the soul of our brother in this lock of hair so that our Mother Earth will bear fruit, and so that our children may walk the path of life in accordance with your wishes." Reverently, he untied the buckskin and removed the lock of dark hair, holding it in the smoke from the sweetgrass so that it might be purified.

"Behold, o soul!" he continued. "Where you dwell on this earth will be a sacred place, and the people will be as wakan as you are. Our children, and our children's children, will walk their paths with pure hearts and sure steps." He went on to beseech Wakan Tanka to permit the soul of O'hiniya he Mani to furnish those who prayed to him with knowledge and wisdom, encouraging them to respect and treat with reverence all of the wondrous gifts of Mother Earth; the animals and the birds, the rivers and the trees, the great prairies, and all of the abundance of nature. He reminded the people that they were all of one spirit, an omnipresent force interconnecting all of creation, and that as a consequence they were brothers with all things, animate and inanimate, implying that they were obliged to protect and live in harmony with the cycle of nature, as the Great Mystery intended.

He turned to face the rest of the band. "Remember this in your hearts. The power of this pure soul will be with you wherever you walk, for it too is the fruit of Mother Earth. It is a seed planted in your midst, which will grow in your hearts and cause all of our future generations to walk in the wakan way."

Returned to the sacred buckskin pouch, the lock of hair was presented to Makawee. "Keeper of the soul, your hands are wakan; use them as such. Your eyes are wakan; when you look upon your people and all things, you should see them as a sacred reflection of Wakan Tanka. Your mouth is wakan, and every word you say should speak in the tongue of the Great Spirit. You should raise your head and look to the heavens often. Look after this soul all of the time, for through this you will remember Wakan Tanka, and from now you will be able to teach others, as they have taught you, because you are wakan. Indeed, it is so. Hechetu welo!"

Makawee was charged with keeping the soul in a special place in her tipi for one year, following which the whole village would build a lodge for the ceremony of Releasing the Soul, and the people would sing and dance with joy, and everyone would be happy again as the soul raced away to join Wakan Tanka.

The sacred rite concluded with a song as the band circulated around the fire. There would be stories told late into the night about the great exploits of their departed brother, but in the morning, there would be work to do, the tribe would have to elect another Shirt Wearer, and the boys would require a tutor to teach them the skills of the hunter and warrior. Life would go on, and the buffalo would continue to lead the band across the plains as they accumulated sufficient stock of food and hides to ensure that they survived the harsh winter in the Rockies.

Chapter 6

March 1865, Fort Leavenworth, State of Kansas

Captain John Gresham stood to attention in front of his General, William G. Murray. The general was beside himself with rage and leaned aggressively across his desk at the young captain, spittle running down his chin.

"You will do exactly as I command you, you impertinent upstart!" he bellowed. "You will take Mr. Colter with you to Platte Bridge Station and you will ask no questions about his purpose, do you understand me!"

Gresham met the general's belligerent glare with steady blue eyes, unmoved by the hysterical outburst. Although only in his late twenties, he was a seasoned campaigner in the United States cavalry, and had endured his fair share of senior officers who sought to run the army from behind their desk, with little or no understanding of the unique idiosyncrasies of the west. Murray could bluster all he wanted, but as soon as Gresham led his company out of the gates of the Kansas fort, his authority would be the only command that mattered.

"Sir, I understand that Mr. Colter is to accompany me and my men, but he must know that he will do so on my terms, and that he will be under the command of the United States cavalry. I will not contemplate a man like Colter traveling with us without it being explicit that he abides by my orders."

"You'll take him with you and leave him to get on with his business or so help me god, I'll have you court martialed!" The general was puce, his face puffy and his eyes bulging, such that Gresham imagined they might pop out of his head at any moment. He ignored the threat, aware that the general was compelled to employ him as the leader of the expedition to Platte Bridge Station. He was being posted to the little fort, positioned close to the waypoint where the newly established Bridger Trail forked away from the Oregon Trail, cutting a route across the northern plains all the way to the new goldfields at Virginia City. It was widely recognized that he was more experienced in dealing with the native Indian tribes than any other officer deployed in the plains region, with a deeper understanding of their customs and means of waging war than any of his contemporaries. The young lieutenants in his company were largely inexperienced in traversing the often dangerous and unpredictable Indian territory and, in any event, were unqualified to assume command of the distant outpost.

"Sir, Colter is a savage and a liability, and the only way he'll travel with me is under my command."

"The only savages around here are those damned Indian barbarians you seem to have so much sympathy for. Colter is in my charge and he'll answer to no one else. Do you understand?"

Gresham realized that in the absence of compromise, the general was in a position to make his life uncomfortably difficult when he reached his new command, where he would be reliant upon support from Kansas. Accordingly, he tried an alternative approach.

"Sir, Mr. Colter may accompany me on the journey, but he must surrender his arms to my custody until we reach Platte Bridge Station. I will reissue his weapons if he has a need to protect himself. I trust this accommodation will suffice. Now, if you'll permit, I have to inspect my men."

Murray was incensed by the young captain's defiance and bristled with frustration, but could think of no practical means by which to assert his authority and force Gresham to capitulate to his wishes unconditionally. His mouth twisted into an expression of bitter distaste, and he forced himself to challenge Gresham's gaze.

"I'll inform Colter that he is welcome to join your company and that you will accord him every support."

"Please convey the conditions, sir. We leave at first light whether he's with us or not."

"Dismissed, Captain!" The general dropped to his seat, attempting to ignore Gresham by diverting his attention to a sheaf of documents on his desk, implying that they were of greater importance, in an effort to regain some semblance of the authority of his rank.

Murray waited for the captain to leave the building and then bawled at his orderly. "Bains! Find Colter and send him to me, now! Try the saloon first."

The young orderly sprang from his desk outside the general's office. He had heard the exchange between the two officers a few moments earlier and, acutely aware that the general would vent his indignation upon his administrators, was grateful to be provided with a means of escaping his superior's wrath. He admired Gresham's determination to resist the bullying of his senior officer and envied the captain's cool confidence. Gresham's reputation as a tough and demanding leader was almost legend, and he was not a man to be trifled with, but nevertheless men followed him without question and queued up to serve under his command.

Bains found Colter in the saloon, as the general had suggested. He was immersed in a game of poker with three unsavory-looking men who were unimpressed at his premature departure, complete with his accumulated winnings, although Colter looked delighted to be presented with good reason to cash in his booty. A fracas almost ensued, but the uncompromising hand Colter placed on his sidearm persuaded the men that his proposal to play a few hands the following day offered their best chance of getting even.

The orderly accompanied Colter to the general's office and observed with distaste the way that he sprawled into the seat opposite his commanding officer, swinging his battered boots up to rest on the edge of the desk. Colter seemed unaware of the revulsion he incited, as he twisted a large calloused finger into his nose and wiped the proceeds idly onto the arm of his chair, belching contentedly as he settled himself.

A stale smell of whiskey, combined with the musty odor of Colter's worn and stained clothing, pervaded the atmosphere in Murray's office. He wore buckskin breeches, a tattered deer hide coat with tasselled sleeves, and his head was adorned with a classical raccoon skin. The epitome of the stereotype of the mountain man of the west, he was unshaven, dirty, and uncouth. He was a man used to living off the land, who did whatever was necessary to assure his survival, irrespective of the expense to others.

"That'll be all, Bains. Now, get out and close the door," Murray instructed irritably, Bains being delighted to take his leave of Colter and the general.

Murray disliked Colter intensely. Every facet of the man's character was exasperating. He was morally bankrupt, stank like a skunk, dressed like a vagrant, and displayed no respect for the institutions of law and order. But, regrettably, he was exactly what Winthrop wanted, a man who understood the west intimately. He was accustomed to trading with the Indian tribes, and consequently was afforded largely unobstructed passage into areas where government agents were not ordinarily free to travel. And, most importantly, he would do almost anything for money.

The general sat opposite Colter and pushed his seat back,

placing as much distance between himself and the mountain man as possible. He rested his hands with deliberate care on the arms of his high-backed mahogany chair and crossed his legs, attempting to adopt an air of elegant composure.

"I've instructed Captain Gresham that you'll accompany him on his march to Platte Bridge Station. He'll be escorting a wagon train of settlers, so the journey will be somewhat slower than usual, but it'll serve your purpose by providing you a degree of anonymity." Colter grunted in acknowledgment.

"You'll need to be ready at first light. I've insisted that Gresham moves out with all haste," Murray continued. He paused awkwardly, considering how best to inform Colter of Gresham's conditions. He was certain that Colter would not entertain surrendering his arms, and the prospect of instigating another argument that he was destined to lose was not appealing. He cleared his throat as he examined his fingernails, allowing himself time to resolve the dilemma, eventually concluding that the management of Colter's compliance was Gresham's problem, not his. "Captain Gresham will brief you," he said evasively. "Now, let's discuss your assignment."

Murray reached for his desk keys and unlocked his top drawer, removing a rolled map, which he spread out carefully. The two men then set to work.

Gresham left the general's office and went in search of his lieutenants, anxious to ensure that preparations for the company's departure were complete. He was mildly irritated by the exchange with Murray, but in truth he was more interested in discovering the nature of Colter's involvement with the United States cavalry. It was evident that Colter possessed an ulterior motive for traveling with his unit, which was a circumstance that certainly would not have been the mountain man's preference. He was a fiercely independent individual, totally at ease roaming the Great Plains, with no need for additional protection. His purpose was a mystery, and the last thing Gresham wanted was a person with dubious intentions traveling with his troop; it made for an unnecessary element of unpredictability.

The day was cold, but bright sunshine bathed the parade ground as Gresham skirted its perimeter. He made a striking figure. Taller than average, with the erect bearing of someone totally at ease with his ability. His strong square-jawed face was chiseled with weathered creases, so that he appeared older than his years, but his wavy blond hair and enigmatic blue eyes, set beneath a wide brow, betrayed his youth. His nose was slender but slightly twisted, having been badly broken in a brutal hand-to-hand skirmish during the Civil War. He enjoyed the authority of command and believed that high moral standards and self-discipline were at the heart of good soldiering. As usual, his uniform was immaculate.

His dress frockcoat was of dark blue wool, double-breasted with nine pairs of perfectly polished brass buttons running from the stand-up collar to the waist and ornate cuffs decorated with three brass buttons and two gold lace braids. Set on broad shoulders, smart rope knots and a central pad embroidered with vertical stripes denoted his captain's rank, and the Seventh Cavalry emblem indicated his regiment. The insignia and two crossed sabers were repeated on the brass buckle of his belt and the pin affixed to his wide-brimmed black hat, which he wore at a purposeful angle to shade his eyes from the sun. Held in place by an elegant black silk trim, three short ostrich feathers fluttered on the left side of the Stetson, which was finished with gold cord, the ends tied at the front and knotted into neat acorns.

His cavalry saber hung at an oblique angle and swung in time with his gait, the polished fittings of the nickel steel scabbard glinted in the afternoon light, and Gresham rested his left hand casually on the elaborate brass handguard and butt cap to steady the movement.

His men were billeted to the rear of the stables, adjacent to the corral, so he left the parade square and slipped between the limestone bulk of the administrative building and the fort's hospital, turned right to walk along behind a group of newly built barrack blocks, and returned to his troop.

His first lieutenant, Isaac Trautman, broke off a discussion with two NCOs and threw a respectful salute as he noticed the captain approaching. Gresham returned the salute, addressing him without breaking step.

"Where are Moylan and Hanley?"

"Lieutenant Hanley's checkin' the supply wagon, and Lieutenant Moylan's in the stables, sir."

"Find them and tell them to be in my office in fifteen minutes. You too, Isaac. Inspection at seventeen hundred hours. Reveille will be at o-four-hundred hours tomorrow. Be ready to leave at o-six-hundred."

"Yes, sir." Trautman responded formally, turning away with a quizzical expression. He and Gresham were veterans of the Civil War, having served with one another for four years on the western front, and both had been posted to the frontier now that the Confederacy was all but defeated.

Despite their differing rank, they were good friends and trusted each other implicitly, so Trautman knew that the formality of Gresham's instructions was a sure indication that something had irritated him. He was bemused. During the troop's muster at Fort Leavenworth he could conceive of no immediate reason for Gresham's agitation and concluded that his superior's annoyance had to be related to his meeting with the general.

He rounded up the two second lieutenants, ensuring that

their NCOs were briefed to prepare the company for inspection, and all three men hurried to the office Gresham had commandeered from the regimental veterinarian. Gresham hated the officers' accommodation, favoring the camaraderie of his field officers and men in preference to enduring the mollycoddling of the administration block.

Trautman tapped on the door, even though it stood open and he could see that the captain was packing a small steel case with documents. Gresham locked the case and beckoned the young officers to enter, close the door, and take a seat.

Resting against the edge of the desk, he addressed them earnestly. "We move out at first light. Our first destination is St. Joseph where we'll rendezvous with a wagon train of settlers bound for Bozeman and the goldfields near Virginia City. There will be farmers and prospectors, nearly five hundred men, women, and children in all, and several hundred head of cattle. We'll be escorting the wagons, but we're there to protect them and to keep order, not to work the livestock. Make sure the men know that."

Trautman was attentive but relaxed. He was a good soldier who had seen his fair share of combat and knew how to lead men when the fighting got tough. He was thoroughly dependable and was a formidable adversary with both musket and saber. Gresham was pleased to have him posted to Platte Bridge Station. They would make a good team.

The other two lieutenants were barely twenty and had joined up from the reserves toward the end of the Civil War. They were both willing enough, but Gresham was concerned that they might struggle to endure the harsh conditions they would encounter in the northern plains.

Hanley looked not much more than a boy, his face still pocked with adolescent spots. He was tall and gangly, and at six foot five they had struggled to find a horse upon which he appeared other than ridiculous. He leaned forward in earnest concentration, like a puppy trying to please, but he was bright and learned fast because he paid attention and was determined to impress.

Moylan was a different proposition entirely. His father, a lieutenant colonel in the Dragoons, had been killed in the Civil War. He hailed from a family with a military tradition and displayed the air of someone who believed that rank accorded him automatic respect and authority.

He was a burly lad with a broad face, deep-set dark eyes, and an unruly mop of curly brown hair. He sat impassive while Gresham briefed them, his bland expression rendering it difficult to assess his thoughts. Self-confidence would not be his problem, but the misplaced assurance of the ignorant could get people killed in the west, and Gresham worried that he might represent a liability unless he began to display greater diligence.

Gresham continued. "The journey to Platte Bridge Station will take about three months, weather permitting, which is time enough for the settlers to cause us plenty of trouble. There will be some hazardous sections of the journey, and people will die. River crossings are dangerous, as are hill descents. We'll have to work with the wagonmaster to ensure that the migrants are disciplined in their approach to these obstacles, because the actions of one careless person can cause the deaths of many others."

He knew that Trautman was familiar with the risks and understood that exercising control over the settlers could be a demanding task. But, inevitably, some people only responded to brute force, and Gresham's company had to be prepared to act decisively to maintain order if circumstances required. His lecture was for the benefit of the two younger officers, and by the time the company reached St. Joseph, he would ensure that both they and their troopers had rehearsed maneuvers designed to confront instances of disorder should they occur.

"You'll need to prevent your men making advances to the women and girls. A man can miss the attentions of a woman in three months, and soliciting another man's wife or daughter will provoke unrest. Make it known that any trooper caught with another man's woman will be shot."

Hanley was shocked at the draconian intolerance, but Moylan's face cracked into a sly grin, and Gresham wondered whether his reaction was induced by lascivious thoughts of taking another man's woman or the prospect of administering Gresham's martial judgment. Either way, he was unimpressed, and he caught Trautman's eye to indicate his reservation about the lad's behavior.

"There will be an inspection of the company at seventeen hundred hours, and I expect the troop to be fully prepared. Any man whose uniform is not regulation standard or has failed to maintain his Springfield properly will carry his saddle for the first day. That includes you.

"Now, I have a sensitive matter to discuss." Trautman looked intrigued. He had guessed that Gresham had a surprise in store, but he had no idea what would be said. "We have a guest traveling with us. A Mr. John Colter."

Trautman was astonished. "Colter? Why would that scoundrel wanna travel with us? Indian territory's his second home. He ain't the kinda man who needs the protection of the U.S. cavalry."

"I'm aware of that, Mr. Trautman. But this time he's traveling with us at the request of the government," Gresham responded curtly.

"He's trouble, John." Trautman forgot his formalities for a moment. "Why's he gotta come with us?"

"I can't tell you why he's riding with us, but he's not going to be any trouble. I'm going to make sure of that." Gresham's jaw tightened and his expression formed a steely mask. "He's going to join us at first light, and I want to give him a suitable welcome." Gresham dropped his voice and explained what he wanted from his lieutenants.

The cavalry company mustered at seventeen-hundred sharp to be reviewed by Gresham. The seventy-two enlisted men wore their dress uniforms and stood in a parade form of four rows of eighteen, each man with his mount saddled and held at his right shoulder. The horses were all Morgans, mostly bay or chestnut, with intelligent broad faces, preferred by the cavalry because of their stamina and inherently courageous nature, both features that made them good war horses that would not flinch from a committed charge.

Each animal was immaculately groomed and tacked with a standard McClellan saddle made of polished rawhide. The pommel and cantle were both high, providing comfort and stability on a long march or in battle, and the saddle was seated on a blue, orange-striped saddle blanket.

Each man stood to attention and an attentive silence settled over the parade ground, interspersed only by the restless shuffle of hooves and the gentle metallic clink of the horses chewing on their curved steel bits.

The three lieutenants were lined up in front of their sergeants and their respective squads, and Trautman handed the reins of his horse to Hanley as Gresham approached so that he could step forward to meet his captain. They exchanged formal salutes, and Trautman fell in beside Gresham as he surveyed the troop with a critical eye. There was no real necessity for him to conduct the inspection, but Gresham knew that some of the men would be unacquainted with the rigors of the Great Plains, and he was determined to reinforce the standard of discipline he required before the company moved out. He would inevitably find some irregularity with a uniform, or the presentation of a trooper's horse, and he would make an example of those individuals to set the tone for the rest of the company.

Trautman had seen this routine several times and understood Gresham's intent. He suppressed a grimace at the plight of the unfortunate troopers who would fail to meet Gresham's exacting standards. It was essential to lead with authority in the conditions the company would encounter on their journey to Platte Bridge Station and on patrol, so the earlier the men learned to respect and respond to orders, the better. The charade of the parade was a small example in isolation and there would inevitably be more demonstrations of the consequences of ill-discipline over the ensuing weeks, but the experience would undoubtedly serve to focus the troopers' minds.

Gresham grunted as if displeased with the spectacle that confronted him, and he moved off to commence the inspection. The first trooper was a young private, newly posted to the company, and he was clearly nervous of the scrutiny. He had prepared his uniform with consummate care, and his horse's coat glistened from the dedicated polish of his grooming brush, so Gresham decided to set the lad at ease as the seventeen-year-old boy reluctantly met his eye.

"You're Cooper, aren't you?" The lad looked stunned that the captain knew his name, since he had barely seen his commanding officer prior to the parade, let alone spoken to him.

"Yais, sir," he responded abruptly in a distinctive drawl.

"Must be your first time out west. Where you from?" Gresham mused that the boy was in danger of rupturing himself if he attempted to stand any straighter.

"Shepherdstown, Virginia, sir."

"You're a long way from home, Private. You care to show me your rifle?"

"Yais, sir." The lad grinned and held out his Springfield.

Gresham took the rifle and inspected it expertly. He flipped open the trap-door breech to admit light into the barrel and held the muzzle up to his eye. The bore was clean and bright and the rifling gleamed. "Well done, Private. You keep it like that. You'll need it in good working order soon enough, you mark my words." The boy swelled with pride, and his relief was palpable as Gresham moved on down the line.

Gresham talked to each of the men as he carried out the inspection, ensuring that he made good eye contact and took time to demonstrate a personal interest. He discovered a few minor flaws, but none warranted a meaningful penalty; still, he pointed out small details of the preparation and care of horse tack and weaponry as he continued the review.

The third trooper from the end of the front row of the parade was the first unfortunate to be subjected to Gresham's wrath. He was a private who had served with Gresham in the Civil War and should have known better. The captain eyed him with exasperation as he turned to scrutinize the man. Crevett had the physique of a bull, with wide muscular shoulders and arms the size of most men's thighs. His forage cap was wedged onto a mop of curly black hair, a wide patch of which was missing on the right side of his head, where scar tissue betrayed the legacy of a musket shot that had nearly taken his life. The tight skin around the healed injury had lifted the flesh on his cheek, creating the effect of a permanent lopsided leer. He had left his family on their farm in Kentucky and become a fine soldier, but he was lazy and required firm leadership to ensure that he pulled his weight.

Gresham looked him up and down. His fatigue blouse was clean enough despite a missing button, but his pants looked as though he had barely attempted to brush the mud off his knees, and he had made no effort to polish his boots. From a cursory inspection of his horse it was evident that minimal energy had been put into grooming his mount and soaping his saddle and headstall.

He bristled with frustration at the veteran trooper's failure to set a better example to the younger and less experienced men, and Crevett sensed his ire, staring doggedly over Gresham's left shoulder in a futile attempt to avoid the inevitable consequences.

"You feeling strong, Crevett," Gresham started obliquely.

"Strong as an ox, sir," Crevett responded, flicking his gaze to meet Gresham's, anxious to detect the reason for the question.

"Good! That's excellent. Care to present your rifle?"

Crevett hesitated, but offered his Springfield, holding it out horizontally, hopeful that Gresham would undertake a brief visual examination. Instead, the captain reached out and grasped the rifle by stock and barrel, forcing Crevett to reluctantly surrender the weapon. Consistent with previous inspections, Gresham opened the trap-door breech, but on this occasion, he wiped the inner surface with his finger, eliciting a smear of dirty, oily black residue. Incensed, he examined the offending substance and smelled his finger, snapping a sharp glare at Crevett, whose focus reverted to a distant point over Gresham's shoulder.

Next, he turned the rifle to inspect its barrel, and once again his face contorted in an expression of bitter distaste. He snapped the breech closed and took a step backward.

"Lieutenant Hanley!" he bellowed over his shoulder.

The company shuffled their feet awkwardly as the young lieutenant scurried to Gresham's side.

"Sir!"

"Lieutenant, take this man's rifle. It's a disgrace. Likely to jam with the first round."

"Sir! Ah'll have 'im clean it, and I'm gonna inspect it mahself when parade's all done."

"Did you explain to Private Crevett that there would be an

inspection at seventeen-hundred hours?"

"Yes, sir. Ah did, sir."

"Thank you, Lieutenant." Gresham turned back to Crevett. "How long have you served with me, Private?"

"Couple o' years, capt'n," replied Crevett, still avoiding Gresham's glare.

"Couple of years. And, the lieutenant here says you were told there would be an inspection at seventeen-hundred hours this evening." Crevett remained silent since there seemed no merit in compounding his position.

"Your uniform is a disgrace, Private. I've seen mules better turned out than your horse, and your weapon is barely functional. Discipline! Discipline saves lives, Private. You ever hear me say that before?" Gresham bawled at Crevett so that the whole company could have no doubt about his fury at the private's breach of acceptable standards.

"Yes, sir. Discipline, sir."

"Well, you discredit the uniform of the Seventh Cavalry, soldier. And I don't accept absence of professionalism in my company," Gresham bellowed.

"Sir! Captain, sir!" Crevett barked obediently in an attempt to appear compliant.

"Sir. Private Crevett wah helpin' to do thah final loadin' of thah supplah wagon," Hanley interjected, hoping to alleviate the captain's annoyance. "Ah'm afraid . . ."

Gresham wheeled on Hanley and cut him off, fixing him with a scowl that required no interpretation. "Are you making excuses for this man, Lieutenant?" he growled. Trautman cringed at the young lieutenant's naive intervention, which fueled Gresham's pantomime and could only end up badly for the young lad.

"No, sir. Jus' tryin' to explain . . ."

"Explain! There is no need to explain, Lieutenant. This man

knew there was an inspection and yet he wasn't prepared. Being unprepared is unacceptable in this company, Lieutenant! Clearly you didn't communicate your expectations with adequate clarity, did you?"

"Yes, sir. Ah mean no, sir." A few of the more seasoned soldiers were beginning to enjoy Gresham's exhibition and struggled to conceal their amusement at the young officer's discomfort.

"Well, Lieutenant. This man is going to learn about discipline in my company. You'll ensure that he cleans and presses his uniform and that his weapons are properly cleaned and maintained. Private Crevett will surrender his horse to Sergeant Riley, and he'll carry his saddle and his weapon on tomorrow's march."

Hanley snapped to attention and his hand shot up into a salute. "Yes, sir. Ah'll see to it, sir."

"Yes, you will, Lieutenant, because you'll carry your saddle too. You clearly weren't capable of impressing upon Private Crevett the standards that you expect, so you'll carry your saddle and consider how you're going to enforce discipline in future. Do I make myself clear?"

Hanley's mouth dropped open in disbelief, and Trautman closed his eyes in silent sympathy for the lad, but Moylan broke into an unabashed grin of satisfaction at the misfortune of his contemporary. Curtly dismissing Hanley, Gresham turned and continued his inspection, eventually consigning two more troopers to endure an arduous foot march with Crevett and the young lieutenant.

Once the inspection of the troop was complete, the parade was dismissed and the men returned to their billet to conclude preparations for their journey, leaving Trautman to accompany Gresham as he strode back to his office.

"Don't you think you were a bit hard on Hanley, John?"

"You think so?" Gresham smiled mischievously.

"He's young. He'll learn to keep his mouth shut in the future when you're tearin' the backside out of one of his men."

"Hmm. I think he's a good lad. Good potential. But he needs to earn respect. If he manages to keep up with the other men tomorrow carrying his saddle for the day, he'll have shared some pain and he'll have shown some steel. I think he'll do it. I don't think he'll let himself fail and, young or not, I think the men will appreciate his grit. He looks like a boy, but he needs to be seen to be a man."

Trautman inclined his head pensively and shot his friend a crooked grin. "You're a wily bird. But it's a big gamble for Hanley."

"You want a wager on that?" Gresham extended his hand to seal the bet.

Trautman puffed out his cheeks and grunted. "I think not! I've lost enough wagers to you already, thank you!"

Chapter 7

Fort Leavenworth, State of Kansas

The 04:00 bugle echoed around the fort, heralding a bustle of activity as the company assembled, preparing to move out at six o'clock. The barracks hummed with the murmur of low voices as the troopers jostled to wash, pull on their boots, and pack up their saddlebags.

Gresham had risen an hour earlier and ensured that his own horse was saddled and ready. He had stowed the steel document box in the supply wagon and packed his saddlebags and bedroll so that he was able to sit quietly on the wall outside his office and watch the fort come to life.

The company organized themselves efficiently, the men eager to avoid joining those of their compatriots condemned to undertake the day's journey on foot so that by half-past five all the horses were saddled, the men were fed, and the canteen was packed away in the supply wagon. Gresham was pleased with what he observed.

Trautman marshalled the two second lieutenants who, accompanied by the NCOs, inspected the men, confirming that each trooper was carrying his quota of ammunition, checking their horses, uniforms, and weapons.

Hanley entrusted his horse to Sergeant Riley, along with the three mounts belonging to the troopers that would accompany him on foot. Trautman felt sorry for the lad, who maintained a brave face as he attempted to organize a mountain of kit into a load that looked decidedly awkward to carry.

"You up for this, Jim?" Trautman enquired sympathetically.

Hanley forced a smile. "No trouble, Lieutenan'." But it was obvious that his bravado was only skin deep and that he was seriously concerned about his ability to survive the day.

"That's the spirit! Cap'n thinks you'll manage, no problem. He's lookin' forward to you showin' the men how it's done."

"Captain said thah?" Hanley retorted in surprise, Gresham's affirmation bolstering his confidence.

"Sure did. I reckon you might even make camp before us."

Trautman laughed, slapping Hanley on the back. "Here, let me show you a couple of tricks for carryin' that lot. I had to do this once or twice myself!" With that, Trautman demonstrated a technique for inverting the saddle over one shoulder, stabilizing the load by gripping the horn, and counterbalancing the thirty-pound weight by placing his saddlebags and headstall over the other, using the strap of his Springfield to sling the rifle across his back. A load of more than sixty pounds in total.

The young lieutenant's height alleviated the problem of the dangling cinch, fenders, and stirrups from interfering with his gait. Nevertheless, his tall spindly frame burdened by the huge load rendered his appearance thoroughly ungainly.

Hanley broke into a broad grin. "Fits like a glove!" But he rolled his eyes and groaned. "Will yer tell ma parents ah died heroic like? Ah'm 'fraid this is gonna kill me!"

Trautman was impressed at the lad's wit and laughed with him. "I'll tell them you carried the burden of your responsibilities with courage and determination. Now, come on, let's get up to the Cap'n's office, we don't wanna be late for our guest."

They rounded up Moylan on their way to meet Gresham and arrived in time to witness the disheveled bulk of the mountain man emerge from the early-morning gloom, lumbering up the hill leading his horse, a sturdy-looking mustang laden with deep saddlebags and a pile of winter coats and other paraphernalia.

Colter drew up and cleared his throat noisily, spitting a large glutinous clod of phlegm onto the ground. He dropped his horse's reins and it stood compliantly, without any apparent need to be tied.

His heavy boots clattered on the wooden steps as he made his way to the office and shoved the door open uninvited. Gresham sat with his hands rested on his thighs leaning casually back in his chair, which was tucked closely up against the desk, and the three lieutenants stepped aside as Colter shuffled in.

"Well, Mr. Colter, it seems we have the pleasure of your company on our route across to Platte Bridge Station."

Colter hooked his thumbs over his belt, the stance exaggerating the size of his ample belly as he inspected the room with idle curiosity. "Yep. Looks so," he responded without enthusiasm.

"Care to explain why you feel the need for the Union's cavalry to provide you with an escort? Doesn't seem your style." Gresham enquired, not expecting Colter to divulge any aspect of his purpose, but intent on demonstrating that he was not trusted.

"Nope." Colter's mouth curled into a conceited smirk. "Guess s'above your pay grade," he chuckled.

Gresham smiled, impassive. "Fine with me. Murray tell you about my conditions?"

Colter narrowed his eyes and studied Gresham, continuing to chew on a piece of tobacco lodged behind his lower lip, but he did not respond.

"I assume the rules are going to need explaining. I'm going to have to ask you to surrender your weapons to Lieutenant Trautman here." Gresham nodded at Trautman.

Colter's expression tightened and his right hand slid around his belt, closer to his side arm. "Ain't no one taking ma gun," he drawled menacingly.

"I was afraid you were going to say that." Gresham looked disappointed but unmoved. "You see, I can't permit you to travel with us if you're bearing arms, Mr. Colter. Lieutenant Moylan, Lieutenant Hanley, would you please oblige Mr. Colter?"

Moylan and Hanley, who had positioned themselves on either side of Colter, stepped in to remove his weapons. The young lieutenants had been briefed about their task and did not anticipate any resistance, given the presence of four cavalry officers. However, they had not previously encountered a man like Colter.

For a large man, he reacted with extraordinary speed, lunging to the right to body-check Hanley, whipping out his meaty left hand to grasp Moylan by the collar and using the young lieutenant's own momentum to yank the lad across in front of him, then stepping sharply backward so that Moylan plunged head first into the unsuspecting Hanley. Having stopped Hanley dead in his tracks with a brawny shoulder, Colter's right hand flew to his revolver and, in a heartbeat, the gun was aimed directly at Trautman, the startled lieutenant too slow to reach for his own firearm.

The Remington Model 1861 Navy was Colter's pistol of choice. Slightly smaller than its army counterpart, accepting a .36-caliber round as opposed to the larger handgun's .44, it had several adaptations developed as a consequence of use in the field, including a solid frame enclosing the revolving cylinder, which reduced the potential for the weapon to jam. The seven-and-a-half-inch rounded barrel, with its sighting post positioned a finger's width from the muzzle, pointed unwaveringly at Trautman's heart.

Gresham was impressed at the mountain man's agility, his

ponderous demeanour having belied the lethal speed of his reactions, and the fighting skills that lent him such a formidable reputation. Based on Colter's mesmeric demonstration, it was easy to understand how he had survived in the west where others had perished.

Colter eyed Gresham coldly. "Like I said, aint no one gonna take ma gun."

Gresham rocked gently back and forth in his chair and nodded his appreciation of Colter's skill. "Thank you for that entertaining display, Mr. Colter, but I'm still going to have to ask you to hand your weapons to Lieutenant Trautman."

"Don't look like that's gonna happen, though, do it?" Colter snarled.

Gresham dropped his chin thoughtfully, peering at the mountain man from under his furrowed brow. "Well, now. That depends how much you value your manhood, Mr. Colter."

Colter looked bemused at the captain's cool bearing and his casual threat, until it dawned on him that Gresham's hands remained out of sight beneath his desk. Gresham watched his eyes flick to the surface of the table and knew that the comment had hit its mark.

"I'm a pretty fair shot, Mr. Colter, and while a Colt revolver will make a good-sized hole in this desk, I dare say it'll make a bigger mess of your marital prospects."

"You wouldn't dare." Colter's confidence began to crack, and his challenge sounded more like a question.

"Oh, I think I'm well within my rights, Mr. Colter. A man comes into my office and threatens to kill one of my lieutenants. I'd say that's self-defense, wouldn't you?" Gresham leaned forward and glared at Colter. "I've wasted enough time, Mr. Colter. I have a company of cavalry to get on the trail. Would you please surrender your weapon to the lieutenant, *immediately*?" The last word was delivered with uncompromising emphasis, and it was evident that Gresham had run out of patience. The two men held each other's eyes, testing one another's resolve.

By now, Hanley and Moylan had recovered their feet, their hands settled on their side arms, but they knew better than to make any attempt to draw their guns.

Colter broke eye contact with Gresham and glanced from one lieutenant to the other hesitantly. Abruptly, he dropped his gun to his side and shrugged. "Guess there'll be time enough to sort this out," he drawled and spun the Remington in his hand, placing it on the desk in front of Gresham.

"Thank you, Mr. Colter. You'll take station alongside Lieutenant Trautman. It'll give you a chance to get to know one another." The altercation concluded, Gresham lifted his hands from under the table and placed them on the desk, pushing himself to his feet. He held no weapon and the two young second lieutenants gawped at him, amazed at the audacious bluff, Trautman left wagging his head in amused disbelief.

Colter's eyes flicked up to meet Gresham's, which sparkled roguishly, and the mountain man smiled, nodding his head respectfully and exploding with a deep belly laugh. "Gonna have to keep ma eye on you," he chortled.

"I don't think so, Mr. Colter. That's my job." Gresham turned to Moylan and Hanley. "Lieutenant Moylan, please see to it that any weapons Mr. Colter has on his person or in his belongings are given into the safe keeping of Lieutenant Trautman. Lieutenant Hanley, I believe you have some preparations to make. That'll be all, thank you, gentlemen." Gresham walked around his desk and placed the Remington in Trautman's hand. "Please be sure to take good care of this for Mr. Colter. We move out in fifteen minutes." He walked briskly past Colter without a second glance and left the four men staring uncomfortably at one another.

★ ★ ★ ★ ★

The company set off as first light broke over the fort, the troopers riding in double file, with the first sergeant at the head of the column. Trautman and Colter were tucked in behind the supply wagon, and Gresham rode to the side of Hanley and the men on foot, who brought up the rear.

His horse was the only black Morgan in the troop, and it was a fine specimen. It held its neck arched with its face almost perpendicular to the ground, imparting a haughty arrogance, and lifted its hooves in a high prancing walk as if struggling to contain its energy.

The air reverberated to the measured tempo of almost a hundred sets of hooves, the chomping of steel bits, and the creak of iron-shod wagon wheels, as the troop and their pack animals passed beyond the sentry posts at the perimeter of the fort, where they wheeled north-east and set a course for St. Joseph on the Missouri River, some fifty-three miles distant. General Murray did not attend the troop's departure, and Gresham was grateful that he was not obliged to exchange pleasantries with his senior officer.

It was early spring and the temperatures were still cool, which was a blessing for the men carrying their saddlery, since Gresham intended covering eighteen miles or more each day, and summer heat would have sapped the energy of Hanley and his troopers.

The first day's route was relatively straightforward, the Kansas plains being largely flat, and although the penalty for his men would be back-breaking, the topography of the land had been in Gresham's calculations when he had allotted their punishment. He was confident that they would all reach the evening camp in one piece.

The troop's progress was largely governed by the speed of the heavy chuck wagon, drawn by four mules, so they averaged only about two and a half miles per hour, and Gresham planned to break for a midday meal, with the intention of setting up camp in the late afternoon, leaving sufficient daylight for each sergeant to practice maneuvers with his squad of ten men. The drills would relieve the monotony of the journey to St. Joseph and constituted essential preparation for the company's responsibilities when they arrived at their posting.

Gresham was very particular about the training of his men, believing that there was no substitute for the relentless repetition of practice drills, which instilled a reflexive response among the men, built their trust in one another, and conditioned new recruits to the tactics of combat. It was his custom to watch the performance of each squad, often delivering withering assessments of their effectiveness and insisting that they repeat routines eight or ten times before declaring his satisfaction.

As the morning progressed, Hanley and the troopers on foot began to lag behind, losing sight of the main column. Hanley's muscles screamed with pain, and he struggled to conceal his torture from the other men as they plodded along.

The four soldiers began to string out as the trail entered a shallow gulch, distinguished from other sections of the plain by a vigorous stand of red cedar, resplendent with its year-round green foliage and displaying the first hint of early blossom. The fittest man, Private Coleman, his sinewy battle-hardened body disguising a tough stamina that the others could not equal, pulled ahead whistling the Garryowen with infuriating nonchalance.

Meanwhile, Crevett and Hanley kept weary pace with one another, but the third trooper, a ginger-haired kid called Solomon Friedman, was suffering badly. He was sixteen, the son of a Boston shopkeeper, unaccustomed to the rigors of outdoor life, much less the hardships of the military. But, although he struggled to summon adequate stamina and strength, he was single-minded in his commitment to the cavalry and in time would make a first-class soldier.

Hanley stopped to cast a concerned glance at the boy, who trailed some four hundred paces behind, valiantly laboring to carry his saddle across his chest. He looked as though his legs might buckle at any moment and Hanley's sympathy was stirred by his sense of responsibility for his troopers.

He considered it unacceptable to abandon one of his men. If one failed, they all failed, and he was determined to ensure that they all succeeded, but it was clear that Friedman would not reach the troop's evening campsite if they continued as they were.

"Private Coleman! Hold up!" Hanley called, but despite the trooper turning to see what the lieutenant wanted, he made no attempt to respond.

"Wait for Private Friedman!" Hanley bellowed, although his voice seemed weak and high-pitched as he attempted to make himself heard.

Coleman appeared unimpressed and reverted to his march, his intention clear. He would struggle on, making his own way rather than being burdened by the inadequacy of others.

"Coleman! Stop! That's an order!"

The private pulled up reluctantly, but defiantly refused to turn around. Instead, he lowered himself to the ground and settled against his saddle, ignoring Hanley. He had seen young cavalry officers come and go, mostly boys with little experience of life, naive to the horrors of war. When the fighting got tough, they were invariably redundant, having little expertise to lead and inspire men. He was damned if he was going to capitulate to this spotty-faced bean pole who barely had the strength to make the day's march.

Hanley was irritated by the private's insolence, but concluded that engaging in a battle of wills to exert his authority would be folly. Accordingly, he allowed Coleman to remain where he was, and after dropping his saddle down beside Crevett, hurried back to meet Friedman.

Seeing Hanley approach, Friedman's endurance crumbled and he stumbled, collapsing in an ungainly heap, tripping over his saddle and tumbling comically head first, grazing his chin and the side of his face.

Hanley restrained his laughter as the lad hurried to recover himself, a smudge of green on his forehead and a trickle of blood forming on his chin. "You fahnd somin' worth lookin' at down there?" he chuckled, the lad looking bashful but grinning at the genial rebuke.

"No, sir. Jus' right clumsy, ah guess."

"Heavy darned things, ain't they?" Hanley enquired.

"Ah'm thinkin' I'm gonna ride bear back if y'all let me, sir?" Friedman retorted, his grin broadening. Instantly, Hanley decided that he liked the lad, and the sentiment reinforced his commitment to ensure that Friedman arrived at the evening camp in good time.

"Come on, grab the other end of yer saddle," Hanley instructed, draping the boy's saddlebags over the seat.

Friedman patted down his pants and they picked up the load to rejoin Crevett, who appeared refreshed by the short break. Hanley mused about the best way to help Friedman. It would be unreasonable to expect one of the other men to carry the boy's saddle for him. Indeed, he and Crevett were already struggling to carry their own loads. But it occurred to him that carrying Friedman's saddle between them had made the load considerably easier, and certainly more comfortable than balancing the weight on their shoulders. He wondered whether they could devise a means of transporting all the saddles between them.

He was annoyed and determined that Friedman would not

be left to struggle on his own. He would not be beaten. Frustrated, he stared at his and Crevett's saddles, lying side by side, willing an answer. At that moment, it dawned on him. Of course, that was it. They needed a method of carrying the saddles side by side.

He scanned the copse alongside the trail. "Come wi' me. Ah've got an ahdea," he urged Crevett and Friedman. "Bring yo' knives."

The two privates looked bewildered, but followed Hanley into the stand of cedar. "Right. Wha' we wan's some right straight whips. They gotta be 'bout three-inch thick, an' 'bout eight foot tall," he directed.

"What d'we want them fa'?" Crevett demanded, demonstrating little enthusiasm.

Friedman bounded alongside, rejuvenated by his lieutenant's assistance. "Carryin' poles! Tha's wha' he wan's! Carryin' poles!"

Hanley was impressed at the lad's incisive mind. "You got it. Tha's what we're gonna do. We gonna tie two saddles together an' put 'em on a couple of poles, so's we can carry 'em on our shoulders. We gonna walk in pairs, two men in front an' two at the back, wi' saddles slung on poles in 'tween us. Gonna be whole deal easier, an' ah reckon we gonna walk faster'n that chuck wagon!"

Crevett was decidedly unconvinced, but grateful to be relieved from lumbering along with his burden, so he set to work to find a suitable young cedar trunk. As they were working, Coleman appeared, impatient to ascertain the reason for the delay to the march, but he soon recognized the merit in Hanley's intent and set about assisting. He had carried wounded men from the field on many occasions, so he was familiar with constructing makeshift stretchers, and the prospect of alleviating the hardship of the rest of the day's march was a welcome thought.

Coleman's vigor inspired the others, and they swiftly cut and trimmed two good stout nine-foot poles, to which they tied all four saddles, laid in two rows of two with the poles slid under the saddles to bear the weight. Each man was assigned to carry one end of a pole, and coordinating the lift, they raised the load onto their shoulders, draping saddlebags over the ends of each pole. Compared to carrying their own burdens, the weight was immeasurably more manageable, and all four men were delighted with the result.

Before resuming the march, they broke out a meager meal of dried meat and refreshed their canteens from the stream in the gulch. Afterward, Hanley paired up with Friedman at the back, Crevett and Coleman bearing the weight at the front, and they set off. Their confidence surged, and they had no doubt that they would cope with the balance of the journey.

The trail was well defined, not simply as a result of the cavalry troop's passage, but deep ruts were cut across the plain, indelible scars left by the continuous stream of heavy wagons that traversed to and from Fort Leavenworth. The afternoon sun was warm and a gently undulating carpet of yellow-brown grass stretched across the plains ahead of the four troopers, rippling in the light breeze.

They made good time, and by midafternoon they caught sight of a steady plume of dust. Their spirits buoyed, and the prospect of overhauling the rest of the troop spurred them on, Coleman blasting out a whistled version of the Garryowen until the rear of the column appeared on the horizon.

Gresham rode with Trautman and the two conversed affably, deliberating upon the route ahead and the challenges that they might encounter. They were relaxed in each other's company, finding it easy to intersperse their discussion with reminiscences from the past, and were engrossed in debating their approach to a particularly hazardous river crossing when a corporal loped up alongside.

"Sir, I thought you would wish to know that Lieutenant Hanley is approaching the rear of the column."

Gresham was caught off guard and gawped involuntarily at the Corporal. "Hanley?"

"Yes, sir. Makin' a good pace too, sir."

Gresham glanced at Trautman, who beamed with amusement and shrugged his shoulders. "Okay, Corporal. Let's take a look." Gresham gathered his composure.

The two officers peeled off and followed the corporal, passing the chuck wagon where Colter sat alongside the wagoner, his horse tied to the tailgate, and returned along the procession of troopers until they reached the tail of the column.

Sure enough, in the distance, Hanley and the other three men could be seen marching purposefully toward them. Hanley's face was a mask of steely determination, but the other men all wore broad grins and were clearly savoring the attention they were attracting.

"Well, I'll be damned," Trautman muttered under his breath.

"In good time, I'm sure you will," Gresham smiled at his friend. "But, for now, perhaps you could ask Lieutenant Hanley to take up station to the rear of the column." With that, he wheeled his horse around and loped away, heading for the front of the troop.

Trautman was entertained by Gresham's inability to publicly acknowledge the achievement of Hanley and the other men, given that their allotted punishment rendered an accolade for success inappropriate, but he knew that Gresham would take great pleasure in the young lieutenant completing his ordeal with flying colors. He jogged slowly back to intercept the men and swung his horse alongside.

"Lieutenant Hanley, if you feel able to keep pace, the Cap'n would appreciate your takin' station to the rear of the column." Trautman forced himself to avoid Hanley's eye, but could see the lad's face crack into a wide smile.

"Sorry, sir. Seemed lahke a nahce day for a picnic. Couldn' resist stoppin' for a whahle. We gonna do our best an' keep up nah." Hanley shot a toothy grin at Trautman who could contain himself no longer, throwing back his head and guffawing as he dug his spurs into his mount's flank and hurried away to rejoin the rest of the company.

The balance of the journey was uneventful, and the troop averaged eighteen miles a day, passing the occasional convoy traveling in the opposite direction, to arrive in St. Joseph three days after leaving Leavenworth.

The plains to the west of the town were seething with humanity, hordes of would-be travelers spilling out across the prairie for as far as the eye could see, complete with wagons, tents, teams of oxen, horses, and cattle. Adding to the chaos the constant trampling of people and livestock had churned the ground into a quagmire, which threatened to ensnare man and beast as families labored to assemble the provisions they required for their migration.

Gresham detested everything about St. Joseph. The debauchery was obscene, and the place oozed with the voracious avarice of men whose motivation centered upon securing their fortune panning for precious metals in the distant Rockies. The homesteaders, in their own way, were no better. Their presence presaged an increase in confrontation with the native peoples, caused by farmers fencing off land that the Indians regarded as part of their sacred hunting grounds. The relentless surge of humanity, intent upon populating and taming the beautiful wild prairies of the west, would change the character of the land and destroy the livelihood of the native Indians forever. Gresham bridled at the thought, but the tide of change was irrepressible. All he could hope to achieve was the brokering of a reluctant tolerance, acting as a voice of reason where possible and resorting to force only when all other avenues failed.

He ordered the troop to make camp three miles southwest of the Missouri River, remaining remote from the chaos, and set off with Trautman to locate the wagonmaster for the convoy they were responsible for escorting.

Chapter 8

Late autumn 1864, St. Joseph, State of Missouri

The Kopps had been in St. Joseph for nearly four months and family life had all but fractured. The railroad journey from New York had turned into a nightmare. Not only had it been unbearably uncomfortable in the stifling heat of the boxcar, but Hans had been relentless in challenging Elena to explain how she had orchestrated their railroad fare.

In an effort to coerce her into elucidating upon her actions, he had at first complimented her on her ingenuity, but when she remained resolute about her story, he became progressively more abusive. He made it plain that he rejected her version of events, being adamant that the railroad would not have accepted a promissory note to receive payment at some point in the future.

By this time, Elena had become sufficiently wedded to her account that she could not envisage a means of confiding what had really happened without provoking even worse repercussions, so their relationship degenerated into a barrage of shouted obscenities.

Hans paced back and forth, slamming his fists against the wooden walls of the boxcar. "You lying bitch," he spat in guttural German, glowering at Elena as she huddled in the corner. "You're going to tell me what you did, or I'll beat it out of you! I bet you let that little runt mount your bony arse!" His venomous spittle sprayed her face as she pleaded her innocence.

"No, Hans. Please. I promise . . ."

He cut her off. "Shut up, you whore. You've always been a whore. You threw yourself at me to get what you wanted, didn't you? Now you've bent over like some bitch in heat for that bastard clerk!" His mouth frothed, and his eyes bulged wildly as he aimed a vicious kick at her legs, prompting Elena to squeal in fear, as much as pain.

Johannes attempted to restrain his father, but was reluctant to be too persistent in his mother's defense, since in doing so it was probable that he would inadvertently find himself the object of his father's rage, and he was not a boy inclined to defend others at his own expense. Carla, on the other hand, screamed at her father, prostrating herself across her mother's lap, and begging Hans to leave her alone.

Elena tried vainly to remove Carla from harm's way, but Hans grabbed the young girl by a clump of hair and yanked her aside, pinning Elena with a throttling meaty fist.

"Get your filthy brat off you," he cursed as he pushed his face up against Elena's. "Tell me what you did, bitch, or so help me I'll wring the life out of you!"

The constant bickering and abusive language had become a feature of the journey for the other occupants of the boxcar and, while they had initially tried to placate Hans, they had established to their cost that he was adept at redirecting his anger if they attempted to intervene. Cowed by his behavior, one of the families, a timid couple from Holland with three young children, sat huddled sheepishly in the opposite corner of the boxcar, attempting to shield their offspring from the big Ukrainian farmer's unpredictable violence.

The other occupants were an older Quaker couple from England. Edward May was in his late fifties, tall and wiry, dressed all in black, wearing baggy shapeless pants and a thick collarless shirt topped with a white linen necktie. His wide, flat-brimmed felt hat, decorated with a deep buckled band that wrapped around the squat topper, was pushed tightly down over long gray hair.

Edward's gaunt and stoic face inspired the impression of a serious and god-fearing man, but his heart was warm and he had been gripped by concern for the poor young woman who was so consistently abused by her brutish husband. The sight of Hans lashing out and choking Elena was too much for him to permit. Unable to contain his fear for her well-being, he pushed himself upright and rushed to intercede.

"Unhand that woman, sir. Let her go, do you hear!" he demanded in a deep authoritative voice.

But Hans was beyond hearing the entreaty, a red mist of fury glazing his manic eyes. He elbowed Johannes out of the way and lifted Elena off the ground by her neck, pinning her to the side of the boxcar as her legs thrashed and her hands scrabbled to escape his vise-like grip.

Alarmed at Elena's distress, Edward stepped forward and grasped Hans's upper arm, using his momentum to spin the farmer around. He was four inches taller than Hans and, despite his lean frame, years of hard work had honed powerful muscles. His weight turned Hans with ease, causing the Ukrainian to lose his balance and release his grip on Elena, who slumped to the floor gasping for air.

Having succeeded in forcing the farmer to let go of his wife, Edward considered that he had achieved his objective. He was not a fighting man, so he simply stepped back and prepared to remonstrate with Hans in whatever way their differing language would permit.

Regrettably for Edward, Hans was a natural brawler, having learned to stand up for himself scrapping with the teenage youths in his local town in the Ukraine. Blind with fury, the object of his anger was immaterial, so correcting a momentary loss of balance, he swivelled his body, rotating his left foot on its heel and bending his knee slightly to adjust his weight, before swinging his right leg around so that he could face his assailant squarely. Simultaneously, he dropped his right hand and balled his knuckles, using the rotation of his body to increase the power of his punch as he rolled his shoulder and twisted his fist, pulling his head down low as his arm shot through with explosive speed and struck the unsuspecting Edward squarely on the chin.

The Quaker was lifted off his feet and thrown backward by the sheer force of the blow, crashing into his wife, who screeched in fear. But her misfortune saved Edward's life as his head was deflected to strike the wall of the boxcar, barely missing one of the wide steel brackets that secured the latch to the sliding door.

Hans was not done, though. He fell on Edward like a raging bull, hauling him to his feet by the scruff of his shirt and flinging him from one side of the car to the other. Again, Edward's wife was knocked to the floor as she tried desperately to intervene, an angry red welt appearing on her forehead and cheek as she tumbled head first.

Horrified at her husband's behavior, Elena wrapped her arms around Hans's leg, attempting to subdue him, and was dragged bodily around the carriage. Carla pleaded with her father to stop his assault and the other children in the car burst into tears as their mother tried to shield them from the rampaging man.

Edward was cast to and fro like a ragdoll, curling his arms about his head to protect himself as he was slammed from side to side. Blood ran from his eye, smearing his cheek, and one of his ribs cracked as he crashed against a steel strut, his knees buckling from the pain. A black haze of semi-consciousness washed over him as his head struck the wall once again.

Hans's eyes bulged wildly and spittle flew from his mouth

through gritted teeth. Johannes was mesmerized. He had never seen such violence, and to his surprise discovered that he was intensely aroused by the experience. The brutality was delicious. He could hear the crack of bones and see the pain on Edward's face. Blood ran unchecked down the Quaker's forehead, blinding his eyes and dripping off his chin to soak his white necktie. It had never occurred to Johannes that he could derive so much pleasure from such a callous exhibition of power, but he yearned to get involved, to draw blood himself, and to hear Edward groan in pain.

The Quaker was cast to the floor again, landing immediately in front of Johannes, and impulsively he whipped his foot back and unleashed a savage kick into Edward's midriff. He heard the crunch of breaking bone as Edward convulsed in agony, blood splattering from his mouth as he bit through his tongue. Johannes stood transfixed. He flushed with excitement and grinned with delight at the man's anguish.

"Johannes! No! No! No . . ." Elena screamed, her voice a whine of desperation, and the animated plea shocked Johannes out of his hypnotic state, so that he retreated to the wall of the carriage, panting.

Carla scrambled to her feet and threw herself between her father and the stricken Quaker. "Mother has money, Father! Mother has money! She paid the railroad! Stop, Father, please! Don't hit the man! Please stop!" she implored, glowering at Hans as she wrapped her arms protectively around Edward's chest.

Carla's appeal registered briefly with Hans and he hesitated, his shoulders heaving as he tried to process the implication of her garbled explanation.

"What? What did you say?" He shook Carla's arm violently, tears streaming down her cheeks and her voice trembling as she was wrenched back and forth.

"Mother has money, Father. She paid the railroad."

"What?" Hans spun to face Elena. "What money? Tell me, you lying bitch!" Hans cast Carla roughly aside and pursued Elena into a corner of the boxcar, where she curled into a ball and cowered.

"Your mother, Hans!" she squealed, her hands flapping defensively in front of her face. "Your mother gave me the money for our journey, Hans." Tears streaked her cheeks as she whimpered. "Please don't hit me. I'll give you the money, my love. Please don't hit me," she begged as she scrambled to reach her bag, crawling along the floor like a whipped cur.

Hans was speechless. In a stroke, the principal obstacle to their journey was resolved, but the deception tore into him like a hot lance. What money? How much? Why hadn't his mother given it to him? The truth left him stunned. His own mother's faith in his self-control had been insufficient to entrust their wealth to his custody. The fight drained from him, and his arms dropped listlessly to his sides as he slumped to the floor.

Edward's wife, Mary, rushed to her husband's side, bending over him and sobbing as she cradled his head. Carla and the Dutch couple hurried to help, relieved that Hans's rage had passed, and Johannes slid slowly down the wall, wrapping his arms around his knees and watching with mystified fascination as Edward attempted to raise himself into a seated position.

Elena shook uncontrollably. She fumbled in her bag and cast the money she had received from the clerk in Castle Garden onto the floor in front of Hans. "There's more," she sniveled. "There's more, Hans, my love." She tugged fruitlessly at the lining of the bag, trying unsuccessfully to extract the remaining gold pieces. "Here, feel. There's more in the lining of my bag, my darling."

Her whine was pitiful, and Hans felt disgusted as he watched her crawling on all fours, her lank hair tumbling across her face in matted clumps and her clothing smeared with filth from the stinking floor of the boxcar.

He gathered up the scattered cash and stared at it vacantly. Gazing around the carriage in numb silence, he noticed the frightened faces of the scruffy children, and the equally unkempt huddle of people attending to Edward. He studied his own hands and his soiled pants, his ragged shirt that had not been washed since they had left the Ukraine. They all looked like a band of destitute vagabonds, stowed away in the squalor of the endlessly jolting train.

He sank against the wall and closed his eyes. "My god, what's become of us?" he whispered, his hand opening to allow the coins to tumble onto the floor.

Elena crept to his side, dragging her bag and sniffing. "We'll be okay, Hans. Don't worry, darling, we'll be all right. I have our money." She pushed the bag into his lap and huddled against him.

"You keep it," he murmured. "Mother was right. You keep it."

Edward was heavily bruised. His broken ribs stabbed with excruciating pain each time he stood up, and whenever the train rattled over a particularly uneven section of track, but fortunately he had suffered no severe internal injuries and given time his bruises would heal. Although not a fighter, he was tough and resilient.

Carla helped Mary tend her husband, acting as a crutch whenever he wanted to rise to his feet, and the older couple soon developed a keen affection for the young girl, who spent most of her days conversing with them in her broken English.

Acutely embarrassed at Hans's assault on Edward, Elena was more reserved, but the Quakers displayed no overt animosity, appearing willing to forgive his aggression in a way that she found difficult to believe, much less understand.

And, after a few days, to Hans's amazement, Edward approached and held out his hand in a gesture of concilliation. Hans was dumbstruck and stood mouthing wordless apologies as Edward informed him that god demanded forgiveness of all his children. Despite not understanding Edward, the inference was clear, and he was left humiliated by the Quaker's generosity of heart.

An uneasy accord settled over the travelers, each sharing their food and water in an effort to foster a degree of mutual dependence, hoping to dissuade the burly farmer from losing control of his temper again.

Edward, who had been a teacher, took it upon himself to equip Hans with some English, while Elena and Mary shared the experience of their respective journeys, empathizing over the hardships they had experienced along the way.

Carla chatted to the other young children and made it her business to entertain them, playing games and singing songs, but Johannes remained remote, brooding over what he considered to be an unwelcome familiarity with the other families.

The Mays were deeply religious and Edward led prayers morning and evening, which were followed by hymns, Mary starting the singing in a soft melodic voice, hands clasped firmly at her waist as she stood beside Edward in her long black skirts and white apron, her kindly round face framed by the decorative pleats of her white bonnet.

The journey seemed endless as the train traveled up through Albany, then on to Utica and Rochester before encountering a day's delay in Buffalo. From there, they rattled along the shores of Lake Erie to Toledo, where there was a further lengthy delay before traversing a new section of line to Elkhart and South Bend, until, at long last, they arrived in Chicago.

Everyone aboard the train was relieved when the doors to the boxcars were opened, allowing brisk gusts of fresh air to disperse the stuffy atmosphere, although the biting autumn wind blowing off Lake Michigan searched its way through the heaviest of clothing, chilling the migrants to the bone.

Feverish activity ensued as the boxcars were unloaded and the travelers poured onto the station, dragging trunks and piling their belongings in untidy heaps. Eager to secure tickets for their onward journey, the chaotic throng of migrants mobbed the railway staff.

Elena left the children watching over their possessions and joined the scrum of people jostling for their travel documents, while Hans, released from his incarceration, pocketed some of the cash his wife had cast onto the floor of the boxcar and made a beeline for the nearest saloon, desperate to find solace in a whiskey bottle.

Edward and Mary noticed that Elena had been abandoned by her husband and hustled her along with them as they elbowed their way through the crowds, but it transpired that the arrangements were quite straightforward and the mayhem proved unwarranted. The station officials were organized, and travelers were able to buy tickets via Hannibal to Quincy, at which point they would be required to disembark to join a small spur-line train to the wharf on the Mississippi, where they could catch a steamboat to the opposite bank. From there, the Hannibal and St. Joseph Railroad ran all the way through to their destination. The ticket clerk was helpful, explaining that thousands of travelers had already passed through Chicago, resulting in the logistics being well rehearsed.

Frustratingly, he informed them there would be a twenty-four-hour delay before the next train departed, implying a long, cold wait, and although Elena would have appreciated the opportunity to find accommodation for herself and the children, the prospect of lugging their belongings around Chicago seemed impractical. Exasperated, she concluded that they would all have to remain at the station overnight. In any event, she was concerned to avoid another of Hans's murderous rages, which was certain to ensue if he was unable to find his family when he returned. That was a prospect she considered to be beyond contemplation.

Mary and Edward felt deeply sorry for Elena and the children, but they did not want to remain in the cold. Mary was yearning for a hot bath and wanted to wash Edward's cuts and bruises, so with regret they embraced Elena and went on their way.

The night was bitter, and by dawn the Kopps were shivering uncontrollably, but, as the sun rose, the station came alive and they joined the other travelers shuffling around, stomping their feet, and rubbing their arms to get warm.

Leaving the children, Elena went to buy some breakfast, returning with bread and ham, and a bag of roasted nuts cooked on a street brazier outside the station, which they all clasped gratefully in their hands, soaking up the warmth. They ate hungrily, and their spirits began to rise as they speculated about the sort of life they would encounter when they ultimately arrived at their new farm. Fueled by the tasty ham, their imaginations ran wild, Johannes envisioning a huge ranch extending over thousands of acres, raising hundreds of head of cattle, with a large double-story stone farmhouse incorporating separate bedrooms for everyone. Carla hoped that they would own lots of horses and she looked forward to caring for the foals, and Elena wanted a practical yard, with flowers and vegetables that Carla could help her tend. The children longed for their father to be happy, imagining that he would sit contentedly at the head of their dining table, laughing and handing out delicious helpings of roast meat derived from their own herd.

By the time Edward and Mary returned, they were brimming

with optimism about the rest of the journey, and the apple pie that Mary supplied only served to further fuel their enthusiasm. They sang and told stories, laughing about the hardships they had endured. It was a glorious morning, full of hope. Even Johannes was in an ebullient mood, although his joviality was subdued by the presence of Edward, for whom he had cultivated an intense dislike. His animosity was incited by the perverse rationale that the Quaker had somehow induced him to inflict the savage kick he had delivered during the fight with Hans, and the unprovoked attack had left him wrestling with a maelstrom of emotions: elation, guilt, power, and shame.

The day passed, and by noon Hans had still not reappeared. Elena became apprehensive that he would not return in time for the train; to appease her concern, Edward suggested that he and Johannes should go in search of him. It was easy to imagine where he might have gone, since there were scores of saloons near the station. The problem would be discovering which of the hostelries he had selected.

There was no sign of Hans in the first three saloons they reconnoitered, and no one seemed to have seen the big Ukrainian, but their fourth visit was more fruitful. The owner of the bar was furious. Hans had brawled with another man in the early hours of the morning, breaking chairs and a table, and the proprietor was adamant that he was due recompense. He had thrown Hans out of the saloon and watched him lurch off along a narrow street to the rear.

Edward managed to extricate himself from the bar when it became apparent that he was not in a position to offer compensation and, with Johannes, he scouted the neighboring streets, searching alleys and doorways where Hans might have collapsed.

After ten minutes, they arrived at an intersection where a bar called Maisie's occupied the opposite corner. The sound of loud music and raucous laughter spilled onto the street as they approached, and a drunken young man stumbled out of the door ejected by a buxom woman dressed in a tight showgirl's dress, her ample bosom advertising the attraction of the saloon. It seemed unlikely that Johannes would be permitted to enter the hostelry, so Edward advised the boy to wait outside while he went to look for Hans.

The bar was dark, with private alcoves set around the perimeter of the room; dozens of young women in showgirl dresses flounced between the tables, serving drinks or smooching with inebriated men who whooped and roared at a troop of dancers performing on a stage at one end of the bar. The whole saloon reeked of cheap perfume and stale alcohol, but it was clearly a magnet for men who had money to burn and a hot passion to quench.

As Edward's eyes acclimatized to the dim light, he was accosted by two young girls, each of whom entwined their arms with his and attempted to steer him to a private booth. Alarmed at their brazen proposition, he shrugged them off, but they were unamused at his entering Maisie's without any apparent intent to sample the goods. They cursed and jeered at him, insinuating that his preference might be for men or young boys, a suggestion that was met with howls of derision from a group of drunken men seated at a nearby table, each bouncing a leggy young girl on his knee.

Edward peered around awkwardly, hoping to spot Hans among the gloom. He was worrying that he might unintentionally aggravate other customers with his unwelcome scrutiny when he heard a blast of anguished German emanating from a dark corner at the back of the room.

He hurried to investigate and was greeted by the sight of two girls perched precariously on the Ukrainian's knees. Hans was blind drunk, his shirt hanging off his sweaty shoulders, revealing a distended hairy paunch. He rolled the girls back and forth, an arm wrapped tightly around their waists as he smothered his face in their breasts and plastered them with hungry lascivious kisses. He grunted, belching out a lecherous laugh as his hand slid down to squeeze one of the girl's backsides. She squealed, partially in pain but mostly in encouragement, while her friend poured whiskey into Hans's upturned mouth.

The prospect of intervening was daunting, since Edward's intrusion would inevitably be regarded as provocative by both Hans and the saloon's owner, and he hesitated, considering how best to interject. However, his deliberation was shattered by an exasperated bellow.

"Get that brat out o' here!"

Edward wheeled around to find Johannes at his shoulder. The boy stood rigid, his mouth gaping in disbelief as he stared at his father. Sensing his son's presence, Hans raised his head, extracting his face from the bosom of the girl seated on his left knee, and peered at Johannes, his watery red eyes swimming in a fog of alcohol.

"Johaniz?" he slurred, narrowing his eyes as he attempted to focus.

The woman Edward had seen throwing the young man out of the saloon stormed up behind Johannes, and grabbed him firmly by the neck. "Out o' here, ya scamp!" she instructed, hauling him roughly toward the door. "An yer awta na betta," she rounded on Edward. "Fancy bringin' a baw in 'ere!"

Edward dithered with embarrassment, stammering to explain that Johannes was not his son, but his protestation was interrupted as Hans's two companions were unceremoniously dumped off his lap and onto the floor.

Bewildered by Johannes's presence and barely recognizing Edward, he was incensed at the sight of his son being dragged away. He shoved himself upright, swaying momentarily before staggering after the madam, bellowing unintelligible German obscenities.

Grabbing her by the shoulder, he swung his fist wildly at her face. But he had more than met his match. The woman, Maisie, owned the bar. Of Irish descent, she had emigrated with her family in the late 1840s, when famine in Ireland had been at its height. She had worked as a showgirl and a prostitute, but she was worldly wise and possessed a keen business head. Soon, she rented her own premises and built a thriving business on the east coast, until eventually she decided to move to Chicago to open Maisie's saloon.

Over the years, she had been obliged to contend with her fair share of drunks and had split up numerous fights. Nevertheless, her reaction to Hans' assault was incongruous to observe. Standing with her powdered face and extravagant long blond hair piled up under a bonnet of garish feathers, provocatively garbed in a revealing burlesque dress and high heels, she gripped Johannes firmly by the scruff and stepped back elegantly to avoid Hans's ineffectual swipe, simultaneously unhooking a short baton from her waistband with practiced skill, which she swung with whirlwind speed to administer a resounding crack to the back of Hans's head. Stunned, he lost his balance as the baton found its mark, spun with the momentum of his punch, and crashed to the floor.

With accomplished agility, Maisie drove the heel of her shoe down hard onto Hans's outstretched hand, eliciting a howl of pain. Then, she turned and pinned Edward with a hostile glare.

"Take the baw an' git awt!" she snarled, shoving Johannes at him while bending down close to Hans's ear, continuing to press her heel relentlessly into his hand. "Naw, ma' darlin'. Yer 'ad yerself a gud tam, an' naw yer gotta settle wi' ole Maisie." She rummaged through his pockets and whooped when she discovered the wad of notes he had taken from Elena. "Well whada we 'ave 'ere? Reckon yer was real 'appy wi' Maisie's gals!" She tucked twenty dollars into her cleavage and shoved a couple of small notes and some coins back into Hans's pockets. "Naw, yer gonna be a gud baw? Yer gonna go nais an quiet?" She stood up slowly, keeping Hans's hand pinned to the floor, took a careful step backward, and released him.

Hans pushed himself upright and sat on the floor gawping at Maisie through bleary eyes. She smiled, bending forward slightly. "Tam t' go big baw."

In response, Hans whipped an open hand at her cheek, the swipe scything harmlessly through the air and causing him to topple onto his side. The second attempt to hit Maisie was not wise, and she aimed a vicious kick of her sharp-toed shoe at his backside before grabbing the collar of his shirt and hauling him onto his hands and knees, amidst whoops of admiration from the other men in the bar.

"Ride 'im, Maisie!" they encouraged.

One of the girls Hans had dumped from his knee recovered her feet and hurried to assist Maisie. Bending low in front of Hans, her provocative dress revealing her ample cleavage, she blew him a big kiss.

"Cummon, soldier!" she cooed. "Come ta Lillie."

Hans's eyes were swollen, bruised from his tumble to the floor, but he leered at Lillie, a trail of spittle running down his chin, and shuffled toward her on all fours as she lured him seductively towards the saloon door, with Maisie providing the intermittent impetus of a good shove up the backside.

Riotous at the entertainment, half a dozen men leaped to their feet hollering each time Maisie pushed Hans and whooping whenever he reached out to grab at Lillie, the showgirl deftly evading his grasp on each occasion. The men guffawed and threw their drinks over Hans as he groveled along the floor, and encouraged by their raucous laughter, Maisie sat astride his back, twirling an elegant gloved hand around in the air and thwacking his backside with her baton. The whole saloon was in uproar, and two overenthusiastic onlookers collided as they endeavored to secure a better view, each causing the other to lurch sideways and collapse in paroxysms of hilarity, tipping two tables on end. Inspired by the revelry, three of Maisie's girls dove playfully on top of the men, and they all rolled around on the floor hooting.

Determined to compete with the din, the pianist hammered at the keys like a man possessed, and the girls on stage joined in the merriment with outrageous high kicks and flirtatious shimmies of their undergarments.

But one of the customers exceeded the point of acceptable entertainment, and as Hans crawled compliantly after Lillie, the man stumbled alongside and unbuttoned his breeches with the intent of urinating over the Ukrainian's head. The idea was ill-advised. Barely had he unleashed his manhood when Maisie dealt it a savage blow with her black baton, causing the man to shriek with pain and fall backward grasping his groin, affording Hans a moment of brief relief from his shame as the screams of laughter were redirected at the unfortunate inebriate who rolled around in agony.

Johannes was bewildered. Initially, he had been appalled at his father's lecherous entanglement with the two young showgirls, recoiling at Hans's shocking disrespect for his mother. But now he was enraged by the humiliation being heaped upon his father. He was speechless that the indomitable man, whom he held in reverent awe, could be reduced to such a degraded wretch. He pleaded with Edward to intervene, but the big Quaker was not inclined to embroil himself in the fracas, and Johannes was furious, instantly attributing the blame for Hans's misfortune to Edward. He lashed out, launching a frenzy of punches and kicks at the long-suffering Quaker.

Maisie was unmoved by the boy's ire, having achieved her objective. Hans crawled out of the saloon, and Lillie stepped deftly aside as Maisie's foot sent Hans sprawling into the street with a final flourish, whereupon she promptly returned to the bar accompanied by a chorus of delighted cheers.

Johannes dropped to his father's side and helped him to sit upright. Hans's face was red and swollen and his hands were bleeding and bruised. He had an egg-shaped lump on the back of his head where Maisie's baton had sent him flying, and his shirt was torn, with most of the buttons missing. His eyes swam, focusing on a distant point, offering no indication that he recognized his surroundings.

It took half an hour to navigate Hans back to the station, since he was obliged to walk largely unsupported, Edward's broken ribs being unable to bear his weight, and consequently he toppled over and slumped to the ground with frustrating frequency.

By the time the trio returned, the men's wives were distraught. They were panicking about missing the train's departure and had been caught in a quandary about whether to load their belongings onto the waiting boxcar until the conductor had insisted that they stood a good chance of being left behind.

Elena was once again mortified with embarrassment at her husband's drunken condition; nevertheless she helped to bundle him onto the train and prop him unsympathetically in a corner of the boxcar. She thanked Edward profusely as he sat panting, exhausted from the exertion, and Carla spread a blanket over her father, who was snoring loudly within moments.

Johannes scrambled onto the train last, still smoldering with rage. His mind simmered with murderous emotions and he would have attempted to kill Edward had a weapon been to hand, but, instead, fuming with adolescent petulance, he resolved to exact his vengeance at a later date.

The camaraderie of the latter leg of their journey did not return, and the remaining passage to Quincy was tense, the families keeping their distance from one another and interspersing long periods of silence with short, excessively polite exchanges.

The Mississippi River crossing was uneventful, but the strained relationship persisted as they traveled via Hannibal to St. Joseph, so the Mays' relief was intense when they were able to unload their belongings and bid a hasty farewell, Mary giving Elena a sisterly squeeze.

Chapter 9

St. Joseph, State of Missouri

The chaos in Chicago was nothing compared to St. Joseph. The area surrounding the railroad station seethed with recent arrivals, and it was clear that the town was struggling to cope with the hordes of humanity that thronged its streets. The prospect of finding accommodation was futile, and the Kopps were directed to join other emigrants setting up camp on the western outskirts of town.

Winter threatened, and the first snows were already falling by the time the Kopps had fully established their temporary camp. They purchased a tent, bedrolls, and several buffalo hides, which they used to insulate themselves from the frozen ground and provide a warm layer of bedding at night, but still they were forced to huddle together to conserve body heat. Elena bought some additional cooking equipment, and she and Carla attempted to make their temporary home as comfortable as was possible under the circumstances.

Hans had acquired a rudimentary vocabulary of English during his journey from New York and encountered fellow German travelers in St. Joseph who helped him to communicate. Subsequently, using his newfound skill, he occupied himself haggling over the cost of a wagon, or the supply of oxen and cattle, but since demand was enormous and traders were subject to little competitive pressure, Hans's efforts were ineffectual. The price asked was invariably the cost to be paid.

Remarkably, he managed to control his excesses, despite the numerous saloons in town, instead focusing his attention on preparations for the journey ahead and developing a deeper understanding of the system of land allocation. Often, Johannes accompanied him, his grasp of English improving by the day, and Hans found, to his surprise, that the boy conversed easily, possessing a disarming charisma that enabled him to garner information about how the wagon trains were organized and how the land registration process worked. Impressed at the lad's enthusiasm and understanding of the intricacies of the planning and administration processes, officials and agents shared their knowledge willingly.

But life was tough, falling miserably short of the affluent existence Elena and the children had envisaged during their delay at the station in Chicago. There was no prospect of embarking upon the passage west until the snows cleared, and the Kopps suffered a long and arduous winter. The saving grace was that St. Joseph was blessed with an abundance of food and other goods, so they ate well and had time to assemble the supplies they needed for their journey.

The town had expanded rapidly, particularly following the discovery of the goldfields at Alder Gulch and, although rudimentary, the facilities were being developed to serve the thousands of transient migrants and prospectors.

St. Joseph had originally been established along the bank of the Missouri River, founded by Joseph Robidoux and sustained by the lifeline of paddle steamers that arrived daily from New Orleans. The Robidoux Ferry supplied the only means of crossing the river, situated adjacent to the extensive wharfs at the end of Jules Street, where flotillas of steamers docked, converging with the new railroad head to deliver every manner of goods required by the Union Army posts and the emigrants' insatiable demand.

The two largest general merchandise stores were imposing brick buildings set alongside the wharf, run by Elias Perry and John Corby, and when the wagon trains were preparing to leave people jostled through their doors in angry throngs, fighting to secure their supplies.

The town had spawned a broad spectrum of outfitters and traders; nine blacksmiths, two saddlers and harness makers, four wagon builders, and several other general stores. And, on the southern outskirts of town, two flour mills had sprung up alongside twin saw mills that provided timber to construct the rapidly expanding sprawl of residential buildings and enable the fabrication of wagons.

As prosperity grew, residents started to build opulent homes on the hills to the north, away from the bustle and filth of the commercial areas, employing the popular Greek Revival style of construction; brick or white-painted ornate buildings with elaborate porticos, front-facing triangular pediments, rounded columns, and facade pilasters. In addition, schools and churches were erected, serving the various denominations of the eclectic mix of nationalities that combined to establish one of the foremost frontier towns in the west.

By contrast, the commercial area was a labyrinth of small streets designed by the town's founder, who had subdivided the original trading post into as many small plots of land as possible to maximize his profit from their sale. The main street was a jumbled mix of timber buildings, all built independently in differing styles and broadcasting their trade with large colorful facia boards. Mercifully, each building provided a duckboard walkway, enabling pedestrians to navigate the street without being obliged to wade through the deep mud, which was inclined to ensnare boots and adhere to ladies' skirts in heavy clods. In most cases, the shopkeepers' family lived in accommodation on the second floor, accessed by an outside staircase, and sometimes they supplemented their income by offering rooms to let.

Numerous saloons remained open day and night, generating a constant stream of occupants for the sheriff's cells, as tempers flared over a game of poker or a dispute arose surrounding one of the many prostitutes who flocked to take advantage of easy pickings among the mass of transient prospectors.

Situated at the north end of town were two sprawling liveries, their stockyards crammed with hundreds of horses, alongside which the blacksmiths' furnace burned twenty-four hours a day, shoeing animals and crafting steel rims for wagon wheels.

The noise was intense, laden wagons creaking as oxen or mules labored to drag them through the cloying mud, the clatter of the smithies' hammer, music and drunken singing spilling out of the saloons, cattle lowing, and the hubbub of countless people shouting at one another to be heard above the din. It was a hell hole, but nonetheless the launch point for a journey to a new life filled with optimism.

As the worst of winter passed, the settlers amassed their final supplies. The wagon makers had used the winter months to build up stocks of prairie schooners, which were now the favored means of transport for the settlers. These wooden vehicles, with their huge steel-rimmed wheels, weighed nearly a ton and a half when fully laden, a fraction of the weight of their forerunners, the Conestoga wagons, which at eight tons had proved far too heavy for the challenging conditions encountered on the plains, often becoming bogged down and being abandoned.

The prairie schooner was a lighter build, featuring a canvas shroud waterproofed with linseed oil, which was stretched over a series of hickory hoops or bows. The body of the wagon was timber paneled, roughly ten feet by four feet, caulked at the joints and reinforced sparingly with steel fittings where absolutely necessary. The rear wheels were nearly six feet in diameter, with the front being about two-thirds of the size, all four requiring a regular soaking with water during the journey, since the scorching summer weather was prone to dry out the timber, causing it to shrink, break away from the snug-fitting steel rims, and fracture.

The money Matilde had entrusted to Elena proved essential, and the Kopps could not have contemplated their onward journey without the financial resources. They traded more of their gold and purchased a wagon and harness for four hundred dollars, together with four oxen at an additional cost of twenty-five dollars each.

The general mercantile supplied the balance of their needs, Hans and Johannes assisting to load their schooner with seven hundred pounds of flour, thirty pounds of salt, two hundred pounds of lard, six hundred pounds of bacon, eighty pounds of fruit, and eighty pounds of coffee, leaving only enough remaining space for their cooking pots, tent and bedding, their trunks, and Hans's father's table. In total, they had expended nearly $700 by the time the wagon was fully laden.

Lastly, Hans bought ten head of cattle that were in calf, and a horse that they agreed to ride in rotation, the family being condemned to walk alongside the wagon since there was insufficient space remaining for passengers.

The burgeoning fleet of wagons and associated livestock soon rendered inadequate the camp on the east side of the river, thus with many other families, the Kopps were obliged to relocate, taking their wagon across the Missouri on the steamer ferry and driving their stock across the wide fast-flowing waterway. It was a sobering initiation, neither the oxen nor the cattle being keen to enter the water, and Hans suffered his first taste of the challenges of traveling through the barren lands of the west. Indeed, without the assistance of a more experienced cattle hand, he would have failed to make the crossing.

As February turned to March, the enormity of the human

migration became apparent, with over a thousand wagons assembled on the plains to the west of the Missouri, each laden with supplies for the months ahead and attended by their beasts of burden.

Novice cowhands struggled to feed and control their cattle, and it was not unusual for camps to be flattened or overturned as a stray herd wandered unchecked among the assembled schooners. The mood was fractious, and everyone yearned for the moment when their expedition would commence.

St. Joseph had become a jumping-off point for several of the overland routes to the west, all starting along the two-thousand-mile Oregon Trail, some eventually branching off to join the Santa Fe Trail to the south, the Applegate Trail as an alternate route to Oregon via California, or the Bozeman or Bridger Trails that led north. The chaotic sprawl began to subdivide into defined groups, each intent upon following one of the respective routes.

Elena was pleasantly surprised to find that Edward and Mary were mustered in her group of wagons, and when the opportunity presented itself she slipped away to give Mary a hug.

Although the mass of migrants gave the impression of an irrepressible tide of humanity, the journey west was becoming increasingly dangerous, provoked by the United States government's determination to promote settlement of the Great Plains. This vision of the political leadership, referred to as "Manifest Destiny," was aimed at extending the sovereignty of the United States to stretch unfettered from coast to coast across the continent.

Policy implementation had proven difficult. The industrial leaders in the east feared that their workers would succumb to the temptation of free land in the west, while in the south there was concern that new States, opposed to slavery, would emerge from the northwestern territories, contributing support to the antislavery movement. Successive frontier strategies failed until the secession of the southern states, following which the Homestead Act was approved by Congress, providing a formal mechanism for settlers to claim, improve, and obtain title to their own land.

However, the policy instigated direct conflict with the indigenous Indian tribes, who insisted that the Great Plains could belong to no man, that the buffalo should be left to migrate freely, and that the land should remain unsullied by cultivation. Frustrated, the government proposed that the Indians vacate the plains and take up residence on allocated reservations, but the natives steadfastly refused, clinging instead to their traditional way of life and running into conflict with settlers who sought to define the boundaries of their homesteads by erecting fenced enclosures.

The Indians foresaw the threat to their very existence, anticipating the destruction of nature's fragile balance, which the white man's influence would inevitably inflict upon the land of their forefathers, their sacred hunting grounds. Appalled, they rallied to oppose the danger, attacking and disrupting supply trains and wagon convoys that attempted to traverse the Great Plains.

For this reason, many wagon trains were accompanied by military protection, particularly those that intended navigating the northern trails, and as they welcomed the first hint of spring, the Kopps and their fellow travelers waited impatiently for the arrival of their escort.

Chapter 10

North of the Greybull River, Dakota Territory

The morning was bitterly cold, winter having arrived with a vengeance, so that trapping was all but over for the year.

Red McCabe was irritated. He had ventured out to check the traps he had set on the nearby ponds, leaving his partner comatose at their cabin. La Brais was a drunkard and had taken to the whiskey bottle to keep himself warm, now that severe weather had set in.

The two trappers had drifted south from Canada in search of wealth. Initially lured by the prospect of gold, it had transpired that they were unable to afford the cost of a stake. So, disillusioned with the prospect of working someone else's claim, they considered alternative options and decided that the fur trade offered potential, given that many of the pioneer trappers had abandoned the Rockies in favor of more abundant beaver populations in California.

Neither of the men were experienced at survival in the wilderness, and the arduous conditions were taking their toll. Rather than joining one of the remaining fur-trapping outfits, which they had concluded would pay a paltry salary and retain the majority of the profits of their labor, they elected to chance their hand as free trappers, hoping to make more money bartering for the best price for their pelts. But the dream was fast turning into a nightmare. Many of the creeks were bereft of beaver, the large aquatic rodent having been hunted to near extinction over the preceding thirty years, and the trapping gear they had acquired was of poor quality.

Additionally, their preparation for winter had been far from ideal. They had bought plenty of coffee, but precious little meat or pemmican, La Brais having spent much of his money loading their mules with cases of whiskey, promising that he would shoot more game than they would be able to eat.

McCabe was a skinny, sour-faced man in his late forties. His face was long and narrow, pock-marked with tufts of ginger stubble, and he had a squint in one eye. His mouth, with a deep scar on the upper lip and a disorderly set of broken yellow teeth, rendered the impression of a permanent sneer. He was a loner, who regarded other people as an unwelcome encumbrance. He had never succeeded in cultivating a relationship with a woman, being content to fraternize with prostitutes in preference, since they demanded no commitment in return.

On the other hand, La Brais was a bull of a man, with a barrel chest and a virtually nonexistent neck. His body was swathed in thick, dark, wiry hair that spouted from the neck of his tunic, enveloped his back, and covered his hands so that they appeared like the paws of a bear. Having declined to trim his beard, it had grown long and full, masking his face and framing his eyes, which were his most striking feature. One iris was black and the other an albino red, presenting a disconcerting difficulty in determining his point of focus.

He was totally self-assured, enjoying the camaraderie of the saloon but equally content with his own company. In his companion, he recognized a weak man who could be manipulated to his advantage, so he had been sanguine about striking a partnership with McCabe to undertake the beaver hunting.

They had scouted the Little Big Horn River during the summer months, diverting west along the Greybull toward its source in the Absaroka Mountains later in the year, where they scoured the creeks in search of beaver. The signs were sparse, but they discovered promising dams in some of the ponds and evidence of the canals that the industrious rodents formed to float harvested willow whips to their lodges. Content that they had identified a favorable area to hunt, they set about building a cabin in the gently sloping vee-shaped valley of a tributary to the Greybull, providing a base from which to operate as they set their traps in early autumn.

La Brais proved to be idle, leaving the hard work to McCabe, but he was an expert shot with his rifle so little game evaded his lethal aim, when he was sober. His skill had at least supplied the little sustenance they had managed to assemble, but as importantly, it provided McCabe with the confidence that they could protect themselves against hostility from Indians, whom La Brais hated with a passion.

Before winter set in, they succeeded in trapping nearly fifty beaver, having ventured deep into the mountains to find ponds. The process involved identifying the points where the beaver entered and exited the ponds, so that they could place their snares in the late afternoon. The objective was to catch the beavers as they embarked upon their busy nocturnal ritual, gathering winter food supplies and marking their territory with pungent scent mounts, each pile of mud impregnated with castoreum secreted from a gland at the base of their flat, scaly tail.

The beavers' behavior was regarded as most predictable during late autumn, when restoration of their lodge became a pressing necessity ahead of winter. The colder temperature caused the lodge's mud cap to freeze solid, providing a protective shield against any predators that might attempt to dig into the warm home that cosseted the families of adults, yearlings, and kits.

Setting traps meant getting wet, placing the snare where the beaver would enter the dam, but also ensuring that the area around the trap was sculpted with dead branches and mud to channel the animal into the snare. La Brais refused to immerse his legs in the icy water, restricting his effort to gathering the materials required for the task, once threatening to kill McCabe when his weasly partner tried to push him into one of the freezing ponds.

In truth, McCabe was frightened of his companion, who had a ferocious temper and was prone to reach for his gun as a first resort. It was rumored that he had nearly beaten a man to death over a disputed card game in Ottawa and had gunned down the husband of a woman with whom La Brais had conducted an adulterous relationship. Consequently, McCabe concluded that it was in his best interest to remain silent, focus on surviving the winter, and assemble as many pelts as possible before decamping to the trading post in spring, where he planned to give La Brais the slip.

McCabe trudged through knee-deep snow along the edge of a frozen pond, careful to avoid the slippery bank. It was possible that the beaver might venture from its lodge, since the weather had improved over the preceding two days, but there was no point in placing traps unless he identified signs of activity. He completed a circuit of the pond to no avail, his trip up the mountain appearing futile, although it had at least provided an opportunity to get away from La Brais for a while. Disillusioned, he decided to return to his horse, which he had hobbled at the treeline.

Situated slightly above the forest on the northerly facing slopes, and shaded from the low winter sun, the pond caught the full force of a bone-numbing wind that whipped down from a long ridge that flanked the southern border of the valley. McCabe felt the gusts pluck at the fur around his neck, reflexively glancing up at the cloudy feathers of snow being blown over the crest of the escarpment.

The bright azure sky accented the ridge with particular clarity, so that even at a distance of a mile or more the detailed contours of the rock formations stood in stark relief. His eyes traced idly along the summit toward its eastern-most promontory where he was surprised to detect a distortion to the natural outline of the craggy edge.

Battered by the howling wind, the top of the mountain was clear of snow, revealing a small man-made structure seated upon the bare rock. McCabe paused and gazed up at the unexpected sight, shading his eyes against the bright sunlight. The shape was not natural. He could discern vertical poles, but at a distance the rest of the structure was amorphous.

Although curious, he put his head down and plodded back to his horse. Having found no sign of beaver, and certainly not minded to get wet setting traps, it seemed sensible to return to the cabin.

His horse stood in the shelter of the trees alongside a mule laden with packs of snares, their heads hanging and their rumps turned to the wind. He hitched the mule and removed the hobbles from his horse, mounted, and traversed the treeline to join the beginning of a trail that led down through the forest and into the valley below.

The thought of spending the day with La Brais was not appealing, so, before entering the forest, he stole an impulsive glance at the strange structure on the ridge. A shaft of sunlight reflected off a horizontal platform, suspended on the vertical pillars, and the sight piqued his interest. He halted his horse, reflecting upon the acrimonious day he was likely to endure if he returned to the cabin, and pulled his cinch tight as he mused his options. One further glance made up his mind. He decided to trek up to the ridge and take a closer look.

Exposed on the barren upper slopes below the ridge, the bitter wind whipped viciously, flailing his skin until it felt sufficiently raw that he had to stop to pull on an extra coat and cover his face to afford more protection from its icy blasts. Continuing, the climb was slow and the snow was so deep in places that he was forced to divert from the path to find a passable route, the mule trailing unenthusiastically, since the animal would almost certainly have broken its tether had he left it behind.

The path advanced diagonally up the escarpment and eventually surmounted the ridge about a mile to the west of the promontory where he had spied the structure. The view was breath-taking. The ridge was roughly two hundred yards wide and largely flat, its sheer southerly face being so dangerously overhung with accumulated snow that he was unable to see into the valley below, but the eastern aspect exposed the expanse of the Great Plains.

The cabin he and La Brais shared lay to the northeast and to the west stood an endless range of peaks, capped with a brilliant reflective crystalline icing. Some of the mountains rose to gently rounded pinnacles, while others jutted sharp spires of sheer gray rock toward the heavens, their precipitous faces glazed with a thin veneer of ice or laden with perilously loose boulders that threatened to break away and plummet to the foothills. It was a wilderness beyond measure, in which a man could lose his way and become disorientated in a matter of hours, and where wolves were masters of the winter realm.

The rugged panorama frightened him and he wheeled away to track hastily along the ridge to the east. The going was easy, the wind having blown away most of the snow, and he hunkered down into his thick coat, pushing his horse on at a brisk walk, so that after twenty minutes he dropped down a small incline and was confronted by the funeral scaffold constructed by the Lakota.

The sight was bizarre. Thick fillets of ice clung to the leeward side of the scaffold, the only snow lying in a deep pile accumulated on the ground at one end. A fluttering bundle of rags lay upon the dais, shedding wisps of white powder in intermittent ghostly puffs. Beyond the structure the ridge dropped away at an impossible angle, revealing an unimpeded view across a low jagged range of mountains, cloaked with thick stands of lodgepole speckled with a sugary icing. McCabe's eye traced the line of the closest valley, knowing that it provided his route to the plains, and thence liberation from his partner.

He sat on his horse gazing out across the prairie, feeling uncharacteristically drawn to the attractions of civilization, which now appeared eminently preferable to the hardship of his present undertaking. He grunted at his discontent and swung his horse around, urging it alongside the platform.

Despite being mounted, he was unable to reach the mound that lay upon the elevated deck. Inspecting the scaffold further, he concluded that it must be some form of altar built by the local savages and imagined that it had been erected to practice their heathen witchcraft, for the purpose of offering sacrifices to their pagan gods. Given the location, he thought it probable that the Indians had thrown their victim off the sheer cliff beyond the scaffold, as part of a macabre ceremony to appease their deity. If so, it was possible that gifts to the gods had been placed on the dais, perhaps valuable gifts, gold, silver or precious artifacts.

He stood tall in his stirrups, trying to acquire a better view of the platform. It was clearly laden with a good-sized assortment of items, but he was reluctant to dig around in the snow-covered bundle without being able to see what he was touching. He had heard stories about the Indians' barbaric practices: eating critter's entrails, drinking the blood of their dogs, making masks from the heads of animals, and rubbing their bodies with buffalo brains. The stories were legend in the saloons where lurid tales of the natives' rituals became progressively distorted as the whiskey flowed.

McCabe's imagination ran riot. He had no desire to inadvertently handle some disgusting carcass the savages had left, but he was determined to establish whether there was anything of value on the dais. He chuckled greedily. In La Brais's absence he would be able to keep anything he found for himself.

After maneuvering alongside the dais and tying the mule securely to one of the stout vertical scaffold posts, he unraveled a rope and fastened it securely around a horizontal rail of the dais. The opposite end he looped several times around the horn of his saddle and swung his horse away from the structure until the rope was taught. The scaffold proved surprisingly strong, demonstrating no sign of breaking, so he backed the horse up a pace and dug his spurs aggressively into its flank, whooping and beating its rump with his hat. The horse sprang forward and the rope whipped tight, causing the dais rail to snap with a rending crack and drag away half of the woven platform so that the load it supported crashed to the ground in a billowing cloud of powdery snow.

McCabe was delighted, and he hooted and hollered as though he had struck gold, his avaricious mind whirling with extravagant ideas of the bounty he had unearthed as he leapt from his horse in a frenzy of anticipation.

The crumpled heap that confronted him still gave the impression of a pile of animal hides and, in the center, as he had anticipated, there lay the gruesome spectacle of a buffalo skull. Disgusted, he aimed a kick at one of the horns, dislodging the headpiece, which rolled away with surprising ease trailing a dark buffalo hide. McCabe staggered backward in shock, as the disfigured and partially eaten skull of a man grimaced back at him. Birds had pecked away most of the flesh, leaving the eyes as gaping empty sockets, but tufts of hair remained around the top of the head and frozen clumps of flesh clung to the jaw, which displayed a ghoulish grin of exposed bone and teeth.

He was certain that he had stumbled upon some form of sacrifice, the victim having been tied to the platform and left to be eaten alive by the huge eagles that patrolled the mountain peaks. The grisly corpse was enveloped in hides and, summoning his courage, McCabe shoved it with his boot, pushing the body clear of the debris that had fallen from the platform. It rolled awkwardly, twisting grotesquely and trailing a partially eaten arm as it fell away from the pile. Snow tumbled off the corpse, revealing a brightly colored shirt decorated with elaborate stitching and curious leggings adorned with ornate pictures. McCabe was fascinated, but reticent to touch the body for fear that it had been imbued with some form of dark magic.

"Filthy savages. Devil worshipers! Kill their own kine," he muttered under his breath.

The sight of the body made him feel uncomfortable, and, since it failed to yield anything of value, he continued to roll it away from the scaffold, administering callous kicks to turn the rigid corpse.

"Git on!" he protested, straining until his foot slipped and struck the back of the skull, which detached with a crack and tumbled free. "Euh! Darn thung. Git away!"

Agitated, he shoved the body until it balanced precariously on the precipitous edge of the plateau, a trail of small bones left in its wake, and with a final brutal flourish, he thrust it unceremoniously into the void. Infused with a sense of triumph, he turned around to be confronted by the hideous mask of the severed head, its animated toothy grin leering at him ominously. He shuddered.

"What yer lookin' at!" he jeered, swinging a well-aimed boot so that the head careered along the ground scattering teeth before bouncing over the edge of the cliff. "Ain't so funny now. Eh!"

Elated by a satisfying sense of victory, he returned to inspect the rest of the items laid at the foot of the scaffold, dropping to his knees to burrow into the snow with feverish excitement. Immediately his hand touched something long and thin, and he brushed the snow away hungrily to reveal a beautifully fashioned bow, topped with a sharp metal point and ornamented with eagle feathers. It was an artifact crafted with skill, and his avarice was piqued.

Further frantic delving revealed a quiver of arrows, the sleeve festooned with drawings of every manner of beast and decorated with colorful tassels that hung from the entire length on one side. Next, he retrieved a wickedly sharp hunting knife, a beautifully crafted small axe, and an ornate spear. They were all interesting items, but McCabe was disappointed. He had expected to unearth precious metals or gems, but he could find nothing of value, so he rose to his feet and scattered the rest of the snowy mound in frustration. Nothing.

Slowly, he wheeled around and noticed the pile of snow he had seen earlier, gathered at one end of the scaffold. Again, he dropped to his knees and plunged his gloved hands into the mound, clawing at the snow to uncover its treasures.

His hand struck a hard, irregular shape, and he wrestled to pull it clear, patting it down enthusiastically to remove the snow, until he revealed a sizeable animal vertebra. His hands sprang open and he threw himself backward, snapping upright and heaving for breath as he tried to make sense of his discovery. Once more he swung his boot, kicking at the snow repeatedly until it tumbled away to reveal the skull of a horse, broken and cracked where it had been chewed by wolves. The carcass had been scavenged, stripped to the bone, so that only the scattered skeleton and a large hoop of rib cage remained.

The sight was enough for McCabe. He had found nothing of significance. His effort had been fruitless, and he was angry at his wasted exertion. Nevertheless, he decided to pack the weapons onto his mule as keepsakes and head back down to the cabin. His desecration of the sacred place of rest was of no significance to him, and he cared little whether the site was of importance to the native peoples.

Chapter 11

March 1865, Sioux village, Greybull River, Dakota Territory

"My heart is heavy, Grandfather. I cannot put aside my part in Father's death. A darkness clouds my mind, and the wonders of nature that made me sing with joy are like shadows to my eyes." Takoda paused. "I am troubled by a dream too. It has come to me often since Father died. In the dream, all the women cried and the children fell to the ground. A huge black buffalo stamped on our fires until the flames died, and the ashes were scattered. As a moth emerges from its cocoon, the buffalo transformed into a great gray iron horse, belching smoke and turning the prairie grass to blood. I stood before the iron horse and saw death piled all around our people. In one hand, I held an eagle and in the other a dove. My legs could stand no more, and a great fear settled upon me. That is where I always awake. I can see the dream with my eyes open as though it is the truth, but I do not know how it ends or what it means." He sat back and gazed imploringly at the Itancan, as if his grandfather might deliver a reassuring explanation.

The Itancan was deeply troubled by Takoda's dream, but there was no merit in worrying the boy further. "You feel guilty, Takoda, but you cannot be responsible for something that Wakan Tanka has ordained. Who are we to question what the Great Spirit decrees? There are things that we can influence and things that we cannot. You must rejoice that your father is with the Creator. But, for those of us who remain here, in the blessed arms of Mother Earth, it is our duty to strive to be the best that we can, and in this way, we will serve our purpose. This, now, should be your focus."

"But I cannot see my purpose, Grandfather. I am like a bird with a broken wing. I walk through the trees and they obscure my view because I cannot fly above the forests and see the truth."

"Takoda, these are deep feelings for one so young. I understand your pain and I hear the words of your dream, but I do not know yet what they mean. Your healing is not something that I can give you. You must heal yourself from within. Pray to Wakan Tanka and I will think upon what you have said. Soon we will speak again."

"Thank you, Grandfather." Takoda stood and left the Itancan's tipi quietly, his head bowed.

The months had passed slowly for Takoda and his brother. It was now well into winter and there was little to keep the boys occupied, deep snow having settled in the valley where they were camped. There was the chore of collecting firewood and the distraction of an occasional hunting party, but at this time of year the band was fairly sedentary, living off the accumulated stock of dried meat and pemmican that they had amassed through late summer and autumn.

Takoda did not mind the winter, the cold wind, or the driving rain. To him, as for the rest of his people, winter was part of nature's cycle. The cold killed the parasites that caused illness and the snow fed and refreshed the mountain streams, heralding renewal of the prairies. But his mind was heavy with the loss of his father. His insatiable love for the wonders of nature, and his thirst to study the behavior of the beasts of the forest and the plains, was dulled. He could not shake off his guilt, despite his grandfather's reassurance, and he felt that his father's death was a precursor to something even more shattering. His dream was recurrent, and he believed that there was a connection between his vision and the events that had befallen his father.

He returned to his mother's tipi, where the fire burned brightly and the smoke rose in an etheric plume. Settling close to the heat, he pulled a buffalo hide around his shoulders and rubbed his hands, holding them to the flames to warm. He was solidly built and although not as strong as his brother, his shoulders were broad and his limbs were lean, beginning to display the bulge of adolescent muscle. His face was round, more so than was normal for his people, with broad lips that curled up slightly at the corners and a straight aquiline nose, but combined with his soft dark eyes, set under a thoughtful brow, he exuded a magnetic warmth, reflecting the meaning of his name, Friend to Everyone. His hair, which fell below shoulder length, was tied in a single ponytail interwoven with thin strands of leather, and around his neck he wore a lace threaded with a collection of animal claws and teeth.

His brother sat beside him, brooding. Howahkan looked surprisingly unlike Takoda, inheriting his father's straight mouth, broad curved nose, and serious eyes. His bearing was erect and purposeful, whereas Takoda often managed to appear slumped. A long vertical scar ran from upper cheekbone to jaw-line on his left cheek, a souvenir from an early hunting trip, during which he had hurried to inspect a wolf that his father had shot, thinking that it was dead. But, although the arrow had pierced the animal's chest, the wolf had still been alive, and had launched a vicious swipe with its sharp claws as Howahkan had dropped down at its side, leaving him lucky to have avoided a more serious injury than the deep scratch to his face.

Howahkan's extra year of maturity showed in his physique. He was lithe and muscular, honed from long hours of undertaking the numerous physical challenges that young Lakota were obliged to endure to build their confidence, strength, and courage. He was a formidable shot with his bow and could hurl his spear with extraordinary accuracy for one so young. The use of guns was not encouraged at his age, so he was restricted to using traditional weapons, which enabled him to develop his skill and bravery, but unquestionably he was gifted with a quality of coordination that suggested he would make a fine shot in due course.

Distinct from Takoda, he swept back his long black hair using a leather thong, looped across his forehead and tied behind his head, with two eagle feathers bound into his ponytail. The Lakota considered the eagle sacred, and because it flew higher than any other bird it was seen as capable of soaring closer to Wakan Tanka, enabling it to commune with the Creator. The feathers that Howahkan wore had been given to him as a reminder that he was destined to be a leader, signifying that he should live at all times in the sacred way. One had been presented by his father, the other by the Itancan, and he had never removed them from his hair since they had been given, regarding their symbolism as a solemn duty.

"I cannot sit and fan the flames of this fire any longer," he looked up at Takoda. "We must get out of the village. I have to smell the forest and taste the mountain air."

"Mahpee will take us to hunt for squirrels soon," Takoda responded, but the comment was half-hearted, and he knew that the old man would not wish to travel far in the deep snow. He also yearned to get out of the village and hoped that exercise and solitude might clear his head.

"We'll be waiting until the snows melt, if we wait for him," Howahkan grumbled.

"I have spoken to grandfather about my dream and he is going to consider its meaning. I cannot go until he speaks with me again."

"We should go to Father's resting place. The spirits may talk to you there and tell you the meaning of your dream." Howahkan stared into the flickering flames of the fire as he spoke.

The simplicity of the suggestion hit Takoda as though he had been punched in the stomach. It was so obvious, he should have thought of it before now. Instantly, he knew that it was the right thing to do. He had no option. Surely, the spirits had talked to him through Howahkan. But the journey would be grueling. The weather would render it impossible to ascend the steep mountain path to the north of the village, so they would have to traverse out of the valley to the east and cut a route north across the plains to approach the ridge from the opposite side. Their challenge would be to find a plausible excuse to leave the village, since neither their mother, nor the Itancan, would countenance them undertaking such a journey alone in the depth of winter.

"What?" Howahkan felt the intensity of his brother's gaze as Takoda stared at him, speechless.

"I know what you say to be right." Takoda whispered. His eyes met his brother's, and without a further word they knew that they must undertake this journey together.

It was two days before the Itancan called for Takoda, having reflected seriously upon his grandson's dream. Takoda was not a natural warrior, but his spiritual sensitivity was unique, many of the band being vocal in their belief that he was blessed with the ability to communicate with the spirits in all their forms, whether bird or beast, mortal or otherworldly. The elders had concluded that his dream warranted grave consideration, and the Itancan felt disturbed by its inference. He wondered whether the dream might be a sign of Takoda's father communing with him, attempting to give the tribe a message of urgent importance.

He had called the elders together, with Makawee, and they had spoken for many hours, considering the meaning of the dream, debating what they should do as a consequence, and agreeing the action that should be taken to help Takoda recover from his melancholy.

Makawee was worried for her son. Takoda had not been himself since his father had died. He was sullen and depressed. He rarely left her tipi and, when he did, he seemed disinterested in the things the other boys wanted to do. Even Howahkan struggled to motivate him, and he was usually the first to make Takoda smile or encourage him to embark upon some hare-brained expedition.

The elders had discussed Takoda's connection with the spirit world, and all were of the opinion that he was wakan, gifted with an ability to communicate with the Creator, and that he was also true to his word. If Takoda said that he had dreamt such a dream, his assertion was not to be questioned. These factors being beyond dispute, they agreed that it was important to consider the significance of the dream. The timing, so soon after his father's death, was unlikely to be coincidental, and the substance of the dream resonated with real concerns that the tribe harbored about the continuity of their traditional way of life.

For several years, the Union government had been in discussions with native Indian tribes about relinquishing occupation of the prairies to settlers migrating from the east. Initially, the Indians had been open to negotiation about shared use of their ancestral lands, but promises had been made and broken so many times that most tribes had concluded that the white man was not to be trusted.

The Indians did not believe that any man could own the land. It transcended life. It had existed for millions of years before they or the white man had appeared on earth, and it would exist for millions of years after these people, who wished to buy the land, would pass from this life. They could not comprehend how anyone could seek to own something so eternally enduring.

Equally, moderate Indians believed that their right to use the land was no greater than that of anyone else. They reasoned that both Indian and white man must be creations of the same Great Mystery, and that Mother Earth provided her abundance for the benefit of all. For this reason, it was incumbent upon them to agree with the white man how they could cohabit.

It was an accepted norm that another band could take up residence on a section of land, once the first band had chosen to move on, such occupation being of a nonpermanent nature. This flexibility was tempered with an understanding that the original band would be entitled to return to the same section of land whenever they wished.

The white man did not share this notion of the possession of land. He believed that once he had occupied the land, he became entitled to its sole use and would permit no other person to enter upon it. Often, he would enclose the land with fencing, signifying some unique distinction between the land on one side of the fence and that on the other, and conferring upon him a greater entitlement to its use. This was not how the Indians regarded the sacred gift of Mother Earth.

At first, there had been few white people. They had traded with the tribes, who had relished the opportunity to swap their furs for horses and latterly guns. The horses and modern weapons had transformed the Indians' ability to traverse the plains and to hunt; changes that were regarded as good medicine by some, although others disagreed, insisting that the traditional ways were better. But, over the years, more white people arrived, and now there was an endless stream of migrants, like a great river in flood, all of whom believed that they had the right to claim land and build their fences.

The white men tore up Mother Earth, rending her surface to

form ditches and plant unusual crops, and they fought over stones that they dug from the ground or blasted from her belly with fire that deafened the ears.

The government began negotiating for small sections of land to be set aside for occupation by white people, and agreements were struck. The sacred pipe was smoked to seal the agreement, and the words of the negotiators' promise rose up to the Great Spirit in the smoke from the pipe, so that those words became the Indians' sacred bond. A commitment not only to the government, but a spiritual vow to the Creator of all things. But the Government broke their bond. They returned and demanded more land. Now they wanted the Indians to leave their hunting grounds and settle upon land that was barren, where the buffalo did not roam. It was a momentous time. The surge of humanity was relentless, and the medicine of the white man was strong.

Young warriors wanted to fight and throw the white man off the land, but the grandmothers warned that Wakan Tanka forbade the taking of another life, and that doing so would only provoke more soldiers to come from the east, resulting in outright war. They argued that the white man's medicine was too strong to resist, and that it was inevitable that the Bluecoats would eventually overpower the Indian Nations; as the heavy winter snow covered the land, so the white man would smother the native peoples. They surmised that the best course of action was to negotiate, agreeing to an accord by which both peoples could live together, while preserving what was possible from the old ways.

To the purists such a proposal was heresy. They perceived a future that constrained their traditional way of life to be a future not worthy of life itself, insisting that it was better to fight and die than to concede one's freedom and live as a shadow, enslaved by the white man's dominance.

Takoda's dream spoke of this future. Already, there seemed

less buffalo, and the Indians' fire was being trampled. The Itancan had heard tales of the white man's great iron horse too, talk that Takoda could not have heard. Tribes to the south told stories of an iron horse that charged across the plains, belching fire and carrying hundreds of people upon its back. The boy's dream was surely a premonition of the threat to the tribe of the advance of the people from the east.

All the elders agreed that this was the substance of Takoda's dream, and they debated the implications for many hours. Since Takoda had said that his dream had occurred repeatedly, having awoken before the dream had finished in each instance, it was their belief that the spirits wished him to know and understand its meaning. They concurred that it was important to discover how the dream ended and concluded that it was likely that a negative energy was blocking Takoda's connection with the spirits, preventing his ability to finish the dream. He required assistance to clear this impediment.

The Lakota method of treating this problem was to undertake a Smudging ceremony. The elders agreed that this should be done to help lift his depression, clearing his vision so that he might see his dream more clearly and thereby restore his bright demeanor and his spiritual peace. The Smudging ceremony also advocated that Takoda would benefit from exercise, and Howahkan was to be instructed to accompany his brother on some short excursions.

Additionally, Makawee was charged with responsibility to undertake the ceremony of Yuwipi. During this ceremony, the medicine woman would pray to the spirits, beseeching their guidance in interpreting the dream and assessing its implications for the tribe. Both ceremonies were to be conducted as soon as possible.

★ ★ ★ ★ ★

Takoda was grateful for his grandfather's intervention, but he was most elated by the proposal that he and Howahkan venture out of the village. This sort of activity was often advised as complementary to the Smudging process, aiding mind, body, and spirit to heal, but in this instance, it provided a legitimate excuse for his absence when he and Howahkan went to visit their father's funeral dais.

Howahkan was delighted with Takoda's news. He was frustrated by the confines of the village and had his own demons to resolve following his father's death. The prospect of some solitude and the opportunity to sit alongside his father buoyed his spirits, so he busied himself assembling a small pack of supplies for each of them, leaving Takoda and his mother to prepare for the ceremonies.

Makawee was encouraged that, having spoken to the Itancan, Takoda immediately started showing signs of his depression easing, and she hoped that the Smudging ceremony would contribute decisively to the relief of her son's unhappiness. She joined the matriarchs to prepare for the ceremonies, both of which would be conducted in the sweat lodge, set at the center of the village and built as the band's communal area for the winter season.

As the afternoon light faded, the band assembled around the village fire, and the elders filed into the lodge to take their places. The Itancan sat cross legged in the center at the back of the lodge, with Makawee to his left, each of the elders taking their place alongside until they encircled the central fire pit. The rest of the band organized themselves in a series of supplementary concentric rings.

Silence fell, and the Itancan started to explain the purpose of the ceremonies, urging everyone to focus the power of their thoughts for Takoda's benefit. He did not discuss Takoda's dream, which the elders had agreed should remain confidential until there was greater clarity about its meaning.

The Lakota considered the Smudging ceremony to be part of a healing process, invoking the spirits to bring about spiritual peace as part of a long-term restorative therapy, rather than being intended to cure a symptom, and the support of the entire band would heighten the communion, adding potency to the effect.

Once the Itancan had spoken, Makawee stepped forward and knelt before the fire where she laid out three bundles of dried plants and a large wooden bowl, upon which she piled fronds of sage, covering them with sweetgrass, and heaping on a small quantity of tobacco leaves. She then placed a stick into the fire, letting it burn until a small flame danced from its end, which she held to the base of the pyre of dried plants in her bowl, blowing gently until they began to smoulder.

The concoction possessed great significance. Sweetgrass was known as the grass that never died. It grew high in the mountains, and its fragrance provided a reminder of the cool, clean air of their lofty peaks. The sage represented the desert, being dry, clean, and aromatic when crushed. And the tobacco acted as a vector when mingled with both scents, the mountain and the desert, conveying the thoughts and prayers of the ceremony's participants into the ether, and thence to Wakan Tanka.

Makawee continued to blow upon the contents of the bowl until they crackled gently in the heat. She piled on more sage and sweetgrass, smothering the flames to produce billowing clouds of smoke. Once prepared, Takoda was summoned to stand before her, wearing only a small deerskin breechcloth tucked into a simple leather waistband.

His demeanor was serious and pensive, but he was pleased that the ceremony was being undertaken. He had a deep knowledge of Lakota medicine and a strong belief in its efficacy, having witnessed remarkable feats of healing achieved by his mother over the years. He sensed the collective prayers of the band and the air in the lodge caused his skin to tingle, as if charged with an invisible force.

Makawee held a small bundle of sage stems over the fire until they started to burn, at which point she blew out the flames, leaving the sage smoldering as she commenced a slow circuit of the lodge, addressing prayers to Wakan Tanka and fanning the smoke over the assembled members of the band as she passed.

"Oh, Great Spirit, who breathes life into all things and hides the Great Mystery in every grain of sand, every tree that grows, and all the winged, four-legged, and two-legged beasts of the world. Help us to hear your voice upon the wind, and teach us to live our lives with open hands and straight eyes. Let us walk in beauty. Cleanse the hearts, thoughts, and spirit of these your children with this fragrant gift of sage, the pure scent of the desert. Banish black spirits of deception, and greed, and of sadness and depression. Lift our hearts from the ground that we shall shine like the sun on a summer's morning. Fill our hearts with love for your creation, and guide our deeds to serve your purpose. Thank you for the gift of this sage that purifies our spirit and banishes the hand of evil." She moved between the rows of people, ensuring that they had all been touched by the smoke from the sage.

Next, she stood before Takoda. He looked up and met his mother's eyes as she lifted the smoldering bowl in one hand, eddies of smoke clouding his vision. In her right hand Makawee held a fan of eagle feathers, chosen because of the eagle's ability to carry prayers to Wakan Tanka. She smiled and began to chant quietly, the rest of the band taking up the song and swaying in rhythmic unison, harmoniously breaking into a traditional prayer.

Oh Great Mystery,
Wakan Tanka, the creator of all that is and will be,
Reveal yourself in my heart, that I might know the truth,
That I may feel your presence and understand my purpose.
Open the eye of my soul to my Sacred Space, so that I might live in blessed peace,
Nurtured in the arms of Mother Earth, humbled by your creation,
Body, mind, and spirit, walking in balance,
For all the days of my life.

Takoda had learned that the Sacred Space existed in the moment between exhalation and inhalation, and that to Walk in Balance was to live with Heaven and Earth in harmony.

As the band chanted the prayer, Makawee used the eagle feathers to push the smoke over her son's body, starting at his feet and working up to his head. Takoda assisted, wafting the smoke against his body and massaging it into his skin as though it were some form of silky oil that would cleanse and nourish, concentrating on his breathing and searching for the comfort of his Sacred Space. The sage would ward off the influence of negative thoughts and the sweetgrass would infuse him with a sense of relaxation, aiding his spiritual calm and enhancing his well-being.

The ceremony ended with a chorus of chanting as everyone prayed for Takoda's good health, and the band's close bond filled the lodge with a pervasive sense of unity. It was central to their culture that the tribe should strive for the benefit of an individual, on the basis that the health of one influenced the well-being of the whole.

It was considered to be every individual's responsibility to act in the best interest of the band. If one person enjoyed a surplus of food, or hides, or horses, while others were deficient, the one possessing excess would be expected to donate all that he was able to those in need, often to his own detriment. Generosity was considered one of the most respected values, and a man could bring great honor upon himself and his family by giving away his most valued possessions. In this way, the Lakota avoided preoccupation with material things and built a mutual dependency founded upon love and harmony.

Makawee, the Itancan, the matriarchs, and six singers remained seated around the fire pit in the lodge in anticipation of the Yuwipi ceremony that would follow, its purpose being to divine a deeper understanding of Takoda's repetitive dream. Meanwhile, Howahkan, Takoda, and the others filed out, returning to their tipis or gathering to prepare the evening meal. The door flap was left open, admitting flickering light from the village fire, and the remaining group shuffled closer together, the singers remaining standing on the west side of the lodge.

Each person was given a sprig of sage to wear behind the ear, so that the spirits might know them during the ceremony, after which Makawee began to assemble an altar alongside the fire pit. She demarcated the ceremonial area with four small containers of earth placed in a rectangular pattern at each quarter of the compass, each bearing a vertically planted cane decorated with colored cloth. Stretched around the canes, a long cord suspended four hundred and five tiny tobacco pouches, hastily prepared by Makawee and the other women in the village, each filled with a pinch of tobacco, and collectively representative of the differing spirits in the universe. Once positioned, the cord delineated the hocoka, the ritual space that would be used for the ceremony, so that it appeared surrounded by a rudimentary form of bunting.

Continuing her preparation, Makawee formed a small pile of earth at the north end of the hocoka, upon which she placed symbols of the sun and the moon. Next, she assembled a bed of sage to lie on, surrounding it with a collection of Yuwipi stones, Yuwipi rattles, the sacred pipe called a chanupa wakan, pipe bag, and an eagle bone whistle. These items served as the instruments of the Yuwipi ceremony, through which the Itancan hoped to receive divine guidance about the meaning of Takoda's dream.

Once the ceremonial space had been organized, stones heated in the village fire were transferred reverently into the fire pit in the lodge, and one of the matriarchs dropped the heavy door coverings to confirm that no light would seep into the lodge. They were plunged into darkness. All was prepared.

The door was reopened to provide sufficient light for Makawee to remove her moccasins and bulkier outer garments, leaving her sitting on the bed of sage in the center of the hocoka, facing west, wearing a light buckskin shirt and skirt. She breathed deeply, composing herself, and ladled several scoops of water onto the searing hot stones, eliciting billowing clouds of stifling steam. The foggy mist eddying eerily around the lodge, she addressed the respected members of the band who encircled her, their serious features appearing distorted and wraithlike in the pale flickering light.

Although those present had attended many Yuwipi ceremonies previously, Makawee explained the ceremony in the traditional way, it being respectful to the spirits to observe the formalities of such an important occasion, one that could have profound implications for the tribe. She was meticulous in her adherence to protocol, for the sake of everyone, not solely for Takoda's benefit.

Over many years, her father had schooled her in the rituals of the Lakota, until he had returned to the Great Spirit. She had demonstrated the same innate connection to the spirit world that Takoda displayed, but her gifts had been characterized by an intuitive knowledge of the medicinal properties of herbs and vivid dreams that always seemed to foreshadow a momentous event. Given her aptitude, the grandmothers of her band had decided that she should train with her father, who had been a respected medicine man. Subsequently, she married O'hiniya he Mani and became the medicine woman to his band.

The Yuwipi ceremony was relatively common, but its use for matters of deep importance could be draining, and its ways intricate and mysterious, employing the collective influence of prayer, song, and the medicine woman's training and spiritual power to invoke the spirits to provide their guidance and insight.

Commencing the sacred ritual, Makawee began to fill the sacred pipe with seven pinches of tobacco, the first four representing the cardinal directions: west being the source of life giving rains and the home of the spirits; north where the great wind blows, helping to develop strength and endurance, truthfulness and honesty; east where the sun rises, giving knowledge and imbuing spirituality; and south where new growth starts, the source of life's bounty from which medicine is derived. The final three directions she acknowledged were the life giving earth, the sun, and Wakan Tanka, the Creator.

The singers intoned the opagipi olowan, the filling of the pipe song, as she observed a careful and methodical process, pointing the pipe in each of the directions, to the ground, the sky, and vertically to the Creator, placing one pinch of tobacco into the bowl of the pipe with each salutation and packing it with a little rubbed sage.

When the pipe was prepared and the song had ended, an elder and one of the singers stepped forward and wrapped Makawee from head to toe in a heavy blanket, tying it securely with ropes and lying her gently facedown on the bed of sage. The lodge flap was closed, and all were plunged into darkness, the singers commencing a melodic chant and beating a rhythmic tone on their drums, evoking the resonance of the depths of Mother Earth herself.

First, they sang the *wicakicopi olowan,* the "they call them" song, beseeching the spirits of the universe to enter the lodge and provide their guidance, and the Itancan and the elders joined in, closing their eyes and blending strong voices with the harmony of the singers, invoking a trance-like state.

Makawee's head tingled and her vision shot with splashes of vibrant color, a great warmth spreading over her body. She concentrated on breathing evenly, clearing her mind so that the wisdom of the spirits would not be confused with a clutter of meaningless thoughts. She felt detached from her body, and a bright white light filled her mind's eye. The singing receded, appearing distant but reassuring, and she prayed to the spirits to enter the lodge and impart their gift of knowledge. She focused on Takoda's dream, rehearsing the account she had heard, and spoke aloud as the prayer song concluded.

"Spirits of our ancestors. Messengers of our great Creator, Wakan Tanka. We ask for your help and guidance. Help us to see with a clear eye. Help us to understand the mystery of your message in Takoda's dream. Share your insight, that we might be wakan and live in your honor."

Makawee entreated the spirits with impassioned prayer, and when she fell silent the singers continued, performing the *wicayujujupi olowan,* the "they untie her" song, which was repeated twice, followed by two dance songs. The drumming ceased abruptly as the song concluded, and a heavy silence fell upon the lodge, interspersed only by the muffled sounds of those busying themselves outside.

During the songs Makawee had become free from her bonds, a process that was a constant source of wonder to the uninitiated, and now she picked up her rattles and shook them in time with an ululating song as she conversed directly with the spirits. She sang and chanted, uttering words that the assembled elders could not discern, her voice at times low like a whisper and at others strong and forceful.

Eventually, her voice trailed away and the singers commenced the *wanagi kiglapi olowan,* the "spirits go home" song, followed by the *inkiyapi olowan,* the "quitting" song, Makawee settling herself in a comfortable position, kneeling with her legs tucked to one side.

Once the singing finished, one of the elders threw open the door allowing the flickering light of the village fire to percolate into the lodge, diffusing the darkness and revealing Makawee sitting at the center of her hocoka, the rope and blanket that had bound her folded neatly at her side, her countenance serene, as if untouched by the ordeals and suffering of mortal life.

The singers sat respectfully outside the circle of elders, one of whom set about rekindling the lodge fire, while Makawee lit the sacred pipe and passed it to the Itancan. The chief pulled gratefully on the chanupa, closing his eyes as he savored the aromatic smoke, before exhaling contentedly. The pipe was passed around the circle and to each of the singers, so that everyone could partake and give thanks to the spirits for their eternal oversight.

The fire crackled into life as women brought a hot meal of elk stew, a unique indulgence for the winter months, and everyone relished the succulent meat and earthy broth of roots and herbs, which warmed their hearts and infused their bodies with a rejuvenating energy.

The ceremony having concluded, the matriarch seated to the south of the door stood and faced her companions offering the salutation, *Mitakuye oyasin,* "All my relations." Then, in succession, each person took their leave.

Presently, only Makawee and the Itancan remained, sitting in comfortable silence as they reflected upon the ceremonies, neither feeling an obligation to speak. It was their custom to respect the value of silence, to consider carefully what others had said before responding, forming one's own thoughts with care so that the words spoken were concise and appropriate.

The Itancan inhaled deeply on the pipe, his eyes partially closed as he allowed the scent of the herbs to infuse his lungs. "I fear for our people. I foresee that the blue tide of the Great Father in the east will overwhelm us and the ways of our forefathers will die forever." He spoke matter-of-factly, but there was a wistful set to his expression. Makawee did not respond, allowing him to continue.

"The white man wants to buy our land, but how can we sell what is everlasting? A man cannot pick up the land and carry it away. One might as well sell the air we breathe, or the rivers that flow from the mountains. Why would we sell what the Great Spirit has bestowed upon all living things? It is not ours to sell, and if we were to sell the land, what would we do with the money? We can't eat money. We can't wear it to keep warm in winter, and eventually it will be used up and there will be no more. In time, we will be left with nothing. Is it not true that the desire to possess material things corrupts the soul? The white man wants to own the land. When he has land, he wants more. And, if you don't give him more he will fight you for it, or he will speak with a forked tongue and trick you into giving it to him. The white man is never happy because he always wants more. We own nothing, but we are honest and everything we need is provided in abundance by Mother Earth. I do not know how we will reconcile these differences."

Makawee listened in silence, pausing before delivering her response. "Father, I have seen Takoda's dream. The great iron horse does indeed speak of the white man's advance across the prairies, and I believe that he will continue his onslaught whatever the Red Nation attempts to do to prevent him. But I see forces for good, as much as those who would cheat us and do us harm. These contrasting influences are represented by the eagle and the dove that Takoda holds in his hands in the dream. We must have an eye for this dove, for it may offer us hope. Takoda also speaks of a crushing weight, and I sense that if we stand before the iron horse we will surely be destroyed. This I believe to be the truth. Those who speak of war with the white man, speak of a future where our people will be consigned to live with shackles upon their feet. The ashes of our fires will be scattered by the onslaught, and our peoples will no longer be as one, but cast to the four winds.

"I am less certain about the meaning of the buffalo's transformation into an iron horse, but I feel a great unrest about this. I fear that a terrible event will cause the plains to be silent, and the buffalo to be no more, but I do not understand this and I cannot see an explanation in Takoda's dream."

The Itancan stared gravely into the flickering flames of the fire. "I feel these things also, Makawee. There is a difference between our peoples that cannot be reconciled. An Indian regards an untarnished natural landscape as his home. Nature teaches us all that we need to know about gathering our food, caring for our young, and hunting. We are at peace in an endless school of mystery and beauty. But the white man fears all that he cannot control and dominate. The prairies and the mountains are not his home. To him they are a trial. Something to be endured and tamed. He would rid the world of all its winged and four-legged creatures, so that in its barren wasteland he might find contentment and safety. We cannot live together because we do not value the same things. The tribal council advocates a treaty of compromise, but this can never succeed. Our only salvation will be to discover new lands, where we can place our tipi wherever we wish and call it home."

Makawee was silent. These were momentous matters. The Itancan was considering rejecting the decision of the tribal council and breaking from the tribe. She knew that all of the Indian nations faced the dilemma of determining their response to the white man's incursion into their ancestral lands, but few had contemplated leaving them altogether. The discussion was always about whether to fight or negotiate, and the Itancan's proposed alternative would almost certainly place him in direct opposition to the will of the council, risking the fracturing of the tribe.

Makawee leaned forward and addressed the Itancan in a whisper. "There is one more thing, Father. I saw more of Takoda's dream than he has seen. I saw a land where the beasts of the plains grazed calmly, and there was a sense of peace for our people. Mother Earth was as a cradle, wrapped around her children, but she was shaking and growling with anger at those who threatened her creation. In this place, she breathed fire upon the earth to protect her children."

The Itancan nodded thoughtfully. "This is of great importance. If there is a place where we can attain peace, we must pray that Wakan Tanka will lead us to it. We will consider all of these matters further with the grandmothers," he concluded. "But, for now, let us sit with the others."

CHAPTER 12

North of the Greybull River, Dakota Territory

Takoda insisted that the snow was too deep to contemplate a long walk, as his healing treatment had recommended, but proposed the alternative of a long ride with his brother. The boys told their mother that they would ride into the forest to trap some squirrels, and persuaded the head of the Akichitas that, since their journey would be brief, they would not require protection. Conceding that winter conditions could be unpredictable, they agreed to take sufficient food to sustain an overnight expedition, plus hides for a small shelter and buffalo skins to keep them warm.

Makawee had confidence in the boys' ability to survive in the wilderness, but was reassured at their precautionary preparation for the possibility that the weather might close in. The forest provided good shelter, being considerably warmer than the plains, so she had no misgivings about their plan.

Howahkan made all the preparations and the boys set off early the morning after the ceremonies, shouldering their bows, their ponies loaded with supplies, and waving a joyful farewell to a gaggle of excited children who made a brief attempt to follow.

They rode south until they were out of sight of the village, so that anyone watching would assume that they intended riding into the forest, and after a mile and a half crossed the river where the bank was low and the waters were shallow, the horses crunching through the thin veneer of ice encasing the freezing green waters that swirled below. Remaining parallel to the Greybull, they turned east, heading for the Great Plains, ploughing through accumulated snow that lay a foot deep across much of the valley. Progress was slow, and they had to be careful that the horses did not fall into gullies deceptively concealed beneath the pristine white carpet that obscured their path.

As the treeline receded, much of the snow dissipated, blown away by the relentless wind, and the landscape opened up to the plains, their vast expanse stretching to the horizon. Dull yellow winter grass poked its weathered blades through a dusty white icing, imbuing the prairie with a rippling buttery light that rolled away in endless undulating contours, reminiscent of the rhythmic swell of the ocean, its smooth surface broken only by occasional ragged bluffs, evoking a sense of dramatic white rollers surging across a stormy sea.

The plains appeared deserted, and the boys hugged the lee of a steep escarpment on their left hand, minimizing their exposure to the bitter northeasterly wind, which plucked at their clothing with icy fingers. The horses tucked down their heads, their long manes and tails fluttering like torn flags, and the boys hunkered into thick buffalo hides that they pulled tightly around their shoulders.

The escarpment rose vertically, running parallel to their direction of travel for nearly ten miles, its precipitous face preventing them from traversing north and forcing them to move out onto the plains to circumnavigate its eastern end, where they curved northwest and followed a tributary of the Greybull River into the arms of a wide valley on the opposite side of the ridge.

The slopes on either side of the valley were heavily forested, dense stands of lodgepole carpeting the mountainside up to the highest elevations, clinging to rocky outcrops along contours where other trees would have failed to find purchase, their slim arrow-straight trunks reaching up a hundred and fifty feet, so that their conical crowns swayed in a rhythmic wave, driven by the prevailing winds. On the lower slopes the lodgepole yielded to Douglas fir, its prolific blue-green needles providing an impenetrable facade to the forest's border.

To the north, a jagged black scar of seared tree trunks cut a swathe from ridge to valley floor, standing like rows of charred sentinels, a legacy of wildfire instigated by a lightning strike during one of the frequent short but violent summer storms. New growth sprouted, displaying the first flush of regeneration, with intermittent stands of whispering aspen being the first trees to recolonize the barren landscape, the chatter of their shimmering leaves carrying on the wind as the boys pressed their way into the valley.

Ahead, the gradient increased steadily, the trail curving to the left before swinging right-handed as it carved its path progressively west, small creeks crossing the route and tumbling down rocky waterfalls to gurgle between crested banks of snow as they converged to form the upper reaches of a lazy river, its surface encrusted with glassy sheets of ice.

The boys observed the wildlife with interest, a fox prowling stealthily across the flat white meadow of the valley floor, tilting its head from one side to the other, listening for the movement of small rodents beneath the snow before stopping and priming itself for an explosive headfirst dive to seize its prey.

They spotted a small herd of cow elk scattered along the treeline to the south, scratching methodically at the snow to scavenge for grass, their distinctive ivory rumps contrasting the dark brown of their winter coats. A lone bull marshalled the harem with restless paranoia, stopping every few minutes to survey the valley and sniff the air, searching for the scent of any potential competitor before shuttling over to smell the hindquarters of one of the cows.

Six hours had elapsed before the brothers reached the head of the valley and identified a suitable path into the forest, by which time snow was falling in a thick blanket, obscuring their view, and they were grateful to enter the shelter provided by the dense canopy of trees.

Protected by the firs, the forest floor was smothered with a compacted bed of decaying needles, topped with a chalky white dusting of snow, shaken from the trees by the wind. Progress became easier, although the heavy foliage conspired to create an eerie twilight world and the intermittent thud of clumps of snow tumbling through the boughs and dropping to the ground contributed to a sense that the forest was alive with movement.

The boys rode in silence, their sure-footed ponies picking an easy path as they wound progressively up the foothills of the mountain. Howahkan was grateful that he had packed enough skins for a shelter, since the journey had taken longer than he had anticipated, and it was clear that he and Takoda would not be able to return to the village until the following day.

But Howahkan's sense of direction was impeccable, and he guided them with unwavering accuracy, so that by late afternoon they broke clear of the upper treeline and were confronted with a steep barren ascent to the crest of a northerly facing slope.

The adverse weather had abated, and the clear sky revealed a shimmering crystalline carpet of virgin snow stretching unblemished from the edge of the forest to the perimeter of a pond flanked by large stands of willow, and thence to the summit of the escarpment to their left. Despite the opaque evening light, Howahkan was confident that their father's dais stood on the ridge, but the boys could see that the route to the summit offered no shelter from the elements, being barren of trees.

The first stars were beginning to twinkle in the steely blue early evening sky, and a crescent of moon rose slowly above the treeline on the horizon to the east. After a brief discussion, the brothers agreed that they would make camp within the fringe of the forest, as close to their father's resting place as possible, where they would be afforded protection from the wind and could make use of wood collected from the forest floor to build their fire. They would ascend to the scaffold early the following morning, with a view to starting back to the village before midday.

Having found a suitable site to camp and hobble their horses, Takoda cleared the snow from a small area in the lee of a fallen tree, where he laid buffalo fleece to provide insulation from the cold ground. Working with practiced efficiency, he placed a large deerskin blanket over the fleece and weighted the side facing the prevailing wind with stones, pushing snow back over the edge of the blanket to prevent the ingress of air.

He used three stout sticks to build a frame, forming a long horizontal bar with two shorter vertical posts, each joint bound together with a leather thong. Once complete, he wriggled the frame under the blanket and lifted it vertical, creating a wedge-shaped shelter with a flap to the front, which could be rolled up to allow access. As with the windward aspect, he flattened the edges of the blanket against the ground on each side of the shelter and covered them with more snow, rendering the interior effectively insulated from the wind on three sides.

Howahkan collected wood and kindling to build a fire before removing a short length of cedar and a fire-stick from his pack of supplies. The cedar had a scorched thumbnail-deep hollow drilled in its upper surface, into which he placed a few shavings of tinder from a pouch carried at his waist. Then, inserting the fire-stick into the hollow, he looped a strand of leather between each of his thumbs and located it in a notch on the top end of the stick. He applied downward pressure with the leather thong and rubbed the stick vigorously back and forth between the palms of his hands, causing it to rotate rapidly and generate sufficient frictional heat to ignite the tinder.

A small wisp of smoke signaled his success, and Howahkan blew gently on the embryonic flame before heaping on more tinder and blowing again. Once the flames flickered with sufficient intensity, he tipped the tinder off the cedar block and onto the ground in front of their shelter, piling on dry twigs until the fire burned intensely.

The boys sat under the canopy of their shelter, warming their hands as they chewed on some dried meat and pemmican biscuits. The forest creaked and groaned in the wind, like a huge beast stretching itself out of a lazy slumber, and the flames of the fire cast a flickering light, encouraging amorphous shadows to dance among the trees and arouse their imagination. The boys were comfortable and content. The forest was their friend, and the eerie sounds spoke to them in hushed tones that evoked memories of their forefathers.

Weary from their journey, they stoked the fire and crawled further into their refuge, curling up and snuggling into their thick insulating buffalo fleeces, where they drifted into a restful sleep.

The dawn light poked its rays between the shutters of the window to the trappers' cabin, and McCabe stirred from an uneasy slumber. His crib was set against the wall opposite his partner, and he was relieved at the separation.

La Brais had been incensed at him returning to the cabin with the Indian weapons, initially refusing to allow him to bring them into the cabin, insisting that they were the tools of devil worshippers and demanding that he burn them. But McCabe had ignored La Brais and placed his trophies in the corner adjacent to his crib, provoking a stormy argument during which La Brais berated him for his inadequacy as a trapper and threatened to abandon him as soon as the winter snows melted.

"I seen bigger beavers 'an you can catch under the petticoats o' the girls in a Vancouver dance hall!" He slurred as he spat the insult, delighted with his analogy, and collapsed in a heaving fit of raucous laughter.

McCabe bridled at the incessant verbal abuse, responding through gritted teeth. "Well, don't stand much chance o' even seein' a darn beaver wi' you 'bout. Smell your whiskey-soaked backside comin' mile away! Best off wi' out yer."

The jibe hardly registered with La Brais, who was getting into his stride. "You ain't got a pecker big enough to stay out in the mount'ns on yer own," he retorted. "Yud piss yer pants at the sound o' the first wolf as howled! Only brought yer 'cos ah needed a woman to clean house!"

He slapped his thigh, relishing his humor, and threw back his head to pour another liberal measure of whiskey down his throat, causing it to strike the wall behind him with a resounding thud. The impact stunned him momentarily, his glazed eyes staring blankly into space until he shook himself and regained his composure.

"Shame yer didn't find some o' them Injun skins an' stuff. Yer'd look jus fine in buckskin skirt, wi' 'em skinny legs an' all. Maybe take yer as a wife maself!" As he howled with laughter at the thought, McCabe settled himself into his crib and rolled to face the wall, simmering at the insult.

La Brais drained his bottle and peered into the neck, mortified that the contents had mysteriously evaporated. He turned the bottle upside down and shook it hopefully, but to no avail. Disillusioned at the result, he peered wistfully at his remaining supply of whiskey, secreted under a stack of blankets piled alongside the door to the cabin, and considered the difficulty involved in navigating the few feet from his crib.

Uncertain of the wisdom of making the attempt, he committed himself to the task, rocking back and forth on the side of the crib to rehearse the process of standing up, continuing to titter at his levity. He was reassured to find that his stance felt firm, and with a little shove of his arms, his confidence surged. Content with the practice and brimming with self-assured aplomb, he spaced his feet squarely, rocked backward to gain momentum, and swung forward, thrusting himself upright.

The result was exceptional, and his knees snapped straight as he came vertical, eliciting a broad grin of satisfaction. But the motion was more than his fragile senses could control, and his body continued to swing forward like a pendulum, until it became obvious that his achievement was destined to be brief.

Perturbed, he attempted to rebalance, swinging his hips forward and spinning his outstretched arms in rapid circles, but the flailing movement served only to disrupt his control over his legs, which abruptly folded, toppling him head first. His eyebrows shot up in alarm and he cursed loudly as he dropped in a sweeping flourish, cracking his heavily bristled chin on the edge of the cabin's makeshift table. His teeth crunched, and his nose and forehead thudded off the rough timber, before he ended up planting his face into the floor in an ungainly unconscious heap, his legs splayed like a frog.

McCabe rose quietly and pulled on his boots, anxious not to wake La Brais, who continued to snore loudly, sprawled where he had collapsed the previous evening. He had no desire to be present when the man stirred and decided to ride up the mountain to check for signs of movement on the beaver pond.

He stoked the dying embers of the fire, made a cup of coffee, and cooked some oatmeal. Having warmed himself and sated his appetite, he hauled on a coat and gloves and went to saddle his horse, the animal stomping its hooves as its breath condensed in wisps of cloudlike steam in the cold morning atmosphere.

The ground was cloaked in a thick layer of fresh snow, tarnished only by the path of a hare that had hopped past the cabin, which was set on the north side of the narrow valley. McCabe swung his mount to the southwest and the horse plodded wearily through the snow, leaving its own deep trail in its wake as they crossed the valley floor and entered the trees on the southern slope.

The wind had died away during the night and the morning air was cold and fresh, but, as McCabe looked up at the sky, he concluded that its translucent white sheen threatened yet more fresh snow. Keen to avoid the bad weather, he urged his horse into the trees and picked his way steadily up the lower slopes of the mountain. Little moved, and the forest seemed devoid of life, other than the twittering call of the birds that skittered among the branches of the Douglas firs.

As he rode, he reflected angrily on La Brais's drunken behavior the previous night, the caustic jokes made at his expense festering in his mind so that he paid little attention to his surroundings on the journey, which had become a repetitive ritual.

Preoccupied, he was surprised to emerge from the forest and find that he had already reached the pond. The ride had passed swiftly as his mind had wandered, rehearsing the sarcastic responses he might have poked back at his partner, had his wit been sufficient. He pulled up and rested his wrists casually on the horn of his saddle, casting an eye around the perimeter of the pond, combing the bank for any evidence of animal trails.

He had become conditioned to expect that he would see nothing, and his visual patrol was conducted without enthusiasm. As anticipated he identified no sign of beaver, but nonetheless he gathered up his reins and rode a short circuit around the pond.

Beyond the trees the snow was deep, and he steered his horse well away from the edge of the pond, ensuring that his mount did not inadvertently slip into the freezing water. The willows were bent over at acute angles weighed down by a heavy crown of snow, and the aspens shimmering rustle was silenced by their powdery coating. Snow began to fall steadily once more, and McCabe pulled his coat high up around his neck.

Satisfied that there was no activity, he wheeled around and trailed back toward the trees, initially ignoring a deep furrow in the snow, which he attributed to a distortion induced by the buffeting wind. But as he looked more closely, he sensed that the contour was unnatural.

Curious, he steered his horse to obtain a better view, surmising that he had probably stumbled across the path of a large animal. In anticipation, he spun his head urgently, searching for signs of a bear or a pack of wolves, until he realized with relief that it was too early in the year for bears and that the straight line of the track was unlike those made by wolves, which tended to weave back and forth along a trail.

The hairs on his neck began to rise, and his heart beat faster. The trail was lined with the unmistakable prints of horses' hooves, their direction of travel clearly moving away from the trees and ascending the mountain to the southwest. Hastily, he swung around in his saddle and scanned the escarpment.

Snow was falling in a steady mist, partially obscuring his view, and it was some time before he was able to discern the outline of two distant slow-moving figures, ploughing doggedly up to the ridge.

He turned his horse to face the slope and shaded his eyes, waiting anxiously for the snowfall to subside and afford a clearer view. The figures remained indistinct, until the snow abruptly abated and with absolute clarity, the outline of two Indians materialized, mounted on ponies, heaving their way through deep snow below the ridge. They appeared to be turning left-handed, ascending toward the scaffold.

McCabe flushed with alarm as he reflected upon the way he had plundered the site, imagining the Indians' reaction when they discovered the desecrated altar. Immediately, he was stricken with the notion that they would descend from the mountain, fired with a savage bloodlust, and hunt him down, intent upon exacting retribution.

Unnerved, he hustled his horse into the cover of the trees to avoid being seen and snatched a final glance up the mountain before turning to speed off down the hill, driving his spurs into his horse's ribs, impervious to the low branches that plucked at his coat and threatened to sweep him from his mount.

His return trip took less than half the time it had taken to reach the pond, and when he reached the valley floor, he drove his horse at a fast lope until he reached the far side, where he wound his way up through a thin stand of trees to reach the cabin.

All was silent, only a thin wisp of smoke from the chimney suggesting any sign of habitation. McCabe's chest heaved from the exertion of his flight as he pulled to a sharp halt and dismounted, leaving his horse standing with slack reins dangling, its ribs pumping like bellows. He stumbled through the snow and burst in through the door.

"Injuns! There's Injuns!" he hollered, expecting to see La Brais sitting at the table.

The Canadian remained comatose, slumped on the floor where he had fallen the previous evening, but La Brais's subconsciousness registered the crash of the door being flung open and McCabe's urgent warning galvanized him from his foggy torpor.

Displaying lightning reflexes, he shoved himself upright, crunching his head against the underside of the table and sending a searing shot of pain through his skull. His feet thrashed wildly as he attempted to gain purchase on the floor, trying valiantly to stand up, eventually kicking over a stool and pulling the hides off his bed before he was able to stagger upright. He swayed unsteadily, staring at McCabe through swollen red eyes as his incoherent mind attempted to recollect where he had put his rifle and handgun.

"Where're they?" he slurred, whipping his head around as if anticipating an imminent attack.

"Up the hill . . . highest pond! Two . . . two o' 'em. Ridin' . . . ridge . . . up to th'ridge!" McCabe panted.

"Vermin!" La Brais hissed, his eyes narrowing and a malicious sneer crossing his face. He staggered, knocking into the table as he fumbled for his coat and almost tumbling to the floor again as he bent to pick up his boots.

"They gonna go to that goddam devil worship place. They gonna see we taken them bows an' stuff. Maybe come after us? Hunt us down!" McCabe implied that La Brais had been party to his ransacking of the Indians' funeral dais, but the trapper ignored the misrepresentation and did not protest.

"We ain't gonna be hunted ba no one!" La Brais retorted, rolling back onto his crib and wrestling to pull on his boots. "Fancy maself bit o' Injun huntin'," he chortled, huffing and puffing at the effort of donning his clothes.

"Buffalo gun'll give 'em somin' to think 'bout." He lurched into the corner of the cabin and picked up a long-barreled sporting rifle. It was his favored weapon of choice, an 1859 model Sharps rifle with a thirty-inch octagonal barrel that fired a .52-caliber linen cartridge, capable of taking down buffalo at five hundred yards. La Brais liked stopping power in a gun, something that ensured you did not have to shoot either man or beast twice. In his view, the Sharps was the best weapon available.

"You sayin' we gonna git 'em?" McCabe sounded uncomfortable with the idea.

"You bet. Nothin' like a bit o' sport to clear the head." La Brais laughed heartily, fumbling with his pistol belt as he strapped it around his waist.

"Not sure you kin see y'own feet, let alone shoot any Injun."

La Brais looked indignant. "Shoot th' eye outta coyote at two hundred paces wi' ma eyes shut," he bragged.

"More like shoot yer own dick off tryin' to pull out yer gun," McCabe chortled at the derision. "Gonna go git yer horse," he followed up, concluding that it was unlikely that La Brais would manage to saddle his own mount.

Despite his mirth, he was not convinced that going after the Indians was a good idea. He had no way of knowing how well the Indians were armed or whether they were seasoned warriors. McCabe owned a gun, but he had to concede that he was not much good at using it, and if put to the test against an adversary with more skill, he was pretty sure that he would end up worse off. On the other hand, La Brais was an excellent shot and although he was still soaked in whiskey, it was probable that they would be able to pick off the savages using his big buffalo gun without having to get close. On balance, given the potential of an incendiary reaction to his vandalism of their place of worship, McCabe decided that there was merit in trying to dispatch the Indians before they attempted to kill him and La Brais.

He left the big Canadian trapper tussling with his thick outer coat and trudged around to the corral at the back of the cabin, lugging the saddle and headstall for La Brais's horse, which stood, looking thoroughly dejected, sheltered under the low branches of a Douglas fir.

Meanwhile, La Brais tucked a large leather-sheathed game knife down the inside of his boot and filled his pockets with a pouch of cartridges and a small bag of percussion caps. He pulled a dark beaver skin hat over his head, securing the ear flaps with a leather thong tied under his chin, and wrestled into his double layer of coats, which added to his already sizeable bulk, the thick hides restricting his movement so that his arms stuck out obliquely at his sides.

McCabe led La Brais's horse to the front of the cabin, where he found the trapper firmly wedged in the doorway. La Brais wriggled and cursed, heaving himself back and forth as he tried to force himself, the rifle strapped across his shoulders, and a heavy set of saddlebags out of the cabin. It was apparent that something was going to have to give way, and McCabe braced himself for the possibility of the entire doorway surrendering.

With a furious wrench La Brais thrust his weight against the impasse, and for a moment it seemed that the barrel of the Sharps would hold him fast, but with a rending snap the gun's strap abruptly succumbed to the load and catapulted him headfirst into the deep snow.

McCabe hooted with laughter. "You lookin' for tracks down there?" His humor fueled his amusement, and he bent over slapping his thighs and wheezing in the cold air, leaving La Brais to roll around on his back, scrambling to regain his feet. His hat and beard were caked in snow, a clump of which hung off one bushy eyebrow, concealing an infuriated scowl.

"Git yerself over here an' git me outta this, else th' Injuns ain't th'only thing gonna get shot 'round here!" he roared, pushing himself onto all fours.

McCabe continued to snigger, but knew better than to incite La Brais's anger, so he dropped the horse's reins and shuffled through the snow to haul the trapper to his feet, leaving La Brais to dust down his coat as he staggered upright and lurched off toward his mount.

"Pick up ma gun 'n bags. Let's git goin'," La Brais ordered.

As he clambered onto his horse with great effort, McCabe

slung the bags over its rump and handed up the Sharps, which the Canadian slid into its leather scabbard before gathering up his reins and wheeling his horse onto the trail without further comment.

McCabe mounted up and followed as they broke into an awkward lope, the horses slipping and sliding as they plunged through the snow. La Brais rode hard, the cold air and strenuous riding helping to clear his intoxicated mind as they crossed the valley and plunged into the trees on the southern slopes, joining a well-used game trail that wound steadily uphill leading to the beaver pond.

Howahkan led the way onto the ridge. The track had been indistinguishable, its route submerged below a heavy fall of fresh snow, so they were forced to weave across the hillside in search of a path that the ponies were able to traverse.

A bitter southwesterly wind whipped against their faces as they mounted the summit, and they were grateful to turn along the ridge to the east so that they could lean a shoulder into the wind to protect themselves from the worst of the chill. They rode close together in silent companionship and eventually dropped down a shallow slope to reach the dais where both boys pulled up abruptly and stared at the broken scaffold in disbelief.

"What's happened?" Takoda whispered.

"I don't know," Howahkan replied, his voice betraying his distress. "It can't be a bear, they're all sleeping." He urged his pony forward and dismounted as he came alongside the scaffold, Takoda following.

Howahkan bent to the ground and picked up a broken spar, snapped by McCabe when he had pulled down the dais, while Takoda searched the scattered remains.

"Father's body has gone, and his bow. His tomahawk too!"

he exclaimed.

"There are marks on the ground, look. The stones have been scraped away, and there are the hoof prints of a horse. This was not done by an animal; it was done by a man." Howahkan's fingers traced the outline of the spoor.

"But who would do a thing like this? And why? This is a burial place. It should be sacred and respected." Takoda's temper flared, and he clenched his fists in fury at the thought that someone had interfered with their father's final resting place. He glared at Howahkan, and could see that his brother was also struggling to control his anger.

"What have they done with Father's body?"

"I don't know, Takoda, but no Indian would do this. This is the work of white men."

They gazed around in despair. There was no indication of what had happened to their father's body, but they walked slowly across the plateau checking the steep edges at the promontory of the ridge. They found nothing, and when they peered over the precipitous drop all they could discern was a smooth covering of unblemished snow.

Under the dais they discovered remnants of hide and the scattered carcass of the horse, but Takoda also recovered bones that he was certain were parts of a hand. Despondent, they collected the paltry remains and placed them carefully with the leather items, using stones to form a small cairn to protect the only lasting evidence of their father. Afterward, they knelt and offered prayers to Wakan Tanka, beseeching him to protect their father's spirit.

"There is nothing for us here, Takoda. We must return and tell the Itancan what has come to pass." Howahkan felt empty, his wrath turning to grief in the absence of a culprit upon whom to exact his retribution and leaving him to reflect upon the implication of the unconscionable circumstances to his tribe.

Takoda was silent. There seemed no point in trying to commune with their father. The purpose of their journey had been defeated by the destruction of the scaffold and the absence of their father's remains. They both rose and gazed out across the vast expanse of the plains, feeling all of a sudden alone and vulnerable. They turned back to their horses and mounted up, Howahkan leading the way as they walked along the southern perimeter of the ridge, stretching to obtain a glimpse of the valley below in the hope of catching sight of their village.

La Brais and McCabe drew their horses up at the treeline by the beaver pond and scanned the mountain slope, searching for any sign of the Indians. An unmistakable trail wound in an erratic path toward the ridge, great furrows of snow having been ploughed by the Indians' ponies as they had searched for a passable route. But the two Sioux were nowhere to be seen.

The trappers dismounted and stood in the shadow of the forest, watching carefully for any sign of movement. The top of the scaffold at the end of the ridge stood out clearly against an ethereal silver sky, laden with the potential for more snow, but the clarity of the morning light accented the ridge with a sharp, clean focus that would make it easy to detect the Indians if they appeared.

La Brais pulled his rifle from its scabbard and slid the retaining catch to the trigger-guard so that he could lever it downward, opening the breech to accept one of the linen cartridges. He blew into the breech and checked that it was unobstructed, took a cartridge from his pouch, and inserted it carefully, snapping the trigger-guard closed and shearing off the end of the cartridge to expose the propellant charge. The rifle loaded, he applied a percussion cap to the hollow firing nipple, which, when struck by the hammer, would project its incendiary charge into the breech, igniting the propellant and firing the

.52-caliber 475-grain projectile at 1,200 feet per second.

He lifted the ladder sights and hoisted the gun, tucking the metal butt of the stock tightly into his shoulder, and lined up the sight to traverse the ridgeline, savoring the snug fit of the rifle. With a sharp intake of breath, he stopped and flinched. A faint motion caught his attention at the base of the dais. He strained his eyes, attempting to pick out the movement again, but could detect nothing and began to believe that his senses had deceived him. Progressively, as if materializing out of thin air, two people stepped to the edge of the ridge and began moving east, pausing intermittently to search the ground.

"They're still up there," he whispered to McCabe, smirking. The other trapper nodded in silent response. "Can they git down off the far end, or they gotta git back same way they come?"

"Reckon only way back's the way they gotten up there," McCabe confirmed.

La Brais smiled maliciously. "Rats in a barrel."

He lowered the gun and removed the percussion cap, slipping the rifle back into its scabbard. "We git up there quick an' they gonna walk right back on'a us." He chuckled and heaved himself back onto his horse. "Cummon."

McCabe reluctantly remounted and followed La Brais out of the trees. The Indians had disappeared from sight again and both men drove their horses up the escarpment with urgency, tracing the path that the Indians had forged. It took half an hour to reach the ridge and the trappers pulled up a few yards short of the crest, heaving and panting from their exertion. Fired with enthusiasm, La Brais dismounted, leaving McCabe to tend the horses as he crawled up to the summit on his elbows and knees, the Sharps cradled in his gloved hands.

Wriggling the last few feet, La Brais was greeted with an unobstructed view along the ridge. He could pick the Indians off with ease when they returned, so he settled himself prone on the ground, concealed behind two large rocks upon which he rested the barrel of the Sharps, placing the cartridge pouch and percussion caps close at hand. Buoyed with bloodlust, he waited.

Howahkan peered over the edge of the precipitous drop, hoping to discern a wisp of smoke from their village fire, but the valley was shrouded in mist, rendering any smoke indistinguishable. Both boys were overwhelmed by the desire to return to the comforting security of their band, and they hugged the southern edge of the plateau eager to discover an alternative route home, avoiding the requirement to trail back out onto the Great Plains.

They discovered the top of the path they had ascended for their father's funeral, but it proved impassable, blocked by the immense wall of snow that shrouded the face of the mountain, and they were obliged to retrace their steps.

Nevertheless, they remained close to the lip of the perilous abyss as they made their way back along the ridge, pausing intermittently to lean out, more in hope than expectation of identifying a potential means of descent.

La Brais stiffened as he saw the Indians' heads appear over the brow of a shallow rise. Riding in single file, they appeared intent upon observing something to their left. The Indian on the lead pony rode in a saddle, whereas the one following was riding bareback, both heavily protected against the weather, wearing thick skins with hoods pulled tightly over their heads. Every few paces they stopped and leaned out, peering over the edge and paying little attention to their direction of travel. La Brais was elated. He was confident that he would remain undetected.

Removing his gloves, he reached for a percussion cap, gently cocking the tumbler of the hammer to the safety position to enable the cap to be placed onto the firing nipple. He judged the range as being roughly six hundred yards, within range for a kill and adequate to permit sufficient time to reload and fire a second shot before either Indian would be capable of getting close enough to retaliate.

Howahkan paused again. He was frustrated, impatient to find a safe route down the southern side of the ridge. He pushed his pony right to the edge so that he could scan the steep drop more carefully.

"There must be a way," he protested.

"It's too dangerous, Howahkan. And, if the snow slides, we'll be thrown down the mountain like twigs. I feel that there's something not right here. We need to leave at once. Please, Howahkan!"

Howahkan knew that Takoda was right, but he could not resist a final glance. He thought he could distinguish a faint shelf of flat snow, running diagonally to the east of where they stood, but he could not determine how far it descended, so he pushed his pony into the snow at the brink of the ridge.

La Brais adjusted the ladder sight to six hundred yards and licked his finger, raising it to the wind to judge its speed and direction. He lifted the sight to his eye, lining up the pin on the end of the barrel so that it hovered at the throat of the Indian on the nearest pony. He settled his breathing, pulling back the tumbler an extra notch to prime the weapon as he took a deep breath and held it.

The wind gusted violently and La Brais waited patiently for the breeze to subside, determined to assure the accuracy of his shot. He watched the Indian push his pony right up to the edge of the escarpment, so that it appeared as though the animal was standing in thin air.

★ ★ ★ ★ ★

The hair on Takoda's neck tingled and he whipped his head around, anticipating imminent danger. On the distant northern edge of the ridge he glimpsed the minute movement of a hand held briefly in the air, but the gesture was fleeting and he strained to distinguish what had caught his eye. Every muscle snapped taught with the premonition of something ominous.

A sudden flash flared, followed by a wisp of smoke and a thunderous bang. Instantly, Howahkan was thrown over his pony's withers, cast out into the void beyond the ridge. For a moment, he hung as if suspended. Then, as Takoda watched with impotent horror, he plummeted from sight.

Chapter 13

Funeral dais, north of the Greybull River, Dakota Territory

"Howahkan!" Takoda screamed, desperately attempting to see over the drop, but it was clear that any attempt to rescue his brother was futile. The precipice was colossal, and there was no possibility of finding a safe way down. Howahkan had gone.

Realizing his own peril, Takoda pressed his hand firmly against the left side of his pony's neck, shifting his balance to lean over its forward right-hand quarter. The pony responded instantly, surging out of the deep snow and launching into a headlong gallop toward the opposite side of the plateau. Takoda's instinct was to race for the edge and plunge down the steep slope with the intention of reaching the treeline where he and Howahkan had camped the previous night. Traversing to the south and east had already proved impossible and the gunshot had come from the west, so his only viable route of escape was to the north.

La Brais had hurried his shot, having been startled when the second Indian had turned and stared directly at him, as if instinctively detecting his presence. He had seen the first Indian fall from his pony and was confident that he was dead, but the second had reacted with astounding speed.

La Brais cocked the trigger guard on his Sharps and hurriedly loaded another cartridge into the breech, fumbling the percussion cap and dropping it into the snow so that he had to reach for a replacement. Once primed, he threw the rifle up to his shoulder, but the Indian's speed confounded his aim and the stones he had used to conceal his position restricted his field of fire. Irritated, he leapt to his feet to obtain an unobstructed shot.

The Indian rode flat out, leaning into his pony's neck and keeping his body low, the second pony in swift pursuit. La Brais swung the Sharps smoothly, mirroring the speed of the Indian's flight, and smiled at the thought that the warrior would have to slow down as he reached the northern edge of the plateau, adjusting his aim in anticipation.

He cocked the tumbler and steadied his breath, but to his astonishment the Indian did not slacken his pace. Instead, reaching the lip of the ridge at a full gallop, he simply leapt off. La Brais snatched at the trigger, attempting a shot, but the pony and the Indian disappeared out of sight, plunging down the slope below and leaving the second pony to pick its way down more carefully.

Takoda had seen the warriors in his band reloading their rifles and knew that he had precious few moments to escape the gunman's range before he became the next victim. He thanked Wakan Tanka for his pony's faithful trust as they launched off the ridge, dropping twenty feet before hurtling into deep snow on the steep slope of the escarpment. The little mare's front legs folded and she crashed onto her chest, rolling sideways and slithering down the mountainside, dragging Takoda in her wake, his bow being wrenched from his back.

The pony thrashed its legs, struggling to recover its feet, but slid for a further hundred feet before managing to dig its hooves into solid ground. Takoda skidded into the pony's back and wriggled around to loop his arm over her neck, stroking her head and whispering reassuringly into her ears.

The mare's ribs pumped like a pair of bellows and she snorted with fear, but Takoda's loving caress soothed the worst of her distress, and she struggled gamely to her feet so that Takoda could remount and hurry on down the slope, plunging from one deep drift to another.

La Brais stood open-mouthed. He had never seen such an act of lunacy and did not know whether to be impressed or angry.

"Cut him off!" he screamed at McCabe, who had begun to trudge up the slope with their horses.

Having seen La Brais stand and take aim, he had concluded that there was no point in remaining concealed, but he was spellbound by the Indian's leap from the ridge and gaped at both man and horse as they emerged from a billowing cloud of snow, apparently unscathed.

McCabe gawped at La Brais, who spun around and stumbled toward him. "Git after 'im!" he spluttered.

"D'yer see 'im jump?" McCabe shouted back, incredulous.

"Thinks he's a goddamn bird. Run 'im down. Git below 'im, an' I'll drive 'im ont' yer!" La Brais was apoplectic.

McCabe fumbled with his stirrups and swung onto his horse, spinning it brutally on its hocks to speed back down the path to the forest. He whipped the horses flank, forcing it to charge down the hazardous trail, his mind focused on overtaking the Indian, without considering what he was going to do if he caught up with him.

Takoda saw the rider break away from the ridge to his left and hurtle down the mountain in pursuit. He was still four hundred feet above the trail he had taken with Howahkan and half a mile from the treeline, but his assailant was approaching at speed, threatening to intercept him, so he urged his pony forward even faster, turning diagonally to reach the sanctuary of the forest rather than seeking to recover the path.

They surged through the snow, slipping and sliding, barely managing to remain upright as the pursuing gunman became impeded by a stretch of particularly deep snow, and with a wave of relief Takoda judged that he would reach the sanctuary of the trees, now only a hundred yards away, before he was caught.

His renewed confidence was shattered when the mare stumbled into a concealed gully, pitching him over her head. They struggled, exhausted by their ordeal, until eventually the pony staggered to her feet, allowing Takoda to heave onto her back once more. His heart pounding, he glanced back up the mountain and, to his dismay, noticed a second horseman partway down the slope, stationary, with a rifle leveled directly at him.

Takoda swung away in desperation, his pony stumbling as they lurched sideways. But the pony squealed and its hind quarters collapsed. The report of a rifle shot echoed off the surrounding mountains.

Once again Takoda was cast into the snow and turned to see his pony struggle to her feet, blood pouring from a laceration across her rump where the bullet had skimmed her quarters. He wanted to comfort her, but it was certain that the first of the gunmen would overhaul him, and the only chance he could conceive of evading capture was to roll away from the pony and bury himself in the snow, in the hope of avoiding detection.

To Takoda's surprise, the first horseman did not attempt to intercept him, but instead charged along the trail and disappeared into the trees, two hundred paces further down the mountain. His pony stood shivering, its eyes dilated with fear. She could go no further, so, given his unexpected reprieve, Takoda scrambled toward the forest, scuttling across the snow and darting into the trees.

He remained close to the upper treeline and decided to follow it east as fast as possible, hoping that his assailants would remain lower down the mountainside. After a few moments, buzzing with adrenaline, he rested to steady his nerves, the brief reprieve providing the first opportunity for him to reflect upon his brother's fate. These men had shot Howahkan in cold blood, without warning, and he could not comprehend why they had committed such an unwarranted act.

The shock of his loss washed over him, sapping his strength. First his father had been killed, and now his brother. Wakan Tanka must surely be very angry at him, his family, or his tribe. He was devastated. Two of his closest family were now dead.

His thoughts drifted to the damage that had been done to his father's funeral dais. Surely, these were the men who had torn it down. If so, it was probable that they were responsible for removing his father's body. He could only guess what they might have done with the sacred remains. His father. His mother's beloved husband. The Itancan's son. The Shirt Wearer to his tribe. It was too much of a coincidence to think that anyone else could have destroyed the grave.

The thoughts stoked Takoda's fury and the teachings of his tribe swirled through his mind. A Lakota should live a life of courage, being prepared to lay down his life to protect or avenge his family. As he considered the brutal murder of his brother and the disrespectful violation of his father's resting place, his resolve strengthened, a steely conviction kindling in his heart, banishing his fear, and forging a cold determination to stand his ground. In that moment, Takoda passed from childhood to manhood. He would not run. He would hunt these men, and he would kill them.

Both of his adversaries would expect him to run, anticipating that he would make his way through the forest and escape onto the plains. Neither would imagine that he might turn and attack them.

He bemoaned the loss of his bow with which he would have had no difficulty stalking and killing the men in the forest. Instead, the only weapon he retained was his hunting knife, so he drew it from its sheath and slid stealthily back through the trees, aiming downhill to intersect the trail where it entered the forest. He lamented his neglect in paying sufficient attention to his father's teaching, conscious of every sound that might give away his presence as he stepped carefully across the forest floor. Nevertheless, edging along cautiously, he descended to the trail in good time, so that he could watch the second horseman hurriedly retrace his steps, approaching the forest along the snowbound path.

La Brais slowed his horse to a walk two hundred yards from the forest and stowed his Sharps in its scabbard, drawing his Colt revolver and easing warily alongside Takoda's pony, which hobbled awkwardly through the snow, hampered by its injury.

Once confident that the Indian was not hidden in the surrounding snow, he turned his attention to the forest, following Takoda's trail as it tracked toward the trees, but stopping short of the dense fringe of lodgepole as he considered the wisdom of further pursuit.

The Indian was on foot and would undoubtedly head east, so La Brais decided that the best strategy would be to overtake and block his escape route, driving him to the upper edge of the forest, where he would have no alternative but to break out across the higher barren slopes of the escarpment. There, he would be exposed and defenseless. He smiled. The chase was on, and the trapper relished the thrill of the kill. Elated, he swung his horse around and hurried down to rejoin the path into the forest.

★ ★ ★ ★ ★

Takoda considered his tactics. His opponent was on horseback, placing him at an immediate disadvantage, added to which the man was armed with a gun. Ideally, he needed to secure an elevated position where he could engineer an element of surprise.

Scanning the trail, he noticed a tree with large branches overhanging the path, its thick growth of needles casting deep shadows across the ground. He crept stealthily alongside its trunk and clambered up onto its lower boughs, careful to position himself so that he remained concealed from the approaching rider. Balancing comfortably in the fork between two branches, he primed himself, his hunting knife in his right hand with the point of the blade thrust downward.

The thick pine obscured his view of the trail, but he could hear the horse jogging steadily toward him, its hooves scuffing the detritus of the forest floor. Moments later, he picked out the intermittent flicker of its outline through the web of pine needles and caught his first clear view of the big bearded man mounted on its back. The rider scanned the forest vigilantly, and Takoda was sure that he detected an unsightly anomaly to the trapper's eyes.

His mouth was dry with anticipation, but he felt no fear. He sensed only a burning hatred for the men who had killed his brother, and the prospect of delivering his revenge swelled his confidence.

As he reached the treeline, McCabe saw the Indian's pony stumble and fall and was sure that he had spied the brave scramble into the refuge of the forest. Having ploughed along the trail for a few hundred yards, he stopped to draw his revolver and listen. The beat of his heart pounded in his ears, and his nerves leapt at every creak of the trees. He was acutely aware of his lack of fighting expertise, and his hand trembled as his eyes searched the opaque twilight for signs of movement.

McCabe dismounted, feeling uncomfortably exposed sitting high up on his horse, and slid off the path to hide behind a large lodgepole, scanning the hillside in an attempt to estimate the point at which the Indian might have entered the forest.

La Brais may have sent him to intercept the Indian, but McCabe was damned if he was going to get himself killed chasing some battle-hardened warrior. His legs felt like lead, and he was gripped by an overwhelming urge to urinate. Terrified, he resolved that he would remain where he was until La Brais returned, but he willed the big trapper to hurry, each minute seeming an eternity as he peered back up the trail yearning for the Canadian to appear.

Still there was no sign of La Brais, and he was considering riding back up the trail to find him, when at the edge of his vision he detected a stealthy movement. His stomach clenched, a wave of fear coursing through his body. Deep in the forest, a silhouette crept slowly downhill, flitting through the trees and hugging the shadows as it moved steadily toward the trail. McCabe held his breath. He could faintly discern the profile of the Indian, cloaked in thick hides, stealing through the forest like a wraith.

He watched, mesmerized, until, with a sense of dread, he realized that the Indian had faded into the shadow of a tree and disappeared. The hairs on his neck prickled with anxiety as he envisaged the Indian killing La Brais before turning to hunt him down. Gripped by a desperate need to warn his companion, he rallied his courage and crept back up the trail, anxious to avoid causing any noise that might alert the Indian to his presence. His progress was painfully slow, and he could smell his own sweat, his finger quivering on the trigger of his gun.

With a feverish sigh of relief, McCabe heard the heavy footfall of La Brais's horse and caught a glimpse of it weaving through the trees as it approached along the trail. But he still had no idea where the Indian had gone. He had vanished.

La Brais came into sight and ducked his head to pass under the bough of a large overhanging tree, giving McCabe the confidence to step out onto the trail to meet him. The adjusted perspective McCabe obtained as he hurried onto the path opened up a view of the tree above La Brais's head and with a rush of horror, he saw the Indian poised to leap. Launching himself up the trail, he screamed a warning, gesticulating wildly at the thick canopy of pine as the Indian sprang from its branches.

Takoda aimed his knife at La Brais's back, driving downward with the intent of severing the man's vertebrae. But La Brais reacted instinctively, ducking and twisting, as he responded to McCabe's shriek of alarm, his rapid shift of position deflecting Takoda's blade so that it sliced through the thick layers of the Canadian's coat and stung the fleshy bulk of his shoulders, failing to cause any serious injury.

Takoda collided with La Brais, his knee driving into the middle of the trapper's spine, the impact throwing them both from the horse and sending them tumbling to the forest floor. His knife lodged firmly in La Brais's coat, Takoda landed flat on his back with a bone-shattering thud. Compounding his misfortune, La Brais crashed down on top of him, driving the breath from his lungs.

The trapper's weight pinned Takoda to the ground, a dizzy wave of concussion clouding his eyes as he frantically gasped for air. But La Brais was also winded from the fall and the effects of the previous night's whiskey dulled his senses as he lay and groaned, unaware that he had fallen on top of the Indian.

Recovering rapidly, Takoda seized his opportunity and

reached around La Brais's neck, pulling up hard and gripping the man in a throttling arm lock. La Brais was spurred into frantic defense, rolling and writhing to evade strangulation. His hands clawed at Takoda's forearm, pulling and punching in a frenzied attempt to release himself, but his gloved hands were unable to obtain adequate purchase.

La Brais heaved sideways, rolling onto his stomach, and pushing himself onto his hands and knees. With immense effort, he threw himself backward, crushing Takoda against the trunk of a tree. Takoda's grip failed momentarily, and La Brais managed to suck in a deep breath before he could recover his grasp.

The respite cleared La Brais's head, and he remembered his game knife. Fumbling to remove his gloves, he stretched to reach inside his boot. Then, using his left hand, he drew the blade from its sheath, swinging it upward and driving it down over his right shoulder.

Seeing La Brais crash to the ground, McCabe was uncertain whether his fellow trapper was still alive and was hugely relieved when the big Canadian started to struggle madly against the Indian's concerted attack. The two opponents being entangled in a ferocious wrestling contest, McCabe was unable to use his gun and he watched with impotent fascination as the two men rolled back and forth in desperate combat.

As La Brais rolled onto all fours, McCabe searched frantically for an alternative weapon, locating a short broken section of branch, which he flexed back and forth as he circled the two men, waiting for an opportunity to take a clean swipe at the Indian. As La Brais thrust his knife into the brave's bicep, the Indian howled with pain and released the trapper. McCabe seized his chance. La Brais rolled free, gasping for air, and he swung the bough brutally at the back of the Indian's head.

★ ★ ★ ★ ★

Everything happened in an instant. Takoda glimpsed a flash of steel as the knife's lightning strike skewered his arm. An excruciating pain shot down his arm, his adversary rolled away, and simultaneously he detected the presence of a second man. The trees whirled overhead and he heard himself cry out. Then, his head snapped forward and darkness washed over him.

McCabe stood panting, and La Brais pushed himself upright. They gaped with open mouths, staring at the inert body of the Indian collapsed facedown between them. McCabe dropped the branch and approached cautiously, prodding at Takoda's prone form with his foot before rolling him over. Both men were transfixed.

"He's nothin' but a kid!" McCabe murmured under his breath.

CHAPTER 14

May 1865, Nebraska Territory

The wagon train rumbled slowly across the plains. It had been over a month since they had set out from St. Joseph, and the first week had been chaotic until the huge party had settled into a routine, but progress was now steady and largely uneventful. There had been no rain, so the ground remained relatively firm under foot, having been frozen solid during the preceding severe winter.

Gresham had anticipated the inevitable bedlam that ensued when the wagon train started to move out. He had experienced similar situations in the past, but was still surprised at the speed at which any semblance of control degenerated.

The inexperienced travelers whooped with excitement as they got underway, having waited impatiently for months, and the competition to take the lead was intense. Despite Gresham personally briefing each family about the dangers involved and explaining the safety measures that everyone would be expected to observe, many people ignored his warnings and attempted to race toward the front of the convoy.

As a precaution, he deployed two squads of his company to each flank under the command of the two young lieutenants, Hanley and Moylan, and dispatched Trautman with two dozen troopers to hold a line a mile or so to the rear. He picked half a dozen experienced men to accompany him at the front of the procession, issuing detailed orders of the actions they should take in the event of a stampede.

In the days leading up to departure, Gresham and the wagonmaster had moved a small number of families whom they felt would be inclined to follow instructions, including Edward and Mary, to the western edge of the huge gathering of wagons, their intention being to use their wagons to set the pace and present an impediment to anyone who attempted to rush ahead.

And, although there was much jostling, their plan operated effectively as the wagon train moved out, the row of slow wagons at the front of the convoy making it difficult for others to push through and the troopers positioned at either side restraining those who attempted to bypass the outside of the line.

Nearly one hundred wagons progressively took up station, stretched out across two miles of prairie, most families walking alongside their schooners, the children dancing and singing, while the men led their mules, horses, or oxen.

A sense of euphoria pervaded the entire wagon train, five hundred migrants strong, supported by the cavalry troopers and accompanied by hundreds of cattle, which lowed gently as they were encouraged to move off, being prodded with sticks or driven by men on horseback who whistled and waved their hats. The ground shuddered with the trampling of the huge migration, but all set off with an easy gait and a deliberate purpose.

Gresham rode on the outer right of the column, scanning the sea of wagons and watching for the first indication of anyone attempting to break forward. Someone always broke ranks, and as soon as one started to make a run, the provocation inevitably spread like an infectious contagion, the scourge of human competitiveness overwhelming good sense.

Sure enough, the pandemonium began after three miles, the instigator of the stampede being positioned to the left of the column so that Gresham was unsighted when the trouble started, but he heard whooping and shouting, followed by the report of two gunshots and screams of panic.

A large covered schooner drawn by four shaggy chestnut horses broke to the left, cutting between two slower wagons that obstructed its path. The teamster, seated on the jockey box, whipped his reins furiously and fired his pistol, urging his horses to charge into a gallop, the wagon bumping and rocking as it lurched over the uneven ground, his wife and children running in pursuit shouting their encouragement.

The gunshots spooked the oxen pulling the more sluggish wagons, causing one set of animals to break left to escape the sound and the other team to wheel right, cutting into the line and crashing into a schooner alongside. Seizing his opportunity, the renegade driver raced through the gap between the wagons, ignoring the mayhem in his wake.

Gresham dug his spurs into his horse's flank and wheeled ahead of the row of schooners at the front of the line, reminding his troopers to abide by their orders as his Morgan danced on its hocks. He instructed each family to restrain their animals at all costs, making it clear that pulling to a stop would only add to the chaos and endanger the rest of the wagon train. Then, having delivered his instructions, he let his horse surge away, hurtling off to the left flank of the convoy.

Frightened, the cattle on either side of the column broke into a steady lope, wheeling away in either direction. Gresham could see that Moylan and Hanley were following their orders, fanning their men out to drive the cattle away from the column, since it would have been impossible to stop the huge herd once the animals started to stampede, and it was only feasible to guide and contain them until they slowed and tired.

The Kopp family were fortunate in being camped close to the western edge of the migrant's temporary settlement, managing to join the first twenty-five wagons as they set off. Hans was used to harnessing and handling oxen, having worked with them on his farm in the Ukraine, and he walked beside his yoke of four, a tether attached to a draw-rope wrapped around the lead oxen's snout, which, when drawn tight, pulled the animal's head down and controlled its pace. Carla and Elena ambled beside the schooner and Johannes followed, plodding along on their elderly horse.

The gunfire erupted to the Kopps' right and their startled oxen shied to the left, knocking Hans to his knees. Had he not rolled to the side, he would have been crushed under the wheels of his own wagon. Instead, he scrambled to his feet and rushed to recover the trailing tether, throwing his weight against the rope before the beasts managed to build up any speed. Thankfully, the noose did its job, pulling the animals back to a steady walk, assisted by Elena and Carla hauling on the harness on the opposite side of the team.

The family to their right was less fortunate. Their wagon was struck by the gunslinger's runaway team, knocking the driver to the ground. His mules panicked and bolted, leaving his family in their wake, who watched in helpless horror as their schooner careered out of control, crashing into other wagons and sending the occupants scattering as they attempted to avoid being trampled.

The mules wheeled to the right, cutting across in front of another wagon and causing its oxen to veer so sharply that it lurched sideways and toppled over. Its heavily laden cargo of stores burst through the canopy and was tossed into the path of the following wagons, which pulverized the mass of boxes, crates, and sacks of flour, sugar, and other goods. The stricken teamster was knocked to the ground and crushed, his body severed in two as the wagon was drawn over his prone body.

Panic spread, and the caravan of schooners fanned out in either direction, some attempting to avoid the chaos and others trying to take advantage of the opportunity to overtake, mistakenly assuming that the sudden surge was incited by the euphoria of setting off.

Women and children screamed, and men shouted and heaved to restrain their startled teams. Confusion erupted in the stampede that ensued, and several inexperienced drovers lost control of their teams, which took off at a tangent, cutting through the caravan of wagons and leaving carnage in their wake.

The pack mules, acclimatized to scavenging the muddy plain around St. Joseph and objecting to being herded away from the familiarity of their temporary home, broke away and galloped back toward town, snorting and braying as they scattered their loads.

Hanley and Moylan dispatched a squad of their troopers to restrain the most wayward wagons, in an effort to regain some control, while continuing to drive the cattle clear of the pandemonium. They made no attempt to slow the herd, but pushed them into a fast lope to make it easier to control the direction of their flight.

In most instances the troopers sent to assist the wayward wagons were able to grab hold of the teams' harness and haul the animals to a standstill. Annoyed at the troopers impeding their progress, a few drivers whipped their beasts to encourage them to break away and continue their charge. But Gresham's orders had been explicit and, following a warning, the troopers readied themselves to shoot the lead animal in the traces of any wagon that the driver refused to pull up.

Only two teamsters failed to capitulate, the reckless drivers aiming their whips at the soldiers and attempting to steer their teams into the cavalrymen's horses. Having been well drilled during their march to St. Joseph, the troopers adeptly swerved out of harm's way and drew their weapons, issuing a final warning before firing a well-aimed shot at close quarters into the lead animal's skull. The tactic was a measure of last resort and the consequences were gruesome, each beast collapsing to the ground as if poleaxed.

The trailing oxen leapt over the body, ripping away their traces as their wagon ploughed into the fallen beast and bursting its stomach open like a ripe melon, eviscerating its entrails.

The second animal to be gunned down was a mule, and the rest of its team were not so fortunate, tumbling over its carcass and snapping their legs as the schooner ran into their felled bodies, its metal-rimmed wheels tearing through their flesh like a knife through butter and casting the wagon onto its side.

Women and children screamed at the horrific sight of the dissected animals, which squealed and thrashed in pain until the troopers dispatched them with a bullet to the brain. In stunned silence, the families started to reassemble their frugal belongings, their dream of a bright future in the opportunistic lands to the west reduced to a hollow aspiration.

Gresham galloped directly for the wagon that had started the pandemonium. He could see the driver leaning forward, oblivious to the mayhem he had caused, manically thrashing his long reins and whooping at his horses, his fervor incited by a team of six mules hauling a schooner that thundered along beside him with a terrified teenage girl bouncing on the jockey seat, desperately trying to slow her beasts.

Concluding that his priority was to stop the reckless drover, Gresham swung in front of the careering team of horses, the animals galloping with their necks outstretched, sweat pouring down their chests below their breast collars, nostrils flared and eyes wild. A swift appraisal revealed that there was little chance of slowing the horses by trying to obstruct their path, so he veered to the side and yelled at the driver to rein in his team, reaching across to grasp the headstall of the lead horse on the left-hand side.

He expected the driver to comply and bring the team under control, but to his astonishment a whip cracked alongside his head, and when he turned to face the wagon he found the puce-faced driver screaming abuse and preparing to unleash a second lick of his long bullwhip.

Gresham dropped the headstall, swerving away as the cat-tail ends of the whip snapped over his shoulder. His surprise turned to cold fury. The teamster's foolishness was certain to result in several deaths by the time his wagon was brought to a halt.

As the team burst clear of the left-hand side of the line, the driver rose to his feet, standing unsteadily on the pitching plate of his schooner, his legs braced and the reins grasped in one hand. He dropped his whip and tugged at his waistband, pulling out a long-barreled revolver.

Galloping alongside the wagon, Gresham glanced across to discover the driver attempting to level the pistol in his direction. He was astounded. The man was past assistance, possessed by a madness that was beyond reason. Gresham could see the feverish lunacy in the wagonners' eyes. He reined his horse back harshly, disappearing from view behind the wagon's canopy as a shot whistled past in front of him.

Gresham considered his options. Having broken away from the wagon train, there was little risk to the other schooners if he allowed the rampant team to continue to run; on the other hand, he needed to arrest the stampede. He was concerned about shooting one of the horses because of the sheer speed at which the animals were galloping. In addition to which it was likely that the lunatic with the gun would attempt to shoot him, if he advanced close enough to get a clean shot at one of the animals. Also, he had to consider the impact of his actions upon the mule-drawn schooner running alongside. He could not risk the two wagons colliding if he shot one of the horses. In a split second, he made up his mind and drew his sword from its scabbard, its razor edge glinting as he swung it high on his right side and urged his horse forward.

The driver was startled to see Gresham reappear, but was unable to take aim with his pistol before Gresham swung his saber in a strong downward flourish. The blade sliced cleanly through the leather of the outer traces, behind the rear of the two left-hand horses, and the sudden change in tension caused the animal to stumble against its right-hand pair. The driver lurched clumsily, managing to prevent himself from falling, but dropped his gun in the process so that the weapon tumbled out of his hand and ricocheted off the whirling spokes of one of the front wheels. The driver screamed abuse at Gresham, but continued to whip his horses with the long reins.

Swinging away, Gresham dropped behind the wagon and steered his horse up its opposite side, almost colliding with a teenage boy who was galloping along on an ungainly horse, attempting to catch up with the mule-drawn schooner. He surmised that the boy must be a family member trying to help the terrified girl he had seen wrestling with her team and nodded a curt acknowledgment. Grateful for the help, he sped to the front of the horse-drawn wagon again, deftly swinging his sword across his body and down to his left, severing the second set of traces.

This time his action had the desired effect, and the four-horse team stumbled into one another, tearing themselves from their harness and breaking free of the wagon, although they continued to gallop for several hundred yards before realizing that they had shed their load.

Falling free of the horses, the hitching shaft impaled itself in the ground, forming a lever that thrust the front of the wagon into the air until the shaft sheared from its fittings and fired into the hooped canopy like a massive spear.

The speed at which the horses broke away gave the driver no

chance and the fractured shaft hit him squarely in the chest, catapulting through his torso like a lance and leaving him transfixed. His eyes wide with shock, the wagon careered on, bumping over the uneven ground as his hands groped helplessly at the tail of timber projecting from his trunk.

When the mules hauling the schooner adjacent to the Kopps bolted, the teamster and his family scattered, fearing that they might be crushed. Hans was unable to help them because he was struggling to control his own oxen, but Johannes was mesmerized by the attractive girl mounted on the jockey seat, fighting to control her spooked team. Immediately, he made up his mind to help and charged after her.

He whipped his old horse into a gallop, pursuing the schooner until eventually he was able to force his way alongside. He was a confident rider, having ridden on his family's farm in the Ukraine since he was a small child, but forcing the elderly steed to maintain its speed required all his skill.

Pulling parallel, he found himself sandwiched in between the schooner and a horse-drawn wagon in full flight to his left. The wagon swung across, narrowing its gap to the schooner and threatening to crush him between the wildly spinning wheels. Abandoning caution, he reached the front of the schooner and caught sight of one dainty foot and the skirt hem of the young girl, who was braced against the footplate, throwing her weight against the reins.

Johannes had no idea what he was going to do to stop the runaway schooner. He was not a courageous person, nor given to putting himself at risk for the benefit of others, but inexplicably he was drawn to the girl. He searched the side of the wagon for an adequate handhold and considered riding forward to grab the halter of the lead mule, but his horse's stamina was failing and the sight of the ferociously spinning steel-shod wheels almost caused him to abandon his rescue attempt.

Unexpectedly, a cavalryman appeared to his left. Their eyes met momentarily and Johannes could see the soldier's surprise, but he was struck by the strength and confidence the man exuded. In a fraction of a second the contact was broken and the soldier surged ahead, wielding a long elegant sword, lost in his focus on the wagon to his left. Inspired to emulate the suave officer, Johannes's commitment was revitalized. He whipped his poor old horse, driving it dangerously close to the wildly spinning wheels, until he could snatch a glance at the young girl, who was hauling on the reins, arching her back with the effort.

The girl gawped at Johannes in disbelief as he launched himself from his horse in an act of wanton madness, his chest crunching onto the footplate and his legs flailing in the air behind him, one shin scuffing the rim of the flying front wheel, which ripped away part of his breeches. The metal rim scraped at the top of his boots and the thick leather saved his leg from being sliced open as he wriggled like a landed seal, his hands fumbling for a secure hold.

Gripped by panic, he felt himself slip. But, as he considered his gruesome fate, a slim hand locked around his wrist and the surprisingly strong grip arrested his fall. He pulled frantically, his biceps searing with effort, until mercifully he succeeded in hooking a knee onto the platform and wrenched himself aboard.

He heaved a gasp of relief, flashing a grateful acknowledgment at the girl who had saved his life. She grinned in response, the full lips of her broad mouth breaking into a bright smile, and Johannes's heart jumped. Her alluring green eyes sparkled, lighting up her delicate round face with its elegant aquiline nose, and he was entranced.

He pushed himself onto the jockey seat alongside her and reached across to take the reins, which she readily surrendered.

Johannes braced his feet and jerked the long straps viciously to slow the mules, looking for the horse-drawn wagon to his left to gauge his progress, only to be greeted by the sight of the wagon's liberated team of horses wheeling out of view, their reduced pace causing the girl's mules to respond to his insistent tugging.

At length, the animals slowed to a walk and Johannes pulled the schooner to a halt. He and the girl sat in silence, the adrenaline of their ordeal coursing through their veins. Their hearts thumped and their breathing was hoarse, but eventually they turned to look at one another and the girl smiled coyly, dipping her chin to conceal her blushes when Johannes beamed in return. Spontaneously, they both burst into a peal of laughter and Johannes threw his arms around her shoulders, hugging her tightly.

To his surprise, she responded eagerly, reaching around to hug his chest and bury her head into his neck. Soft curls of her hair fell against his cheek, and he was roused by the delicate smell of her skin, the pit of his stomach clenching with excitement. But the delicious sensation was interrupted when she looked up and their eyes met, both acutely aware of the unexpected intimacy.

Their self-conscious discomfort was compounded as Gresham pulled up alongside and misinterpreted the youngsters' embrace. "That was a brave thing you did there, son. Your sister was putting up some fight with those mules." He waved his hand at the team, their heads hung low and their ribs still heaving as they recovered from their breakneck charge.

Johannes was caught off guard. "Ah . . . no. Is n-not sister," he stammered.

Gresham was perplexed, having assumed Johannes to be one of the girl's family, dashing to her rescue. "Well, she ought to be mighty grateful," he addressed Johannes eyeing the girl curiously. "Looks like you've made a new friend, anyway."

Johannes blushed, stumbling to find an appropriate response. "I hiv getting back viz mine family," he mumbled, resisting the urge to turn and look at the girl, but intrigued and elated by the soldier's assessment.

Before Gresham could respond further, a trooper rode up, deflecting his attention as he issued orders to keep the wagon train rolling and detailed men to assist those families who had lost livestock or been injured during the stampede.

Refocused on the wagon train, Gresham tipped his hat respectfully and swung away. Alone again, Johannes immersed himself in the soft warmth of the girl nestling against him, until their privacy was disrupted by a tall fair-haired man with a close-cropped beard and Scandinavian features who collapsed against the step plate. He was panting heavily, his face red from the exertion of chasing after the runaway schooner, but he squinted up at Johannes and puffed his gratitude.

"Thank you, sir!" he wheezed. "You saved our wagon, young man, and our daughter." He shot a concerned glance at the pretty blond girl at Johannes's side, relieved to see that she was unhurt. "You risked your life jumping from that horse," he followed up.

Johannes was embarrassed by the plaudit and uncomfortable at the girl's affectionate embrace in the presence of her father. He pushed himself to his feet, leaving the girl sitting awkwardly on the bench seat. "I must getting back to family, sir," he explained, lowering himself from the wagon.

The man grasped him by the hand, shaking it vigorously. "I can't thank you enough. I don't know what to say," he declared.

Unsure how to respond, Johannes was looking at his feet when a distraught woman enveloped him in a bear hug, her attractive angular face streaked with tears and her body shaking with emotion.

"Mary-Jane, are you all right?" she enquired urgently of the girl on the wagon, releasing Johannes and gasping to recover her breath.

"She's fine, Ma. Not a scratch on her, thanks to this young man," the girl's father commended.

Overwhelmed, the woman turned to Johannes and squeezed him again. "Oh, thank you," she cried. "We were so scared. Mary-Jane's never driven a wagon before." She planted a kiss firmly on Johannes's cheek and he went rigid with humiliation.

Fumbling for a response, he nodded and smiled weakly, wriggling to extract himself from the woman's clutches. "Is no trouble," he blurted. "Must go now, sank you." He backed away waving a hurried farewell, concerned to locate his horse.

His departure was too much for the young girl, who scrambled to the edge of the schooner. "My name's Mary-Jane!" she shouted unnecessarily, shooting a hopeful smile. Johannes was delighted and grinned back at her, waving idiotically.

"Johannes!" he called in response.

"Thank you!" she cried, bouncing excitedly. "Thank you, Johannes!"

The troopers worked hard to keep the wagon train rolling. Hanley and Moylan drove the cattle several miles ahead before they eventually slowed, leaving a dozen of their men to tend the herd, while they led the balance of their troopers back along the trail to help restore order.

The men who had been dispatched to restrain errant wagons had done a fine job too, and Gresham's troopers managed to keep the majority of schooners moving, so that collectively they succeeded in forming the entire wagon train into an orderly procession.

Setting their minds to helping the families whose wagons had been damaged, troopers dismounted and assisted the migrants where possible, but it was clear that most of those affected would have to return to St. Joseph to repair their wagons and replace lost provisions. For several, the journey ended before it had really begun, and those migrants were condemned to wait for the next wagon train.

Sweeping the rear of the line, Trautman and his men busied themselves catching stray mules as they bolted back toward St. Joseph and helped to free a few of the schooners that became bogged down in the churned mud.

Two people died as a result of the stampede and there were several injuries, but given the chaos it was miraculous that more people had not been killed. Once order had been restored, Gresham dispatched a trooper to summon the undertaker from St. Joseph, who duly arrived to collect the bodies of the deceased with his open-topped wagon, the hopes and dreams of the families affected having been brutally extinguished.

The cavalry surgeon attended to cuts and bruises, twisted ankles, and a broken leg. But all of the injured elected to resume their journey rather than return to town, so that within a few hours the plains to the west of St. Joseph were deserted, only remnants of broken crates and split sacks left to betray the passage of the huge convoy.

Gresham rode back down the line, checking each schooner to assess damage and gauge people's morale, and he was pleased to be met with robust enthusiasm, leaving him confident that most people would not only sustain their commitment, but would have learned from the traumatic experience.

During the inspection, he found Colter riding alongside a heavily laden schooner, tended by four unsavory-looking men whom he introduced as gold prospectors intent upon reaching Virginia City. And, although Gresham did not like the look of the pioneers, he could see why Colter might have been attracted to their company, since they were the kind of hard-drinking sourdoughs who harbored an appetite for gambling.

The mountain man appeared amused. "Looks like you got yer work cut out, soldier boy. Gonna have t' look after maself, since seems like you gonna have yer han's full, keepin' yer flock alive." He chuckled at his own levity and leered with ghoulish fascination at the undertaker's wagon as it passed, returning to St. Joseph, surrounded by the grieving families of the dead men.

Gresham bridled at the unnecessary jibe, but was determined not to give Colter the satisfaction of seeing that the barbed comment had hit its mark. "You do that, Mr. Colter. I'd rather not have to be your nursemaid too."

"An' ah thought you'd bin s'tructed t' look after me real nice?" Colter chortled.

"Safe passage, Mr. Colter. Those are my orders. After that, you're on your own. Now, I'd be obliged if you and your colleagues would keep your wagon rolling. Good day." He tipped his hat and rode toward the front of the convoy.

CHAPTER 15

Oregon Trail, Nebraska Territory

Each day the wagon train became more organized and its routine more established. The migrants soon realized that there was no material advantage in being at the front of the procession, other than avoiding the worst of the billowing plume of dust. In any event, much of the dust problem could be mitigated by fanning the wagons out across the plain, and it was obvious that those who had passed before had employed the same strategy, rows of well-established sets of rutted tracks running parallel for mile after mile.

The ground was firm, enabling each family to master the art of leading their teams in conditions that were relatively undemanding and presented few significant challenges. The migrants walked alongside their schooners talking happily, singing songs or playing games to keep themselves occupied. The dry weather continued and the sky remained a bright blue, stretching unblemished from horizon to horizon, although occasional late-spring flurries of snow sent everyone rushing for their thick coats to wrap up against the sudden snaps of bitter cold.

Gresham and Trautman accompanied the wagonmaster as he visited groups of the travelers each evening once the wagon train had made camp, the three men using the opportunity to explain the nature of the obstacles they would face further into the journey, warning of the risks, and briefing each family about the preparations they would need to make to ford rivers and successfully negotiate hill descents.

Many of the travelers absorbed the information readily, clarifying ambiguities and ensuring that they knew who to ask for help if they got into trouble, but more importantly the discussions provided the opportunity to identify the migrants that possessed the most relevant experience and competence, those least able, and those whose cavalier attitude might present a liability to the safety of others.

The three men debated their impressions of each family and arrived at a consensus opinion of the individuals that they felt should be appointed as marshals, in each instance selecting people that they deemed responsible, competent, and authoritative, the appointments being confirmed by the wagonmaster. The selected men were each entrusted with accountability for the leadership of twelve schooners, and the wagon train was progressively broken into these smaller units over the course of a week, with the least-confident teamsters being allocated evenly between each group. The arduous trail would necessitate effective teamwork, so it was critical that an understanding of relationships, responsibilities, and dependencies was established at an early stage.

The Kopps fell into the regimented routine. They woke early. Elena and Carla busied themselves with the cooking and Johannes became adept at collecting fuel for their fire, often working with others to build a communal fire since fuel resources were scarce. Hans tended the cattle, intent upon avoiding the more mundane chores.

The daily march was ponderous, the heavy schooners struggling to achieve much in excess of two miles an hour, and soon Hans's initial euphoria was displaced with an irksome boredom. But although he found relief in the company of the other men in his group, he considered their conversation tedious and yearned for the thrill of some good gambling or the revelry of the saloon.

Johannes was delighted, however, because Gresham had recognized the boy during his briefing with the Kopps and concluded that there would be merit in pairing his and Mary-Jane's families in the same marshal's group. While there had been a little devilment in Gresham's decision, recollecting the chemistry he had witnessed between the two youngsters, he had concluded that the trust established as a consequence of Johannes's actions would only serve to reinforce the solidarity of the group.

The first evening the new unit was formed, Mary-Jane's father brought his family to the Kopps' schooner to introduce themselves, reiterating their appreciation for Johannes' bravery. Elena instantly liked them and was delighted to have someone to talk to, since Hans was becoming increasingly withdrawn and argumentative. She shared johnnycakes, a bread made with cornmeal salt and milk, and brewed coffee while they all sat around the fire and discussed their dreams for a new life in Montana Territory.

At first, Johannes and Mary-Jane were too embarrassed to even acknowledge each other, managing only furtive sidelong glances, but Carla was smitten by the attractive blond girl and avidly embraced her company. She sat close to Mary-Jane, monopolizing her attention, and the two girls' easy conversation relieved the tension for Johannes, enabling him to sit and listen as he soaked up every snippet of information about the entrancing young woman.

The evening visits became a regular event and Johannes sat deliberately close to Mary-Jane, the two exchanging conspiratorial smiles as they fought to overcome their mutual awkwardness. But it became clear that Hans had little in common with Mary-Jane's father, Todd, and he became adept at finding excuses to absent himself. Consequently, Todd's attention focused on Johannes, to whom he expounded his analysis of business, farming, and politics. He talked about the advent of technology and the marvels of engineering that would eventually enable the railroad to breach the Rockies, completing the transcontinental integration of the country. He was gratified to discover that Johannes possessed an astute mind and a keen understanding of the principles of sound business, including a detailed appreciation of the intricacies of land title, derived from his discussions with officials at the land office in St. Joseph.

Johannes's grasp of English had improved dramatically during the winter months, and he was blessed with a unique charisma for a young man of his years. Todd enjoyed their discourse and, being impressed by Johannes' intellect, was content to permit the subtle flirting between the boy and his daughter.

Nevertheless, Johannes found the inability to be alone with Mary-Jane agonizing. They were always surrounded by the suffocating claustrophobia of other people, which made him self-conscious about engaging Mary-Jane in conversation. He had never had a girlfriend before and found himself fumbling for appropriate words, causing Carla to laugh at his clumsy interventions and compound his embarrassment.

He was confused by his feelings for the girl. She made his stomach churn and tied his tongue in knots. He was able to converse confidently and expound his opinions upon any range of subjects with entire strangers, but his conversational abilities seemed to dry up with Mary-Jane, his mind rendered blank so that he was unable to think of anything relevant to discuss.

Unexpectedly, the solution presented itself. Elena and Mary-Jane's mother decided to prepare an evening meal for the two families: cornbread, beans, fried meat, and gravy, washed down with some fresh warm milk from their milking cows, and coffee.

Hans left to join his friends, Todd was busy undertaking a repair to his wagon, and Carla was occupied with the task of making the cornbread, so Elena asked Johannes to go and collect fuel for the fire. They were camped below a wooded bluff, its slopes cloaked in a thick forest of pine, and having burned buffalo chips and cow droppings for several days, Elena hoped that they might be able to scavenge some firewood. Indeed, people from other parts of the wagon train were already hurrying off to search for timber.

"I'll go with him. Two of us can carry more wood," Mary-Jane suggested, causing Elena to beam with delight as she noticed Johannes's eyes light up at the prospect of spending some private time with the pretty young girl.

"Zat vould be velly nice to you, Mary-Jane. Sank you. I im sure zat Johannes vould like dis." She sighed wistfully, watching the two youngsters as they set off side by side, reflecting upon the heady days of her early relationship with Hans.

The walk up to the edge of the forest was arduous, the ascent from the plains proving steeper and further than it had looked, and Mary-Jane's long skirt constantly snagged on the rocky ground, so that by the time they reached the treeline she and Johannes were both puffing wildly. Exhausted, they stopped to peer back down the hill, catching each other's eye and grinning at their breathlessness.

"You vant sit down to a minute?" Johannes panted.

Mary-Jane nodded, giggling at his pigeon English as she dropped onto a large boulder. "Phew! Look at the view."

Johannes stumbled for a response, hypnotized by the sensuous shape of Mary-Jane's body, her full hips and shapely buttocks evident as she swept her skirt behind her knees to sit down, and his eyes gloating over her narrow waist and prominent breasts, which heaved up and down as she fought to regain her composure. Nervous that she might notice him staring, he spun his head and followed her gaze.

"Oh, ya. Is velly amazing," he stuttered, surprised at the beauty of the panorama, endless miles of plains stretching to a distant hazy border of mountains, making the wagon train appear small and insignificant, camped at the foot of the escarpment.

Mary-Jane looked up and patted the rock she was sitting on. "Will you sit with me for a moment?" she smiled, the alluring effect enhanced by her glittering green eyes. Johannes was captivated, and he sank down gratefully beside her while she entwined her arm with his.

"Look, you can see the beginning of the sunset," she murmured, leaning into his shoulder.

Johannes gazed out across the plains, watching the first hint of orange reflect off a thin layer of cloud low on the horizon, but his senses tingled at the touch of the girl at his side, and he pressed gently against her, soaking up the warmth of her body and the fragrance of her scent. The confusion he had felt about broaching conversation, and his awkward anticipation of their first touch, evaporated in an instant with Mary-Jane's relaxed intimacy.

They sat quietly, watching the restless wanderings of the migrants and their animals on the plains below, milling about like a colony of industrious ants until, with regret, they realized that daylight would soon fade. They stood up, Mary-Jane slipping her hand comfortably into Johannes's palm and walked into the trees.

Suffering from the attentions of previous wagon trains, much of the perimeter of the woods had been thinned and felled, the forest floor cleared of any material worth collecting for firewood. But Johannes was determined not to return empty-handed, so they pushed deep into the woods until eventually they discovered a fallen tree, its dead branches lying in shattered pieces that could be broken into lengths short enough to carry.

Mary-Jane skipped around, loading timber onto Johannes outstretched arms, until she could hardly see his face over the pile. Amused, she selected five good-sized sections of branch to carry herself, and they started to retrace their steps through the woods.

Daylight faded as they picked their way between the twisted roots of the big trees, taking care not to stumble in the gloom. Mary-Jane talked excitedly about the terrifying way her mules had bolted on the day that they had met and the thrill of seeing him jump onto the schooner to help her. And, listening to her recount the events, Johannes basked in the warmth of her praise for his bravery, which fanned his voracious ego.

They laughed at what had happened and joked about the difficulty they had experienced in talking while in the presence of their parents, oblivious to the pervasive darkness enveloping their path, until with an eerie melancholy, a nerve-tingling howl echoed through the woods. The mournful call of a wolf reverberated through the trees, hanging in the air before falling silent once more.

Horrified, they stopped and whirled around to face the sound, the hairs on the back of their necks bristling with anxious anticipation. Their eyes met, wide and startled.

"A volf!" Johannes whispered, but he could see from the haunted look on Mary-Jane's face that she was all too aware of the origin of the sound. Momentarily they were rooted to the spot. Then, the first call was answered by a second, this time closer, to their right. They gawped at one another.

"Run!" Johannes hissed.

Mary-Jane dropped her stack of wood and lifted her skirts, sprinting off like a startled rabbit, but Johannes held on gamely to his burden, wrestling to keep his balance as he crashed through the trees.

"Keep run down ze hill," he panted, twisting and stumbling as they hurtled toward the lower fringe of the woods.

The wolves howled again, this time closer than before, and Johannes's imagination conjured an image of the pack running them down, pouncing from the shadow of the trees and tearing them limb from limb. The prospect fueled his instinct for self-preservation, abandoning any concern for Mary-Jane's safety, his sole focus centered upon his own ability to reach the open ground below the woods.

He saw Mary-Jane stumble and crash to the ground, but continued his flight unchecked, mildly relieved to glimpse her scramble to her feet and plough on down the hill. Again, the wolves bayed. This time the sound came from the left. They were encircled. Johannes's heart beat furiously and his mouth was dry. He was oblivious to the strain of carrying his burden of firewood, and his legs pumped madly as he leapt over the tangled mass of twisted roots and scrubby undergrowth.

Unexpectedly, he burst out of the trees and onto the barren hillside, Mary-Jane trailing fifty paces behind. Together, they raced down the rocky slope, slithering and stumbling until eventually their fear receded and they pulled up, buzzing with the heady exhilaration of their escape. They stood peering back up the hill, panting, searching the shadows until they were confident that they were not being pursued.

Turning to face one another, Johannes saw tears streaming down Mary-Jane's cheeks and noticed the dirty scuff marks on her clothing where she had fallen. He sensed her shaking hand rested on his forearm and was overwhelmed by a rush of desire. He dropped his stack of firewood and pulled her to him, kissing her with frenzied urgency.

Shocked at his passion, Mary-Jane baulked at the intensity of his embrace and wrestled to pull away, but slowly his fervor eased and she began to relax, searching between his lips with her tongue and pressing herself gently into his chest.

They clung together, exploring each other's bodies with fumbling caresses, and Johannes's head whirled with an unquenchable lust. He could feel his stiffness pulsing against his pants, and was possessed by the desire to force her to submit to his pleasure. He had to have her.

To his astonishment, Mary-Jane broke off their embrace and pushed him gently away, her eyes wide and her breath hoarse. "We have to get back," she croaked. "It's dark. They'll be worried about us."

Johannes's anger flared. Her rejection, inflicted at the height of his incendiary passion, incited a bitter resentment. Had she been able to see his face, Mary-Jane would have been shocked at the raw fury of his expression, but her soft husky tone and the gentle caress of her hand served to placate what might otherwise have been a violent riposte.

Johannes stood brooding, silently watching Mary-Jane as she bent to pick up the wood he had dropped, reloading his arms and gathering a few sticks to carry herself. The moment had been lost, but the yearning burned fiercely in his loins as he watched her dainty movements. He longed to conquer her.

There was a flurry of concern when the youngsters returned to their schooners, Mary-Jane's parents being relieved to discover that they were both unharmed, although the tale Johannes told of their flight from the wolves made for a welcome bit of excitement around the campfire.

By the following morning, Johannes resolved to deploy all his charm to woo Mary-Jane, mindful that excessive pressure might scare her off. Over the following days, he committed himself to attending to her every need, serving her food and fetching drinks, helping her with her chores, and keeping her company as she walked alongside her schooner. He told colorful stories about his life in the Ukraine, his journey across the Atlantic, and his family's preparations for their migration across the Great Plains once they had arrived in St. Joseph.

He told her about Hans's drinking and violent outbursts, explaining with emotional regret that he had been forced to protect his mother from physical abuse and how he had intervened to protect a man his father had attacked during their journey on the railroad. He embroidered his lies with elements of truth, describing the knowledge he had gained about the mechanism for acquiring land, learned from the land agents he had met at St. Joseph. Intent upon securing Mary-Jane's affection, he articulated an alluring set of qualities to ingratiate himself with her parents. He advocated high moral values and promoted his keen business mind, anxious to demonstrate that he was the sort of man who would assure the success and security of his family when they reached their new home.

During the day, he lent Todd his assistance, and, in the evening, he sat holding Mary-Jane's hand, a blanket spread around their shoulders as they huddled close to the fire. But his obsessive lust for her body remained a coiling serpent of longing, twisting in his stomach as he watched her every move; the gyration of her hips, the flick of her hair, or the sunshine of her smile. She would be his, and he could barely wait.

CHAPTER 16

Platte River, Nebraska Territory

On the evening of the thirty-fourth day, Gresham and the wagonmaster called together all the marshals to brief them about two major challenges they would have to negotiate over the ensuing few days. The first was the river crossing at the South Platte fork, the confluence of the north and south tributaries to the great Platte River. There was no ferry and the river would be deep in places, swollen by the spring thaw.

The wagonmaster explained the risks he anticipated, and the marshals were invited to discuss the arrangements they planned to put in place to assure the wagon train's safety during the crossing. Of particular concern were the teams of oxen and the other beasts of burden hauling the schooners. While much of the journey across the Kansas plains had been uneventful, the availability of fresh water had been sparse, and there was a high degree of probability that the animals would stampede once they smelled the river. To that end, Gresham reminded the marshals of the heavy cost some of their kinsmen had paid resulting from the loss of control that had occurred at the outset of their trip and implored them to plan for the worst.

The second obstacle would be a steep hill on the approach to Ash Creek, the convoy's first challenging descent, a three-hundred-foot acute slope over the edge of an escarpment into the North Platte valley below. It was one of the significant bottlenecks along the trail, where schooners would have to condense to single file, restrain their teams, and allow each wagon to clear the bottom of the slope before permitting the next to follow. The consequences of a heavy schooner breaking free and careering down the hill, to collide with the one in front, did not bear consideration.

The mechanism for lowering the wagons required each team to be unhitched to prevent the animals from being run over by their own wagon, and the settlers controlled the descent using ropes, rough-locking the rear wheels of their schooner by sliding a strong pole through the spokes.

Each marshal was charged with coordinating the arrangements for the schooners in their charge and was dispatched to make preparations with their group. The following day, Gresham, Trautman, and the wagonmaster circulated the wagon train and listened to each marshal's proposals, providing advice and suggestions where they felt that the risks had not been adequately considered or mitigated.

Two days later, the convoy made camp six miles east of the Platte crossing, Gresham and the wagonmaster having selected the location to allow the huge caravan the benefit of a full day in which to approach and cross the river. Their intent was to ensure sufficient daylight during which to manage any potential stampede, as opposed to exposing the wagon train to the risk of arriving at the river in poor light, later in the day.

The night was restless and families worked late, unloading their belongings and caulking splits that had opened up in the bed of their wagons, damage caused by the stress inflicted by a month of lumbering across the plains. The purpose of creating a watertight bed for each wagon was to ensure that the schooner floated as high as possible in the deeper water of the river, reducing the potential for its cargo to be washed away. But weight was also a consideration, and many families chose to leave behind the least necessary of their belongings, contributing to the mass of discarded possessions cast aside along the trail by preceding convoys.

As dawn broke, Gresham deployed a cadre of his troop, commanded by Lieutenant Hanley, to assist the cowhands in driving the herd to the river, having agreed with the wagonmaster that separating the cattle from the wagon train during the crossing would mitigate an element of risk.

The marshals directed the caravan to spread out across the plain, avoiding the potential for collision in the event of a stampede to reach the river, and each group set off at quarter-mile intervals, reducing the number of schooners that would reach the banks of the Platte concurrently.

Comprising nearly two hundred of the settlers' milk cows and six hundred head of breeding stock, the consolidated herd moved at pace once the cattle detected the tantalizing aroma of water. They loped along, lowing gently, pausing only occasionally to grasp a mouthful of the scrubby grass on the overgrazed trail.

Having broken camp at six in the morning, the cattle were all drenching themselves in the muddy shallows of the Platte only an hour later, the cowhands allowing them to wallow lazily as they cooled off, sucking hungrily to fill their bellies with the refreshing water.

The river was nearly a mile wide, countless islands of verdant grass interspersing a meandering maze of silt-laden channels, hazardous to man and beast. And, at its western bank, a confluence of faster running water had carved away a deep channel where the river's raging current swirled dangerously.

Rising above the torrent, the far bank was steep and undercut in many places, presenting an impassable obstacle to cattle attempting to haul themselves out of the river. At intervals, previous wagon trains had cut a series of well-used landing slopes, enabling both animals and wagons to escape the river if driven across with care and accuracy.

Hanley assembled the cowhands, discovering that several were experienced cattlemen, and after a short debate a tall stocky man with a long drooping moustache called O'Halloran, whom everyone referred to as Hal, was elected to take charge. Garbed in a grubby faded red flannel shirt and dark woolen pants, a rugged well-worn coat, and a pair of six-guns slung at his waist, he projected the air of a tough and uncompromising man.

Hal hailed from Illinois and, having worked several of the Texas Longhorn drives, he was intent upon establishing his own ranch in western Montana Territory, along with his wife and five children. But, for now, he was in his element organizing eight hundred head of cattle.

He made a show of his horsemanship as he took control of the drive, and his spritely black gelding danced excitedly in anticipation as he divided the cowhands into teams and allocated their tasks. "You boys hold on tight to the horn o' yer saddles, now. Don't want none of yer takin' a swim gettin' 'cross this puddle." He scowled, inciting the men to action once he had issued his instructions.

The less experienced quailed under his steely glare, but one seasoned hand leaned out of his saddle, unimpressed, and spat at the ground. "You gonna talk 'bout this all day, or we gonna git on with it?" he grumbled, prompting the other hands to laugh.

Hal grinned broadly. "Okay, boys. Like the man says, let's get at it!" Satisfied, he spun his horse on its hocks and set them all to work.

Commencing the drive, the cowhands moved the cattle slowly upstream before attempting to cross the river. This was done to ensure that any animals washed past the first cut-out on the opposite bank would have access to several further landing points downstream before being swept away.

Hal stationed troopers and stockmen at each cut-out on both banks, their job being to encourage the cattle into and then out of the river. The men with most experience of using a lasso were positioned at the final landing, as a measure of last resort to recover any beast that failed to make the crossing.

On the east bank, a team of cowhands lined the flanks of the herd, whistling and beating their lassos against their legs to encourage the cattle to keep moving, the thick, deep silt sucking at their hocks as they navigated the shallows, so that the herdsmen were obliged to allow the animals time to recover before driving them into the fast-flowing waters.

The first cows to approach the river bunched up as they began to lose their footing, so Hal picked a dozen strong men to cut out some of the more dominant beasts and drive them across the river first, their example designed to prompt the rest of the herd to follow. With encouragement, the lead animals launched themselves into the swirling water, pumping their legs furiously as they were washed downstream, and the rest of the herd plunged into the river in pursuit, forming a diagonal swathe of snorting and heaving cattle as they struggled against the current.

Hal whipped his lasso around the neck of a large shorthorn and took a couple of loops around the horn of his saddle, slipping off his horse and swimming alongside so that he was able to drag the cow briskly toward the opposite bank. Once Hal's mount regained its footing, he swung back into the saddle and urged the horse onto the landing, gathering up the tension on the lasso and dragging the shorthorn onto the bank, a group of other cattle tucked close up in its wake.

He did not allow the shorthorn to rest but pulled it up the bank and out onto the prairie above the river, stimulating the other cattle to follow and clearing space for the following herd to make firm ground. He whooped and whistled as he slackened the lasso, flicking it over the cow's horns and coiling it up with masterful technique before wheeling away to rejoin the drive.

Half the cattle lurched gratefully onto dry land at the first cut-out, the rest being swept past, thrashing wildly against the vertical bank until they reached the next landing, where many were able to lunge their way to safety. Meanwhile, Hal and the cowhands west of the river made a fine job of lassoing struggling cattle and hauling them to the bank, their horses dripping with sweat as they worked feverishly back and forth.

Amidst frenetic whooping and hollering, the spectacle unfolded, with a dwindling number of increasingly desperate cattle being washed further and further downstream, the cattlemen driving them relentlessly toward the far bank as they approached each of the cut-outs.

In the midst, Johannes rode around lethargically on his old horse, both he and Edward May among the herdsmen remaining on the east side of the fast-flowing channel of the river. But Johannes's horse was of little use. It struggled to keep its footing in the heavy silt, and he resigned himself to making as much noise as possible, waving his hat furiously, seething with envy at the men mounted on more nimble steeds as he watched them deploy their roping skills with casual aplomb.

Compounding his irritation, Edward's horse, a game little dun mare, appeared to possess a natural aptitude for working with cattle. It danced from side to side, cutting off any cattle that tried to turn away from the river, Edward sitting effortlessly astride its back, so that, eventually, the little mare's confidence prompted even the most stubborn cattle to capitulate to its tenacity and resume the crossing.

As the herd thinned out on the east bank, Edward pushed his horse into the shallows of the fast-running river, encouraging any wayward cattle to keep swimming for the far bank, and the other cowhands followed his example, between them managing to push nearly all the herd across the river, leaving those that struggled to be rescued by Hal and his team of ropers.

There was a sense of jubilation as hundreds of exhausted cattle spread out across the plains beyond the Platte, and the cowhands on the east side of the river focused their attentions on rounding up any stragglers.

Johannes's old horse lacked sufficient stamina to chase cattle, so he remained by the river and watched the others work, cursing his inadequacy. Irritated, his mind turned to the future, his avarice and pride fueling his desire to acquire the means to purchase the best roping horses that money could buy. He was determined that his stock would be the envy of the other ranchers, and that he would not be condemned to sit again in embarrassed ignominy, as he was now.

Distracted by his self-absorbed thoughts, it took several moments for him to register the cries of men shouting at him.

"Get that cow, son! What yer doing? Get the darned cow!" Two of the hands closest to Johannes bawled at him, while on the opposite side of the river, Hal was furious.

"You deaf or jus' damned stupid, boy?" Hal bellowed. "Get y' arse after that cow!"

Snapping back to reality, Johannes spun around, his startled eyes searching for the focus of everyone's attention. To his chagrin, no more than five yards away, a young heifer was struggling in the turbulent river, fighting upstream against the strong current.

Without assessing its plight, Johannes turned his horse and hurried into the shallows, his mount reluctantly immersing itself up to its belly. Removing his hat, he waved it frantically, yelling at the cow for all he was worth, shooing it across the river.

"Wha! Ha! Ha! Go!" he screamed, causing the heifer, alarmed by Johannes's frenzied behavior, to veer away into deeper water, its eyes wide with fear and its nostrils snorting as waves swirled over its face.

"No! Not in the river, y' idiot!" Hal bawled.

"Catch her, son!" shrieked another of the cowhands, desperately forcing his horse across the muddy shallows toward Johannes.

The pleas failed to register with Johannes and he continued shouting at the cow, hoping that it would steer itself across to the opposite bank, without realizing that it had already passed beyond the final landing and was in danger of being swept away.

Hal was apoplectic. He threw his lasso repeatedly, attempting to rope the stricken cow, but the animal was too far from the west bank and the lariat dropped short each time. Several cowhands converged on Johannes, the first to arrive being Edward, who raced past and drove into the river on his game little mare.

As they plunged into deep water both Edward and his mount disappeared below the surface momentarily, before striking out into the river after the little heifer. Johannes was dumbstruck, confused by Edward's sudden intervention, but slowly he absorbed the reality of the circumstances and recognized that he had compounded the cow's danger.

He cringed with embarrassment, sensing the disbelief of the other cowhands at his stupidity. As usual, he reached for excuses. It was not his fault. He would have managed to save the cow. It had not been necessary for Edward to interfere. His humiliation flared to anger. It was Edward's fault. The Quaker had made a fool of him again. Attempting to redeem himself, he urged his horse to follow Edward into the river, but the old nag steadfastly refused to enter the fast-flowing current.

The Quaker steered his horse with deft hands, swiftly overhauling the heifer and grabbing it around the neck, simultaneously urging his little mare to swim back into the shallows. The speed of the river's flow increased as the channel narrowed downstream, approaching a sweeping set of tight bends. For a moment, it seemed that Edward and the two animals might be swept away, but his horse stretched out its neck and pumped its legs ferociously, inching toward the bank until a hoof struck bottom and it was able to lunge clear of the deep water, almost causing Edward to lose his grip of both the mare and the cow.

With a few more powerful strides the horse reached the bank, dragging Edward and the little heifer in its wake. The cow staggered unsteadily into the shallows, its ears flat against its head and its eyes staring vacantly, and Edward held it upright as he encouraged it to stumble onto a small island of grass, where it stood shaking, its legs splayed and its chest pumping.

As he consoled the exhausted cow, several of the herdsmen pulled up and dismounted, clapping him on the back and bombarding him with congratulations. But Edward's diffidence left him feeling awkward about the commendations. His purpose had been to rescue the heifer, no more.

"Son of a gun! You got balls o' steel!" one of the cowhands slapped Edward's shoulder.

"Need a prize fa' best dive o' the day!" another chortled.

"Gonna have a drink on strength a' that!" A throng of men surrounded Edward laughing and joking, until Hal reminded them brusquely that they still had work to do. Johannes's shame was complete. Edward was heaped with praise as disapproving glances were thrown in his direction. His resentment boiled, and once again he saw Edward as the architect of his misfortune. He did not know how, but he was determined that he would find a way to exact his retribution.

Hans had little interest in driving cattle, so having dispatched Johannes to help, he joined his drinking partners. His group of schooners would have to wait to take their turn crossing the river anyway, so he figured there was ample opportunity to socialize before his assistance was required.

He found the prospectors sitting in the lee of their wagon, shading themselves from the early-morning sun, accompanied by a short round-bellied man who looked out of place in his gray flannel suit. They all greeted Hans warmly when he presented a bottle of whiskey, and six tin mugs were thrust at him in anticipation. Chortling contentedly, he dispensed a measure of the liquor into each cup, taking one for himself, and sat down beside the short man, greeting him with an affable slap on the back.

"How is dee land baron dis day?" he joked in his fast-improving pigeon English.

The little man smiled, peering at Hans through thick circular eyeglasses and knocking their mugs together amiably. "You jus' made it a whole lot better." He took a long draught and nudged Hans's arm to encourage him to pour another shot.

"Ha. You is drunk bum. Better drink dis all before dat vixen is come." Hans referred to the man's wife, who disapproved of the company he kept and regularly appeared, castigating him for his debauchery until he was forced to return to his own schooner.

The man, Jefferson Hardwick, was a Kansas land agent who was traveling out to the emerging town of Bozeman to take up a new post administering the allocation of land to migrants settling in the area. He was in his early forties, although he looked older, dressed like a city banker in his suit and fob watch, but he had a taste for gambling and whiskey, which meant that he gravitated toward spending time with less-reputable men.

"She eat your arse, ya?" Hans laughed as he poured the land agent another good measure. He was confident that Hardwick was frightened of his wife, who was a wiry gray-haired lady with a ferocious temper.

"What she don't know, don't harm her," Hardwick protested, closing his eyes and savoring the harsh flavor of the coarse spirit.

Despite their differences, Hans and Hardwick enjoyed each other's company and often sat together ruminating about their respective lives. Both men were dissatisfied with their lot, each struggling to maintain a cordial relationship with his respective wife.

Hardwick had been hopeful that moving out west would represent a fresh start, allowing him and his wife to consign to history the fractious life they had led in Kansas. But the hardships and close confines of the journey were doing little to improve their marriage, and he slipped away regularly to escape their quarreling. Appreciatively, he sat with Hans, making the best of his opportunity for respite ahead of the river crossing.

Chapter 17

Platte River crossing, Nebraska Territory

The wagon train reached the river before noon and the process of orchestrating the crossing began.

The oxen and mules were unhitched and taken across the river ahead of their schooners, guide ropes being attached to each lead animal so that they could be hauled by the beasts that had already made the crossing. The wagons were floated across the river, roped up to a strong team of oxen on the west bank, with an anchor tether on the east side of the crossing to prevent the wagon slewing in the current.

Contrary to Gresham's recommendation, several schooners were prepared at a time, and teams of oxen were doubled up to drag the heavy wagons through the thick mud and silt of the shallows. The beasts strained in their traces, and families pushed and shoved as their schooners became bogged down, the wheels threatening to stick fast in places.

The first accident happened when a wagon lurched forward unexpectedly as its wheels broke free of the mud and a young boy, pushing against the spokes of the rear wheel, slipped and fell in the treacherous conditions, crushing his hand beneath the steel rim of the wheel. In similar circumstances, a man shattered his knee, but worst of all, an elderly grandmother slipped as she alighted from her schooner in an effort to reduce its weight and fell under the wheels, where she was killed as the wagon surged over her prone body.

Despite the efforts of the marshals, the river claimed the most casualties. Two small children, clinging to their schooner during the crossing, were swept away by the treacherous current, the river swamping their overladen wagon and their father nearly losing his life in a desperate effort to save them.

Compounding the carnage, a rope used to haul one of the schooners snapped, causing the heavy wagon to slew sideways, the swirling river sending it crashing into the side of another schooner making the crossing in parallel. The upstream wagon drove into the second, flipping it over and casting its cargo and all six passengers into the river.

Twisting and turning in the churning water, the schooners locked together and the oxen hauling them on the west bank were dragged off their feet by the enormous combined weight, being wrenched from the landing and cast into the river. In the eastern shallows the oxen securing the anchor line dug their hooves into the mud but were towed along, slithering on their sides, until the overturned wagons snagged in the silt, coming to rest in a swamped heap of splintered timber.

Seven members of the families aboard the schooners died, their bodies swept away by the river, and five oxen were drowned. A father and two teenage sons were the only survivors, left clinging to the side of their damaged wagon.

Crossings were suspended to enable a review of the methodology, and Gresham insisted that the wagonmaster only permit one schooner to cross the river at a time. The marshals took personal responsibility for checking the stowage of each schooner and attaching the hauling lines, together with a contingency rope, and a squad of troopers was assigned to supervise each crossing, ensuring that people remained clear of the wheels of the wagons as they were dragged through the churned mud of the shallows.

Gresham set a camp to the west of the river, drawing the

schooners into circles, and organized a field hospital to tend to the injured, the company's surgeon being required to perform two amputations and treat several fractures.

The mood of the migrants was somber, the enormity of their undertaking revealed in stark perspective, and by the time the river crossing was complete the cumulative number of deaths suffered on the route from St. Joseph amounted to twelve, with more than twenty injuries, some serious. The most sobering thought was that the Platte River was only the first of many hazards that the wagon train would have to navigate before reaching its destination, and there was still the potential of encountering hostile Indians, not to mention the risk of disease, dysentery, cholera, and typhoid being the most prevalent.

There were funerals for those whose bodies were recovered from the river and ceremonies for those who had been lost. At Gresham's order, the graves were left unmarked and placed in the line of travel of the wagon train, ensuring that any trace of the burials would be obscured as the schooners passed over them, since it was reputed that some Indians dug up the bodies of the dead to obtain clothing and jewelry, and Gresham was determined that the graves would remain the final resting place of the loved ones of the bereaved.

Unfortunately, the attention devoted to improving the safety of the river crossing had a detrimental impact upon the supervision of the cattle. Since the river blocked their retreat to the east and a steep escarpment ran parallel to the trail, its impassable slopes ascending vertically to a dramatic crest of sandstone pillars, preventing passage to the north, the herd scattered across the plains to the west and into the hills to the south.

The shallow valleys to the south intertwined rugged bluffs, their promontories littered with haphazard heaps of boulders that evoked a sense of their seismic history, but the grass was lush compared to the scrubby growth to be found on the overgrazed plains. Good early-season growth of tall blue-green turkey grass bounded a sea of wispy purple threeawn, with buffalo grass bursting from its honey-brown winter hue into the pea green of early summer.

Tempted by the better quality of grazing, most cattle had meandered into the valleys, so that following the two-day river crossing they were now distributed in small groups across an area of nearly ten square miles.

Hanley and Moylan, together with half the company of troopers, were assigned to help the settlers round up the herd, the balance of Gresham's command remaining with the wagons as a defensive force. And, much to Johannes's annoyance, Hans instructed his son to join the roundup, the big Ukrainian electing to play cards with Colter's motley group of prospectors instead, the men now firmly established as his preferred companions.

Colter chose to join the cowhands, Gresham giving him discretion to carry firearms for the occasion, and following Edward's prowess at the river, the Quaker was encouraged to join the roundup. So, early on the morning after the final wagon had crossed the river, the troopers and stockmen dispersed in twos and threes, armed with their carbines and shotguns, to retrieve as many cattle as they could find.

The area to the west of the Platte was Pawnee country, a tribe of Indians who lived in large oval mud lodges along the banks of the river, cultivating the land and growing bountiful crops of corn, squash, pumpkin, and beans. In the summer months, the tribe packed up their tipis and moved out onto the plains to hunt buffalo, but in late spring they remained close to their winter lodgings.

Undetected by the wagon train, the Pawnee had observed the frenetic industry of the river crossing from vantage points on the surrounding hills. They watched the cattle disperse, and recognized the chance to replenish their supply of meat, the focus of the cavalry being centered upon the welfare of the emigrants.

Capitalizing on their opportunity, they dispatched small hunting parties to locate the cattle, drive the animals further from the settlers' camp, and kill them silently, using bows rather than rifles to avoid attracting the soldiers' attention. Each hunting party was composed of two or three warriors, and one or two women who were responsible for butchering the animals killed.

Johannes ambled along on his old horse following Hal and a seasoned trooper, the two riding together telling lewd stories about the loose women they had frolicked with at saloons and military waypoints on their travels. They laughed heartily at each other's bragging, embellishing their accounts with details of increasingly improbable experiences, their raucous hilarity almost causing Hal to fall off his horse.

Johannes was treated as though he did not exist. He felt ignored and isolated. He had wanted to confide in Mary-Jane about his experience at the river, but had been too embarrassed to admit what had happened and had lapsed into petulant behavior instead. He had yearned for her embrace, but Mary-Jane had been confused by his conduct and responded by distancing herself, making him feel resentful of her apparent rejection.

Adding to the sense that he was being treated like a child, Hans had not permitted him to carry a gun like the other men, leaving him feeling vulnerable in the event that he encountered Indians. He had argued with Hans, until it became obvious that persistence would be rewarded with his father's fist, so reluctantly he had capitulated, resorting instead to pocketing the Cossack knife that had belonged to Johannes Senior, his grandfather. He had tucked the curved knife, with its razor-sharp blade, inside his shirt, and could feel its sheath and ornate handle thumping gently against his chest with the roll of his horse's gait.

Shortly, it became apparent that Johannes's mount was unable to keep pace with the other horses and he excused himself, his companions being dismissive of his departure. Rather than returning to camp, he pulled his old horse to a standstill and waited until the two men were out of sight. Content that they had disappeared along one of the numerous canyons that wound through the rugged hills bordering the plains, he turned south. He had no desire to sit with the women in camp and doubted that Mary-Jane would welcome his return, so he decided to explore one of the alluring little valleys before making his way to the river and tracking back north.

Although picturesque, the craggy bluffs appeared harsh and inhospitable, strewn with shale and loose rock, making it difficult to scale their slopes. But the dramatic contours were interspersed with large expanses of buffalo grass erupting in a sea of succulent fresh spring growth, and Johannes plowed through the tall stands, some touching the withers of his horse, as he wound his way along an indistinct animal trail.

The sun was high, and he took his hat off to savor its warm rays. The canyon was soundless, disturbed only by the rustle of a soft breeze fluttering the swaying heads of grass, and two hours rushed past without him realizing how far he had traveled. His mind drifted, self-indulgently replaying the injustices of the preceding days, attributing blame to those he felt had disparaged him.

Particularly, he thought about Mary-Jane. Her attitude before he had left the camp seemed unfair. He had needed her understanding and wanted her to reinforce his self-worth, but instead she had rejected him. With a surge of excitement, he recollected the embrace they had shared when they had fled from the wolves, the memory conjuring the delicious sensation of her touch.

He fantasized about her submitting to him, satisfying his lustful desires, and dutifully fulfilling her role as his wife. She was a beautiful young woman and he would be proud to have her on his arm. Men would be envious of his good fortune, and he would display his trophy with conceited gratification. There was every reason why she should submit to him too, since he had saved her life. He owned her, and he would ensure that she did his bidding.

Daydreaming, his eyes faintly registered a dark patch on the ground as he passed, and the raw stench of fresh cow dung penetrated his hedonistic thoughts. He hauled on his reins and peered down at the splatter of feces, startled by the unexpected sign of cattle. Tracks emerged from a small ravine to his left, the grass knocked flat and grazed clumsily where the animals had passed, but further along the trail he could see intermittent piles of dung and trampled areas where the cattle had stood ruminating or laid in the sun.

His thoughts raced. If he could round up some cattle and drive them back to camp on his own, perhaps he could redeem some of the prestige he had lost. His stomach fluttered at the prospect and he pushed his horse on, hoping to catch up with the stray cows, concluding that they could not be far ahead.

After a further half hour, he became despondent. The cattle continued to elude him, although the smell of their droppings still saturated the air. He paused, considering whether to continue or turn back, unsure how much daylight remained. The sun had passed its zenith, and since it was clearly early afternoon, he concluded that he would have to return shortly.

The footfall of hooves roused him from his thought, and he strained to determine the source of the sound, which emanated from the right, some distance away. It sounded like several animals and he felt an urge to rush forward and round up the cattle, but caution restrained him from haste, mindful that he might cause the animals to bolt, so he dismounted and led his horse slowly along the trail, remaining concealed among the tall grass.

Four hundred paces away the ground rose, a path leading up the slope and over the crest of a bluff, and he was considering whether the cattle might be following the trail when he detected movement, the rhythmic bobbing of a group of heads emerging from the long grass at the foot of the slope. Watching with bated breath, he was astonished to be greeted by the spectacle of a small group of Indians. There were four Pawnee riding in single file. Three looked to be men, bare-chested and sporting brightly colored Mohicans, their hair shaved to the scalp on either side. An Indian girl trailed along behind them, leading two further ponies, burdened with large bundles.

Johannes was entranced, mostly from fear, but partly out of curiosity. He had seen many Indians along the trail, trading their furs and crops, and most had displayed signs of their interaction with white people, wearing conventional European clothing, but these were the first Indians that he had seen who appeared untouched by civilization. The stories of the natives' savagery that he had heard around campfires and the streets of St. Joseph swirled through his head, and he instinctively ducked down into the grass, concerned that his horse might whinny and give away his presence. But the Indians continued up the trail and passed out of sight over the horizon.

Cautious, he waited to ensure that the Pawnee did not re-appear before creeping further along the track, leaving his horse tethered to a stout bush so that he was able to weave silently through the long grass without the risk of his mount scuffing a stone or making some other unwanted noise.

After a hundred paces, the buffalo grass started to thin, revealing the perimeter of a broad flat glade, and Johannes stepped gingerly toward the fringe of the clearing, careful to remain concealed. His heart pounding, he drew up sharply at the sound of movement a few paces to his right, stiffening as a flicker of tan-colored clothing passed on the far side of a thick stand of grass and holding his breath as a slim figure materialized.

The shapely form of a young girl emerged, her back turned to him as she moved slowly to the left. She hummed quietly, a rhythmic ululation, and her hips swayed gently as she immersed herself in her musical serenity. Her hair was long and dark, hanging in a single plait that stretched almost to her waist, and her limbs were long and slender, their soft brown tone exuding health. She bent to place an object on the ground and Johannes gasped, mesmerized by the alluring swell of her buttocks as they pressed against her buckskin skirt.

The involuntary exclamation alerted the girl to his presence and she whirled around to face him. Her dark eyes were wide with alarm and Johannes saw that she was young, about his own age. Her lips parted as if she might scream, but she stood motionless, staring back at him as though struck rigid. Johannes was captivated by her raw beauty and equally unable to speak. His eyes searched her face, taking in her delicate features, until the discomfort of his gaze prompted her to stumble backward.

Alarmed by her sudden movement, he ran forward instinctively, stretching out his arms and imploring her not to run. "No, don't go. Don't be frightened," he blurted in German, but the girl was clearly terrified and staggered away even faster.

"No! No! Don't go, please," Johannes implored, hurrying after her.

His pursuit only reinforced the girl's fear and she turned to flee at the same time as Johannes reached out and grasped her shoulder, his attempt at restraint causing her to weave and duck as she tried to escape his clutch. Insistent, Johannes threw himself at her, attempting to prevent her flight, and she bucked like a wild animal, rolling her shoulders and flailing her arms to rid herself of his grip. Her tunic tore away, revealing her shoulder and the smooth contours of her back.

Johannes caught the fragrant smell of her scent and a thrill of excitement rushed through his loins. He wrapped both arms around her torso, throwing his weight onto her so that they both crashed to the ground, where she twisted and writhed, turning onto her back and inadvertently exposing the soft curve of her breast, its dark nipple brushing against Johannes's chest.

Whilst they wrestled she made virtually no sound, but as Johannes gloated at her naked body she let out a long high-pitched wail. Panicking, he slapped his hand over her mouth and her eyes flashed wide with fear.

With lightning speed, she picked up a stone and swung it with brutal force at Johannes's head. He saw the blow coming and managed to duck at the last moment, causing the rock to hit him with a glancing blow. A searing pain shot down his neck and a wave of dizziness numbed his senses. Impulsively he lashed out with his fist and abruptly the girl fell silent, her body inert.

Dazed but still sentient, Johannes realized that he had reached a fever pitch of arousal. His penis strained in his breeches, and his mouth was dry with sexual anticipation. He gawped at the girl, who seemed to sleep peacefully, and his hand moved to caress her bare breast. His breathing came in short rasping breaths and, kneeling back on his haunches, he noticed that her skirt had ridden up, the smooth tanned skin of her upper thighs beckoning toward her pubis.

As if in a dream, he fumbled to undo his breeches and release his impatient manhood, before hitching her skirt higher and forcing himself into her. Eyes pressed tightly shut, he thrust wildly, until with a sudden relief he burst into her and cried out.

"Oh, Mary-Jane, I love you!"

Johannes collapsed onto the girl and lay panting, until she slowly began to stir. Her eyes flicked open and she stared at him, uncomprehending. Horrified, her hands flew up to push him away, her head flicking from side to side desperately. Her legs flailed and, as her attempt to escape built to a frenzied panic, she let out a blood-curdling shriek.

Shocked, Johannes fought to smother the ear-splitting screech, terrified that the warriors would come racing to her aid. His attempt unsuccessful, she continued to twist and writh as if possessed, her scream unabated.

"No! Stop! Be quiet!" he implored urgently. "Don't scream! Please! It's all right!" But his plaintive pleading had no effect and his effort to silence her became more frantic. An initial fear turned to anger. She was rejecting him too. He had made love to her. He cared for her, and she was spurning their intimacy. He rolled to and fro, trying to pin her to the ground and silence her, when her knee drove hard into his groin. He jerked forward, gasping in pain, and his grandfather's knife fell out of his shirt onto her belly.

Instinctively, Johannes lunged for the knife, drew the blade, and thrust it into the girl's chest in one fluid movement. Her breath erupted in an explosive burst, her eyes transfixed upon the hilt of the blade, and in a final attempt to cast off her assailant, she bucked and thrashed with all her remaining strength, screaming a high-pitched wail of terror.

Her response stunned Johannes, provoking him to thrust the knife repeatedly into her chest in a manic delirium, until she fell silent, her body lifeless and her eyes still.

Johannes sat up, panting from the exertion of the fight, and gaped in revulsion at the gory corpse. Blood welled from puncture wounds to the girl's chest, and the contorted angle of her arms and legs made her look like a macabre mannequin. For the first time, he looked about the clearing and saw the carcass of a cow the Indians had been butchering, its skin laid out alongside the bones, which were stripped bare of meat.

Why the girl had been left on her own was a mystery, but Johannes surmised that she might have been required to remain with the kill to deter the unwelcome attention of coyotes, while the other Indians transported the meat back to their village. If so, the warriors would surely return sooner or later, placing him in extreme danger.

He had to get away, but he could not leave the dead girl where she lay. He had to try to conceal her corpse, if only to buy himself more time to escape when the Indians returned. Lifting her easily, he retraced his footsteps along the trail to where he had left his horse. There, he found a shallow gully concealed by high stands of buffalo grass in which to place her body.

Lowering her gently, Johannes bent to stroke her hair, feeling a rush of affection. She was beautiful, young, and nubile, and he wanted to cherish her memory; to retain something to remind him of the intimacy they had shared. Carefully, he selected a lock of her lustrous black hair and cut it off with the sharp curved blade of his grandfather's knife, curling it into a neat swirl and placing it into the pocket of his breeches.

Afterward, he scouted the area for brushwood, which he placed over her body before returning to the glade to try and extinguish the most obvious sign of the brutal assault. Gathering handfuls of the dusty soil, he scattered it over two areas where the girl's blood had splattered the ground and used a fan of sage to obscure his tracks, both in the clearing and along the trail toward his horse.

Content that he had concealed the girl to the best of his ability, Johannes mounted his horse and pushed it into a fast jog, tracing back along the track and turning to the northeast, following the trail the cattle had taken rather than retracing the route by which he had entered the canyon.

Soon, he was swamped by tall grass, screening him from potential observation, but although he felt safer he continued to urge his old horse along. The canyon was narrow, its steep sides lined with pillars of craggy sandstone that reflected the afternoon sun, and within half an hour he was pouring with sweat. Unable to sustain the pace, he slowed, allowing himself and the horse to cool down, when to his astonishment he ran straight into a group of five longhorn cattle, all ruminating contentedly as they chewed on the lush grass.

Johannes could not believe his luck. He had been concerned that he might be asked to account for his long absence from camp, imagining that he might be subjected to an inquisition about where he had been and what he had done. But finding the cattle provided the perfect explanation, and he concluded that rounding up the beasts might even garner some acclaim.

Relieved, Johannes took off his hat and slapped it gently against his leg, weaving his horse back and forth and clicking his tongue to encourage the cows to move off. To his delight, the cattle responded compliantly so that in no time he had them moving steadily along the trail.

Chapter 18

West of the confluence of the north and south forks of the Platte River
O'Halloran and the cavalry trooper, who was fast becoming his new best friend, meandered with little purpose among the low-lying hills, far more interested in sharing their lascivious stories than tracking down stray cattle.

They stopped to shelter from the intensity of the midday sun and O'Halloran produced a bottle of whiskey from his saddle-bags, which the two men drank heartily, their joviality increasing in like measure. In due course, they remounted and rode southwest, traveling further from the wagon train. They wandered aimlessly, finding no sign of cattle, and drifted miles off course as they continued to drain the whiskey, with the alcohol dulling their commitment to the search.

As afternoon faded into early evening, they should have turned back, but the combination of whiskey, lack of food and water, and the intense heat of the day rendered them both hopelessly drunk. Eventually, they pulled to a halt in a shallow canyon carpeted with course scrubby grass and slid from their horses, slumping beside a bubbling spring that spouted from a cleft in the rocks.

O'Halloran took a long draught of the refreshing water and ambled back toward his horse, wiping the drips off his chin with the back of his hand and leaving the trooper to gulp down his own rehydration. Stumbling away from the spring, O'Halloran spotted a large white-tailed jackrabbit as it popped out from the cover of a sage bush. Immediately, he reached for his Colt, and with a casual flourish fired a shot at the animal. Miraculously, the bullet hit its mark, striking the rabbit in the hind quarters so that it squealed with pain and writhed on the ground, attempting to drag itself along with its front legs.

"Whoa, soldier boy!" O'Halloran drawled at the trooper, lurching unsteadily and pointing at the rabbit. "Yer see that! Got it wi' ma first shot!" He waved his pistol at the helpless jackrabbit and fired again, his aim adrift by several feet on this occasion.

"Ha! You got ush dinner." The trooper slurred. "Gonna cook that son a bitch!" he cackled, staggering after O'Halloran, so that both men bumped into one another and reeled off in pursuit of the rabbit.

"I'm gonna git it!" the trooper whooped, his arms outstretched purposefully.

"Not if ah git it first!" O'Halloran hooted, jostling the other man's shoulder.

Once close enough, they both dived simultaneously, landing in a heap on the jackrabbit and causing it to squeal with terror until O'Halloran clumsily snapped its neck. Delighted, the cowhand pushed himself to his feet, leaving the trooper rolling on his back like an upturned beetle, and lifted his prize so that he could admire his handiwork. The animal was over two feet long with huge chestnut and white ears, a dark gray-brown body, and a pale gray underside. It would make a hearty meal.

The prospect of grilled jackrabbit galvanized the men to work, so despatching the trooper to gather firewood, O'Halloran set about skinning and gutting their catch using a hunting knife he carried on his belt. In a short time they had a good fire going with the rabbit cooking on a makeshift spit.

O'Halloran went to his horse and returned chortling happily as he brandished a fresh bottle of whiskey, after which the two men settled companionably to tuck into their meal, washing it down with the heady liquor before lying back and falling asleep.

Colter accepted the request to participate in the roundup as a means of escaping the claustrophobic confines of the wagon train, and because he was granted the return of his pistol, but he had no intention of doing cowhands' work. Instead, he took himself off along the river, following its meandering course until he caught sight of the Pawnee camp, its cluster of circular Mandans nestled high on the bank.

He smelled fire smoke long before he saw the village and was careful to remain concealed, but he stood and watched with interest. Women were busy slicing and smoking meat from the cattle that they had killed, and small groups of warriors came and went from the village intermittently, provoking a flurry of excitement among the children each time they deposited their spoils.

Skins were either strung up to dry on a framework of wooden poles or were scraped to remove the hair, a job performed by a group of older women seated around a central fire. The unexpected windfall of fresh meat was clearly providing a welcome chance to replenish food stocks following a harsh winter, and the village was making the most of the opportunity.

He smiled grimly at the thought of the Indians profiting from the settlers' misfortune, and when he had satisfied his curiosity he meandered further into the hills for several hours before returning north, keeping to the ridges to afford himself the best view of the surrounding land. After an hour of slow riding, he spotted movement at the mouth of a valley close to the river and observed a young man mounted on a weary-looking horse as he emerged from the canyon driving five longhorn cattle. Colter had no wish for company, so he stopped and watched the lad ride directly to the river, dismount, and remove his clothing as the cattle watered themselves.

The youngster appeared agitated, scrutinizing his shirt and breeches, washing them vigorously before setting the clothes out to examine them with care. Apparently dissatisfied, he washed them a second time, eventually laying the garments on the bank to dry while he rinsed another object in the river. Colter could not see the article he was attempting to clean, but the boy tucked it inside his shirt when he replaced his clothing and made a point of ensuring that it was secure.

As the lad turned from the river, Colter recognized him as Hans's son. He had seen the boy at the prospectors' wagon on several occasions, usually sent by his mother, bearing a plaintive request that the big Ukrainian return to his schooner.

Johannes followed the river northeast, rehearsing the account he would tell of his afternoon tracking the cattle. The Indian girl's death seemed like an illusory event, and he found that he was able to put the memory to the back of his mind, as though irrelevant.

Within the hour, he spied the outline of the wagon circles on the horizon, plumes of smoke rising in lazy spirals from the campfires and groups of children running around energetically playing games with a hoop and stick. He sat tall in his saddle, making an exhibition of driving the longhorn, whistling and weaving his horse to encourage the cattle along.

The main herd was being reassembled to the west of the wagons, a contingent of cowhands standing like sentries to prevent the animals from dispersing again, and as he approached, a horseman came up from his station to intercept him, Johannes recognizing the cavalryman as one of the young lieutenants.

Hanley smiled broadly as he loped toward Johannes. "Good work. Looks lahke you done real well theyre," he called over.

"Where d'yer find 'em?"

"I was thinking I was not having luck, zen on de vey back in camp I am find ze trail. It is head to de river, zo I follow and der is dees cowz. Dey is happy as ever can be!" Johannes hurriedly recounted his rehearsed story.

"That's real good. Let's get 'em pushed in wi' th'others. You look lahke you could do wi' some decent chow." Hanley fell in alongside Johannes, who took the opportunity to develop his alibi.

"O'Halloran and dee Quaker man, I sink he is name Edvard May. Dey is check ze walleys to ze souse-vest." Mischievously, Johannes was prompted to imply that the Quaker had been in the area where the Indian girl had been killed. "My horse it is old and is not keep up, zo I decide is best to make back to camp. But, on vay, I see many cattle shits vich is make to ze river, zo I sink to look dere. It take me many time to get cows and bring zem back."

"Good job ya didn' ha' run in'a any Injuns. They been watching us ahll day, an' seems they gone an' killed a good few cattle. Yer shouldn' really ha' been out theyre on ya own."

The mention of Indians rattled Johannes and he was unsure how to respond. "Indians? Ver is Indians?" he stuttered.

"Oh, they bin sittin' up top of them hills roun'bout. Jus' watchin' ah reckon."

Johannes was relieved. For a moment, he had a vision of the massed tribe of Pawnee sweeping down upon the wagon train in retribution for the murder of the girl he had killed.

"Yer got a gun?" Hanley enquired.

Johannes did not hear Hanley at first, his mind conjuring images of the Mohican-headed braves thundering across the plains on their ponies, showering the wagons with deadly arrows.

Hanley tried again. "Yer don't seem to ha' a gun?"

This time the question shook Johannes from his reverie. "Oh, zorry. No. My fazzer is not let me have gun."

"How old're you?"

"Sixteen," Johannes replied, straightening his back.

"Well, ah reckon at sixteen a mayn should know how to use a gun out here. Ah'll speak to yo' daddy if ya lahke. Tell him ah'll teach yer how to use a gun, and how to look after it rahit. Yer lahke thait?"

Johannes broke into a broad grin. "Ya. Pliz! Zat vould be much good."

Hanley laughed. "Okay. That's wha' we gonna do!"

Once they reached the rest of the herd Johannes handed over his cattle and took his leave.

Colter watched the boy turn away from the cavalry officer. He was intrigued. And, intent upon satisfying his curiosity, he loped toward the Kopps' wagon, arriving slightly ahead of Johannes.

Elena offered him a mug of coffee when he told her that he was looking for Hans, which he accepted, plonking himself down so that he was concealed from view and could observe Johannes surruptitiously climb into the back of the schooner upon his return. The boy fumbled in a pile of clothing, glancing furtively around to check that he had not been seen. Assuming that he had not been observed, Johannes clambered down, straightened his shirt self-consciously, and walked around to the front of the wagon, where his mother leapt to her feet and berated him.

"Where have you been? You've been gone all day!" she complained, addressing him in German. "You shouldn't leave me alone all day. There are chores to do. I can't do them all myself. You're as bad as your father, selfish. No thought for what needs to be done." She protested with a petulant toss of the head.

Johannes ignored his mother, who stomped off belligerently,

and eyed Colter warily, nodding an acknowledgment.

Colter fixed him with an uncompromising eye, sipping at the coffee Elena had provided. "You had a busy day, son?" he narrowed his eyes, searching Johannes's face.

"Ya," Johannes responded, nodding his head and busying himself with the fire in an effort to avoid conversation with the mountain man.

"That you I seen comin' in from the river wi' five o' them longhorns?"

Johannes's vanity was piqued by the recognition that he had rounded up the cattle on his own. "Ya, is me," he bristled with pride. "Dey is velly difficult to find."

"Where d'ya catch 'em?" Colter retorted as Johannes recoiled from his implacable gaze, the big man's beard concealing any form of facial expression, his eyes cold and threatening.

"Oh, I find in small walley. Is near de river."

Colter peered into his coffee cup. "Looks like you gotten yersel' wet," he mentioned casually.

Johannes's head snapped up in alarm. "Vhat? Vhat is you mean vet?" his hands moved instinctively to feel his shirt, confirming Colter's suspicion that he had been up to no good.

He gave Johannes a penetrating stare. "Oh, I reckon its nothin'. Jus' looks like yer shirt took a soakin'." He held Johannes's startled gaze as the boy wrestled to think of a response.

At that moment, Elena reappeared, unaware of the awkward exchange, and instructed her son to go and find Carla so that they could all prepare their evening meal. Johannes did not need a second invitation to absent himself from Colter's company and responded with alacrity. As he turned to leave, Colter stood and addressed him purposefully.

"Guess I'm gonna have to keep ma eye on you. Out in Injun country on yer own, an' brought in five cattle. Seems like there's more t' you than meets th'eye?"

A chill ran down Johannes's spine, and he nodded hurriedly to Colter before dashing off, leaving the mountain man to return his empty cup to Elena.

"Fine boy," Colter ventured. "Thanks for the coffee. Be sure an' tell yer husban' I was lookin' for 'im." He touched the brim of his hat and stepped over the wagon tongue, leaving Elena to attend to the cooking pot.

Taking a casual glance around to confirm that he was not being watched, Colter lifted the schooner's canopy adjacent to the position that Johannes had stashed the mysterious object he had been carrying. Inside there was a jumbled pile of clothing and it took a few moments before Colter located the hidden knife, which he pulled clear so that he could study the ornate scabbard and bone handle, inset with distinctive red and green gems. But the knife's most impressive aspect was its long, thin blade, an inch across at the hilt and curved to a point as sharp as a porcupine quill, its edge honed like a razor. It was lethal. A weapon to be used with considerable care.

Colter slid the blade back into its sheath and buried the knife under the clothes once more. *That boy's been up to no good,* he thought, slipping away stealthily.

Chapter 19

May 1865, the Executive Mansion, Washington, District of Columbia

"Mark my words, there'll be nearly five hundred thousand new citizens land on the shores of our great country this year, Mr. President, and half of those fine people will be set on traveling to the west. The architects of our agricultural growth. We have a responsibility, sir. We must protect those people. They are disciples of our ideal. They will transform the wilderness of the Great Plains. They will cement the continuity and integration of our continent, from the east coast to the western seaboard. They are the means through which Manifest Destiny will become a reality. Certainly, we will have railroads and commerce, but we also need towns and cities; civilization where before there was none. It is our responsibility to ease their endeavor. Safety, security, access to land. Realization of our goal depends upon these factors." Winthrop's tone was earnest and insistent.

"Abraham Lincoln passed the Homestead Aict in '62, so thait the laind in the weyst could be allocated to saittlers on generous terms, so the principles of availability of laind aren't an issue," the President responded in his southern drawl. "Ah shaire your ambition for Manifest Destiny, Theodore, really ah do, but ah haive to face realities. Ain't been but a month since we've come to the aind of a bloody civil war, thank the Lord. Our military and our finances are depleted. We simply don't haive the means to go to war with the Indian nations to protect a few would-be farmers. We haive to think about what's best for the whole country at this taime."

The two men sat informally, lounged in high-backed studded leather chairs, illuminated by the flickering light of the fire in an anteroom to the President's office in the Executive Mansion. They knew one another well. Winthrop had been one of the first to congratulate Andrew Johnson on his succession to presidency, following the deplorable shooting of Lincoln a month beforehand.

The President had been governor of Tennessee before becoming Lincoln's running mate for his candidacy for a second term in office, and for many years Winthrop had cultivated his relationship with Johnson because of the man's influence in the southern states, where a substantial portion of the senator's wealth was accumulated.

Winthrop had identified the commercial opportunity presented by a mass migration of settlers. He was familiar with many parts of the west, including the Rocky Mountain region, having been a director and significant shareholder in the Hudson Bay Fur Trading Company, and understood the challenges associated with organizing logistics into such an inhospitable and inaccessible part of the continent.

As the decline of the fur trade became inevitable, driven by depletion of beaver stocks and changes in European fashion, he had diversified his interests. Utilizing contacts introduced by Johnson, he founded a steamer business at the mouth of the Mississippi, which transported freight up river to frontier trading posts on the Missouri that served both the settlers and the military outposts. He considered the southerners' passion for sustaining slavery to be abhorrent, but their business ethics were malleable, and he was able to acquire the facilities and consents he required in return for a promise of influence in the capital.

Business had been brisk. In a matter of a few years, Winthrop's company had established a near monopoly in the shipping of supplies along the busy waterway. Many of the trading posts were desperate for continuity of supply, and Winthrop's agents undertook to ensure that they were properly stocked in return for a sizable share in the profits of their enterprises.

Inevitably, some irate traders attempted to resist Winthrop's domination, cutting him out and making their own supply arrangements. However, they inevitably found that their merchandise failed to arrive, the third-party steamers often encountering unexplained incidents, mechanical failures, or even sinking.

Winthrop was prepared for the inevitable demise of those traders that defied his dominion, and when they eventually faced bankruptcy, the senator's land agent would acquire their store for virtually nothing, enabling him to reopen the business as a hundred-percent-owned enterprise.

His influence and wealth expanded exponentially and he soon realized that the west held little interest to many of the legislators, who were preoccupied with the secession and subsequent reintegration of the southern states. There was big money to be made, and little scrutiny over how it was done.

Partially as a cover for his interest, Winthrop became evangelical about the attainment of Manifest Destiny and the importance of the west in fulfilling that ambition. He actively canvassed the President to entrust him with greater authority for matters related to the west, finding that many in Congress were happy to abdicate the responsibility. In the meantime, senators and the House of Representatives became preoccupied with the more political issue of ratifying a new Civil Rights Act and debating the provisions of a controversial Fourteenth Amendment proposal, as well as running constitutional conventions and establishing new state legislatures in each of the southern states.

There were two major issues for Winthrop to resolve in order that he could assure the security of his burgeoning empire. The first was to profit from the progression of the railroads across the continent, which threatened to erode the revenues of his steamers as they started to move freight out west from the east coast.

The second was the Indians. Profit growth was a product of the volume of settlers and the frenetic fever created by the discovery of gold and other precious metals. The initial treaties agreed with the Great Plains tribes were hopelessly inadequate in Winthrop's opinion, presenting unacceptable restrictions upon the occupation of the land and the ability to traverse it freely. And it seemed unlikely that the treaties could be renegotiated to his satisfaction, many of the tribes being divided about whether the original treaties should have been signed in the first instance.

"My concern isn't about the availability of land for settlers, Mr. President," Winthrop lied with implied indifference. "My concern is for the safety and security of the people. The incidence of contravention of our treaties is almost daily. Emigrants are being slaughtered in their homes, and their livestock stolen in droves. We need to take more draconian steps to enforce the treaties effectively, otherwise they become meaningless. And, on a practical level, the source of gold for the Federal Reserve is almost entirely dependent upon the west. California, Colorado, and now Virginia City. We need safe and unfettered ability to traverse the Great Plains, for the prospectors as much as for the transport of gold. The time has come for robust measures to be enforced. Our Indian policy should be positioned in a more federal context. The Great Plains are a part of this continent, an entire continent now administered from and by Washington. For this reason, there is an overriding imperative to ensure the right of passage across our nation, the right to build and use roads and railroads, a freedom of movement enshrined in our constitution. But, instead, people are attacked, their property stolen, and their lives taken. If the Indians aren't going to comply willingly with the spirit of our treaties, then, with the Lord's grace, we shall have to enforce them, if necessary relocating entire tribes. The Indian Appropriations Act enables us to apportion discrete sections of land to the Indian nations in areas where they won't come into conflict with settlers."

"Hmm. Ah appreciate the subtle nuances of repositioning the politics, Theodore, but thaire simply is not enough of ain imperative at thiys moment for us to allocate further resources, aind that's ma final word. Perhaps if you discuss the matter with General Grant, he maight be able to provide you with a little more hailp." The President put his brandy balloon down and took a long drag on his cigar.

"There'll be a massacre at some point if we don't act decisively against these incursions," Winthrop ventured. "You've entrusted me with responsibility for matters pertaining to the west, and I simply wish to avoid the distraction of an atrocity committed by the Indian Nations detracting from your presidency, Andrew. Anti-Indian sentiment is high, and it wouldn't take much to fan the flames of discontent in Congress. As you say, our energy should be focused upon reintegration of the south."

The President looked thoughtful. He knew Winthrop was presenting him with a veiled threat, and had used his first name to infer that the comment had been made with his personal interest at heart, but there was some substance to his assertions.

Johnson's authority with Congress was marginal. He was obliged to navigate a precarious course through the process of reintegration of the southern states, ensuring that he retained the personal support of their leadership but also placating the staunch republicans in the north, who were determined to prevent former rebel leaders returning to positions of influence and authority. A crisis in the west would only hand republicans ammunition to challenge his competence, further undermining his ability to achieve compromise.

Winthrop relished the President's discomfort and decided to advance his second priority. "I appreciate that you'll want to give the matter some thought, Mr. President, but while you consider the options, perhaps I could mention another matter. The president of the Northern Pacific Railroad, Henry Stevens, has approached me. A hard-working and earnest man. As you know, his company is forging ahead with construction of the new railroad from Minnesota, a railroad that will provide a continuous connection between our east coast cities and the west, Oregon and Washington Territory. But alas, they are running out of resources to fund construction, and I fear there is a real prospect that the company might fall into bankruptcy.

"Mr. Stevens came to me, Mr. President, since the company's operational base is in Minneapolis, and because I am his representative in the Senate. I have taken a considered view of the finances of his company, and I have to concur with his assessment. The Northern Pacific will fail before it reaches even halfway across the Great Plains.

"As you know, Mr. President, this railroad is fundamental to the establishment of our transcontinental commerce, and I think you'll agree that it would be a source of deep embarrassment if the company were to collapse.

"The Pacific Railroad Act was conceived to address financing of the continental railroads, but the Act is not explicit about the Northern Pacific's qualification for funding. Financial instruments were specific to the Union Pacific and the Southern Pacific. But I believe that the principles are identical, and the omission is simply the consequence of the limited scope of construction envisaged at that point in time.

"If you are in agreement, Congress would have to approve a minor amendment permitting the Northern Pacific to benefit from the provisions of the Act. I see it as an administrative matter rather than agreement of a new policy position.

"I've told Stevens that he'll need to agree to free transport for the mail service and for our military forces, and that his company will be bound by the terms of the Act with respect to repayment of government bonds and the associated interest. Speed is now of the essence if we are to safeguard the liquidity of the company, and it will be important for Congress to give consideration to the matter timeously." Winthrop reached into the pocket of his jacket and placed a document on the table to the side of the President. "I've taken the liberty of drawing up a draft Amendment to the Bill for your consideration. It would be of great assistance if you could afford the time to look at the proposal, and perhaps lend it your support."

Johnson was grateful to be diverted from the dilemma of Indian policy, the task of building railroads to fuel the growth of commerce being far more appealing. "Ah'd heard the Northern Pacific maight be strugglin', aind ah agree thait we need to ensure they remain solvent. Leyt me haive a look at yo' Amendment tomorrow, aind ah'll test the water for support. Ah imagine the proposal shouldn't meet with resistance, siynce completion of another transcontinental link cain only send a strong political message."

He paused to gather his thoughts. "On the subject of yo' Indians, ah'll reconsider yo' suggestion if there's ainy significant increase in aggression. In the meantime, ah'll haive General Grant provaide me with an update of our military strength in the region." With that, he rose and looked meaningfully at the clock on the mantelpiece, which indicated that it was nearly midnight. "Taime for some shut-eye, ah thaink. Good to see you, Theodore, as always."

Winthrop shook hands and took his leave.

The following morning the senator sat in his study, reflecting upon his interest in Virginia City. He was energized by a thrill of anticipation at his audacious plans. He would have to craft the circumstances to suit his intentions, and there were many variables to consider, but friction between the military and native Indians in the Great Plains might well play into his hands.

The gold rush town was awash with prospectors, the forecast gold reserves predicted to be enormous, and the frontier town was lawless, beyond the scrutiny of any meaningful legal jurisdiction, both factors that conspired to his advantage.

Of particular significance, the Federal Reserve would covet the output from the gold seams at Alder Gulch, requiring that it be transported to the federal mint for production of currency. Consequently, it had been necessary to build facilities in Virginia City where the gold traded by prospectors could be accumulated and safely stored in readiness for shipping.

Winthrop had recommended a man to oversee the development of such a facility. A Minnesotan banker of good repute, whose bank carried a national charter, enabling its subsidiary branch in Virginia City to offer the assurance of financial security for prospectors depositing their funds. The components of his plan were falling into place. Now, he had to orchestrate an important sleight of hand.

He summoned Stone and turned his mind to drafting a series of telegraphs, while awaiting the arrival of his emissary. First, he sent an update and a set of instructions to the banker in Virginia City, following which he crafted a message to General Murray in Kansas.

"William. Believe AJ will give support if we follow through. GG to be asked for status. Sending Mr. Stone to assist. Must act with speed and precision. TW."

Tobias Stone responded to the senator's message immediately, appearing in his study within half an hour. He wore his habitual blank expression, accentuated by the drooping moustache that concealed his mouth, but his eyes were alive with interest. Winthrop closed the door and invited Stone to pull up a seat close to his desk, leaning forward so that they could converse in a conspiratorial tone.

"We are on the brink of historic events, Tobias. But we must be meticulous in the execution of our plan. I need you to take instructions to Murray in Kansas and to find Colter. I can't go myself. It would be inappropriate for me to be seen taking a direct interest in military affairs. You'll have to be forceful with Murray, though. He'll try to brush you off with his supercilious attitude, so I anticipate that you'll be obliged to demonstrate the importance I attach to the actions I require of him. If he elects to disregard my request, you must remind him of the obligation he owes me and impress upon him the fragility of his privileged rank and respectability."

Stone flashed a lop-sided smile. "I've dealt with Murray's type, sir. Don't worry, I know how to get his attention."

Winthrop studied the man opposite him with a paternalistic gaze. "Yes, I believe you do, Tobias," he nodded, satisfied. "Now, here's what I want Murray to do."

Winthrop spent the next hour briefing Stone on his detailed requirements, insisting that he repeat the instructions and rehearse the manner in which he proposed to convey the rationale. It was a prerequisite that all communications should be verbal. No trail of evidence was to be left that might lead back to the senator.

Stone was a master at conveying Winthrop's missives. His

memory for detail was exceptional and his loyalty unwavering, so the repetition of the instructions proved unnecessary, it being clear that Stone had meticulously committed to memory precisely what was required. There would be no mistakes.

Chapter 20

Sioux village, headwaters of the Greybull River

The impact of the shot was immense, the momentum of the projectile easily throwing Howahkan from his saddle. He had never experienced such overwhelming pain. Like a lightning strike, a searing heat radiated from his shoulder, stifling his breath and leaving him unable to utter a sound in response.

Time froze. He saw Takoda race to the edge of the cliff and watched his brother scream in horror, but he could hear no words and could shout none in return. Cast into the void, he fell. An endless drop, with the prospect of death seeming inevitable, until, with a jarring thud, he struck the ground and darkness swept over him.

The shadowy periphery of consciousness teased Howahkan's senses, like an early-morning dream, intertwining elements of reality with the invention of the subconscious. There was a ringing in his ears and a heavy numbness to his limbs. The hint of light, but no clarity of vision. A pervasive lethargy encouraged him to relax and sink into the comfortable embrace of sleep. It would be easy. No more effort. No more pain.

A jolt of agony stabbed through his shoulder, clearing his head and wrenching him back to reality. Of course, he had been thrown from his horse. No, shot. He must have been shot. But he felt crushed. Trapped. The feeling made no sense.

Panicking, Howahkan arched his back and lunged with his legs until one foot burst clear of the oppressive weight and he realized with a sense of terror that he was buried. The blankness of his vision was not an illusion, but the consequence of a slight percolation of light through the snow piled above his head. If he failed to unearth himself, he would suffocate.

He tried to spit and the glob of moisture dropped back onto his face, indicating that the surface of the snow was immediately above his head. He had to create an air hole, but pain coursed through his body in agonizing waves when he tried to move his left arm. Nevertheless, with urgent movements, he wriggled his right mitten until it touched his cheek, working his arm free and punching upwards with all the energy he could muster.

At first, the compacted snow resisted Howahkan's efforts, the power in each lunge being pitiful, but he persevered doggedly until eventually a space opened up above his head, and with a thrill of relief he felt his fist burst clear of the snow. Elated, he gulped at the fresh air fluttering against his face.

Extricating himself from the snow proved an onerous task, and the exertion drained him of energy, so while he recovered he sat and examined the source of the pain in his shoulder. Palpating the flesh below his collar bone, he found the entry and exit wounds left by the bullet that had hit him. Miraculously, the shot appeared to have missed the bone, and he could detect only minimal bleeding, so it appeared that no major blood vessels had been severed. The wound was painful, but he had been lucky.

Howahkan understood intimately the challenges of survival in the wilderness and knew very well that exposure would kill him in a matter of hours if he did not act promptly. The injury to his shoulder only served to compound his vulnerability, so he had to find shelter and warmth as fast as possible, but first he had to establish his location.

When falling, he had been fortunate to be thrown clear of a jagged fringe of rocks surmounting the sheer drop. Had he struck them he would undoubtedly have been killed, but instead he plummeted over a hundred and fifty feet. And, rather than striking firm ground, he had brushed the top of a precipitous four-hundred-foot field of snow, clinging like a huge blanket to the acute face of the mountain. The angle of the slope dissipated the force of his impact, slowing rather than arresting his fall and knocking him unconscious. However, he continued to plunge down the mountainside, drawing an avalanche of unstable snow in his wake until the slope began to level out, slowing his descent, so that he eventually rolled to a stop in a cloud of powder.

The huge fall had carried Howahkan nearly two-thirds of the way down the escarpment, leaving him only sixty feet above the narrow path the tribe had ascended to conduct his father's funeral. Above, the face of the mountain loomed in an almost vertical white cliff, impossible to scale, and he marveled at his providence in surviving the fall. He could not climb back to the ridge, and he would die of hypothermia if he remained where he was. His only option was to make his way down.

Peering at the sky, he gauged the time of day. It was mid-afternoon and the light would not last for long, but there was a hint of blue sky and the worst of the snow had passed. Gingerly, he eased himself as close as he dared to the edge of the ledge where he lay and surveyed the valley below. The crowns of the trees were shrouded in thick snow, but he could discern the twisting line of the river winding its way along the valley. His village was out of view beyond a shallow ridge, but his heart leapt at the sight of a thin trail of smoke that rose above the trees in a gentle spiral.

Immediately, Howahkan's hand touched a pouch he carried on his waistband. Removing his mittens, he pulled out a flint and reached to check that his hunting knife was still attached to his belt. He wondered whether he could attract the attention of someone from the village, but to do so he had to act before the light faded. And he needed some luck.

Howahkan scanned the mountain. Clumps of conifers clung precariously to the cliffs in several places, anchored tenaciously to their inhospitable surroundings, and he selected an accessible cluster of lodgepole that offered the potential to forage enough wood to make a fire. He set off cautiously toward the trees, cradling his injured arm and retreating from the perimeter of the snow field for fear of it collapsing and sending him tumbling to his death.

By the time he reached the sanctuary of the pine, he was exhausted. The pain in his shoulder had drained his strength, and the cold was beginning to seep into his bones. He longed to curl up and close his eyes, but knew that succumbing to the craving would spell disaster.

Mustering his determination, he scoured beneath the trees, searching for anything suitable to use as tinder and, remarkably, he found the solution. Not on the ground but tucked in among a tangle of low branches. It was a tiny nest, lined with a ball of dry furry material, woven into a cozy home for the young fledglings it had once housed.

Howahkan gathered a stack of dry wood and dead pine needles and unearthed a collection of slightly damp detritus, which when piled onto a reasonable fire would smolder, producing good smoke.

He cleared a small patch of snow in a sheltered position outside the lee of the trees, placed the little nest in the center, and set to work. Holding the flint with his right hand, he struck the back of the blade of his hunting knife, but the knife spun out of his left hand as a burning pain flared in his shoulder and he struggled not to scream. Gritting his teeth, he picked up the knife and continued the tortuous process. Occasionally, a spark fell onto the tinder and fizzled out, at other times it was blown by the wind, dissipating its heat before it settled.

His actions became more and more desperate as he beat the flint against the back of the blade, howling with pain and frustration until he slumped from fatigue, his eyes closed and his head hung low over the nest.

Howahkan's breath was shallow, exhaustion sapping his resolve. He wanted to cry, but such indulgence would dishonor the memory of his father. Disillusioned, he sniffed at a drip hanging from the end of his nose, and his eyes flicked open in surprise as he detected a faint smell of burning. In the center of the nest a pinprick orange glow emitted a tiny trail of smoke. Hastily, he cupped the nest in his hands and blew gently. Nothing happened. Then, suddenly, a spark leapt and a flicker of flame crackled into life. His heart fluttered with excitement and he blew again, coaxing the flame to take hold, until the fire caught and started to consume the nest.

Howahkan worked fast, feeding the flames with small twigs and dry pine needles, placing each piece meticulously so that he did not smother the fragile fire, but ensuring that he added sufficient fuel to sustain its heat.

In a short time, the flames burned brightly and a welcome heat began to seep into his body, penetrating the numbness in his fingers, which began to tingle with the revitalizing flow of blood. His spirits rose, and for the first time he began to believe that he might survive to return to his village.

Once confident that the fire was hot enough, Howahkan heaped on a mound of needles and branches, the damp material immediately producing a fog of billowing gray smoke. But, unfortunately, the smoke was far from ideal. Preferably, he wanted to create a denser black smoke, it being easier to detect against the backdrop of the mountain's wintery cloak, but he had no oily material to burn. Resigned to work with the materials available, he removed his thick outer coat and rubbed it in the snow to prevent it from catching alight before placing it over the smoldering fire. He let the smoke accumulate for a few moments and pulled the coat aside, releasing a thick cloud that rose gracefully into the sky.

He cursed as a gust of wind swept the smoke away and hurriedly placed the coat over the fire again, collecting more smoke to make a second signal. Ordinarily, he would have liked to release the signals in sets of three, signifying a call for help, but given his limited supply of fuel, his priority was to produce as many puffs of smoke as possible, while the light remained sufficient for them to be seen from the village.

Much of the smoke was thin and light, and even when Howahkan succeeded in releasing a good cloud of smoke, the wind contrived to render it almost imperceptible. Doggedly, he persevered until daylight faded, taking occasional breaks to don his coat and warm himself by the fire, despondent that he had been unable to detect any movement in the valley below.

As the fire faded to its final glowing embers, Howahkan resigned himself to the unenviable alternative of attempting to find a route down the perilously steep face of the mountain. Thus, with the moon rising he decided to get moving, knowing that remaining where he was foreshadowed certain death and that attempting the descent presented at least a chance of survival.

He had saved one piece of timber for this purpose, a bough that he had stripped of all but one of its smaller branches, the broken stub forming a hooked point at one end of the stout staff. His intention was to use the rudimentary tool to test the depth of the snow and to provide an anchor in the event that he started to slide by embedding the sharp hook into the snow.

The moon cast a blue-gray light over the mountains, their surface exuding the luster of polished gunmetal, reflecting the color of the night sky. The full moon afforded welcome light but prompted a hard crust to form over the day's snowfall, which crunched underfoot as Howahkan started to move. He was cold to the core, hunching his shoulders as he shivered uncontrollably and numb to the pain of his wound, but he trudged slowly west, crossing the face of the mountain to a position where he hoped that the descent would prove less precipitous.

Each step was a struggle, conditions underfoot being treacherously slippery, but eventually he traversed to a point where the indistinct line of the mountain path ran close below. Looking down, the only route to the trail appeared almost vertical, so he sat on the snow and anchored himself with his staff, resigned to sliding down the remaining pitch in the hope that the hook would provide an adequate means of arresting any potential fall.

For the first twenty feet, he regulated his progress with success, digging his feet into the snow to supplement his control, and his spirits buoyed as he felt a surge of confidence that he might accomplish the perilous descent. But his faith was misplaced. The snow gave way to ice, and the sharp point of the staff struggled to sustain its fragile hold. Progressively, the crag revealed bare rock, and Howahkan scrambled to find a secure hold, most of his weight suspended from his arms and his badly injured shoulder.

Without warning, his left foot slipped on a sheet of slick ice and his traction failed. Immediately, he spun sideways. His safety hook lost its purchase and he tumbled head first, bouncing away from the cliff face and dropping vertically toward the path below.

Instinctively, Howahkan stretched out his right hand to absorb the impact of the fall, and his arm penetrated the deep snow until it struck hard rock, the jarring blow snapping his wrist. The agony shot up his arm, melding with the pain in his shoulder, and his vision blurred as he was overcome by a wave of nausea.

A drift of snow cushioned the rest of Howahkan's body from further injury, but every muscle ached as he lay trying to recover his senses. He blinked, forcing his eyes open. He was on the path, and although it was desperately narrow, for the most part it appeared passable. With enormous effort he sat up and pushed himself to his knees. "Fight to the end," he told himself. "No honor in death without courage." The image of his father's face swam before his eyes, urging him to continue, and he struggled to his feet and took a step forward, his foot plunging into the knee-high snow. He progressed another step. One tortuous pace at a time.

Perception of his surroundings began to diminish, morphing into an impenetrable wall of white, his sense of direction defined by the sheer face of the mountain and the precarious edge of the path, delineated by ornate swirls of snow that rolled out deceptively over the void below, enticing him to step onto their fragile surface.

Howahkan's movements were mechanical. He began to count each pace, starting again every time he reached the tenth step. His eyes scanned the snow for the safest place to set his foot, but fatigue made the precaution superfluous, and he stumbled forward wherever his feet landed, lurching unsteadily from one side to the other.

Howahkan dreamt of his family. He remembered the comfort of his mother's tipi and the laughing of the little children in the village. His heart was happy. He loved his people, and he savored the peaceful consolation of their memory, a feeling that soothed his being like the warmth of the sun on a summer's day.

Something brushed his forehead and his eyelids fluttered

open. A face morphed into focus, gazing at him with concern. His mind swirled. Maybe it was the dream. But, as his vision cleared, the blurred but unmistakable features of his mother were revealed.

Makawee was relieved to see her son stir. His fever had raged for three days since the warriors had discovered him, half frozen at the bottom of a steep cliff, their search prompted by the sight of tendrils of smoke rising from the mountainside, spotted by one of the children in the village. The signals had created much excitement, the band being mystified by the presence of fire on the sheer face of the mountain, and the Itancan had dispatched a contingent of Akichitas to investigate.

It had required all of Makawee's medicinal skills to save her son's life. Howahkan had broken a leg and fractured a wrist, and the bullet wound in his shoulder was swollen with infection. Broken bones were easy to set and would heal in time, and the infection in his shoulder was potentially dangerous if not treated promptly, but it was hypothermia that posed the greatest risk to his survival.

Howahkan had been lucky that the bullet from the rifle shot had passed through the muscle of his upper shoulder instead of lodging in his flesh. The infection could have been worse, but Makawee was able to clean the wound and pack it with a poultice of curly dock and passion flower laced with echinacea, treatments that helped to cleanse and heal. She also succeeded in administering a small draught of an infusion of valerian root, which acted as a sedative and relieved some of his pain.

She leaned over so that Howahkan could see her face without having to move his head, and saw the flicker of recognition in his eyes. His fever had broken that evening, his temperature easing so that he no longer shivered and twitched, and she was encouraged that the worst of his struggle seemed to be passing.

"You are home, my son," she soothed. "You must rest."

Howahkan's face contorted as he tried to mouth a response, but no words passed his lips. He tried to move his arms, attempting to sit up, but he did not have the strength and the pain was too intense. Tortured by his urgency, he attempted to speak again.

"Oda . . . ko . . . a," but he was unable to form any meaningful sound.

Makawee's small gaunt-faced aunt, Chapawee, rose silently, leaving the tipi to inform the Itancan that Howahkan had regained consciousness. For two days, the band's leader had maintained vigil at his bedside, hoping that his grandson would awaken, but he had begun to fear that the boy would not recover. With a heavy heart, he had resumed his duty, to ensure the well-being of the rest of the band, and entrusted Makawee with her ministration.

By the time Chapawee reappeared with the Itancan, Makawee had changed the poultice on Howahkan's wound and bathed his body with warm water. He had managed to say Takoda's name a number of times and was looking more alert.

Makawee felt a twist of dread every time Howahkan uttered her younger son's name. The band had searched the foot of the mountain to no avail after they had found Howahkan, hoping to find his brother. Two warriors had even attempted to scale the lower slopes, assuming that Takoda might have become stranded higher up the cliffs, but the Itancan had been decisive in preventing others from risking their lives, given that there was no certainty he had been on the mountain anyway. The mystery of the boy's whereabouts, and the question of whether he was alive, were festering concerns that occupied the prayers of the whole band.

The Itancan sat down close beside the boy's mother and looked at her expectantly. "His heart is like a bear," she whispered quietly.

He studied the boy for a few moments. "You speak the truth. Has he said anything about Takoda?" he asked.

"He has mumbled his name, but no more."

Howahkan sensed the presence of another person alongside his mother and turned his head with great effort. The stoic face of his grandfather, with his dark thoughtful eyes, gazed back at him, and Howahkan felt a surge of deep respect for the strength of the old man, whose features softened as he acknowledged his grandson.

"Fa . . . fath . . . r g . . . grave. Gone. Bro . . . ken," he stammered. "White . . . man." His eyes closed and he slumped back, drained by the exertion.

"You've been to your father's grave?" the Itancan responded in astonishment, uncertain whether he had understood Howahkan's inference correctly.

The boy nodded in confirmation. "Gone," he repeated.

"Has the grave gone, or has your father's body gone?" the Itancan asked softly. If the grave had disappeared it was likely that someone had destroyed it, but if only the body had vanished he wondered whether some divine intervention had occurred.

"Grave . . . Bro . . . ken. Father . . . gone. White man," Howahkan stuttered, becoming more lucid with every word.

The Itancan sat in stunned silence. He had assumed that the boys had simply embarked upon a reckless ascent of the mountain, resulting in a near fatal fall, but the absence of their horses had perplexed him. Now, the semblance of an explanation began to materialize. It sounded as though the boys had gone to their father's grave, and since they could not possibly have scaled the cliffs, it seemed logical that they must have circumnavigated the mountain, which explained why the horses were nowhere to be found.

"What happened?" the Itancan demanded.

"Shot. Fell." Howahkan was overwhelmed by exhaustion at

the thought.

It was clear that his grandson had been shot, but if Howahkan was implying that he had fallen from the top of the mountain, his survival was truly remarkable. And, if the boy had been shot by a white man, the Itancan was concerned at what might have become of Takoda. Maybe he had been shot too, or perhaps he had been captured?

"Takoda? What happened to Takoda?" the Itancan leaned forward, unable to suppress the urgency of his question.

Howahkan shook his head. "Not . . . know." He whispered, the agony of the uncertainty of his brother's fate causing the words to choke in his throat.

Makawee and the Itancan exchanged a troubled glance. They had no idea whether Takoda was dead, but at least they now knew where to look for him. The Itancan studied his grandson carefully, nodding as if deriving confidence in his recovery, and satisfied that he had overcome the worst of his physical struggle. He turned to Makawee and assessed her pale features, so reminiscent of her grandmother's appearance. She was clearly exhausted, the emotional toll of recent events having drained her of vitality. First her husband's death, and now this trauma with her sons, was more than most people could bear.

She sat tending to Howahkan with her head cast down respectfully, aware that she was being scrutinized. She knew that, irrespective of her demeanor, there would be no criticism from the Itancan. She could break down and sob her heart out, and he would understand. His persona was not one to judge, but he would take careful note of her emotional and physical well-being and ensure that she received the support he deemed appropriate.

Chapawee sat opposite Makawee, silently mirroring her niece's comportment as they straightened the thick skins laid over Howahkan. The old woman was a good person and would keep a watchful eye over Makawee, sharing her pain and assisting with the boy's care until he recovered.

"I must speak to the elders now. The Akichitas will search for Takoda, but we must discuss how many warriors to send. There may be danger," the Itancan said softly. "I will return when we have decided."

Given the weather conditions, the elders concluded that only a small group of Akichitas was required to protect the village, and that their greatest concern should be to ensure that Takoda's search party was of sufficient strength to defend itself if confronted by an aggressive group of white men. Thus, on the second morning after Howahkan awoke from his fever, a party of thirty warriors rode out of the village.

The previous day had been occupied with preparations, packing supplies and weapons in case the task resulted in a sustained search or battle. The most senior of the Akichitas was selected to lead the party, a hawk-faced young man called Otaktay, whose name appropriately means "Kills Many." He chose the men he would take, including Mahpee, who was revered as the most accomplished tracker in the band.

Howahkan explained his memory of the route that he and Takoda had taken, and Otaktay was interested to determine whether they had detected signs of the presence of other people. He insisted that Howahkan recount the detail of what he and Takoda had found when they reached their father's dais, his principle concern being to avoid inadvertently leading thirty of the band's warriors into a trap.

Chapter 21

The trappers' cabin, north of the Greybull River

A crushing pain filled Takoda's head. He forced his eyes open, but his vision was blurred and even the dim light inside the cabin sent a stabbing pain to the back of his skull. His arms ached, and he found that they were tied behind his back, the knot so tight about his wrists that his hands pulsed with a dull throb. His left arm felt as though it was on fire, a searing pain radiating from the wound in his bicep.

He tried to move, but a wave of dizziness swept over him. Cast on his knees in the corner of the cabin, with the top of his head leaned against the outer wall, he was unable to even twist his body. He listened to the muffled sound of a hurried discussion between two men, although he had no idea what they were saying, but as he strained to hear their conversation, his memory of the desperate flight down the mountain began to return.

At first the recollection was piecemeal. The image of a man riding into the forest ahead of him. A sensation of jumping. Attacking a second man. A steely determination to kill. Then, with a flood of grief he remembered the shot that had hit Howahkan and the sight of his brother being thrown from the cliff. A wave of dread hit him like a war club as he realized that Howahkan was almost certainly dead. His eyes welled with tears, and nausea surged up his throat as he fought to contain his tortured emotions. Inadvertently, he groaned.

There was a pause in the muted conversation. "You hear

that?" McCabe enquired. He stared at the Indian crumpled in the corner, detecting small movements as Takoda wrestled with the edge of consciousness. "Well, what'ya know. Looks like he ain't dead after all."

La Brais gave Takoda a distasteful scowl. "Don't know why y' bothered. I say we should ha' finished 'im off afore. A Injun's only gonna bring us trouble."

"Might be the only thing keeps us 'live if there's more Injuns 'bout," McCabe retorted.

The two had quarrelled constantly since La Brais had recovered from Takoda's attack, the big trapper insisting that he should kill the Indian. But McCabe had argued that it was dangerous to kill the boy if more of his tribe were likely to be in the area, and he had succeeded in staying his partner's murderous hand.

From the moment McCabe had seen the Indians tracking up to the dais, he had been concerned that more would follow, the initial pair simply being an advance party. Now, having killed one of them and captured the other, the demons of his imagination were working overtime, and he had whined consistently about the risk of encountering more of the tribe.

"Ain't safe to stay here," McCabe insisted. "They won't let two o' their kind disappear wi'out doin' somin' 'bout it."

"You fuss like an ole woman," La Brais protested, but despite his objection he was beginning to think twice about McCabe's prediction.

"They gonna be from some tribe 'round here. Reckon the boy an' th'other Injun ain't on their own. They got reason to be here. That place, up on th'mountain. Some kind o' worship place is what it is. Reckon rest o' 'em's not far behin'. Maybe they was both boys. Gonna come lookin' for 'em if that's what they was. I tell yer, it ain't safe now."

"Let 'em come lookin'. Got a hankerin' to shoot me a few

more Injuns anyhow's." La Brais chuckled half-heartedly.

"You think you gonna shoot a whole damn tribe o' Injuns? Ain't gonna be safe in this cabin, no sir! Like as not, they gonna burn us out. You wanna die o' burnin'?" McCabe waved his arm around the cabin as if the roof might spontaneously combust.

"Well, what d'yer sugges'? We go out there, we're like as gonna freeze t' death."

"I say we take the Injun boy. If we see Injuns, we kin barter wi' 'em. We give 'em the boy if they let us go. We take jus' what we need an' high tail t' nearest fort fast as we can."

"You think Injuns gonna let us go if we give 'em the boy!" La Brais laughed contemptuously.

"Reckon s'our bes' chance. An' I guess they gonna want the boy 'live more 'n dead." McCabe retorted.

La Brais sat down at the table and chewed on a strip of dried elk meat. He had planned to rid himself of McCabe when winter broke and guessed that it was only a matter of days before he would have considered moving out anyway. Before the autumn trapping season, a man in a saloon in Fort Laramie had approached him to join up with a group of buffalo hunters. At the time, he had felt there was more profit to be gained from beaver pelts, but the pickings had been sparse and the option of hunting buffalo now seemed more appealing. His only reservation was that he did not really want to take McCabe with him.

But La Brais was inclined to agree with his partner. He was pretty certain that more Indians would come looking for the boy once his disappearance was noticed. He and McCabe had limited time remaining if they wanted to escape undetected, and if they left now there was a good chance that the continued snowfall would obscure their tracks.

He made up his mind. "S'pose there ain't nothin' left for us here. Ain't gonna be no more beavers now. Reckon we oughtta go southeast. Make for Laramie. Some folks ah might wanna see along the way."

McCabe was so relieved at his partner's sudden change of heart that he almost missed the inference, but the mention of 'seeing some folks' provoked a prickle of apprehension. It sounded as though La Brais's decision was motivated by something other than the risk of their current predicament.

"What folks?" he enquired curtly.

"Oh, maybe nothin'. Heard there's some folks prospectin' near the Bighorn Moun'ns. Could be a place to rest up an' git some hot chow. That's if we kin find 'em." La Brais was reluctant to divulge more detail.

"How come yer ain't said shit all 'bout 'em afore?" McCabe was suspicious.

"Didn't have no cause, did I?"

"You gonna say who these 'folks' are that yer didn' feel no need to mention?" McCabe sounded petulant.

La Brais's frustration simmered. He was determined not to tell McCabe any more than was necessary, since he was uncertain whether the job he had been offered would still be available, and was concerned that McCabe's presence might represent a liability. Despite his misgivings, he appreciated that he had to coerce his partner into compliance, rather than engage in a debate about their destination.

"There yer go agin. Behavin' like an ole woman. Always full o' questions. You wanna git goin' or not?" He pushed himself up from the table and started to fill his saddlebags.

McCabe studied the other man skeptically. La Brais was hiding something, but he knew better than to push the Canadian further, fearing the repercussions of his furious temper. There was no merit in provoking his ire at this stage. Vacating the cabin, and putting as many miles as possible between themselves and any Indian search party, was more important. Swallowing his indignation, he set about gathering his own belongings.

As McCabe turned toward his crib, the young Indian caught his eye. He remained slouched on his knees, but his eyes were open and he was staring at the bow and tomahawk leaning against the wall nearby. There was an unmistakable look of recognition on his face. The items were known to him, McCabe was certain, and a shudder ran down his spine as the Indian boy turned and glowered at him. His expression was one of absolute contempt, and McCabe had no doubt that, had he not been trussed, the Indian would have attempted to kill him.

Fear twisted in McCabe's gut, inciting him to swing a venomous kick at the boy's backside, which elicited a satisfying thud as his boot made contact. But, to his surprise, the Indian failed to react to the assault; instead, his eyes simply smouldered with even greater animosity. Not to be defeated by the defiance, McCabe spat at him and turned away to pack his bags.

Takoda had never felt such cold rage. Having seen the unmistakable bow and tomahawk, he now knew beyond doubt that these were the men who had destroyed his father's grave. They had killed his brother and desecrated his father's final resting place. The raw hatred he experienced was beyond description, and he vowed that he would kill them both for what they had done to his family.

For the balance of the day, the trappers sorted through their haul of beaver furs and decided which of their belongings they would retain, their mules only being capable of carrying a limited proportion of their possessions.

Keen to leave, McCabe rose as the first hint of dawn began to seep over the horizon and started to load the mules before La Brais had even dragged himself from his crib. The light was poor, the wind blew fiercely from the north, and the sky was heavy with the threat of further snow, all of which McCabe welcomed for a change, the adverse conditions providing the benefit of concealment.

La Brais eventually emerged and went to retrieve his horse from the corral. He threw heavy bags up behind his saddle and stuffed his remaining bottles of whiskey in among his rolled-up clothing to prevent them from breaking.

McCabe had caught both of the Indian ponies the previous day, and he made use of them as additional pack animals, loading them with furs and tying them into the center of the mule train. He did not want to allow the young Indian to ride his own pony, fearful that he might attempt to escape, so he left sufficient space on one of the mules to accommodate the boy. The decision incensed La Brais, who suggested that the Indian should be tied behind the last mule and made to walk, but McCabe was insistent that such treatment would simply hamper their speed.

Soon, Takoda realized that the men were packing to leave and began to resign himself to the possibility that he would be killed. But, when the trappers displayed no overt aggression, he started to consider the possibility that they planned to take him with them. That being the case, he decided that he should attempt to leave a sign that he had been in the cabin, so that if his people came in search of him, they would know that he had been there.

Takoda's hands remained tied tightly behind his back, and he was unable to move them sufficiently to create a mark on either the walls or the floor of the cabin. He tried to force his mind to think, but his head still reeled from the blow he had received and he struggled to concentrate, fighting to take in the detail of his surroundings and conceive some means of leaving a sign.

To his alarm, the big trapper noticed his scrutiny of the cabin and stopped to look at him. "What you lookin' at, Injun?" the man snapped, giving him a violent shove so that he fell and struck his head on the floor. Takoda rolled with the blow, cushioning its impact, but his necklace fell forward and the sharp animal teeth scratched his chin painfully.

He cursed at the trapper's senseless aggression and wished that he was able to rub his bruises. Then, an idea sprang to mind. That was it. His necklace. Many of his tribe would recognize his unusual necklace. He had to break it loose. Excited, he rolled onto his knees, glancing sideways to check that he was not being watched. Both men were busy loading the pack animals and ignored him as they lumbered in and out of the cabin, so he set to work.

Tilting his head forward, Takoda felt the necklace touch his chin, the sharp teeth pricking his skin slightly as he rotated his jaw, attempting to manipulate the necklace toward his mouth. Several times the necklace fell back and he was forced to start again, until eventually he was compelled to kneel with the crown of his head resting on the floor.

The discomfort in his arm made him want to cry out, but he knew the sound would serve no purpose, so he focused on the necklace and tried to put the pain aside. Eventually, a single tooth dropped over his lower lip and he was able to grasp it between his teeth, sucking vigorously to draw the leather lace into his mouth. Slowly a second tooth eased over his lip, and a third, until he was able him to clench the leather firmly. Now, all he had to do was to chew through it.

He sat up and faced the wall, anxious to ensure that the trappers were not able to see what he was doing. The lace was tough. It had been well cured and dried and was exceptionally strong, but Takoda ground his teeth relentlessly, determined to soften the leather and sever the cord. His jaw ached and the sensation of his teeth grinding on the leather made him shudder, but he persevered doggedly.

"That's it," McCabe shouted to La Brais. "We gotta git goin'."

La Brais untied his horse and mounted up. "Better git yer

Injun, since yer so set on takin' 'im with yer." He demonstrated no intent to help and sat with his hands draped casually across the horn of his saddle, regarding McCabe with disinterest.

McCabe shot him a sneer and tramped into the cabin to fetch Takoda. "C'mon, boy." He grabbed Takoda under the arm and attempted to lift him to his feet, but, to his exasperation, the Indian resisted, forcing himself to the floor and pressing against the wall.

"Git yerself up, yer son o' a bitch!" he yelled. "I ain't gonna kill yer." He wrestled his hands under Takoda's armpits, but the boy wriggled free with impressive strength.

"Tarnation! Goddamed Injun. Yer gonna git up if I gotta pull yer outta here with ma goddamned horse!" McCabe bawled at the back of Takoda's head.

"You want that I come in there an' shoot 'im?" La Brais called from outside. "S'only a boy. What yer foolin' round at?"

McCabe hauled on Takoda's shoulders, but he continued to struggle, desperate to chew through his neckpiece before he was dragged from the cabin, there being little chance of his tribe finding the teeth if they fell into the snow once he was outside.

McCabe's frustration boiled over. Infuriated, he aimed his palm at the boy's head and struck him with a full swing of his arm. Takoda's head cracked against the wall and a rush of darkness flooded over him, but his jaws snapped together at the impact and one of the animal teeth slipped free of the leather cord and dropped onto his tongue. The necklace had broken.

Satisfied, McCabe sensed the Indian capitulate and heaved him upright. Takoda reeled on unsteady feet and, as the trapper spun him around, a shower of small objects scattered across the floor. Disinterested in establishing what the Indian had dropped, McCabe hustled Takoda to the door and led him to the mules, La Brais chortling with amusement.

"Good t' see yer kin get the better o' a boy," he taunted,

contorting himself with laughter and erupting in a spasm of coughing.

McCabe loosened the bonds around Takoda's wrists, having noticed that his hands were almost purple, pushed on his mittens, and helped him onto one of the doleful-looking mules. Takoda shivered. Although still wearing his heavy winter furs, freezing tentacles of wind searched through the layers of hide and chilled his skin. The wound in his arm throbbed incessantly, and he could feel the sweaty onset of infection starting to soak his body.

Once prepared, McCabe pulled himself into the saddle and nodded to La Brais, who leaned over and spat a glob of spittle into the snow, giving his partner a disapproving glare as he wheeled away.

"You'd best hold up the rear, so's yer kin keep an eye on yer friend," he growled.

Content to distance himself from La Brais's insults, McCabe took up station at the end of the line as they trailed down into the valley, hugging the northern treeline, and plodded east at a steady pace. Visibility was poor, the snow falling thick and fast, and McCabe was heartened by the thought that their tracks would be eradicated within a matter of hours.

Chapter 22

North of the Greybull River

Otaktay pushed the warriors hard and was gratified to find that their progress was substantially unhampered by snow once they cleared the valley, enabling them to travel at a steady lope. Strong winds had blown the remaining snow into gullies, forming crested drifts around boulders and the thicker stands of sage, lending the plains the impression of a yellow sea interspersed with a choppy foam.

By midmorning they rounded the spur of the mountain and started into the valley to the north, tracing the southern treeline. The sun was bright, set in an icy blue sky, shot with towering bundles of fluffy white cloud that raced toward the horizon hastened by a brisk northwesterly wind.

The snow cover increased as they advanced further into the valley and they moved with caution as they approached the treeline at its westerly fringe, traveling in single file with rifles to hand in readiness for any potential confrontation. The mountain was quiet. They observed deer and elk meandering lazily, scratching through the snow in search of grass, but there was no sign of smoke from a campfire, and they discovered no tracks other than those made by the purposeful scavenging of the herbivores and an occasional itinerant coyote.

Entering the forest Mahpee took up the lead as they stalked along a well-defined animal track, meandering steadily uphill. The tracker's dark eyes, set under his heavily wrinkled brow, scanned the ground and the foliage as they passed. He noted where the grass had been flattened by an animal that had rested in a small glade and saw where a stone had been dislodged by an elk as it had flitted silently through the trees like a wraith. The story of the wilderness was all around him and it read like a book, so the others followed patiently, keenly aware of the old man's intuitive ability to locate the tracks of his quarry, a sixth sense developed over a lifetime of diligent observation.

Midway through the forest Mahpee stopped and dismounted from his pony. He stood quietly and closed his eyes for a moment before continuing tentatively. After a few steps, he paused and turned to Otaktay.

"There is something close. I feel it. We must walk with care now."

Otaktay dismounted and indicated that his men should do likewise, detailing three of the warriors to remain with the ponies while the rest of the search party crept slowly forward behind Mahpee, maintaining single file.

The old man hunted the ground as he moved. At first he was hesitant, but progressively he became more certain and strode ahead with great purpose, covering a full two hundred paces before bending to inspect a depression in the bed of pine needles strewn across the forest floor. Before sharing his discovery, he circled the forest on either side of the path seeking confirmation of the meaning of the spore.

Otaktay waited, letting the old man complete his inspection uninterrupted, until Mahpee stood up and pointed to a trail of tracks, using his arm to indicate their direction of travel.

"White men went this way." He pointed along a faint path that diverted away from the main trail, descending to the northeast. "Two horses with iron on their hooves, leading two more horses that did not wear iron. Ponies I think."

Mahpee returned to the track. "We should go this way." He

pointed up the hill. "The sign may be clearer if we retrace the tracks." Without waiting for a response, he set off up the hill, keeping to the side of the path so that he did not step on any imprints.

Otaktay followed, and in places he could make out faint depressions that might have been made by the shoe of a horse where it had compressed a patch of soft soil, but for the most part he wondered what the old man was able to detect with such certainty.

After a short way, brighter light began to percolate through the upper fringe of the forest and Mahpee became more animated. Staring up the path, he sidled behind a tree and ran his finger along a broken branch that projected from its trunk. He inspected it carefully and smelled it, dropping to the ground and shuffling around as he fingered the bed of needles, selecting one to examine meticulously.

"A man stood here with his horse tied to the tree," he declared before continuing up the path and bending to pick up a short, stout bough that lay at the base of a tree.

The old man signaled for Otaktay to come forward. "There was a struggle here." He pointed at the forest floor and handed the bough to Otaktay. "See, the ground has been flattened here, and the needles pushed to one side. Someone has held this bough too. It does not belong here." He gestured at the piece of wood in Otaktay's hand. "It is hard to tell what happened because the sign is several days old. I think two men fought here. Maybe one of the men tied his horse at the tree back there, or maybe there was a third man." He waved his arm back down the path.

Otaktay studied the old man carefully. There was no semblance of doubt in his eyes. He was uncertain of the detail of what had taken place, but he knew with unwavering conviction that some form of conflict had occurred at the spot where they stood. And, since there was no evidence of a corpse, it appeared that no one had been killed.

Otaktay did not know whether Takoda had been involved in the fight, but the tracks they had found further back along the trail implied that two Indian ponies might have been led down into the valley. He made up his mind and divided his band into two groups. An experienced young warrior named Kohana was instructed to lead one party up the mountain to inspect the funeral site, while Otaktay and Mahpee retraced their steps with the rest of the band to follow the tracks to the northeast.

The old man led Otaktay and his men down through the forest until they were about to emerge into the valley, and although the hoof prints left by the horses had become obscured by fresh snow long before they reached the treeline, Mahpee was certain that the men had followed the track.

The Indians paused under the cover of the trees and waited while the old tracker sat silently astride his pony, his eyes narrowed against the wind and the sun. He guessed from the gait of the horses that the men he was following knew where they were going and he was confident that they had not turned from the path, but now he had to reach for his intuition to guide him.

The snow lay deep across the valley floor, and there was no chance of finding tracks to follow. Indeed, they had been lucky that the forest canopy had protected the spoor on the higher ground, preventing the sign from being obliterated by fresh snow, otherwise despite Mahpee's remarkable skills, they would likely not have found the trail they were following at all. Otaktay waited patiently. These were not matters that could be hurried, and he was content to rely upon the old man's skill to guide him and his companions.

Eventually, Mahpee stirred and nodded his head slightly. "Over there." He pointed at the far side of the valley, a little way into the trees, under the lee of an outcrop of rock.

"You are sure?" Otaktay questioned.

Mahpee regarded the young warrior with disdain, and Otaktay immediately regretted the impertinence of his question. He studied the location that the old tracker had identified and scanned the surrounding area. There was no sign of movement and no fire smoke. Nevertheless, he was cautious about advancing, mindful of the possibility of encountering the men who had shot Howahkan, the valley offering ample potential for an ambush and the rocks under the bluff providing an ideal field of fire for anyone intent upon defending their position.

Otaktay squatted with his warriors and discussed their strategy. It was probable that the white men were camped on the far side of the valley, so they had to conceive a plan of assault that surrounded the camp; one that cut off any route of escape and enabled the warriors to approach undetected.

After a brief debate he split the group into three, sending six men back toward the plains, where they would cross the valley floor out of sight of the white man's camp and return through the forest on the north side of the valley, approaching from the east. Another six warriors were sent into the forest to work their way around to the west, leaving Otaktay, Mahpee, and a warrior named Mato to advance directly across the valley.

Without further comment, the warriors mounted up and hurried away, having been instructed to indicate their readiness by reflecting the sun in Otaktay's direction once they were in position.

As he waited, the young Akichita sat quietly at the edge of the forest, maintaining an attentive vigil and checking his rifle as he waited for his companions' signals. His demeanor was composed and methodical, and Mahpee was interested to observe his preparation for battle. He showed no apprehension or uncertainty, only a calm resolve.

In less than an hour a sharp stab of light glinted from a position three hundred paces to the left of the rocky outcrop, indicating that the first group of warriors was in place, and a little later a bright flash appeared to the right. Otaktay stood and indicated that Mahpee and Mato should follow him. Carrying their rifles, they led their ponies out of the trees on foot and started to trudge their way through the snow, walking at their mounts' shoulders to minimize the target they presented to any potential assailant and trailing one another in single file.

Otaktay kept his head low, as though protecting himself from the wind, but his eyes moved restlessly, alert to any hint of movement or flicker of light that might betray a man's concealed position. He detected nothing and they crossed the valley, reaching the opposite treeline without event.

As they reached the edge of the forest, Mahpee let out a soft croak to catch Otaktay's attention, imitating the harsh call of one of the large mountain crows, and pointed at a small gap between the firs that formed the start of a well-used track.

Otaktay and Mato handed their ponies to Mahpee and crept forward, their weapons ready as they slid quietly through the trees, careful to stay off the path as they scaled the hill, stealthily approaching the bluff.

Within a hundred paces the carpet of snow began to clear and Otaktay could see the clear imprints of the hooves of numerous animals. He moved closer to the path and whistled softly to Mahpee, who appeared within a few moments to inspect the tracks, some of which were hock deep.

"They have left," he said with certainty. "Eight or ten horses, all carrying heavy loads. A few days ago."

Otaktay looked furious and turned to bound up the path, leaving the others in his wake. Moments later, he emerged into the small glade where the trappers had built their cabin and knew instantly that it had been abandoned, the door hanging open and a thick layer of snow laying across its threshold. He let out a shrill birdcall, and his warriors materialized like a wave of ghosts from either side of the camp, stepping warily into the clearing.

"They are gone," he informed them. "Mahpee, what does the sign tell you?" he demanded, gesturing for the old man to come forward.

The tracker walked slowly around the front of the cabin and completed a circuit of the corral before returning to Otaktay. "There are signs of pack animals and two horses that wear iron, but I see sign of ponies too. Maybe two ponies, but I am not sure. The sign is confused and snow has covered many of the tracks."

Otaktay nodded without comment. "We must look in the lodge. Come." He beckoned Mahpee to follow and the two Indians stepped hesitantly through the doorway, peering cautiously inside.

The cabin looked as though it had been ransacked, a collection of pans and skins cast onto the floor and empty bottles strewn in every corner, but as Otaktay scanned the cots at either side of the cabin, an item alongside one of the cribs caught his eye. He hurried forward and stooped to pick up a beautifully crafted bow, which he offered to Mahpee optimistically.

"I know this. It belonged to O'hiniya he Mani," he hissed.

Mahpee studied the bow and nodded. There was no mistaking the exquisite carving and the eagle feathers. "The tomahawk!" he whispered, casting his eye around the cabin and pointing to one of the corners.

Otaktay followed the old man's gesture and saw the tomahawk leaning against the wall. Again, there was no doubt. It was the axe that Walks on Air had carried. Otaktay had seen both weapons placed alongside the revered Shirt Wearer's body at his funeral, and it was obvious that the men who had occupied this lodge had destroyed the dais and taken the weapons, as Howahkan had surmised.

He put his rifle on the cot and picked up the tomahawk, feeling the weight of the skilfully crafted axe, and his desire for retribution flared. Memories of the achievements of the Itancan's son turned over in his mind, and he fumed at the sacrilege of defiling the funeral site of the great warrior.

"They will pay for this," he murmured the commitment to Mahpee. "Can you follow them?" He turned and glared at the old tracker.

"They have been gone three or four days. I don't think we will find them now," he responded with a distinct lack of confidence.

"We must search for our brother. If Takoda is alive, he may be with these men. We must try." Otaktay spoke with grim determination, and Mahpee could see that there would be no stopping him.

They turned toward the door and Otaktay gathered up his rifle, his thick moccasin snagging against something on the floor. Assuming it to be a stone, he kicked it away in frustration and strode out of the cabin.

But Mahpee had been a tracker all his life, and his senses were attuned to notice things that were out of place. Grass that bent in the opposite direction to the wind, a stone dislodged with its weathered side to the ground, the flutter of a group of birds when there was nothing obvious to disturb them.

Instinctively, his eye fell to the floor, following the object that Otaktay had brushed aside. He was intrigued at its odd shape and bent down and picked it up, turning it over in his fingers. It was a tooth. It looked like a large molar from a whitetail or mule deer, but holding it up to the light he could see a tiny hole drilled through the tooth with great care and skill. This was not the relic of a white man's hunt.

He rolled the tooth thoughtfully in his hand and turned back toward the cot, wondering why such an item would be in the lodge. His eyes searched across the floor, intuitively rather than with conscious purpose, and settled on a cluster of small objects scattered under one of the makeshift beds.

He knelt down and scooped them toward him, feeling a sense of euphoria as he swept them into the light. Lying before him was a string of irregular and misshapen teeth, carefully threaded onto a dark leather thong, together with two or three loose teeth that had fallen off what was obviously a neckpiece.

As he inspected his discovery Otaktay appeared in the doorway, bridling with irritation and mystified to find the old man kneeling on the floor. "What are you doing? We have to leave now."

"Takoda was here." Mahpee turned to face Otaktay holding the broken neckpiece in his hands.

The Akichita was transfixed. "What?"

"This is Takoda's neckpiece. I know it. I gave him two of the bear teeth myself," Mahpee explained.

Otaktay hurried over and squatted beside Mahpee so that he could see the neckpiece clearly. "You speak the truth," he murmured. "Do you think he is alive?"

Mahpee was examining the frayed end of the leather thong meticulously. "He bit through this. It was not torn from him. Look." The old man held the leather up to the light and both of them could clearly see that it had been chewed. "He is alive," Mahpee declared with absolute conviction.

Once Kohana and his group of warriors had returned from the funeral dais Otaktay considered how he should proceed. Given the prospect of Takoda being alive, he concluded that he should send ten warriors back to the village with Mahpee, who would explain to the Itancan what they had found. He would take the remaining warriors and attempt to track the white men. Two of his braves, besides Mahpee, were noted for their exceptional tracking skills and they would have to undertake the task in the old man's absence, since it was unreasonable to expect him to embark upon an indeterminate pursuit across the plains.

Otaktay gave Mahpee the tomahawk and bow they had recovered from the cabin, Takoda's neckpiece being tucked into a leather pouch at the old tracker's waist for safe keeping. Then, the band rode down into the valley, splitting into separate groups when they reached the plains to further their respective undertakings.

Chapter 23

June 1865, Kansas City

Stone stepped off the train in Kansas and was met by a short bespectacled man, who fidgeted with the impatience of a person unaccustomed to waiting for others. His name was Seth Jones, and he was one of Winthrop's most trusted business associates. He ran the General Stores in Kansas, situated in the bustling commercial area of Westport, on the confluence of the Kansas and Missouri rivers.

The shopkeeper had been one of Winthrop's earliest business partners, when as a junior investor in the Kansas Town Company in the early 1850s, the senator had been instrumental in incentivizing the settlement of the area and had risked much of his embryonic fortune in developing the Westport Landings to accommodate the first of his Mississippi steamers.

Jones ran the largest store in the city, stocked with every form of merchandise that the townsfolk and transient population could require, and under Winthrop's guidance he had diversified, strangling competition from other traders by cutting off their supply routes. The disparate enterprises, besides the general store that served Kansas and Fort Leavenworth, now included a men's clothing shop with a sister store in the emergent town of Denver, a business that sold wines, liquors, and groceries run in partnership with an industrious man by the name of William Dalton, and a shop that sold cigars and tobacco under the management of the Haas brothers.

Seth Jones presided over all of the senator's retail ventures, his diminutive stature concealing an intelligent business mind and a ruthless competitive drive, and Winthrop rewarded him well for his loyalty and hard work, recognizing that he needed a man he could trust to nurture his arm's-length investments.

Stone wore a dapper three-piece suit with an elegant timepiece tucked into his breast pocket, but his brawny stature and the obvious bulge of his revolver betrayed his business-like image as an unlikely pretence.

"Mr. Jones, it's good to see you again and most accommodating of you to meet me like this," he greeted the shopkeeper respectfully.

Jones peered at Stone through his round spectacles and cracked a hint of a smile. "No trouble, Mr. Stone. I heard you was in a hurry, so thought it best to git you on yer way with all haste."

Jones was not afraid of Stone, being acutely aware of his own value to Winthrop, and was confident that the senator's man would accord him appropriate respect. Nevertheless, he knew very well that Stone specialized in dealing with some of Winthrop's more unsavory business matters and was keen to ensure that the assassin did not remain in Kansas any longer than was necessary.

"Most thoughtful of you. Tell me, how is business?" replied Stone, falling in step as they walked to a horse-drawn buggy standing alongside the station.

"Always an opportunity to do better," Jones responded matter-of-factly. "Trade in Denver's buildin' pretty good, but we gotta find new premises and stop Mathewson and Cartwright gettin' a foothold. They're haulin' stock in by railroad, now the senator's boys messed up their supplies out o' New Orleans. They're strugglin' some right now, but they gonna get better at managin' their supply lines."

Stone nodded quietly as the shopkeeper elaborated upon the successes and challenges of each of his enterprises, so that the journey to the livery passed before there was an opportunity for the conversation to touch upon Jones's family, a subject he would have found distasteful to discuss with Stone.

"Gotcha good horse and the other supplies you wan'ed," Jones confirmed as they pulled up outside a large barn and smithy. "Looks like you gonna be travelin' light."

Stone was accustomed to the west, and he was a man who had no need for unnecessary comforts. He had asked for little more than a thick coat and gloves, a set of large saddlebags, and one of the new Winchester rifles with several boxes of ammunition. He wanted to be able to move fast and unencumbered.

Jones stepped down from the buggy and went to find the owner of the livery, who ensured that Stone was equipped with everything he requested, enabling him to mount up and get on his way without delay. It was thirty miles to Fort Leavenworth, and he hoped to arrive before dark.

Murray was irritated. Winthrop's messenger had been waiting in the headquarters when he had arrived at eight o'clock in the morning and, although his adjutant had prevented the man from barging directly into his office, he found the two men engaged in disturbingly jovial conversation. Compounding his annoyance, the senator's emissary had conspicuously checked his timepiece before making a derogatory comment to the effect that officers should be at their station just after dawn.

Ushered into Murray's office, Stone sat impassively, his bearing erect and assertive as he watched the general compose himself. Murray, by contrast, found Stone unsettling. He knew of him by reputation and was aware that Winthrop used his services extensively, but he had not met him previously. Stone was a man who was distinctly difficult to read. His moustache concealed his expression, and his eyes seemed to possess a cold gray veneer that rendered them detached and unemotional.

"Can I offer you coffee, Mr. Stone?" Murray enquired.

Stone shook his head. "We have business to discuss, General. Would it be appropriate to dispatch your staff on some errand, so that we can be certain we're not overheard?" The question was not one that appeared to have an optional response, and after an awkward visual duel Murray rose and sent his outer office staff to conduct an inspection of the store's inventory.

Stone unrolled a map of the Great Plains region as Murray reseated himself and fixed the general with a dispassionate expression. "Has Grant asked you for an assessment of the current Indian threat yet?"

"That would be a military matter, Mr. Stone," Murray retorted tersely.

"Don't play games with me, General. I haven't come all the way from Minneapolis for my health. We both know that the senator gave you advance notice that Grant would demand your appraisal. Have you received the request?" Stone's eyes bored into Murray with a fiery intensity that was an alarming contrast to his previously cool demeanor.

"How dare you! You are in a military facility, not some backstreet saloon. I command Fort Leavenworth, Mr. Stone, and if you don't afford some respect I'll have you thrown out on your backside!" Murray bristled with indignation.

"General, Senator Winthrop is not a patient man. I have important matters to discuss with you and little time in which to do so. Now, I know you're the commander of the United States forces in the Great Plains region, and I have no intention of detracting from that lofty status, but I need to be clear whether you've had a request from Grant and whether you have responded. The senator is most insistent on this matter and would have me remind you of the fragility of your rank and respectability. Remember who sponsored your promotion and who helped to bury that unfortunate episode with the Ordnance Bureau?"

Stone watched the general's pompous facade crumble when he mentioned the Bureau. Murray had originally served as a junior officer of the United States Ordnance Bureau, where he had met and worked for Major Josiah Gorgas. The two had become firm friends, and when the Union Blockade was put in place at the start of the Civil War at the behest of President Lincoln, Murray had found himself unwittingly assisting Gorgas to supply blockade running vessels with weapons provided by the British.

Gorgas later declared himself a sympathizer and sided openly with the confederacy, by which time Murray's involvement in gun running had become known to Winthrop, who maintained shipping interests in Liverpool, England, where the orders for supply of munitions had been placed.

Murray had believed that he was submitting orders on behalf of the Union, but in fact the weapons were being delivered to Nassau in the Bahamas, where they were loaded aboard smaller vessels to attempt the risky enterprise of navigating their way between the Union fleet to deliver the arms to the confederate military.

A loyal Unionist friend alerted Winthrop to the numerous munitions orders bearing Murray's signature, and he confronted the young officer with the evidence of his treachery, ultimately blackmailing Murray into providing military information and resources in return for sponsoring his career and preserving the secrecy of his previous naive indiscretions. As Murray's career blossomed, his debt to Winthrop and fear of the revelation of his unintentional betrayal had rendered him a reluctant but compliant servant.

Murray's shoulders dropped in defeat. "Yes, I received orders yesterday to provide a full report by the end of the week," he conceded weakly.

"Good. Now, I'm sure we'll make first-rate progress." Stone maintained eye contact with Murray until the general's gaze faltered. "Show me where your forces are deployed and brief me on their strength." He leaned across the map so that he could see clearly as Murray pointed out the permanent forts and explained the patrol activity for each of the military posts dotted across the plains.

The major installations were along the Oregon Trail at Fort Kearny, Fort Laramie, and Platte Bridge Station. In addition, patrols were increasingly being deployed to protect wagon trains using the troublesome Bozeman trail to the east of the Bighorn Mountains. The general explained that the latter task was unsustainable without establishing intermediary fortifications along the route, since the distances involved were enormous and difficulty in maintaining supply lines meant that patrols were generally short in duration and largely ineffective.

Plans were under consideration to build a resupply point in the Powder River basin, and there had been some initial discussion about construction of two additional forts further north, but no decisions had been taken.

"Where would you build the fortifications?" Stone enquired.

Murray pointed to two locations along the trail. "The surveyors and our field officers have recommended here and here."

He indicated a position at the southeastern end of the Bighorn Mountains as the proposed location of the resupply fort and a further point two-thirds of the way along the mountain range to the north, adjacent to De Smet Lake. Murray explained that the lake was the largest expanse of water in the Powder River Basin, named after a Belgian priest who had traveled the region on a mission to spread Christianity.

"This would need to be a substantial garrison." He pointed at the location near the lake. "It's in the heart of Sioux hunting grounds, and Red Cloud is vehemently opposed to any incursion by prospectors, settlers, or military. He has vowed to rid the plains of the white man and is orchestrating systematic attacks on any patrols or wagon trains. But, assuming that we could build the fort and control the area, there would be merit in constructing a further fort here." He dabbed his finger at a location where the Bozeman Trail crossed the Bighorn River before continuing northwest toward the Yellowstone.

"What will happen if you don't get the resources to build and operate those fortifications?"

"We'll have to prevent travelers going through the Powder River region and send them along the Oregon Trail to Fort Bridger, where they can cut a course north to Fort Hall on the Snake River. The problem is that people know about the Bozeman Trail now and they're in a hurry to get to Virginia City. They're willing to risk confrontation with the Sioux in return for the reward of gold."

"The senator wants military control of the Powder River Basin. He believes that emigrants and prospectors should be free to traverse the continent without fear of hostility. He is insistent that your response to General Grant is colorful and provides irresistible motivation to sanction the allocation of further resources to combat the Sioux, so you'll need to elaborate upon the extent of their aggression." Stone rehearsed the instructions he had been given by the senator.

"Why is Winthrop so worried about a few settlers? There are thousands of people pouring across the prairies, and it seems unlike him to be concerned about a few casualties. Surely he's got bigger fish to catch in Washington?" Murray was scornful of the senator's motives.

"You know very well that the Union needs every ounce of

gold it can get its hands on. Subduing the natives means that work on the railroad in the north can proceed with less disruption, and that will provide a more secure means of transport for the gold from the Montana goldfields."

"So, this is about the railroad?" enquired Murray.

"A strong offensive in the Powder River Basin will certainly assist progression with the railroad. If Red Cloud and Sitting Bull are kept busy defending their precious hunting grounds, it will distract them from interfering with the construction of the Northern Pacific, but there's a principle at stake here too. It wouldn't be good for the army to be seen to be failing to control the Indian nations. There's a lot of bad sentiment toward the Plains Indians in Congress, and it would reflect badly upon both the administration and the military if the safety of migrants or security of the transit of gold were to become problematic. I'm sure you wouldn't want the responsibility for that failure to land on your shoulders?" Stone presented the issue as one of personal risk to Murray.

"I can only achieve a limited amount with the resources at my disposal!" Murray bridled at the inferred slight to his competence.

"That's the point, though, General. There's no value in being a silent hero. Magnify the risk. Persuade Grant and Johnson to allocate the resources you need for the task. Then, having forced their hand, once you crush Indian resistance, you'll take the credit for having liberated the west. The challenge is getting Washington's attention while Congress is focused on the southern states, but the senator's assessment is that the timing is now optimal to secure extra resources and strike a decisive blow against the Indian nations. You know he'll champion your cause if you respect his interests." Stone paused for emphasis. "And, on this occasion, your interests and those of the senator are perfectly aligned."

Murray eyed Stone suspiciously but he recognized the logic in the man's argument. He was already struggling to provide adequate protection to those migrating west and had lost nearly forty men engaging with the Sioux, the Cheyenne, and the Arapaho over the preceding six months. Animosity between the tribes and settlers was escalating to unprecedented levels, and he was worried that the situation had the potential to boil over into a full-blooded confrontation.

Part of his rationale for sending Gresham to Platte Bridge Station was to use his unquestionable talent for working constructively with the native tribes to try and break the Northern Cheyenne's allegiance with the Sioux and perhaps broker a discreet treaty. But to set about building permanent fortifications along the Bozeman Trail was bound to strengthen the coalition between the tribes.

He faced a difficult choice militarily. On the one hand, he could invoke a balanced negotiation, supported by visible displays of military strength, designed to encourage the Sioux to endure grudging acceptance of transit through their land. This was a strategy that found elements of support within the Indian nations, but was an anathema to Red Cloud, who commanded increasing allegiance among his people and some allied tribes. Murray was less than certain that the strategy had any chance of succeeding, although it was the path of least risk and effort.

Alternatively, he could employ a strategy of confrontation, entering the Sioux's sacred lands with permanent garrisons and deploying sufficient military manpower to beat Red Cloud into submission, or at the least render his raids ineffective. But Murray considered that it would require several thousand soldiers, and an equal number of civilian resources to build the fortifications required. The tactics would certainly incite a violent riposte, although it was likely that the army would be capable of securing safe passage for the majority of migrants and transit for the shipments of gold from Virginia City, both of which he recognized as politically sensitive issues.

The general enjoyed the privileges that rank afforded and the respectability that came with seniority. He had no desire to be at the center of a political storm and was inclined to believe that the more palatable of his options was to be charged with responsibility to quell a native uprising, rather than risk accountability for the death of civilians or the loss of federal gold. Besides, he had to consider Winthrop. The man had a truly ruthless streak, and Murray was certain that the senator would be more than willing to expose his procurement of confederate weaponry if he did not get what he wanted.

"General Grant won't roll over on this," Murray mused. "He'll need more convincing than a handful of costly engagements with renegade bands."

"The senator appreciates the politics, General, and suggests the orchestration of a couple of high-profile incidents to support the validity of your assessment."

Murray watched Stone settle back in his chair, irritated at his passive expression. "What exactly does the senator mean by that?" he probed apprehensively.

"You need an event that touches a raw nerve in the corridors of power. Something the senator can use to engender support for your proposals. There will be a gold train traveling from Virginia City at the end of July. If that were to fall foul of the Sioux, it would certainly cause a stir." Stone proposed.

"How do you know that? The timing of the gold trains is shrouded in secrecy." Murray looked astounded at Stone's brazen proposition.

"Shall we say that the senator enjoys a productive relationship with First National Bank?"

"It seems the senator's influence knows no bounds!" Murray protested. "Those gold trains are a priority for military protection. They can be carrying up to $400,000 in gold. In any event, they're less attractive targets to the Sioux. They move fast, there are no livestock, and they invariably have a strong military escort."

"True, but I'd wager that Red Cloud wouldn't let them pass without a fight if he knew their value to the U.S. government?" Stone retorted.

"And how might he come to know that?" Murray cast his mind back to the request he had received from Winthrop to provide safe passage for the mountain man, John Colter, and immediately wondered whether his presence was connected with Stone's proposal.

Stone ignored the question. "What we need is an impetuous young officer. One who is likely to exceed his orders when confronted with the chance to strike at the threat of a small group of opportunist Sioux. Do you have someone appropriate?"

"You're asking me to send my troops to their death," Murray spat with contempt.

"I think we're talking about a small sacrifice for a higher cause," Stone replied evenly.

"You must be mad if you think I'd countenance doing a thing like that. It's outrageous!" Murray stood and thumped the desk with his fist.

Stone remained seated, holding the general's eye with an unwavering steely gaze. "As I said, General Murray, the senator is most insistent in this matter. He's asked me to remind you of your vulnerability."

Stone slipped two folded sheets of paper from his pocket and opened them out, placing them on the desk so that Murray could see them. One was an Ordnance Bureau order for weapons bearing Murray's signature, the other a shipping manifest for the munitions to be dispatched to Nassau.

Murray knew exactly what the papers were. He had last seen them many years previously when Winthrop had first confronted him with the damning evidence, documents that the senator had characterized as tantamount to treason, if misinterpreted. Winthrop had seemed entirely reasonable, professing to recognize the obvious deceit of Major Gorgas and Murray's unfortunate entanglement. He had proposed a mutually beneficial business relationship and offered to sponsor Murray's career, describing him as a talented young officer, in return for a few minor favors. The blackmail had been subtle but nonetheless clear, and Murray had felt a sickening wrench in the pit of his stomach, although subsequently he had done little but profit from the arrangement. But now, the sensation came flooding back as he snatched a glance at the documents. He had always harbored an unsettling premonition that something atrocious would come of his arrangement with Winthrop, and this appeared to be the moment. His mouth was dry at the prospect of sending a contingent of his men into a deadly trap.

Stone could sense Murray's capitulation and rose from his seat. "You clearly have work to do, General, and I'll not detain you longer. Shall we review your draft report to General Grant tomorrow morning? I'll be here at seven." He picked up the two documents and replaced them purposefully in his jacket pocket, touching the brim of his hat before striding from the general's office.

The following morning Stone went through Murray's draft report. It contained an assessment of the risks presented by the army's highly charged relationship with the Indian nations, the current and forecasted volume of people and livestock migration, their increasing numbers swollen by the lure of the gold found at Alder Gulch, and a summary of the skirmishes that had occurred with Sioux war parties over the preceding months, together with a list of casualties.

Murray had masterfully synthesized the information into a compelling case for additional resources, setting out his prediction for the likely intensification of hostilities and his proposals for subduing the native aggression. The consequences of failing to act were presented as a series of potential permutations, summarized in a factual and unemotional manner that rendered them all the more compelling.

Stone was impressed at the general's eloquence and understood for the first time why Winthrop had invested energy in advancing Murray's career. Although not an inspiring leader, he was intelligent, highly articulate, and tactically astute, qualities that would get him noticed in the United States army.

They made minor amendments to the report, adding proposed timelines that emphasized the priority that should be attributed to each of the recommendations. Stone also insisted that the importance of the Powder River Basin as a route for transporting gold should be accorded elevated prominence.

By midmorning they had completed the revisions and Murray sealed the report, instructing his orderly to dispatch it to General Grant with utmost speed and confidentiality. Stone took a transcribed version of the report to send to Winthrop to ensure that he obtained his own copy concurrent with Grant's receipt of the assessment.

"A truly excellent piece of work, General, if I might say," ventured Stone. "Have you given some thought to the other matter we discussed?" He eyed the general coolly.

Murray was unmoved by the plaudit. He felt nothing but contempt for Stone, although he knew that Winthrop's man was unlikely to leave without an answer to his question. "I have one or two options," he responded brusquely.

"The senator would like to know who you choose," Stone pressed Murray. "I'll be leaving Leavenworth first thing in the morning so I'd like to know your decision before you retire this evening."

"I'll tell you when I'm damned well ready!" Murray exploded. "Now get out of my office." His tolerance of Stone had reached its limit.

But Winthrop's emissary stood ominously and placed both hands on the general's desk, leaning across so that his face was inches from Murray's. "Is that what you'd like me to report back to the senator?" he hissed.

Murray felt a prickle of fear run down his spine as the gray eyes bored into him. He could smell the man's musky sweat and sense his ruthless determination. He said nothing.

Stone held his eye, "By tonight, General." he whispered uncompromisingly.

Chapter 24

Confluence of the north and south forks of the Platte River

Each group of schooners had drawn up into a circle at Gresham's instruction, the emigrants huddled together behind the relative safety of their defensive formation, accompanied by a sergeant or corporal and two squads of troopers. The menfolk readied their weapons—shotguns, pre–Civil War muskets, handguns of every manner, and even a few modern carbines—and poised themselves to give their best to protect their families.

At dawn a party of over a hundred Pawnee, mounted on their ponies, had taken up position along the ridge of one of the bluffs to the south of camp, and Gresham was perturbed by their behavior. The Pawnee were regarded as a peaceful people, who benefited from trading with the migrants that passed through their land. He viewed their aggressive display of strength as most unusual and was determined that he would not permit the wagon train to break camp until the Pawnee withdrew, since it would be easier to mount a defense while the convoy remained stationary, in the event that the Indians proved hostile.

Colter was summoned to provide his assistance as an interpreter, but he was not enthusiastic about accompanying Gresham to meet the Indians, and a visceral exchange ensued, the mountain man insisting that it was not his responsibility to protect the wagon train. But, when presented with the alternative of a firing squad or the permanent return of his revolver,

Colter capitulated, readily agreeing to take up station at Gresham's side to ride out and establish the Pawnee's intentions once his weapon had been handed back.

As they approached, the Indians descended the bluff and fanned out across the plain, drawing up about half a mile from the schooners, where two Pawnee broke away from the rest of the war party and advanced a hundred paces to meet them.

The larger of the two Pawnee was impressive, his stature amplified by the size of the bright green porcupine roach attached to the scalplock that adorned his head. His face was painted red with a large black handprint covering his chin and lower cheek. Similar handprints were repeated on his horse, which Colter recognized as symbols of his prowess in hand-to-hand combat. His chest was bare and decorated with a series of black symbols, and a band of rabbit fur was strapped around each arm above the elbow. His leggings were of buckskin with decorative tassels, and his moccasin-clad feet hung loosely at his pony's sides. He carried a large war club and wore his bow and a quiver of arrows across his back.

The second Pawnee was less imposing, but he was also painted, his face yellow with similar black handprints, and when Colter and Gresham pulled up a few feet away the Indian's grave expression betrayed his anger.

The four men stood assessing one another until the yellow-faced Indian pushed his pony forward, screaming abuse at Gresham and Colter in his native tongue, and hurled his spear. The point embedded itself in the ground and the shaft twitched back and forth, Gresham's horse flinching at the thud of its impact, although the captain held his seat calmly and maintained eye contact with the Pawnee leader.

"What did he say?" he asked Colter without averting his eyes.

"Seems some'n killed his daughter. Says one of th' emigrant

folk done it." Colter threw a disaffected sidelong glance at Gresham.

"Tell him we're sorry to hear of his loss, and ask him why he thinks someone in the wagon train is responsible." Gresham continued to face the Indians as he addressed Colter.

The mountain man relayed the message, which was greeted with a further tirade of abuse, the yellow-faced Indian waving his hand wildly in the direction of the hills close to the river.

"Says they trailed a white man's horse an' some cattle out o' hills yonder," he nodded in the direction the Indian had pointed. "Came from where they found the girl, dead. Says she bin cut up bad an' raped." Immediately, Colter recalled the sight of Johannes washing his clothes in the river and the knife he had found stashed in the boy's wagon. The reason for the lad's furtive behavior now seemed blatantly apparent.

Gresham gazed at the hills, considering his response. "Tell this man," he nodded toward the leader, "that a lot of people have been trying to round up their livestock, and that we have found many of our cattle have been killed by Indians, which has made the migrants very angry. But tell him that murder is also a crime in our society, and that if someone in our number has broken the law, I will hold them to account. I give my word, and if he would allow, I'd like to see the girl's body so that I can investigate what has happened."

The mountain man looked dismayed. "You sure you wanna git involved in this?"

Gresham surveyed the large band of Indians. "Looks like we're already involved, whether we like it or not. Besides, no one's got the right to take an Indian's life, any more than they have the right to kill one of us. If there's been a murder, I want to know who's done it. If a man's killed once, he might kill again."

To the surprise of both men, the Pawnee leader intervened in

English, addressing Gresham directly. "You speak with straight tongue. I not wish fight. But, this man, he must make pay for kill daughter. You come village. You only."

Colter threw Gresham a look that conveyed his skepticism of the Indian's proposal, but he watched with interest to see how the captain reacted.

Gresham's face remained impassive as he regarded the Indian thoughtfully. "Are you the leader of these people?" Gresham's eyes described an arc, as he indicated the line of warriors assembled behind the two Pawnee.

"Great chief, Ishcatape. He at village. Warriors me follow," the leader replied in straightforward explanation.

Gresham ignored the yellow-faced man, who continued to bark explosive insults at him and Colter. "I will come with you, but two of your warriors will stay with Mr. Colter here until I return."

The Pawnee held Gresham's steady gaze for a few moments before calling one of his warriors forward. He issued brisk instructions, which were greeted with an air of apprehension, but the man returned to the war party and selected two grim-faced warriors whom he dispatched to join their leader.

But as the warriors approached, a disturbance broke out to their left and several Pawnee turned to ride slowly toward the hills to their rear, accompanied by a barrage of excited shrieking.

Turmoil ensued, and Gresham stood up in his stirrups to try and obtain a better view of the subject of the Indians' interest. Colter's hand slipped to the pistol at his hip, and the measured calm of the parley disintegrated into a tense stand-off, the yellow-faced Indian interpreting Colter's movement as a threat and howling a warning as he knocked an arrow to his bow and took determined aim at Colter's chest.

Gresham was unable to identify the motivation for the sudden commotion, but he understood the potential for a full-scale conflict to ensue. Concerned that his troops might assume he and Colter to be in imminent danger, he spun his horse and picked out Trautman, thrusting his hand into the air to indicate that his men should hold their fire.

Having changed position slightly, Gresham was afforded a better vantage of the hills to the south and immediately observed two riders racing diagonally across the plain. One was a cavalry trooper and the other looked to be a cowhand. The two were hurtling toward the wagon train, their weapons drawn as they attempted to evade a party of Indians hurrying to intercept them.

"Stop your warriors!" Gresham barked at the Pawnee leader, who was watching, intrigued. "I'll stop these men!"

Gresham dug his spurs into his mount's flank and surged away, gesticulating wildly at the two fleeing horsemen to lower their weapons, and the Pawnee leader spun his pony to instruct the balance of his warriors to refrain from the pursuit.

The Indians displayed their natural horsemanship as they chased the two riders, fanning out into a skirmish line and lifting their rifles without any obvious command, steering their ponies with subtle changes in balance and deft touches of their legs. Gresham pursued them at a gallop, but he had no chance of catching the Pawnee, and his frantic instructions to the trooper and cowhand went unheeded.

O'Halloran noticed the Pawnee turn toward him and his worst fears were realized. He had been confident that he and his companion would be able to sneak past the party of Indians, remaining undetected for long enough to enable them to reach the safety of the schooners.

But the trooper had been less certain, asserting that they should remain concealed in the hills until the Indians returned to their village, and had been aghast when O'Halloran had unexpectedly broken cover and raced off across the plain, leaving him with no alternative but to follow.

To the cavalryman's dismay, he and the cowhand were seen within moments of clearing the head of the valley, rendering a return to the hills an unsafe option and leaving the security of the wagon train as their only hope of salvation. As a result, they dug in their spurs and pushed their horses into a headlong gallop.

They had no idea whether the Indians were hostile and drew their weapons in the interest of self-protection until the Pawnee adopted a skirmish line, when O'Halloran concluded that he would be obliged to fight. He and the trooper hollered at the soldiers hunkered behind the wagon circles, pleading for covering fire, and when no response was forthcoming, frustrated, O'Halloran pointed his pistol into the air and fired a shot, desperately hoping to draw the attention of Gresham's men.

The shot was a fatal mistake. The Pawnee assumed that they had been fired upon, and a salvo of gunfire ensued. The trooper's horse collapsed, launching him cartwheeling over its head and sending him crashing to the ground with bone-crushing force.

Realizing his peril, O'Halloran leveled his gun and fired ineffectually at the approaching Indians, their speed and angle of attack presenting an awkward target, and the Pawnee responded so that the sound of gunfire and the smell of cordite filled the air.

Gresham galloped flat out, pursued by the yellow-faced Indian, and could see that he would not reach his fallen trooper before the Pawnee overran the man. He watched the soldier struggle to his feet, hobbling on a broken leg and clutching a dislocated shoulder as he lurched across the uneven ground, frantic to retrieve his weapon, which lay several yards from where he had fallen. He was going to be too late. The warriors would easily reach the man first. But the Pawnee refrained from finishing off their quarry and, to Gresham's intense relief, they satisfied themselves with barging the trooper to the ground with their ponies.

The shooting ceased abruptly, the cowhand's pistol empty and the Indians' ammunition spent, but a headlong chase across the plain continued. O'Halloran discarded his handgun and pulled his rifle from its saddle scabbard as the Pawnee came within range to use their bows. The cowhand aimed his weapon at the nearest Indian, and Gresham screamed a desperate warning, imploring him not to shoot.

The instruction carried to O'Halloran, who glanced around to see the captain rushing toward him, and Gresham wondered whether the cowhand's expression betrayed a hint of recognition of his own folly as his eyes registered both surprise and confusion. At that instant, O'Halloran's head snapped backward, three arrows plunging into his back, one emerging through his chest, and a fourth skewering cleanly through his right arm. He slumped and his head tipped forward, his chin bouncing off the shaft of the arrow protruding from his chest as his horse began to slow.

The Pawnee split into two groups, one of which peeled away to surround the trooper, who sat crumpled helplessly on his knees, the other pulling up O'Halloran's horse, whereupon the cowhand's limp body slid sideways and fell to the ground.

Gresham yelled an order at his trooper, instructing the injured soldier to raise his hands in submission, and as he and the yellow-faced Pawnee slid to a halt alongside O'Halloran the warriors moved aside, shouldering their bows and standing attentively surrounding the two fallen men.

Leaping from his horse, Gresham dropped to his knees beside O'Halloran, who lay with his head twisted at an awkward angle, blood bubbling from his lips. The cowhand's chest heaved uncomfortably as he tried to suck air into his punctured lungs, pierced by the Pawnee's arrows and rapidly filling with his own blood. He whispered a few unintelligible words as Gresham bent over him, his eyes blinking helplessly.

Gresham recognized the man, recalling that he had seen him organizing the stockmen that drove the herds of cattle. "Hal, it's Captain Gresham." He bent low to ensure that he was heard, feeling the need for practicalities as the spark of life drained from O'Halloran fast. "Hal. Can you hear me? You're dying, Hal. Is there a message you want me to give to anyone?"

O'Halloran's eyes closed and he nodded, so that Gresham knew that he had understood the question. "Lou. Love . . . Lou," the words were painfully slow. "Wife."

"Okay, Hal. I'll tell her." Gresham responded sympathetically. "You're not going to die alone, Hal. I'll be here." The light faded from Hal's eyes, and Gresham cradled his head, bending close so that the cowhand would be aware of his presence. But at the periphery of his vision he was aware of the yellow-faced Indian, studying O'Halloran with interest.

He turned briefly as he felt the Indian yank at something attached to O'Halloran's belt. It was a small skinning knife, and the Indian held it up to the light. It was smeared with blood, the sight of which provoked the Pawnee to let out a blood-curdling screech.

Without warning, the Indian drove his knee into Gresham's ribs and threw him aside. Grasping a fist full of O'Halloran's hair, the Pawnee hauled the cowhand off the ground and drew the knife brutally across his neck, the force almost severing his head from his body.

Gresham bellowed in horror, scrambling to O'Halloran's defense, but it was too late, his lifeless body dangled from the sinewy remains of his neck. Compounding the barbarity, and as an unwarranted act of vengeance, the Pawnee yanked back Hal's forelock and sliced off a long section of scalp in one deft movement, leaping to his feet and thrusting the blood-soaked flesh high in the air for all the other warriors to see.

"You blood-thirsty bastard!" Gresham roared, launching himself at the yellow-faced Pawnee. But he was brought up short by three warriors who stepped in his path.

The Pawnee turned and taunted Gresham, dangling the scalp in his face as the warriors fought to restrain him. The yellow-faced Indian shrieked in his own language, his face contorted with venomous hatred for the man that he believed had killed his daughter. His retribution complete, he fell silent and glared at Gresham before spitting on O'Halloran's inert body and striding away.

Gresham was beside himself with fury. He thrashed against his captors, punching, kicking, and screaming contemptuous condemnation, desperate to get his hands on the Indian. But he was held fast until the Pawnee warriors unexpectedly stood back and he was released, allowing the red-faced leader to push his horse between Gresham and the yellow-faced Indian.

The leader dropped lightly from his pony and peered down at O'Halloran, his face serious as he stood staring at the cowhand for several minutes before nodding and turning to Gresham.

He pointed at the yellow-faced Pawnee. "He say this man kill daughter. Is done." The statement was made with finality.

Gresham fought to supress his anger, balling his fists to control his emotions. "How can he know that this was the man who killed his daughter? A man is not necessarily guilty of murder because he carries a knife!"

"He say is man," the Pawnee responded, as if the simplicity of the explanation was all that was required.

"That isn't proof of guilt, and your warriors had no cause to attack these men." Gresham gestured at his trooper and O'Halloran.

The leader was about to respond when one of his warriors gesticulated over Gresham's shoulder in alarm, the other Pawnee swiftly marshaling their weapons and leaping onto their ponies, ready for battle.

Gresham turned to see what had provoked the Indians' agitation and was confronted by the sight of Trautman and thirty troopers riding out from the corral of wagons. Once again, he recognized the potential for the confrontation to escalate into conflict, so he hurried toward the troop, barking an order for the squad to pull up and return their rifles to their scabbards.

Trautman was apprehensive, but he complied with the instruction and brought his men to a standstill, leaving them under the command of one of his most experienced sergeants as he advanced on his own.

"You okay?" he enquired as soon as he was close enough to converse.

"Yes." Gresham responded curtly. "They've killed O'Halloran, and our trooper's in a bad way, but I think the fighting's over. They think O'Halloran murdered a young Indian girl, so they've got what they came for, damn it."

"O'Halloran? Don't see him as the type to go 'round killin'," Trautman mused, dismounting and accompanying Gresham as he returned to the dead cowhand, where Colter now sat alongside the Pawnee leader.

"I know. It's not justice, but O'Halloran's sacrifice may have saved a more costly fight with these Pawnee."

Gresham halted alongside O'Halloran, and Colter leaned out of his saddle to get a better view of the cowhand's corpse. "What they gone an' scalped 'im for?" He displayed no semblance of concern for Hal's fate, posing the question out of idle curiosity.

"They say he killed the girl," Gresham replied, glaring at the

Pawnee leader.

Colter sighed and leaned back, resting his hands on the horn of his saddle in his characteristically indifferent manner. "Well, s'pose that means the fightin's all done," he murmured. "Have t' git yerself a new man t' drive the cattle."

Colter glanced toward the wagon train, his attention drifting back to Johannes. *That seems to have got him off the hook,* he thought. *Reckon he's gonna be mighty pleased if I don't say nothing.* He surmised that the Indians had got their scalp and saw no point in complicating matters by telling Gresham what he knew about Johannes. Besides, he had often found that a bit of distasteful information could prove useful, so he smiled inwardly at his knowledge of the boy's dark secret.

"Lieutenant Trautman, please have your men assist trooper Lorimer and organize a detail to recover Mr. O'Halloran's body." Gresham addressed his second in command formally, maintaining eye contact with the Pawnee leader, and Trautman responded obediently, returning to organize his men.

The Pawnee leader nodded almost imperceptibly. "We go," he said, and without further comment he placed a hand on his pony's withers and leapt up onto its back in one fluid movement. Remounted, he signaled to the rest of his party and they sped off toward the hills in unison.

Gresham ordered Colter and Trautman to keep the allegation of the Indian girl's murder confidential. He was troubled by the accusation, though, since it was not in the interests of the Pawnee to ride out and confront a wagon train of nearly five hundred people, with a military escort, without sound justification. Additionally, he was not convinced that O'Halloran was the kind of man to commit murder.

And, for the sake of the cowhand's family, he wanted to prevent Hal's name becoming tarnished by rumors of an ugly crime.

Following some deliberation, he concluded that it would be better to allow people to believe that the cowhand's death had been the result of an unfortunate misunderstanding. Consequently, he used the marshals to spread word that the Pawnee had assumed Hal to be attacking them when he had fired a shot during his attempt to return to the camp. The story was credible, and most of the migrants were simply relieved that the Indian threat had been alleviated, few being motivated to enquire about the reason for the original confrontation.

The following morning, Gresham conducted a brief funeral service, affording Hal's family the opportunity to ensure that he was granted the dignity of a Christian burial, although he instructed the wagons to drive over the cowhand's grave as they pulled out, rendering his final resting place unidentifiable.

There was a palpable sense of relief at leaving the treacherous river crossing and the proximity to the Pawnee, and Gresham's precautionary measure of deploying his troop to protect the wagon train's southern flank provided welcome reassurance to the travelers.

The schooners were underway once more, but Gresham and Trautman resolved to maintain a watchful eye over the men in the wagons that had camped nearest to the river, one of whom was almost certainly guilty of rape and murder.

CHAPTER 25

June 1865, Fort Laramie, Dakota Territory

The trail from the Platte River to Fort Laramie sapped the migrants' endurance. The grazing was poor and more than thirty carcasses of their precious cattle were left along the trail, most being Hereford or Angus stricken with tick infestation transmitted by the Texan longhorns.

A bout of dysentery also beset six families, who were compelled to remain behind, too weak to continue. Gresham sent the troop surgeon to minister to them, who explained the need to drink plenty of water, advising that they should boil it first since the latest scientific guidance implied that the disease was caused by contaminants in poor-quality water. Despite his best advice, however, half of those smitten with the illness succumbed to the complications of dehydration and died.

Furthermore, notwithstanding the marshal's extensive planning, the hill descent into Ash Hollow resulted in the wreckage of two wagons, one schooner breaking its shackles and careering down the hill, where it exploded in a cloud of splintered wood as it struck another wagon at the bottom of the steep grade. Fortunately, no one was killed, but several people received painful injuries from flying shards of timber.

There were also uplifting interludes along the trail, the emigrants being excited to reach the notorious landmarks of Jail House and Courthouse Rock, and eventually Chimney Rock, its immense Brule clay and Arikaree sandstone spire towering three hundred feet above the surrounding plains. And, morale peaked as the schooners navigated the final difficult incline before reaching Fort Laramie, Mitchell Pass, following which the wagon train adopted a carnival atmosphere.

At Laramie, Gresham agreed with the wagonmaster that there would be a four-day rest period, enabling the travelers to recuperate, replace their depleted provisions, and write letters to their families back home. The wagon train embracing a period of recuperation, he and Trautman set out to survey the congregation of humanity surrounding the fort.

Laramie was composed of an eclectic group of structures. The original fort, once named Fort John in memory of one of the officers of the American Fur Company, stood with its back to a high bluff at the confluence of the Laramie and North Platte rivers, the last sanctuary for migrants to summon their resolve before embarking upon the long arduous climb to the High Plains and South Pass, gateway to the Rocky Mountain trails.

The fort's adobe walls were formed from hand-crafted blocks made of local sand and clay mixed with straw, and surmounted with four guardhouses that provided an unobstructed panorama across the surrounding land.

Its entrance was double gated, enabling the sentries to interrogate anyone wishing to enter the fort without permitting access, and once inside, the inner compound was divided into two, the larger portion comprising a compact parade square surrounded by offices and barracks, while a smaller area provided space for the quartermaster to assemble and protect the station's mules and horses, if required.

The garrison bristled with military strength; two companies of the Eleventh Ohio Cavalry, G Company of Sixth Infantry, and nearly a full company comprised of former confederate prisoners of war. Its resources had rapidly outgrown the cramped confines of the aged fort, and the facilities now extended onto the surrounding plain.

Gresham studied the familiar officers' mess, built in the Greek revival style of timber and brick, accented with elaborate decking that encircled the ground and first floor. He frowned at the thought that the building was increasingly becoming renowned for its raucous parties, lending it the ungracious but appropriate name Old Bedlam. In his opinion, such a reputation was unbecoming of the cavalry, and he mused about the changes he would impose if the garrison ever fell to his command.

The old fort was supplemented by further barracks, stables, a warehouse, and a bakery, all built of stone whitewashed with lime and organized around a new parade square. Encircling and protecting the northern aspect of the fort, a new defensive ditch had been excavated, interconnecting battery redoubts and gun embrasures.

As they meandered through the civilian area, Gresham and Trautman passed the burgeoning trading post, swollen by the insatiable demands of a constant stream of migrants. At its center the general store was the dominant building, seething with customers attempting to trade surplus belongings or purchase new supplies.

An eclectic assortment of people jostled through the doors, uniformed cavalrymen alongside travelers of every conceivable nationality, intermingled with groups of native Indians who pestered the migrants to buy their furs and hides.

Gresham watched the scrum of merchants and wagged his head in dismay, switching his attention to the vast assembly of tipis that stretched across the plain toward the confluence of the Laramie and Platte rivers. The fort was now home to hundreds of Indians, whose traditional way of life had been ceded to the lure of the trading post and the unfortunate seduction of the "white man's firewater."

He was alarmed at the scale of the community. The concentration of itinerant people was a recipe for disease in the absence of adequate sanitation, and evidence of the erosion of cultural tradition was everywhere. Almost all of the Indians wore white man's clothing, but the men sat idly in sedentary groups leaving the women to work their hides and barter. And, from a security perspective, it was impossible to differentiate those who might present a threat, from people who simply wished to buy and sell. Fort Laramie was no longer a military installation, it was a bustling commercial town.

A runner appeared shortly after the wagon train arrived, bearing an invitation to join the garrison commander in his office at Gresham's earliest convenience and, although he was uncertain whether the request was intended as an instruction or a courteous welcome, he confirmed his acceptance.

The commander was a colonel by the name of George Sibley, whom Gresham and Trautman knew reasonably well. He was an experienced man, scarred by the ravages of the Civil War, who was ill-suited to the task of commanding a challenging frontier post, since he was unlikely to be disposed to observing the rituals and traditions inherent in dealing with local tribes, interpreting the subtleties and nuances of native communication and negotiation. Instead, he would tend toward intransigence and brute force, believing that the Indians would quail at the scale of power wielded by the Union Army and capitulate when threatened.

During his tenure, there had already been several notable instances of negotiations with Red Cloud breaking down, and it was rumored that Sibley was now misguidedly dealing with an opportunistic group of tribal headmen appropriately referred to as the "Laramie Loafers," who exerted no influence or authority over the Sioux, Arapaho, or Cheyenne elders.

Reaching the administrative building, Trautman and Gresham were escorted to Sibley's office, where they found him hunched over his desk studying a stack of papers through his circular eyeglasses, his bald pate shining with sweat in the stiflingly hot room.

"Capt'n Gresham, a real pleasure to see you ag'in." Sibley's greeting was effusive, and he waved the two men toward the chairs at the opposite side of his desk. "And, Lieutenan' Trautman, too. You boys're a welcome sight. How's the trail bin?"

"Good as can be expected with one of these big wagon trains," Gresham replied. "Although, I'm afraid the cost of people's dreams has been high for some. But it's good to see you, Colonel. Last time was Nashville, I think?"

He recalled the savage battle with confederate forces the preceding December, led by Lieutenant General John Bell Hood, and the bitter criticism of the Union commander Major General George Thomas by both General Ulysses Grant and President Lincoln himself. Thomas armed with inferior forces, but safe within the fortifications of Nashville, had taken his time to engage Hood on his own terms. The ensuing battle had raged for two days, before the battered and brutally depleted Union army had grasped a vital victory, routing Hood's forces and signaling an end to the conflict in the west. Sibley's regiment had been in the vanguard of the battle and almost all had been killed, leaving Sibley among the few wounded survivors.

"Hmm. Bad business." Sibley muttered. "As if we ain't had enough fightin', now we got these belly-achin' Injuns to deal with."

"Looks like you've got your own tribe settled outside the fort," Trautman ventured.

"Mostly waifs and strays." Sibley gazed blankly out of the

window. "The menfolk're here mainly for the whiskey, and the women're tradin' their skins while the men git blind drunk. It's a pretty unsatisfactory state of affairs, but if we was to try an' in'ervene the jailhouse 'ould be overflowin', and the men 'ould only take up arms. It's a question o' the lesser o' two evils really."

Gresham remained silent, fearing that any comment might be interpreted as criticism and, given his fractious relationship with Murray, he had no desire to compromise the camaraderie he hoped to cultivate with the commanding officer of the closest garrison to Platte Bridge Station.

Sibley returned his attention to his two guests. "Oh. I oughtta show you why I sent for you," he smiled, handing Gresham a communication that lay on his desk. "Had a telegraph from General Murray couple o' days ago. Were for yo' attention. Looks like the general wants one of yo' officers."

Gresham's brow creased quizzically as he took the telegraph and started to read. "What on earth's this?" he simmered with annoyance. "He's assigning Lieutenant Moylan to join a deployment to Virginia City." He passed the telegraph to Trautman and fixed Sibley with a steely eye. "I don't suppose there was any explanation?"

Sibley had anticipated a degree of frustration, but was surprised at Gresham's belligerent reaction. "I'm 'fraid I got no idea. As yo' kin see, it's a straightforward order. Didn' have no reason to question it. All I know is yo' lieutenan's gotta telegraph Major Kearny at Fort Leavenworth to git his orders."

Trautman put the telegraph down and looked at Gresham, mystified. "Why would he want to send a young lieutenant all the way up to Virginia City?"

"It doesn't make sense." Gresham turned to Sibley. "I'd be obliged if you'd permit me to use your telegraph office, Colonel. I'd like to clarify these orders with General Murray."

Sibley looked sheepish and wrung his hands uncomfortably. “I’m ’fraid I had separate orders from General Murray. He asked that the lieutenan’ be ’structed to report direct to me. I’m to take ’im to git ’is orders. I’m sorry. It’s all kinda embarrassin’.”

Gresham shot to his feet, sending his chair crashing to the floor. “That’s outrageous,” he blurted, his face puce with rage. “The lieutenant reports to me, and if he’s to receive new orders I will give them to him.” He was astonished that Murray would treat him so dismissively.

“I don’ appreciate yo’ shoutin’ at me, Capt’n.” Sibley bridled at becoming the object of Gresham’s irritation. “They’s ma orders. Don’t know why the general ’sisted on Lieutenan’ Moylan reporting to me, but I don’t propose to question his ’structions. Seems pretty simple, an’ as I understan’ it, with Mr. Trautman here, there’s three lieutenan’s in yo’ company, so I reckon yo’ shouldn’ be missin’ one anyways.”

Gresham felt Trautman’s light touch on his arm and the gesture helped him to regain his composure. There was no merit in alienating Sibley. Murray’s behavior was not the colonel’s fault, so he took a deep breath to control his anger before responding.

“I apologize, Colonel. General Murray’s orders are an unusual departure from protocol, and I’m concerned that Lieutenant Moylan is being put in a position he’s not ready to handle. He’s a young man with little experience and a hot head. I’ll have the lieutenant report to you, sir, but if you deem it appropriate I’d appreciate understanding the nature of his orders once they become clear.”

Sibley felt genuine empathy with Gresham. He had no idea why Murray’s instructions had been so perverse, and felt awkward being asked to usurp the young captain’s authority. Their shared campaign in Nashville, with all its associated horrors, forged a bond of solidarity that transcended any division of rank. The memories were indelibly etched in Sibley's mind, and he reflected upon his sense of fraternity with the man who stood before him, compared to the animosity he felt toward the general in Leavenworth.

He waved away Gresham's apology. "I appreciate yo' understandin', Capt'n. I ain't sure 'bout lieutenan's orders yit, but if there ain't no need for no secrecy, I'll be sure an' letcha know."

"Thank you, Colonel." Gresham touched his hat and dismissed himself, leaving Trautman to scurry after him.

The lieutenant hurried to catch up as Gresham strode back toward the wagon train, plowing his way through the throngs of people loitering outside the general store, his hand grasped firmly around the brass hand-guard of his saber.

"Hold up, John!" Trautman puffed as he drew level. "You're gonna knock someone flyin' in a minute if you don't slow up."

Gresham marched on despite Trautman's protest. "Damned man!" he growled. "I'd knock him flat if he was here. General or no general."

Trautman threaded past two Indians, who scuttled out of Gresham's way. "What do you make of the orders for Moylan?"

"Lunacy! What idiot would send a boy like Moylan all the way to Virginia City on his own? He hardly set foot out of Ohio before being posted to Leavenworth. Murray should be given a desk job in Washington. He's got no understanding of the west. He's a damned liability."

"Any idea why he might wan' a lieutenant to go up to Montana Territory?"

"No idea. But it won't be an idle purpose." He stopped abruptly amid the bustle of people and faced Trautman. "It's obviously something he doesn't want to explain. That's why he's got Sibley doing his dirty work. He knows I'd want to be told what Moylan's being sent to do, so he's bypassing me. The man's a snake. I don't like it!"

"But why would they wan' a junior officer in Virginia City? There's no garrison there. And if snakes is what you want, you'll find a whole nest of 'em there."

"That's what worries me." Gresham set off toward the wagons again. "Find Moylan, Isaac. Bring him to see me. I need to talk to him before he meets Sibley."

Trautman nodded in confirmation and disappeared to summon the young lieutenant, leaving Gresham to return to the tent he was using as his command post.

Moylan looked nervous as he ducked into Gresham's makeshift office, Trautman at his side. He took off his Stetson and ran a hand through his untidy mop of dark hair in an unsuccessful effort to smarten himself up.

Gresham looked up from his improvised desk and greeted him. "Ah, Samuel. Come in."

Moylan relaxed visibly as he was addressed with the familiarity of his first name, but nevertheless was apprehensive about being summoned to the captain's tent. He was more accustomed to his commanding officer accompanying him on his rounds, probing his relationship with the men under his command and enquiring informally about his home or his father's military career. This encounter appeared decidedly different.

Gresham appreciated his discomfort and indicated that he and Trautman should take a seat. "Nothing to worry about, Samuel, but it looks like your services have been requested elsewhere, so we're going to have to get along without you."

Moylan looked confused, snatching a glance at Trautman for reassurance, but the lieutenant sat impassively alongside. "Sir, I don't understand."

"Well, it seems that General Murray would like you to make haste to Virginia City in Montana Territory. You ever been there before?" It occurred to Gresham that there was a possibility Moylan might have some prior association with the gold-rush town.

"Virginia City? No, sir. Why would the general send me there?" Moylan's broad brow furrowed with anxiety.

"The army works in mysterious ways, Samuel. I'm sure the general has good reason. You know anything about the gold fields?"

"No, sir. Bunch of crazy prospectors grubbin' 'round in the mud's what I heard. Am I joining another detachment, sir?" Moylan enquired.

Gresham was satisfied the boy had no connection with Virginia City that might explain his orders. "The commander here at Laramie is Colonel Sibley. He'll organize for you to telegraph Major Kearny at Fort Leavenworth, who'll provide your detailed orders. Isaac will take you up to the fort. When you're properly briefed, you can come back here and we'll see what we can do to help you prepare."

"It's nice to be asked, sir, but I'd rather stay with your company," Moylan pleaded. "Couldn't they send someone else?"

"Not my call I'm afraid, Samuel. Now, you'd better get going. Let's talk again once you've got your orders. Don't worry, we'll help you as best we can." Gresham stood up and ushered Trautman and the lad on their way.

Trautman escorted Moylan to the fort and left him with Sibley's orderly, who informed the young lieutenant that he would have to wait until the colonel was available to see him. Despite his dislike of the boy, Trautman patted Moylan on the shoulder and wished him well.

He skirted the offices, walking briskly along the decking that wrapped around the outside of the building, its pitched roof shading him from the hot midday sun as he navigated the shortest route to one of the guard blocks mounted on top of the thick adobe walls of the fort, hoping that it would afford him a good view of the surrounding area.

The ground floor was comprised of a series of offices, where administrators orchestrated the affairs of the bustling frontier post. All of the windows were cast open allowing air into the stifling interior, so Trautman snatched a glance as he passed each room.

Sibley's office was at the far end of the building, and Trautman saw Moylan waiting anxiously as he passed the colonel's orderly. To his surprise Sibley's window was open too, and he could not resist a sidelong peek as he passed.

Seated opposite the colonel was a bear of a man, dressed in a weathered hide jacket, his face masked by a thick stubbly beard and his head adorned with a full racoon skin. Colter sat slouched in a chair as Sibley engaged him in animated discussion.

Trautman kept walking, averting his eyes to avoid either man thinking that he had seen them, but he noticed that the colonel appeared less than happy and wondered what business Sibley might have with the mountain man.

Intrigued, he made haste for the guard block, his interest no longer centered on enjoying the view. Instead, he guessed that the elevated post would afford a good vantage point from which to monitor activity within the walls, without being seen.

Reaching the guard post, Trautman bounded up the stairs and engaged the two sentries in polite conversation, encouraging them to identify each of the fort's internal buildings and provide an insight to their respective function. The guards were pleased to receive a visitor from another regiment and listened avidly as Trautman talked about his journey from Fort Leavenworth, allowing him to observe the inner fortifications covertly.

After ten minutes the door to the administrative offices opened and Colter sauntered into the sunlight, pausing to hitch up his breeches and casually scan the fort. His eyes settled on a rustic structure on the far side of the parade square and he aimed purposefully toward it, causing Trautman to break off his account of the wagon train's tribulations and enquire about the building's use.

"That's the telegraph office," one of the young soldiers explained enthusiastically. "Used to be Pony Express office afore telegraph arrived. That were somethin', Pony Express. One rider come in wi' mail jus' three days after he left St. Joseph. Wouldn't think it possible, would yer? Now, s'all gone. Instead, telegraph's same as talkin', only the folks as listenin' might be th' other side of the country." The boy spoke with the wondrous tone of someone seeing a miracle unfold before his eyes.

Trautman continued to make light conversation as he watched Colter step into the telegraph office and waited for him to reappear. After twenty minutes, the mountain man ambled out, a telegraph clasped firmly in his hand, and sat down in the shade as if waiting for something.

Trautman watched from his concealed position, reminded of the dangerously deceptive demeanor that Colter portrayed. The impression he exuded was one of a scruffy vagabond, but careful scrutiny revealed the man's acute awareness of his surroundings. His eyes moved restlessly, examining the detail of everything he observed, and his posture enabled him to reach for his gun while still appearing relaxed and disinterested.

As Trautman studied him, Colter stiffened, his eyes fixed intently on something at the opposite side of the parade square. Trautman followed his gaze and was surprised to see Moylan walking down the steps to the administrative building, accompanied by Colonel Sibley, who led the way to the telegraph office. He flicked his attention back to Colter, who retreated into the shadows at the foot of the inner wall of the fort and moved away, but it was evident that he continued to watch the two men.

Colter's behavior was distinctly suspicious and Trautman wondered whether there might be a link between General Murray's orders for Moylan and Colter's meeting with Sibley. He considered following Colter, but with unnerving ease the mountain man slipped out of sight and disappeared, so Trautman decided to take his leave of the guards and return to the cavalry billet.

Gresham was concerned by Trautman's report. "I don't like what's going on here, Isaac. Murray's up to something with Colter, and it doesn't feel official. Moylan's not going to be up to handling those two rattlesnakes. He'll get drawn into something he doesn't understand." He paused, turning his writing quill in his hand thoughtfully. "This is beginning to smell bad."

"I agree. It was strange, though. Colter hid when he saw Moylan and Sibley. I'm pretty sure he was waitin' for them, or at least one of them."

"Sounds like he didn't want to be seen. My guess is he was waiting for one of them and had to move off when they appeared together. From what you say he'd already talked to Sibley, so there would be no sense in waiting to see him again, and anyway why would he need to conceal himself from Sibley? No, I think he was waiting for Moylan and didn't want Sibley to see him meet the lad."

"Makes sense. But what would he want from Moylan?"

"I don't know, Isaac, but I think we should find out. Let's assume Colter will continue to try and accost Moylan. You'd better find the boy and keep an eye on him. Stay close but don't make it obvious you're watching."

"No problem." Trautman nodded and ducked out of Gresham's tent to search for Moylan, passing the line of picketed horses where his squad was camped. There was no sign of the lad, so he made his way up the well-worn path toward the fort's main gate.

Crowds of people were gathered outside the general store blocking the route, and Trautman had to push his way through several large groups, initially asking people politely to make way, but eventually having to resort to shoving folk aside when they failed to move. Engrossed in clearing his path, he almost missed Moylan approaching from the opposite direction, looking up in surprise as another cavalry uniform brushed against his shoulder.

"Oh, Lieutenant, there you are! I was comin' to find you. You've been gone a good while."

Moylan offered a condescending sneer in return. "That'll be Captain Moylan, Lieutenant!" he spat, holding himself erect and giving Trautman a haughty glare.

"What d' you say?" Trautman was momentarily knocked off guard by Moylan's arrogant manner and grinned back at him. "You catch too much sun, boy?"

Moylan's brow creased into a frown and his mouth tightened. "I said it's Captain Moylan, Lieutenant! Now, if you'll get out of my way, I have business with Captain Gresham."

He pushed past Trautman, who was left stunned, and had to race in pursuit to grab the boy's shoulder and spin him around. "Now, hold up, you pompous little shit!" his face was inches from Moylan's and his voice quivered with fury. "What the . . ."

Moylan interrupted, his face plastered with a conceited smirk. "You want to take this up with General Murray?" he taunted. "Promoted captain, effective immediately." He held up a telegraph for Trautman to see. "And, if you don't get your hand off me, I'll have you put on report, Lieutenant." He glanced sideways at the hand that was clamped to his shoulder.

Trautman was astonished. It was unprecedented for a second

lieutenant to be promoted straight to captain, but Moylan's face betrayed no hint of ambiguity.

"I don't know how or why you've come by your stripes, but they ain't gonna mean jack-shit when you get out there on your own," he nodded in the direction of the mountains. "You'll need men who'll follow you because they trust and respect you, and you'll not get that by bein' an arsehole!"

Moylan twisted, scowling dismissively at Trautman's hand before turning to meet the lieutenant's furious glare. "If I want your advice, I'll ask for it, Lieutenant. Now, get your hand off me." Incredulous, Trautman released his grip, and Moylan gave a self-satisfied sneer as he marched off toward the camp.

Trautman would have preferred to warn Gresham about the young upstart's inexplicable promotion, but hurrying ahead would only have reinforced Moylan's sense of self-importance. Consequently, he arrived at Gresham's tent to witness his commanding officer's incredulous expression as the boy swept in uninvited.

Gresham leaned back in his chair to appraise Moylan. An extraordinary change in his demeanor was patently evident. "Samuel, how did you get on?"

Rather than seating himself, Moylan pushed his thumbs into his waistband and sauntered over to the pot of hot coffee that Gresham's steward had delivered, nonchalantly helping himself to a cup while the captain snatched a perplexed glance at Trautman.

"May I introduce Captain Moylan!" he responded with bitter sarcasm, rolling his eyes.

Moylan spun around, suppressing a smug grin, and countered without glancing at Trautman. "Yes, John. A very satisfactory meeting with Colonel Sibley, thank you." He puffed out his chest and leaned back casually against the center pole of the tent. "Promoted to captain with immediate effect. I am to lead a top-secret mission to Virginia City." He beamed at Gresham, who remained impassive, ignoring the use of his first name.

"Well, Samuel, it seems like congratulations are in order. I don't suppose you know the nature of your new command yet?" Gresham played to the boy's ego, indicating to Trautman that he wanted him to leave, and although the lieutenant was incensed at being dismissed, he knew Gresham well enough to read his game. The question cut straight through Moylan's bravado, and he stumbled to contrive an answer that demonstrated he knew the details of his mission.

The colonel had formally briefed him that he was required to leave his company, but Sibley's further orders only extended to ensuring that he received a confidential communication and to providing him with twenty troopers, horses, and supplies.

Sibley had done as requested and escorted Moylan to the telegraph office, where the room had been cleared and the young lieutenant left alone with the telegraph operator. Moylan had received two communications. The first confirmed his promotion to the rank of captain with immediate effect and reiterated that he should liaison with Colonel Sibley to assemble a squad of men and supplies. He was instructed to make haste to Virginia City in Montana Territory and told to contact Major Kearny at Fort Leavenworth by telegraph when he arrived, who would provide supplementary orders.

The second message was a real surprise. It requested that he make contact with the mountain man, John Colter, who would act as his guide for at least part of the route from Laramie along the Bridger Trail. He was specifically instructed not to share the details of this communication.

"The . . . er, details are confidential." Moylan responded hesitantly.

Gresham nodded, acknowledging Moylan's obligation to maintain his discretion. "Well, if there's anything I can do to help you prepare for the journey, let me know. How long are you going to be up in Montana? Is it a long-term posting or a short-term assignment?"

Moylan fidgeted uncomfortably under Gresham's studious gaze. "I . . . er. I'm . . . not at liberty to say, sir." He immediately kicked himself for addressing Gresham as sir. The captain had a disconcerting ability to provoke a sense of inadequacy when he posed a question, and his penetrating eyes seemed to unveil one's thoughts.

"Hmm. I see." Gresham mused unconvincingly. "As I recall you haven't traveled up through the Powder River region before. Have you got a scout?"

Again, Gresham made Moylan squirm. The question was a difficult one to answer. It would be ridiculous for him to suggest that he could find his way to Virginia City without a scout. On the other hand, he did not want to infer that Colter would be leading him. First, it was obvious that the captain held the mountain man in low regard and, second, it would be apparent that Colter had been instructed to scout for him by either Sibley or Murray. The latter would prompt unwelcome questions about the reason Colter had been asked to guide him, and in truth, Moylan had no idea why Murray had selected the mountain man. In any event, it was information that he had specifically been instructed not to disclose.

"Colonel Sibley is arranging for a scout, and I believe we're going to take the Bridger Trail," Moylan mumbled.

"That sounds sensible. There's a good risk the Sioux would attempt to prevent any cavalry movements through the Powder River, but we don't patrol the Bridger Trail so Sibley must be sending a civilian scout. Do you know who he's using? I know most of the better scouts out here." Gresham watched the boy's face as he wrestled with the question. Moylan knew more than he was saying but was unsure how to respond, and the hesitation reinforced Gresham's impression that there was something improper about Murray's orders.

"Not yet." Moylan adopted a more assertive manner, thrusting out his chin in an ineffectual attempt to boost his confidence. "The colonel's selecting twenty troopers for my command and we'll commence preparations this evening. I expect he'll assign a scout too." He looked smug at his answer and sidled past Gresham's desk so that the captain had to turn in his chair to maintain eye contact.

Gresham seized on the statement, though. It was the piece of information he had been searching for. "Twenty troopers? So you're not being posted to a permanent garrison. Twenty men wouldn't be enough, and if you were being deployed to an existing company, you wouldn't need twenty of Sibley's men. Sounds like an escort detail. Do you know who you'll be escorting?" He smiled inwardly at the lad's naiveté, but maintained an air of serious concern.

Moylan cursed himself. His statement had seemed innocuous, but he had not thought through its implications. "I can't say," he blustered. "It's confidential. I . . . have to go. Sorry . . . thank you, sir," he stammered as he hurried to leave, eager to extract himself from Gresham's uncomfortable inquisition.

"Samuel!" Gresham's voice sounded like a command, and he waited for Moylan to turn and face him. "Don't get into anything you might regret." He remained seated, his bearing relaxed and assured as Moylan reluctantly met his eye before ducking out of the tent without further comment.

A few moments later Trautman reappeared. "Well?" he enquired impatiently.

"Well indeed!" Gresham responded, pushing himself to his feet. "I don't think he has any idea what he's being sent to do. I'm pretty certain he's not going to a permanent post because Sibley's providing him with twenty troopers."

"Sounds like escort duty," Trautman ventured.

"Exactly what I thought. And, he either doesn't know or won't tell me who's scouting for him. I don't think he's ever been up to Montana Territory before, so he'll need a scout."

"You think it's Colter?" Trautman questioned. "He'll eat Moylan for breakfast."

"I don't know, but I think we ought to find out, if we can. I need you to watch Moylan, Isaac. See what he does and who he talks to. I'm going to pay Sibley a visit and try to find out what he knows."

"Why you so bothered, John? Moylan seems happy with his orders, and you've said previously that you were concerned about how he'd cope out here, more so than Hanley. You might be better rid of him."

"I don't like being manipulated, Isaac. Besides, irrespective of what I think of Moylan, anything that has the potential to further frustrate the U.S. cavalry's relationship with the Indian Nations is of interest to me, and I have an unsettling feeling about this. Murray's trying to be covert about his orders to Moylan, which means he doesn't want me involved. That's a good enough reason to be concerned."

"Any idea what you think he's up to?"

"No. But why pick such an inexperienced man to run an escort, if that's what it is?"

"I see your point. I'll keep my eye on Moylan and let you know what I find."

They both left the tent and turned in separate directions, Gresham striding off toward the fort as Trautman went to commence surveillance of Moylan.

Chapter 26

Fort Laramie, Dakota Territory

Colonel Sibley was in conference with two of his officers when Gresham arrived, but he dispatched them unceremoniously when he was informed that the captain wanted to see him. He ushered Gresham into his office with a genial slap on the back and proffered a steaming mug of black coffee. "Well naw, John. Yo' wagon train 'bout ready to roll? I guess yo' gonna want to git 'em movin' agin pretty soon."

Gresham indulged the small talk. He liked Sibley and understood the mental scars the colonel was compelled to endure following his years of fighting in the south. "We're about ready, I guess," he responded. "Some of the families have had a hard journey, and we've lost more people than I'd hoped along the way, so they've earned a decent break. The worrying thing, though, is that they've not even crossed the most difficult sections of the trail yet. But they become more experienced with every day that passes, so with god's grace I hope most will make good progress from now on."

Sibley peered thoughtfully into his coffee. "S'hard country out there. Harder 'an all the ballyhoo back east 'ould have yo believe." The comment was imparted with a depth of feeling that betrayed Sibley's own experiences. "They a whole heap too many wagons rollin' west, y' know." He studied Gresham, continuing with a despondent air. "We can't protect 'em all, John, an' I'm worried they gonna be some helluva bustup if we let mo' folks cross in'a Bighorn."

"Have you asked for more men?" Gresham replied.

"Oh, yeah, plenty times! But th' general keeps on sayin' all o' Grant's resources a' committed, an' I jus' gotta make do wi' what I gotten. S'politics, y' know. They sayin' they wanna make the American con'nent one country, but when it come right down a'it they a trade-off 'tween what voters in the east wan', an' the money they kin 'fford to win the west."

"You know the Indians'll never stand aside and let white men settle in their hunting grounds," Gresham observed bluntly. "Winning the west means defeating the Indian Nations, and to do that you'd need to destroy them. There are no half measures. There are only two long-term choices: give them their lands and protect them from incursion by settlers and prospectors or wipe them out. It's ugly, but true, I'm afraid. The treaties we have are a temporary measure, simply postponing the inevitable. There'll never be an adequate compromise."

Sibley was shocked by Gresham's forthright summary and leaned forward in his chair apprehensively. "I hope yo' don't go roun' promotin' that kinda talk, John. Wrong people hear they 'pinions, yo' gonna git yo'self thrown out the army."

Gresham appreciated Sibley's sensitivity, but he was not minded to be overly conciliatory. "You and I are going to have to work closely together, Colonel, so I think that between the two of us it's better to be candid. That's my assessment, and I'm no warmonger. I've seen enough bloodshed to last me several lifetimes, and frankly I have more respect for the Indians than I do for a lot of the greed I see flocking west. That said, I'll do everything I can from Platte Bridge to foster good relations with the plains tribes and enforce our treaties. But we need to be ready to act when things start to go badly, so I think we both need to know where we stand, don't you?"

The colonel mused on Gresham's comments. He certainly

lived up to his reputation as a straight-talking man. Sibley liked him, and for the first time in many months, he felt as though he might have found an ally that he could rely upon to share the burden of the onerous task of keeping the peace on the Great Plains. He nodded slowly and smiled, a tired but grateful expression. "I guess we understan' one 'nother, John. Yo' feel free to ask fo' any help yo' need when yo' git t' Platte Bridge. An', why don' yo' call me George?"

"Thank you." Gresham stretched out his hand to clasp Sibley's. "To good sense and even better luck." He paused for a moment before continuing. "There was something else. I was wondering whether you have been able to establish more about Moylan's orders. The whole situation seems very unusual to me."

Sibley grimaced. "I'm pretty much in the dark, I'm 'fraid. I understan' boy's bin pr'moted cap'n an' 'structed to make his way to Virginia City. The orders come from Major Kearny, not Murray, though general done ask me t' send twen'y troopers wi' yo' man."

"Doesn't seem like he's my man anymore," Gresham grumbled. "Moylan tells me you're going to provide a scout, since he's never traveled up to Montana Territory before."

"Don't know nothin' 'bout that," Sibley retorted. "Thought 'bout it, though, since th' boy looks like he ain't seen backside o' a barn afore. Picked two good s'perienced men to go wi' 'im. Sergeant Ames knows Powder River Basin pretty fine. He's 'scorted through Bozeman trail couple a times. Then there's a corporal who wa' a scout afore he joined up. He rode wi' Jim Bridger for a few years. Know's land to west o' Bighorn Moun'ns."

"Sounds very sensible. You haven't heard John Colter's name mentioned, though, have you?"

Sibley's nose wrinkled at the mention of Colter. "Y'all know 'im? I sure ain't taken wi' th' smell o' the man, or 'is manners! General asked to git 'im a message jus' 'bout when yo' hauled on in'a Laramie. Well, he come right on in wi'out a by yo' leave. Put 'is damned boots on ma desk!" Sibley eyed the corner of his writing table as if it had been violated.

"Yes, he's sure something, isn't he?" Gresham laughed. "But he's a dangerous man and he operates to his own agenda."

"I guessed that. He gotta big reputat'n an all, an' I sure ain't comfortable wi' 'im bein' in these par's wi'out knowin' what in hell he's doin'. Had masel' quite a bustup wi' yo' Mr Colter when he come in here all high an' mighty. Asked him what he's plannin' on doin' an' where he's goin', but he don't tell me a dang thing. Said he ain't 'countable to no U.S. army, an' s'a free country to do like he wan's." Sibley's irritation at Colter's intransigence was obvious.

"Do you know what Murray wanted with Colter?"

"Well, that's the thing. On one hand, he gone an' say he don't have no 'countability to the army, an' on the other Murray's gotten me runnin' 'im messages. If he's workin' fo' the general, I wanna know what the deuce he's doin'. But he reckons he met Murray in Leavenworth an' general's jus' passin' on a message from a business 'quaintance." Sibley lifted the palms of his hands in defeat and rolled his eyes.

"What does Murray say?"

"General says Colter's free agen'. Got nothin' to do wi' the military."

Gresham frowned. "That's an interesting way of responding. He hasn't said he doesn't know what Colter's up to, and he almost sounds as though he's defending him."

"What's yo' concern?" Sibley scratched his mottled crown.

"I'm not sure yet, but I wouldn't be surprised if Colter leaves with Moylan, and if that happens, I think it will have been at Murray's instruction. If that's the case, I'd like to know why. I don't trust Colter, and I think his presence means trouble for us."

"Why don' we see if ma telegraph operator kin remember wha' Colter's message from Murray said?" Sibley ventured.

"That's a fine idea. Can you do that?"

"Well, not s'posed to in'erfere wi' telegraph an all, but let's see wha' we kin git anyhow."

Sibley sent his orderly to summon the telegraph operator, who looked like a startled rabbit when he appeared in the colonel's office and reluctantly shared what he could recall of the message Colter had received.

"Said somin' bout a lieutenan', an' said TW said was real important. Reckon there was somin' 'bout more instructions bein' delivered too, but don't know nothin' 'bout that." The telegraph operator was nervous and unsure about the content of the message, making it clear that he processed so many communications each day that it was difficult to recollect any of them with a reliable degree of certainty. He scuttled away looking relieved the instant that he was dismissed.

"I guess the lieutenant will be Moylan, but do you know a TW? Do those initials make any sense to you?" Gresham looked ponderous.

Sibley wagged his head. "Nope. Don't mean nothin' to me." He looked equally bemused.

"Hmm. We'll have to watch and see what happens, I suppose." Gresham shifted the conversation back to Moylan's assignment. "How well do you know Ames? Is he loyal to you?" Gresham enquired, draining his coffee.

"Yeah, I know Ames real well. He's the kinda man yo' kin trust, and I s'pect he ain't gonna be too taken wi' yo' greenhorn capt'n!"

"Good. Maybe you could instruct him to telegraph you from Virginia City so we can find out what happens on the trail and what Moylan does when he gets there."

Sibley nodded in agreement. "I'll make sure he knows wha' he gotta do. I hope yo' wrong, John. Life gonna be hard 'nough out here wi'out havin' to second-guess different 'gendas."

"I've got Isaac Trautman shadowing Moylan, so if he gets cozy with Colter hopefully we'll know about it. I'll let you know what happens." Gresham rose and shook hands with Sibley.

Trautman concluded that it would be easier to watch Moylan undetected than to attempt to keep Colter under surveillance. The mountain man had an uncanny ability to disappear into shadows, and Trautman suspected that his years in the wilderness would have refined his ability to detect when he was being followed.

Instead, he observed Moylan relocate to the fort, organize his new uniform, and give orders for the preparation of the supplies his squad would need for their journey. But, for most of the time, Trautman was able to observe him without difficulty as he loitered around Old Bedlam without any apparent sense of urgency.

For the rest of the day Colter made no attempt to contact Moylan, and Trautman nearly missed him intercept the young captain as he trailed the lad toward the fort at dusk, having begun to believe that he had misinterpreted the mountain man's earlier behavior.

Moylan walked with purpose, swaggering with arrogance at his newly appointed seniority, but as he passed through the gates he came up sharply, looking confused. He stepped briefly into the shadows and emerged a few moments later to hurry into the fort, the confidence having gone out of his gait.

Trautman concealed himself and waited. Fifteen minutes passed without event, and he was considering leaving his hiding place when a ghostly figure slipped away from the gates and made its way stealthily along the outer wall of the fort, before disappearing in among the sprawl of Indian tipis. It was too dark to make out the man's face, but Trautman recognized the profile as Colter.

The contact had been brief and clandestine, and Trautman was more certain than ever that the contact between Colter and Moylan had been orchestrated by Murray. Gresham's concerns seemed well founded and, once Trautman had returned and debriefed him, the two concluded that they should attempt to keep Colter under surveillance, difficult as that might prove, to see if they could establish his motive.

Chapter 27

Fort Laramie, Dakota Territory

Stone rode hard for a week, changing his horse twice each day at the small trading posts along the Oregon Trail, and by the time he rode into Fort Laramie he was almost unrecognizable. His smart three-piece suit had been rolled up and tucked into his saddlebags, and he wore a set of buckskin breeches and a woolen capote as a jacket. He was covered in dust, had not shaved for a week, and looked every inch a man of the frontier.

He had completed the journey in almost record time for a civilian and, although physically exhausted, he remained focused on the purpose of his journey. Winthrop had been explicit that he had to catch up with Colter before the mountain man left Laramie, after which he would be more difficult to locate.

The balls of Stone's feet and the insides of his knees were rubbed raw from hard riding and he longed for a good square meal, but he dismissed his physical discomfort and immediately went in search of Colter, despite the late hour.

Murray had said that Colter would be traveling with a wagon train under military escort, so he started his quest by identifying the largest congregation of schooners, which was camped to the west of the fort and attended by a company of the Seventh Cavalry.

He dismounted alongside the nearest wagon, tied up his horse, and approached a companionable gathering of migrants to enquire where he might find John Colter. It was clear that everybody knew the mountain man, but few ventured an opinion of his whereabouts. Nevertheless, he was proffered a few suggestions that seemed hopeful, and his search was rewarded when he encountered a rough-looking prospector who directed him to a schooner where some of the men gathered to indulge in hard drinking and gambling.

Sure enough, once Stone found the wagon, he picked out seven figures gathered around a makeshift table playing cards by the light cast from a series of lanterns. Colter was easy to identify, and although Stone had never met him in person, his appearance accorded exactly with Winthrop's description. He was unmistakable.

Stone worked his way around the schooner so that he could approach Colter inconspicuously, his uninvited appearance prompting hostile glares from the mountain man's companions as he stepped out of the shadows.

"You'd better have good reason for sneakin' up on a man," Colter growled.

"Senator Winthrop sent me. We need to speak," Stone bent to whisper in his ear, unmoved by the threat.

"Heard you was comin'. Hope you ain't plannin' on interfering with this here game o' poker." Colter's attention remained focused on his game.

"I've ridden sixteen hours a day for the last week to speak to you, Mr. Colter. We need to talk, now!" Stone hissed, fixing the mountain man with an obstinate grimace as Colter turned, bristling with infuriated disbelief.

To Colter's surprise, the face that met him was hard and implacable. Stone showed no indication of the fear Colter managed to instill in most people, and the two locked eyes, testing each other's resolve.

"*Now,* Mr. Colter." Stone whispered, his intransigence unmistakable.

Colter regarded him dispassionately for a few moments, shrugged, and turned to his gambling colleagues. "Gonna sit out a couple o' hands, boys. Don't go gettin' any ideas 'bout runnin' off with the purse now."

Stone retreated into the shadows, leaving Colter to follow him.

Trautman followed Colter, remaining as inconspicuous as he was able, and secreted himself among a group of migrants camped close to where the mountain man and his companions were ensconced so that he could maintain an attentive vigil.

The lanterns around the improvised card table emitted enough light for Trautman to scrutinize Colter, and it was clear that the whiskey was flowing, although it looked like the mountain man was getting the rough end of the pack, judging by the scowl on his face.

On several occasions he contemplated taking his leave of the migrants, since it appeared that there was little to be gleaned from Colter's entertainment, but he was relieved that he had not retired early when a tall scruffy man appeared from the shadows.

The murky light made observation difficult, but Trautman felt that there was something unusual about the mysterious newcomer. His appearance looked out of place, and he carried himself with assurance, approaching Colter without hesitation. He either knew Colter well or he was not afraid of him. Certainly, his behavior was not subservient.

Quietly, Trautman left his hosts and melted into the darkness, intent upon circling around to obtain a closer look at the man Colter had slipped away to meet.

★ ★ ★ ★ ★

Stone waited in the shadows, clearing his throat quietly to indicate where he was standing as Colter stepped out of the light.

"This better be good," Colter grumbled.

"You're getting well paid, Mr. Colter, so I suggest you listen up." Stone was in no mood for petulant behavior. "The senator has some work that requires your attention."

"Who the hell d'you think you are?" Colter bristled.

Anticipating Colter's lack of cooperation, Stone held out a small leather pouch. "This should help you understand. Compliments of the senator." Colter took the bag suspiciously and opened the drawstring to examine its contents.

"That's a thousand dollars in gold, Mr. Colter, and another two to come if I have your attention."

In the pervasive darkness, Colter was unable to confirm the contents of the pouch, but he had no doubt that Winthrop's man spoke the truth. "Follow me," he muttered, retying the cord on the bag and leading the way toward the schooner he shared with his prospector friends.

When they arrived, Colter shooed away two men sitting alongside the wagon and invited Stone to seat himself on a stool by the fire, hunkering down beside him and depositing a good slug of whiskey into two tin cups.

Stone accepted the coarse alcohol gratefully and took a long, satisfying draught. "You made contact with Lieutenant Moylan?"

"Seems like he's Capt'n Moylan now. Why, you know something 'bout that?"

Stone ignored Colter's question and continued. "Moylan's been selected by General Murray to run escort to the gold train out of Virginia City at the end of July. They'll be shipping over four hundred thousand dollars of gold."

"Seems a bit wet behind th'ears for that sort o' job," Colter grunted.

"Their route will take them through the Powder River Basin, and the senator wants to encourage Red Cloud to seize the gold. He thinks you could help with that."

Colter had been unsure what to expect from Winthrop's messenger, but he was astounded at the outrageous proposition and stared at Stone dumbfounded. "The senator wantin' to start a goddamned war?"

Stone was unmoved. "Can you do this?" He locked eyes with Colter, and it was clear that he was deadly serious.

Colter wagged his head in disbelief. "Gonna cost you more 'n three thousand dollars t' git that done!"

"There's two thousand dollars for ensuring that Red Cloud attacks the gold train. The other thousand is for a different job. Need I remind you, Mr. Colter, that your share of the profits from your buffalo enterprise is at the discretion of Senator Winthrop. He can and will find someone else to run the hunting operations if you feel your remuneration is inadequate." Stone's tone was hard and uncompromising.

"Son of a bitch! You tryin' to threaten me!" Colter was speechless at the brazen effrontery. No one had ever spoken to him with such disdain, and his blood boiled.

Instantly, his hand dropped to his gun belt and he ripped his pistol from its holster, intent on frightening Stone into a more conciliatory frame of mind. He was well known for his prowess with a handgun, and few people would consider attempting to draw their weapon against him. In fact, everyone who had done so previously now lay beneath a wooden cross.

But, to his astonishment, Colter found himself staring down the eight-inch octagonal bore of a Remington Model 1861 Army revolver. The speed at which Stone drew his gun and cocked the hammer was extraordinary. Colter barely recalled noticing

Stone's hand move before the weapon was pointed between his eyes, his own pistol barely clear of its holster.

An ardent devotee of the Remington, Stone liked the balance of the revolver. He found that its reliability was better than many alternative handguns, some of which suffered from frame distortions, a problem that was alleviated by the Remington's solid frame design. In addition, despite requiring the use of percussion caps, unlike some of the more modern revolvers, the Remington offered the advantage of being able to remove and exchange a complete cylinder, which enabled rapid reloading, a feature that could mean the difference between life and death in certain circumstances.

Stone held the revolver leveled between Colter's eyes. "I didn't come here to argue with you, Mr. Colter. We both have jobs to do, and I came to give you the senator's message in good faith. Do we understand one another?"

Colter seethed at the ignominy. He had never been beaten to the draw by anyone and was unaccustomed to being upstaged, but he sensed that Stone was a very unusual man and his features softened, until, with a sudden eruption, he burst into laughter.

Relaxing, he reholstered his gun and pushed Stone's Remington aside. "You're som'in!" he chortled. "Well, I'll say this, the senator knows how t' find good fightin' men!" He guffawed heartily and reached for the whiskey bottle to replenish their cups, wagging his head. "You gonna have t' show me how yer did that. I ain't never seen no one pull a gun that fast afore. What d'yer say yer name was?"

Stone slid his revolver into its holster and swallowed a slug of the liquor proffered by Colter, resting his elbows on his knees and leaning toward the fire so that they could talk in a conspiratorial tone. "Name's Stone. Now, tell me about Red Cloud."

Colter grunted. "Him? He's a wild one. Reckons Powder Basin's sacred to the Sioux. No way he's gonna back off that land. U.S. army'll have t' kill 'im first, an' that's easier said 'n done. Mean as hell an' cunnin' as a fox!"

"Will he attack the gold train if he knows what's on it?"

"Reckon! He'd attack it jus' for bein' there. Don't need no excuse. But he'll take some convincin' it's not a trap if I go shoutin' ma mouth off 'bout it."

"Can you persuade him?" Stone drilled Colter with his penetrating gaze.

"Have t' be me as does it. Mind, not sure he'll trust me much more'n anyone else, but if I push 'im for a cut I guess he'll figure I'm in it for the money."

Stone mocked him. "And you were complaining about how much you were getting paid a couple of minutes ago!"

Colter chuckled. "Fair day's pay for fair day's work. Figure senator'd understand that." He took a slug of his whiskey. "What else our schemin' leader want?"

"Before we talk about that, how long will it take to reach Red Cloud? The gold train will be coming through at the end of July."

"Guess I'll start off with the cavalry boy next day or so. Git 'im set on Bridger Trail. Reckon I'll cut south o' the Bighorn, make a straight run fa the Powder River. Should git there couple o' weeks afore our boy passes through." He peered at Stone to gauge his reaction.

Winthrop's man nodded in confirmation. "That'll work. Once you're done, come back through Laramie and telegraph Mr. Seth Jones at the General Store in Westport, Kansas. If Red Cloud buys the plan, you telegraph 'transport delayed.' If not, you say 'transport on time.' Sign off with your name. You got that?"

Colter nodded.

"The second job is to run disruption on a Denver trader's supply wagons. Seems there's a couple of guys muscling in on the senator's business, Mathewson and Cartwright. They're hauling goods in to Kansas by railroad, and overland from there. You give them a headache getting their merchandise through, enough to encourage them to move on to some other town, and you get the other thousand bucks."

"Senator's got a finger in every pie," Colter shook his shaggy mop in admiration at the extent to which Winthrop's tentacles managed to influence trade in the frontier. "I got some boys could make a deal o' trouble fa yer shopkeepin' folk. Maybe make it look like th' Indians done it."

"They'll need to stop more than one supply train. Might be a few months of work in it." Stone wanted to confirm that Colter understood the need for a siege on supply, not a one-off strike.

"Yeah, I get it. Don't worry. Boys'll want payin' up front." Colter tested Stone's resolve again.

"Your men'll get paid on results. No advance payments. We want them focused on the supply wagons, not playing poker in the saloon. The senator will pay five hundred dollars for each Mathewson and Cartwright supply train that fails to reach Denver."

"Don't seem like much for the trouble," muttered Colter. "I'd say a thousand."

"Seven hundred, and Mr. Jones will confirm the validity of each claim before it's paid."

Colter sniggered and spat on his hand, offering it to Stone. "That's a deal, Mr. Stone."

"Excellent. Now tell me about the buffalo. Have you got started yet?"

"What 'bout 'em?" Colter was immediately guarded.

Stone regarded him carefully and dropped his voice to a whisper. "We both understand the tension the buffalo hunting's going to stir up with the Indians, but the senator would like a report on your progress. There haven't been any shipments of hides yet, and he wants proof that you're fulfilling your side of the bargain."

Colter shuffled uncomfortably. "Ain't that simple. S'dangerous work."

"Mr. Colter, you've been commissioned to undertake this assignment for six months. What have you actually done?" Stone almost snarled the challenge.

Colter took a long pull on his whiskey and settled back on his stool, his self-assurance returning. "You kin tell Winthrop to bide his time, Mr. Stone." The words were slow and deliberate. "This is ma world out here. Ain't easy pullin' together thirty hired guns an' a team o' skinners without gittin' noticed. Now, you tell Winthrop I'll git the job done an' he's gonna git what he wants."

Stone was reassured by Colter's more bullish attitude, his nonchalance implying that he was confident he had the matter under control. Stone nodded thoughtfully. "Thirty guns, you say? Is that enough?"

"It'll do t' start. Got four o' 'em on this here wagon, an' 'nother six over yonder." He pointed toward a nearby schooner. "That's why I hadda git Murray t' let me ride with the wagon train. Make sure these boys don't git no ideas 'bout turnin' tail when they git halfways out along the trail. Captain o' the train thinks they're no more 'n regular prospectors."

"Where are the rest?"

"Got a cabin up on Nowood Creek, west side o' Bighorn. Boys're holed up there 'til snows clear. S'a good spot for gittin' out on the plains, an' near enough on the trail down t' Bridger's for haulin' hides out t' Kansas."

"Sounds good. I'd like to see it."

"Yer doubtin' ma word?" The request was unexpected, and

Colter bridled at the inference that Stone felt obliged to confirm the authenticity of his account. He would have pistol-whipped any other man for the slight.

"No, nothing like that, Mr. Colter. My responsibility is to check on the senator's investments and help out where I can. Besides, I'd like to bag a couple of buffalo myself, and I figure you wouldn't mind an extra gun?" He smiled at Colter for the first time and patted him amiably on the knee to assuage his obvious ire.

Colter glowered at Stone skeptically, but eventually concluded that the proposition might work to his benefit, so he sniggered and clanked his tin cup against Stone's.

"Okay, fella. Let's drink t' that!" He gulped down the rest of the whiskey and set out his proposal. "I gotta leave in a couple o' days with the cavalry boy, so I figure you kin keep an eye on our hired guns. Make yerself useful." He shot Stone a lopsided grin. "Keep 'em poin'ed north wi' the wagon train 'til yer reach Ten Sleep canyon. Like it sounds, s'about ten days from here. Yer pretty much follow Nowood Creek outta the Bridger's. One o' the marshals'll know Ten Sleep. Indians use it as a stopover. Big red bluff they call Signal Cliff right nearby. Can't miss it.

"Once yer git there, tell the marshal you an' the boys wanna do some prospectin' in the canyon. Say you'll follow on later. That'll give yer good excuse to cut loose from the wagon train." Stone nodded his understanding. "Follow the canyon east couple o' miles, then turn south aways. You'll find the cabins with the rest o' the boys. Trails real easy t' find. Might be they's out on the plains 'bout now, but yer kin bet there'll be bunch o' folks workin' hides. If yer git on an' do that, I'll hit the trail t' Red Cloud."

Stone liked the plan, anticipating that Colter's absence would enable him to get a better feel for the way the hunting operation was being run. "Who's in charge out there?" he asked.

"Oh! You'll like him," Colter hooted. "Real hard ass. Boyd Harrison. Southerner outta Galveston. Shoot yer in th' foot soon as shake yer hand. He's in it for a couple o' cents a hide delivered in'a Kansas, so he's gonna git some lead flyin'."

Colter drained the bottle of whiskey into their mugs, and they set about finalizing their plans. When the details had been agreed, Stone left Colter to stretch out on the ground by the fire where he tucked his bag of gold into his waistband and promptly dropped into an intoxicated sleep.

Exhausted, Stone retrieved his horse and made his way up to Old Bedlam, where Murray's orderly had reserved him a room. The stewards were busy attending to the late-night revelry, but at Stone's insistence, they provided a deep hot bath to wash away his aches and pains and a good square meal to assuage his appetite.

He slept like the dead and woke early, refreshed. After breakfast, he attended the telegraph office to send a coded message to Winthrop in Washington, confirming that arrangements were in place for the escort from Virginia City and that Colter had consented to undertake his allotted tasks.

Winthrop received the information with unprecedented euphoria and immediately dispatched a telegraph to his contact in Virginia City, advising of the good news.

Trautman watched Colter's encounter with the stranger, but their conversation was sufficiently muted that he had been unable to discern the nature of their discussion. Nevertheless, Gresham was intrigued by the lieutenant's account when he returned to deliver his report.

"That's quite a tale, Isaac. Any idea who this man is?"

"Can't really say. His name's Tobias Stone. Took a hike up to Ole Bedlam an' got the housekeeper's tongue waggin' some." Trautman explained his detective work. "Telegraph from

Murray's orderly booked his room, but beyond that no one seems to know anythin' about him."

"Murray? Well, what do you know? He reassigns Moylan, insists on Colter accompanying the wagon train, and now he's making arrangements for the mysterious Mr. Stone." He paused, considering the coincidence. "I'll ask Sibley if he's been briefed about Stone tomorrow. But you think Stone pulled a gun on Colter? And he's still alive?" Gresham was incredulous.

"Not simply pulled a gun. I've never seen anyone draw a gun so fast. Nor has Colter, judgin' by the expression on his face. Thought there was gonna be bloodshed, but Colter didn' seem pissed 'bout it. Laughed, like the two o' them was best buddies!" Trautman recollected Colter's capitulation.

"You think he knows the guy?

"No, don't think so. But I reckon he's not a total stranger. Certainly seemed to carry some sway with Colter, more 'n the speed of his draw too."

They hypothesized about the relationship between the two men and debated the possible subject of their discussion, but their theories were mere conjecture and Gresham's only practical option remained to establish whether Sibley knew who Stone might be or what he was doing with Colter. Unfortunately, the enquiry would have to be cursory, since his priority was to prepare the wagon train to roll out the following day, which would absorb most of his attention.

CHAPTER 28

Great Plains, west of the Bighorn River

The string of horses and mules plodded steadily across the plain. La Brais led the way, hugging the north bank of the Greybull River, and McCabe brought up the rear with Takoda mounted on one of the mules immediately ahead of him.

The weather improved dramatically as they cut a path across the plains, the snow starting to clear and clusters of fresh spring growth bursting through the thin dusting of frost that encrusted the barren land.

During the day, the sun rose high, the sweltering heat causing the trappers to strip off their outer coats. At night the temperature plummeted, a bitter northwesterly wind whipping across the open plain and causing the travelers to shiver under their blankets.

McCabe noticed that the young Indian appeared increasingly weak. It was obvious that he needed medicine, but McCabe did not have the skill to tend his wounds and La Brais considered it immaterial whether the Indian lived or died.

They averaged thirty miles each day, trudging almost directly east, and La Brais divulged that he intended shadowing the Greybull until it merged with the Bighorn River, where they would turn south. But, beyond that snippet of information, he remained tight-lipped about their destination.

The Greybull was a torrent, its waters swollen from the first spring thaw on the prairie and run-off from the network of mountain creeks that fed its headwaters, the combined volume causing the river to overspill its banks in several places. But the terrain close to the river was the first to bloom with fresh growth and early flowers, and in his fevered condition Takoda searched its margins for the plants and herbs his mother had taught him to use to treat his ailments. He knew that the two trappers would have neither the skill nor the inclination to treat the infection in his arm, so he resolved to find his own remedies, hoping that he would be permitted to minister to himself.

They rode on through the third day, the sun beating down on their right flank as it reached its midday zenith, and the two white men stripped off their coats and rolled up the sleeves of their shirts, shedding clothing in an effort to cool down. Takoda was left to swelter in his winter coat, drenched in the sweat of his mild fever, waves of nausea and dizziness causing him to reel back and forth in the saddle.

The trail dropped to the right and swung alongside the river, crossing a sheltered depression lined with stands of white willow and juneberry, the trees soaking up the annual glut of floodwater that revitalized the desolate landscape.

Takoda scanned the oasis of foliage with tired eyes. For two days, he had longed to catch sight of the feathery green fronds of yarrow, a plant that provided his tribe with their most effective treatment for battle wounds. He had spied new shoots of porcupine and buffalo grass and clumps of switchgrass and rye, but no yarrow. Initially, he had been confident in locating the plants he needed, but now his optimism had diminished, having been thwarted so often along the trail.

La Brais pulled up and dropped off his horse, lured to soak himself in the cool waters of a shallow stretch of the river. He fell to his knees and thrust his hat into the water, ladling it over his head and neck and bellowing with relief as he swept his long wet locks off his brow. McCabe followed suit, and the two men immersed themselves in the shallows like a pair of indulgent buffalo.

Takoda's vision swirled as he watched them, his eyes drifting along the bank in either direction. The growth was verdant and fragrant, bursting with new life, and under different circumstances he would have sat contentedly, soaking up the rebirth of the plains. But in his tortured condition the wonders of spring held little appeal.

Takoda's attention settled on a cluster of color that contrasted with the subtle jade and absinthe green of the grasses. It was a flush of flowers, their crisp white petals encircling bright yellow centers, and they seemed somehow familiar. He knew that he had to pay attention to their significance, but his mind wandered and his vision faded in and out.

Momentarily, the flowers came into perfect focus and recognition hit Takoda with a jolt. He had been searching for the long feathery leaves of the yarrow, but it was spring and warmer on the plains than in the mountains, so the plants were blooming earlier than he might have expected. A burst of optimism bolstered his fragile strength as he comprehended the opportunity to gather the leaves of the medicinal plant.

Although Takoda was not tied to the mule, his hands remained bound in front of him and the animal's burden of beaver pelts prevented him from swinging his leg from his saddle, rendering dismounting problematic. In the absence of assistance, he was left to slide sideways from his mount, dropping to his right and landing with a bone-jarring thud.

The impact winded Takoda, and he lay motionless as he tried to suppress the pain that racked his body. The trappers did not hear him fall, remaining engrossed in their indulgent wallowing. Once he had recovered, Takoda struggled to his feet and shuffled over to the flowers. Reflecting on his gratitude for Mother Nature's gift, he dropped to his knees and inspected the green-leafed yarrow.

Picking a dozen large fronds, Takoda stuffed them into his tunic and turned his attention to study the bank of the river with more care. For the first time, he noticed the species of the trees and was elated to identify a stand of white willow, the leaves of which his tribe used to relieve discomfort, the salicin in their tissue acting as a powerful painkiller.

Takoda pushed himself up and stumbled across to the trees, sliding his hands down one of the whips to strip its leaves. But as he grasped the next stem, he was brought up short by an aggressive bellow and the explosive sound of a gunshot, the bullet whizzing past his ear and sending a cloud of splinters spinning into the air as it embedded itself in the trunk of the tree. Instinctively, Takoda dropped to the ground, curling himself into a defensive ball as he heard one of the men splash out of the river and run toward him.

"Hey! Injun! Hold up, yer son o' a bitch! Move an' I'm gonna kill yer!" La Brais was in full flight, his revolver trained on Takoda's prostrate body.

"What yer hollerin' 'bout, he ain't doin' nothin'," McCabe bawled, hurrying to calm his partner.

But La Brais swung his boot as he reached Takoda, striking him squarely in the stomach so that the air erupted from his lungs. Not content that he had inflicted sufficient pain, La Brais grabbed Takoda by the scruff of his tunic and forced the barrel of his handgun into his cheek.

Takoda coughed as he fought for breath, the aggressive grip on his neck steeling his desire for revenge. He thought of his brother and his father and thrashed against La Brais's grasp, glaring at him through bloodshot eyes.

The trapper bent low and Takoda could smell the stench of his whiskey-soaked breath. "That's right, I see the hate in yer eyes. Like a wild animal." He laughed. "Well, boy, I ain't gonna kill yer now. I'm gonna tame yer. Yer hear." He cocked the hammer on his revolver and pushed it hard against Takoda's cheekbone, breaking the skin so that a trickle of blood ran down toward his jaw.

McCabe rushed up and pulled at La Brais's shoulder. "What in hell yer doin'? He ain't runnin' away. Look, he's jus' pickin' a bunch o' leaves." McCabe pulled at the yarrow tucked into Takoda's tunic and waved the foliage at La Brais. "Reckon he's lookin' for medicine. See!"

La Brais peered at the yarrow leaves with a contemptuous scowl, holstering his gun and grabbing them from McCabe's hand. "Yer want these?" He pulled Takoda's face within inches of his own. "Yeah! You want 'em, don't yer!" He glowered at the boy and pressed the leaves to his mouth.

Attempting to avoid the brutal force-feeding, Takoda writhed and twisted his head, but La Brais was determined. He thrust Takoda onto his back and sat astride him, grabbing his nose brutally and shoving his head back while attempting to ram the leaves into his mouth.

The trapper's weight was crushing, and as much as Takoda mustered what remained of his tenuous stamina, he was unable to dislodge La Brais. He was frantic to gasp for air, but knew that as soon as he opened his mouth the trapper would stuff the yarrow further down his throat and attempt to choke him.

McCabe hauled at La Brais's shoulders and implored him to abandon the savage attack, but the trapper was enjoying his entertainment too much and would not be deterred. Takoda's lungs were at bursting point, and when he could hold his breath no longer, he opened his mouth to gulp for air, uttering a scream of defeat.

La Brais seized his opportunity and, letting out a satisfied snort, he shoved the leaves between Takoda's teeth, using his fingers to push them deep into the top of the Indian's throat.

Takoda panicked at the sense of suffocation and bit down hard on La Brais's hand in desperation, his teeth sinking into the horny flesh of the small finger and eliciting an agonized yelp as the trapper tried to pull away his hand. Seeing La Brais's face contort with pain, Takoda focused on his only means of attack and bit deeper and harder.

The trapper's laughter turned to alarm, and he struggled with frenzied urgency to release his fingers from Takoda's clenched jaw, feeling the boy's teeth break the skin and drive into his flesh.

"Aargh! Yer bastard! Let go ma hand, yer cock-suckin' coyote!" He screamed, hammering his fist hysterically against Takoda's forehead.

Encouraged and calling upon his last reserves of strength, Takoda bit down harder, until with a surge of satisfaction he tasted the distinctive metallic tang of fresh blood as it washed across his tongue. La Brais screamed and yanked his hand, Takoda's teeth sliding along the finger and settling into one of the joints. Immediately, he ground his jaw from side to side, driving his teeth between the bones and severing the finger at its last joint, causing a flood of blood to fill his mouth.

La Brais jumped backward, clasping his damaged hand, and Takoda spat out the amputated piece of finger, spluttering as he expelled the leaves crammed into his throat. He glared at the big trapper defiantly, who fumbled to draw his pistol in an effort to shoot him. But McCabe threw himself at La Brais's arm and the pistol discharged with a thunderous blast, driving a bullet into the ground inches from Takoda's head.

"Son of a bitch!" La Brais wheeled around at McCabe. "Injun's gone an' bitten off ma darned finger!"

"Well what'ya expect if yer go shovin' yer hand in 'is mouth!" McCabe retorted unsympathetically.

"You tryin' t' defend 'im?" La Brais fumed. "I oughta kill the both o' yer!" He swung the pistol at McCabe, but the searing pain in his finger made him drop the gun and grab his damaged hand.

"Argh, go stick yer hand in th' river, yer dumb ass!" McCabe growled, bending to pull Takoda upright. "That's it, boy." He picked up some of the leaves Takoda had collected and shoved them into his lap. "Guess you'll wanna do somin' wi' 'em?"

La Brais soon dismissed the Indian, becoming absorbed in washing and dressing his injured hand, and McCabe decided to set camp for the night, breaking out some food and making a fire, since neither of the trappers were in the mood to continue riding.

Eventually, when La Brais's finger had stopped bleeding, McCabe used a knife to cauterize the wound, heating the blade in the fire until it was red hot before pressing it against the ragged stump. La Brais looked decidedly apprehensive at the treatment, and the bellow he emitted would have rivaled a bull elk in rutting season, so McCabe was unsurprised when his companion stumbled off to drag a bottle of whiskey from his saddlebags.

Relegated to sit to one side, Takoda chewed on some willow until McCabe invited him closer to the fire and pointed at the leaves he had gathered. Although Takoda was unsure whether to trust the man, McCabe was insistent, so cautiously he indicated that he wanted to use some of the water the trapper had boiled when making coffee earlier.

He worked slowly, his hands remaining tied, and crushed the leaves of the yarrow between two stones, immersing the pulp in a cup of hot water until it formed a thick glutinous mush. McCabe helped to collect a few sprigs of sagebrush that Takoda wanted and watched with interest as he soaked them with the yarrow before draining the fluid into a separate mug and tipping the pulp onto a strip of material that he tore from his breechcloth.

Once the treatment was prepared, Takoda indicated that he needed to reach the injury on his arm and McCabe reluctantly untied his hands, swiftly picking up his rifle to discourage any attempt at flight. With extreme discomfort, Takoda wrestled off his tunic and studied the bright red swelling around the puncture wound in his bicep.

The flesh was intensely painful, and the incision seeped with yellow pus. Working methodically, he soaked a piece of cloth in the liquid he had set aside and used it to clean around the injury, summoning sufficient courage to probe the laceration and swab away the infected excretions. He gritted his teeth against the pain, and McCabe was astonished that he did not cry out as he worked tenaciously at the wound.

When he had cleaned the injury to his satisfaction, Takoda pressed the pulp of crushed leaves onto his arm and, with McCabe's assistance, tied the poultice in place using the strip of breechcloth. The dressing would provide a powerful astringent and antiseptic, attacking the cause of infection, closing up the wound, and promoting healing.

McCabe permitted Takoda to scoop more water from the river, which he used to brew a willow leaf infusion, the decoction being beneficial in easing his pain and fighting the pernicious fever.

The following morning, they rose early having endured a fitful night's sleep, and set forth on their journey once more. La Brais gave Takoda a murderous glare as he mounted his horse, but said nothing and rode off before McCabe had time to finish packing the mules.

By midday they struck the Bighorn River, where they rested before fording the Greybull at its lowest point and turning south, a bitter wind battering relentlessly against their backs, despite the sky remaining clear and the sun warming their faces.

They continued south for two days, hugging the banks of the Bighorn until they reached a confluence with a broad creek that joined from the east, where La Brais instructed that they camp for the night in advance of fording to the far side of the river the next morning.

As they sat around the embers of their fire, La Brais brooded about his prospective employer. The big southerner had provided rudimentary directions to the location of a hunting camp. La Brais was to make his way to Nowood Creek, a tributary to the Bighorn River, where he had to cut southeast until he reached a prominent red cliff, the encampment being a few miles along a narrow canyon that led off to the east. But, despite being confident in his navigation skills, the trapper harbored misgivings about the wisdom of attempting to find the hunting party. Although not easily intimidated, he regarded the man he had met as someone to be treated with caution. His name was Harrison, and he spoke with a slow Texan drawl, although much of his communication appeared limited to the brace of Colt revolvers that he wore slung low on his waist.

La Brais had witnessed Harrison beat a man half to death for bumping into his chair in the saloon and causing him to spill his whiskey, and it was obvious that he possessed an incendiary temper. In truth, La Brais had rejected the hunting job in favor of beaver trapping because of his reluctance to work with Harrison, but now circumstances were different and, after a lean winter, the offer of paid employment seemed to outweigh the risk.

His immediate apprehension centered upon Harrison's potential reaction to McCabe and the Indian. McCabe was a pussy, but could shoot well enough to hit a buffalo, which was likely to render his presence tolerable. By contrast, La Brais was not convinced that he wanted to be associated with bringing an

Indian into camp.

He pondered the problem. If the presence of the Indian incited trouble, La Brais would feel no compunction in dispatching the filthy prairie dog. But there was the possibility that he might prove useful, since it was reputed that Indians possessed remarkable tracking skills. Alternatively, he could leave McCabe and the Indian behind and make his own way to Harrison's camp. He was sure that he could give his partner the slip, the skinny little runt having no idea of the hunters' location. Or, his most draconian option was to simply shoot them both and tip their bodies into the Bighorn, it being unlikely that their corpses would ever be discovered.

After much thought, he concluded that he would take both men with him. Although he had no reservations about killing the Indian, he did not consider himself a cold-blooded murderer and had no desire to shoot McCabe, as much as he found him a pain in the backside. And, he concluded that McCabe would almost certainly try to stop him if he attempted to kill the Indian. Pragmatism suggested that his best decision would be to take them both to the buffalo hunting camp and deal with each based on Harrison's reaction.

The trail ran alongside the creek for another two days, leading progressively closer to the foothills of the Bighorn mountains, and La Brais began to doubt whether he had taken the correct route until a distinctive red cliff began to emerge from the surrounding landscape on the west bank. The sight of the startling landmark proved a source of immense relief and signposted the mouth of an impressive canyon, into which they turned, tracing its rugged contours to the east.

McCabe sensed that they were nearing their destination and moved up alongside La Brais, probing him with incessant questions until eventually the Canadian relented and conceded that he was endeavoring to locate a buffalo hunting outfit where he had been offered a job. He refrained from mentioning Harrison or expressing his misgivings about the manner in which his companions might be received, but his answers served to placate McCabe's immediate curiosity.

Within an hour, they reached a fork in the canyon and picked up a well-worn trail that tracked south along the foot of a steep bluff. The trail skirted a broad plain that funneled them progressively toward its southerly border, where the treeline converged upon the entrance to a concealed ravine, the faint scent of wood smoke and cooking reaching them on the cool breeze.

La Brais was delighted at his prowess in locating the remote camp, having traversed unguided across so many miles of the Great Plains, and, for the first time in days, a surge of optimism moderated his concern for the reception they might receive. He was savoring the moment when a volley of bullets tore into the ground ahead of his horse and the animal leapt sideways, almost unseating him, prompting a hoot of crazed laughter.

"Step any closer an' next one'll be 'tween yer eyes! What yer wantin' here, stranger?" a shrill voice cackled.

La Brais collected up his horse and patted its neck to soothe its alarm while McCabe ducked out of sight, using the line of mules to shield himself, nervous that the gunman might open fire again. Takoda, whose fever had subsided slightly, sat immobile and impassive.

"What yer do a damn fool thing like that for?" La Brais yelled back, his irritation plainly evident. "I come t'see Harrison!"

There was a brief silence before the voice responded. "What's yer business?"

"Harrison gimme a job huntin' buffalo when we was back in Laramie," La Brais bellowed. "Now stand aside, I'm comin' in."

Without waiting for a response, he urged his horse through the narrow entry into the ravine, prompting a skinny lad to step out of the shelter of a small cleft in the rock, a floppy felt cowboy hat perched at a jaunty angle on his mop of straggly blond hair.

He pointed his rifle at La Brais. "All right, yer kin come on in, but keep yer hands offa yer guns."

As he passed, La Brais gave the lad, barely in his twenties, a dismissive growl. "You put up that damn rifle, less yer wan' it shoved down yer throat!"

"Whoopie do! We got ourselves a cock fighter!" The lad flashed La Brais a toothy grin and rolled his eyes, letting out a loud whistle and bursting into peals of laughter.

Ignoring the idiotic lookout, La Brais picked his way down into the ravine and led his companions into a small clearing sandwiched between the rocky backdrop of the bluff and a thick stand of cedar, a bubbling creek running along its western border. Set in the center of the glade were four hastily assembled cabins positioned around a well-established fire pit, with two large Mandans being set purposefully apart, adjacent to a corral packed with horses and mules.

Seated around the campfire, a motley group of disreputable-looking men interrupted their conversation to scrutinize the new arrivals and a tall, broad-shouldered man, with two low-slung revolvers holstered at his sides, ducked out of the doorway of the nearest cabin. He stood watching as they pulled to a halt.

The man's eyes were narrow and shaded by bushy eyebrows, but even at a distance McCabe could tell that his face was hard and unyielding. He gripped a tin cup of steaming coffee in a brawny fist, exposing calloused knuckles and two foreshortened fingers, souvenirs from a knife fight where his assailant had wound up dead.

Poker-faced, Harrison sauntered from the cabin, his attention fixed on La Brais. "Well, lookie here! If it ain't the fearless trapper. Beginnin' t' think we wasn't good enough for ya." The comment was made without humor and invited an explanation, but the trapper remained mounted on his horse and met

Harrison's challenge with a level gaze.

"Got trappin' finished early an' figured I'd come see if yer still lookin' fa a good gun." La Brais felt no need for preamble or familiarity. This was a man who was simply interested in what he was getting and whether it was to his benefit.

Harrison sipped his coffee, considering La Brais's response, and appraising the rest of his party. He offered no indication as to whether he was content or annoyed by the intrusion, and La Brais almost succumbed to an urge to provide further explanation.

The silence was unnerving and McCabe toyed with apologizing for their imposition, hoping for an opportunity to turn around and high-tail it back to the plains, but he could see that Harrison was focused on La Brais and was loathe to invite unnecessary attention.

Eventually, Harrison nodded, taking another draught of his coffee. "What 'bout ya partner and the Injun?" He cocked his head toward McCabe and Takoda.

"Partner'd make another fair gun, an' been wond'rin' what t' do with th' Injun." He dropped his hands casually across the horn of his saddle in a gesture of conversational informality.

Harrison nodded again, looking pensively at the ground as he employed silence to test La Brais's nerve. But the big trapper made no further comment, instead sitting patiently to await the hunter's considered reaction.

"Okay, ya in. Pays a dollar a day an' two cents a hide shared 'tween everyone." Harrison seemed satisfied. "Mind, there ain't no slackers here, an' no one as comes in leaves less I tell 'em they kin leave. Ya pull ya turn on chow, wood cuttin', an' camp duty. Ya break the rules an' I'll have ya bull-whipped, or put a bullet in ya belly ma'self. Ya un'erstand?" He glared from La Brais to McCabe and back again.

Nodding his agreement, La Brais swung down off his horse.

"Sounds like a real party. Bin a long ride. Yer got any more o' that coffee goin'?"

Harrison ignored La Brais and turned his attention to McCabe. "You?"

The trapper was petrified by the big Texan's demeanor, but was too scared to turn and run, thinking it improbable that the hunter would let him leave alive. Cursing La Brais, he stammered his acceptance of the terms, knowing from the smirk on Harrison's face that the man could smell his fear.

Harrison shot a glance at Takoda. "We're short o' skinners so Injun's gonna have plenty of work." He ambled over to Takoda's mule and peered up at him, Takoda maintaining a defiant indifference. "Hmm. Boy's got spirit. Gonna have ta break that."

McCabe watched the interaction with concern and was relieved to see Harrison walk away from Takoda, assuming that he had lost interest in the boy. To his dismay, however, Harrison set his cup down and swept up a coiled bullwhip, spinning around in one fluid motion and delivering the lash expertly so that it cracked around Takoda's neck. The shock and pain caught Takoda off guard, and he let out a piercing yelp as the whip's cattail split crackers flailed his skin, instantly raising a series of angry red welts. Harrison tugged at the whip and, stunned, he lurched sideways, crashing to the ground and landing hard on his left shoulder.

The men sitting around the campfire let out a chorus of cheers and jumped to their feet to watch as Harrison set about Takoda's prone figure, sending a second searing lash of the whip across his legs before driving his foot into the boy's ribs and rolling him onto his back.

Takoda convulsed with pain as the savage blows compounded the trauma inflicted upon his battered body. The whipping stung like the bite of a rattlesnake, his chest felt like it might cave in, and the injury to his bicep sent shooting pains down his arm and across his shoulder. Every muscle and sinew felt as though it was on fire.

He closed his eyes and searched, as his father had taught him, for the dark place within himself where he could hide from the pain, erecting a mental barrier between the physical agony and his deeper consciousness.

Like all the older boys in Takoda's village, he had been schooled in the skills of hunting and fighting. The tribe prepared all the boys with meticulous care, setting them arduous tasks that developed their endurance and strength, and teaching them to stalk their prey using traditional weapons as a means of enhancing their stealth and precision. But, most significantly, his father had drilled into him the importance of tolerating pain beyond the point at which others might succumb.

In battle, or when hunting, his father believed that a warrior gained invaluable advantage through the ability to endure hardship for longer than his adversary. He had coached his sons from an early age, encouraging them to undertake tasks that tested their capacity to resist pain, and had progressively taught them how to detach their minds from the sensation of physical discomfort. Now, Takoda reached into that safe place, deep inside, and observed the vicious assault as though from a distant hilltop.

Harrison glowered at Takoda and pressed his boot down on the boy's neck, blocking his windpipe. Takoda gasped for air, and Harrison drew a revolver, shoving the muzzle into Takoda's mouth and chipping one of his teeth with the brutal force. He was impressed that the boy had uttered no sound since the first whiplash had caught him off guard, and although the Indian was clearly distressed, his eyes still burned with an unquenchable hatred.

"Doyle, get over here." Harrison called over his shoulder, prompting a short man with a limp, dressed in heavily weathered buckskin clothing, to hurry over and peer down at Takoda.

"Tell hym, he makes any trouble, I'm gonna cut his eyes out an' make hym eat 'em."

Doyle pulled the stub of a cheroot from his mouth and spat on the ground. "You Sioux, boy?" He addressed Takoda in broken Lakota and waited for a response. Takoda glared at him.

The man nodded slightly. "Huh. Don't matter no how. I'm gonna tell yer this anyway. See, this here man. He's gonna cut yer eyes out if yer go makin' trouble. Reckon he's gonna make yer eat 'em too. Evil fuck, yer know!" Doyle cackled with laughter at the thought of Harrison forcing the Indian to eat his own eyes.

"Tell hym he's gonna skin an' clean buffalo hides every damn day till 'e dies." Harrison's foot remained pressed tightly across Takoda's neck, his face a mask of malevolent intent as he drawled the instruction.

Doyle laughed again. "This here gentleman, he's gonna give yer a job fa life! Yer gonna work buffalo hides 'til yer no more use 'n a stinkin' racoon." He bent down low over Takoda's face. "Understan', boy?" He stretched out his hand and patted Takoda's cheek affably. "That's right. Yer understan', don't yer? Yer work every minute o' every day, or this here man's gonna kill yer, right." He glanced at Harrison and smiled. "Reckon he knows the score, boss."

Harrison lifted his foot and reholstered his handgun, allowing Takoda to curl over onto his side and gulp air into his lungs.

"Pick 'im up an' give 'im t' Scratch." Harrison ordered, turning to La Brais and McCabe, the latter shocked at the brutal exhibition he had witnessed. "You boys bunk over yonder." He waved his hand at the furthest cabin, tucked close under the bluff. "Mind, don't go gettin' too comfortable, we move out first light in a mornin'." Dismissing them, he tossed the dregs of coffee from his cup and sauntered back to his own cabin.

The hunters rose early the following morning and saddled up to ride out as Harrison had instructed. Five men were delegated to remain in the camp accompanied by half a dozen Pawnee Indians, the latter having volunteered to join the hunting party and traveled from Laramie with the rest of the men.

La Brais joined the hunters, McCabe was instructed to stay behind, and Takoda was set to work with the Pawnee, his task being to assist in stretching and cleaning a mountain of buffalo hides stacked alongside the corral. But, before leaving, Harrison made it clear to McCabe that he would be held responsible for any trouble caused by Takoda. The trapper cringed, gripped by a tight coil of fear as the big southerner drilled him with his cold blue eyes.

After a few days, the camp settled into a steady routine, and in Harrison's absence McCabe began to relax. There was little to do, the daily chores being mundane and the Pawnee being charged with undertaking the more onerous work. Relieving him of even further obligation, Takoda was largely supervised by the Indians, who viewed him with as much contempt as La Brais had done, the Pawnee harboring little affection for the Sioux, who constantly encroached upon their hunting grounds along the Platte River and were prone to abducting their women.

Takoda was given a blade of sharpened bone and compelled to clean the inner surface of the hides, removing residual meat, fat, and membrane, while the Pawnee stretched the scraped skins in the sun, and dehaired them using a solution of wood ash and hot water. The prepared skins were softened with pounded buffalo brain soaked in warm water, the Indians working methodically to rub the emulsion into the hides before rinsing and stringing them up on a wooden frame to dry.

The enormous stack of skins was a source of deep concern to Takoda. Hunting was an activity practiced by his people with a spiritual reverence, but the Lakota only killed as many animals as they required to survive and always ensured that every part of the animal was put to good use.

By contrast, the huge volume of hides stacked in the hunter's camp suggested a slaughter of massive proportions, and Takoda felt a heart-wrenching sense of despair at the loss of so many of his brother buffalo. Compounding his anguish, it was apparent that the hunters stockpiled only the hides, and he presumed that the meat and other parts of the carcass had been discarded, since there only appeared to be sufficient meat in camp to provide short-term sustenance. As he worked, he mused about the purpose for such a hideous orchestrated massacre.

Presently, the animosity of two of the Pawnee began to soften, acknowledging his youth and sensing the ordeal that he had endured, and they offered to tend the wound on his arm, dressing it with a fresh poultice and preparing regular infusions of willow to ease his pain.

Takoda worked all day, the Pawnee untying his hands so that he could use his tools, but he was provided with some basic food and slowly began to recover his strength. Each evening, conscious of Harrison's warning, McCabe sat him against a post driven into the ground a few paces from the campfire, where he was tied securely to the stake, his feet bound and his hands lashed under his knees, leaving him in full view so that he could be watched throughout the night by the men who stood guard.

The Pawnees reward for their labor was fresh meat and a slug of whiskey each evening, with the promise of a share of the proceeds when the hides were sold in Kansas, although Harrison had no intention that they would ever receive any of the earnings. But, as the days faded into weeks, they worked relentlessly. There were over a thousand buffalo skins stacked by the corral, and despite toiling from first light until dusk, the pile barely diminished.

Takoda twice managed to release the bindings around his ankles and attempt to escape, but each time he was caught, trapped in the narrow ravine and beaten by McCabe or one of the other hunters for his recalcitrance. Nevertheless, he endured the arduous work and suffered the vicious assaults, the abuse serving to toughen his body and fuel his determination to break free and exact his revenge.

Six weeks passed, until one day, as Takoda was scraping a particularly stubborn piece of sinew from one of the skins, his bone scraper split down the center. Falling forward, he cracked his knuckles against the ground and drew blood. His misfortune provoked a scowl of disapproval from one of the Pawnee, but otherwise the incident went unnoticed and he was able to secrete one-half of the scraper inside his moccasin. Thereafter, keen to avoid drawing attention to himself, he worked diligently for the balance of the day, returning to be tied to his post when dusk fell, where he retrieved the piece of bone and examined it surreptitiously.

The fracture had occurred along a hairline crack in the bone, leaving a rough serrated edge, which he tested gingerly with his finger, pleased to detect an angular break that would sharpen easily when worked against a suitable stone. The following day, walking to his work area, he noticed a small stone that would suit his purpose and thereafter began to kick it slowly toward the lashing post each time he returned.

On the third evening, he succeeded in knocking the stone sufficiently close that he was able to reach out, grasp it, and place the abrasive rock firmly between his heels. When the camp was quiet he took the bone from his moccasin and began the slow process of sharpening its broken edge, being careful to minimize any noise that might attract the attention of the guards, who rotated shifts, maintaining a largely ineffectual watch. He worked the bone with tenacious determination, and it became apparent that sharpening the blade undetected, in his contorted position, would require several nights' work.

CHAPTER 29

Reaching Fort Laramie, Dakota Territory

Johannes had been sullen ever since the wagon train had left camp at the river Platte crossing, and although Mary-Jane had tried to cheer him up, he had spurned her attempts, even appearing to find her caress disconcerting. She was left feeling confused and angry at his offhand manner and unable to understand why he made no attempt to explain his behavior.

The confrontation with the Pawnee on the morning after he had murdered the Indian girl had thrown Johannes into a panic. He had been terrified that the Indians would somehow identify him as the person who had killed the girl and had found that he was shaking with fear.

His anxiety was further compounded when he noticed Colter accompanying Gresham to meet the Indians, since he was sure that the mountain man knew he had done something terrible and was worried that his secret would be exposed. He was certain that the murder he had committed was the cause of the Indians' hostility and believed it unlikely that the Pawnee would retreat without the perpetrator being handed over.

Keeping an anxious eye on the captain's parlay through the narrow gap between the canopy and the wagon's seat, Johannes hid inside his schooner, the coil of fear in his stomach unleashing a wave of dread when he spied a group of Indians galloping off across the plain. He envisaged that a full-blooded attack on the wagon train would ensue. But his apprehension turned to euphoria when he saw O'Halloran cut down, and he gawped with morbid fascination as the Indians gathered around the cowhand's body.

As the Pawnee withdrew to the hills, Johannes crawled weakly to the rear of the schooner and dropped to the ground, elated, heaving several deep breaths as his senses cleared and a wry smile creased the corners of his mouth. He was going to be safe, and the thrill of eluding discovery was intoxicating. In a few days' time the wagon train would arrive at Fort Laramie, a bastion of military strength, and in a few weeks, they would reach their final destination. Colter would have no bearing on his life, and the incident with the Indian girl would be forgotten, confined to the past. No one would ever find out what had happened.

Johannes joined his mother by the campfire and accepted the cookies and warm milk she proffered, slumping down and munching contentedly. However, his relief was short-lived, and he almost fell into the fire as he heard the footfall of a horse draw up behind him. A flash of fear ran down his spine, and he spun around to find Colter peering down at him, a sly leer on his weathered face.

"Reckon you bin up to no good, son. Nearly had ourselves a' all-out battle with the Pawnee there. Seems a young girl bin killed." He stared intently at Johannes, whose face drained of color.

Colter took a look over his shoulder and mused. "Seems Injuns reckon O'Halloran done it. Got a notion I might leave it that way." He cocked his head meaningfully at Johannes. "Wha' d'ya say, boy?"

Johannes's jaw dropped, his mouth flapping soundlessly. He felt cold and sick. "I . . . I don't know . . . sir." he stuttered, avoiding Colter's eye.

"Yeah. I guess we'll keep it 'tween you an' me." Colter gave a lopsided grin and casually turned his horse to ride away.

Dumbfounded, Johannes held his breath as the mountain man left, stumbling to the back of the schooner and retching as soon as he jogged out of sight. He emptied his stomach until all he could produce was bile. He was convinced that Colter knew what he had done, and the implied threat to reveal his crime endowed the mountain man with even greater menace. But he could not understand why Colter had remained tight-lipped, and he found the guilt and fear as suffocating as a hangman's noose. Unable to think of anything else, and terrified that Colter might expose him at any moment, he was rendered unable to speak even to his family.

Since Mary-Jane was clearly confused and upset by Johannes's sudden inexplicable indifference, Carla made a deliberate point of keeping her occupied and they walked alongside the schooners together, engrossed in conversation as they studied the plentiful wildlife. Countless different species of birds flitted around the riverbank or hopped through the scrubby grasslands along the trail, so the girls started to document their sightings, drawing pictures, recording their behavior, and noting their songs and courtship rituals.

Carla's enthusiasm was infectious. She found interest in everything, pointing out the variety of differing grasses and delighting at the sight of an unusual flower. To Carla the prairie was a treasure-trove of wonders awaiting discovery, and Mary-Jane immersed herself in Carla's world, appreciating the diversion from the daily drudge of toiling alongside the wagons.

Arriving at Laramie, the two girls immediately ventured into the Indian village, much to the discontent of their mothers. They marveled at its vast array of tipis, adorned with elaborate patterns, drawings of animals, and symbolic stick-shaped men and horses that depicted important events in the lives of the occupants.

The Indian women were friendly and welcoming, and when Carla expressed an interest in their quillwork, she found herself being taught how to pull the quills through her teeth to flatten them out for weaving. But the sad contrast was the Indian men, who seemed unapproachable and often appeared drunk, even early in the morning.

Nevertheless, Carla enjoyed sitting with the Indians. They had a wonderful ability to craft beautiful clothes, blankets, and baskets and were often singing and smiling as they worked. Groups of the women congregated together, their labor a cheerful but industrious communal activity, which Carla considered much at odds with the instinctively mercenary behavior displayed by the emigrants in the wagon train.

She noted that each Indian family occupied their own tipi, in the same way that the migrants each possessed their own wagon, but it was evident that the Indians lived as a single community, sharing tasks between one another with an unspoken acceptance. The behavior juxtaposed the culture to which she was accustomed, where families preferred their independence and shared work often required organization or coercion, resulting in a sense of indebtedness to those who had given of their time and effort.

Thinking that the intrigue might help to lift his mood, Carla attempted to persuade Johannes to join her and Mary-Jane in exploring the Indian camp, but his reaction to the suggestion was apoplectic, and she was genuinely frightened by his aggressive vitriol, so quickly dismissed the idea and left him to brood.

Colter had one problem to resolve before taking up his chaperon duties with Moylan. He wanted to recover his rifle. He was not superstitious, but he was a man of habit and was loathe to be parted from his precious sixteen-cartridge Henry. However, Gresham had made it patently apparent that the rifle would only be returned in the event that he left the wagon train, and Colter was reticent to provoke unwanted questions about the reason for his premature departure.

Colter knew that the rifle had been placed in the secure armory locker on the chuck wagon drawn up alongside Gresham and Lieutenant Trautman's tents, and he contemplated the possibility of breaking in to recover the gun. But a sentry was permanently posted to guard the wagon's cargo and the proximity of the officers' sleeping quarters rendered the idea unattractive.

Additionally, Colter had to obtain the weapon without Gresham being aware of its disappearance, and the finger of blame was sure to be pointed in his direction if the lock on the armory cabinet was found smashed with his rifle being the only item missing. He needed the keys, which he knew that Trautman kept tucked into one of the leather cap pouches on his Fair Weather ammunition belt.

Wrestling with the frustrating dilemma, Colter weighed the odds of being caught, until an idea occurred to him. He could get someone else to do his dirty work. He smirked at the thought. The German boy with a dark secret to hide presented the perfect solution. He was certain that he could coerce the lad into doing anything. He simply had to threaten to reveal the boy's involvement in the murder of the Pawnee girl.

Colter went in search of Johannes and eventually found him checking the hobbles on his old horse as he prepared to retire for the night. The mountain man crept up stealthily and set a brawny hand on his shoulder so that Johannes almost jumped out of his skin.

"Got a job for you," Colter whispered surreptitiously, steering Johannes away from his schooner.

Johannes cringed. Colter scared him, and his tone sounded obdurate. "Vhat?" he whined. "Vhat is you doing?"

"Need a rat to sneak 'round the soldiers' camp an' git somat."

"I no vant do dis! Vhy me?" Johannes was appalled at the suggestion.

"Cos yer don't wanna have no one blabbin' 'bout yer killin' no Injun, do yer?" Colter hissed.

Johannes was dumbstruck. He was uncertain whether to deny Colter's insinuation or to run. "I not know vhat you mean," he stuttered unconvincingly.

"Oh, come on, son. We both know what yer bin doin' with that fancy knife, don't we?"

The color drained from Johannes's face and he felt sick. He wagged his head furiously. "You mad! I no speak viz you." He wriggled to free himself from Colter's grasp.

"You wanna go have a little word with the capt'n? Reckon he'd be mighty interested in what I got to say," Colter snarled, cocking his head at Johannes, who fell limp, his resistance dissolving. "Thought so!"

Colter dragged Johannes into the shadows and explained what he wanted. He would set up a diversion to attract Gresham and Trautman from their tents, leaving Johannes to retrieve the keys to the armory locker from the lieutenant's quarters, recover Colter's rifle, and return the keys, hopefully remaining undetected.

Quivering with fear, Johannes was unable to speak. He nodded his understanding of Colter's instructions, but his bowel felt as though it might erupt at the thought of entering an army officer's tent uninvited and stealing his keys.

But he was far too scared of Colter to argue and reluctantly followed him to the cavalry camp, so that the mountain man could point out Trautman's bivouac and ensure that the boy knew where the armory was located on the chuck wagon.

The camp was quiet, a lamp burning in each of the officer's

tents, and a sentry stood leaning in a lugubrious pose against the rear of the wagon. They watched for several minutes until Colter nudged Johannes, silently indicating that he was departing to instigate his diversion.

Johannes was left sweating. His mouth was dry and his nerves tingled, but in Colter's absence he began to experience an exhilarating thrill of anticipation. The feeling was unexpected, and he started to grin as he savored the excitement. Compared to the monotony of daily life on the wagon train, the thought of breaking into an army store to steal something was like a heady narcotic. He reveled in the sensation.

Johannes waited. Nothing happened for what seemed like an eternity, and he was beginning to wonder whether Colter had changed his mind, when a flash of light erupted two hundred yards away, accompanied by the whooshing sound of fire taking hold of tinder-dry canvas. A schooner burst into flames, a woman screamed, and, in an instant, there was pandemonium.

A mother and father leapt into the back of their wagon to rescue their sleeping children as the schooner's canopy swiftly turned into an inferno, the family barely escaping with their lives. Roused from their slumber, neighboring migrants stumbled from their beds and helped to untie the mules hobbled alongside the burning wagon before hastily moving their own schooners, anxious to prevent the fire from spreading.

Men rushed to fill buckets with water, shouting at one another to form a chain as they attempted the futile task of extinguishing the flames, the dry wooden bed of the wagon fueling the ferocity of the fire.

Disturbed by the chaotic screaming, Gresham and Trautman stormed out of their tents and rushed to offer their assistance, summoning a cadre of troopers to help move wagons and assist with the firefighting.

Johannes was mesmerized. He had not expected Colter to

create such a spectacle. The panic the fire caused was breathtaking, and the impact was exactly as Colter had envisaged. The two officers vacated their tents, and the sentry posted by the chuck wagon followed them immediately, accompanied by several more troopers.

Johannes shook himself from a state of stunned paralysis, his body stiff with apprehensive tension, and eased from his hiding place. Bending low to the ground, he crept to the side of Trautman's tent and confirmed that he had not been observed before slipping inside.

An oil lamp cast a flickering light over the dim interior, and Johannes could see the lieutenant's uniform laid out neatly across his saddle, his saber and his holstered pistol lying at its side. Hurriedly, he knelt down and lifted the cartridge belt, snatching a guilty glance over his shoulder before opening the cap pouch and probing inside. His fingers brushed a single key, and he turned the pouch upside down to shake it into his hand, smiling with satisfaction.

Returning to the entrance flap of the tent, Johannes peeped through a slit in the fabric to ensure that he remained undetected and slid out, tiptoeing to the armory cabinet located at the opposite side of the chuck wagon to the burning schooner.

The solid structure of the big wagon loomed above him, and he slid his hand across the surface of the cabinet door attempting to locate the keyhole. His fingers skimmed the lock plate as he fumbled to insert the key, twisting it anti-clockwise so that with a loud click the armory door swung open.

The cabinet was packed full of wooden ammunition cases, each box bearing a stenciled description of the calibre of cartridge it contained, and Johannes paused to scan the stockpile of munitions enviously. To him they symbolized power and maturity, and he was seized by an avaricious desire to steal a box for himself.

Concentrating on his task, he leaned into the cabinet and found Colter's rifle strung from a nail on the left-hand side. He stretched up to unhook the weapon, his nerves buzzing with trepidation at being discovered, alert to the need to distinguish between the frantic sounds of people fighting the schooner fire and the potential of someone approaching.

He lifted the Henry down, savoring its weight in his hands, his confidence bolstered by its deadly capability. The lever action breech was cool and smooth, the polished stock solid and sleek. He yearned to fire the rifle, intoxicated by the thought of killing something, and caressed the weapon lovingly.

"Gonna hurt yerself, if yer play wi' toys yer ain't man 'nough to handle." Colter snatched the weapon out of his hands and Johannes leaped backward, flushing with a cold sweat as he was left quivering, his jaw hanging open.

"Now, lock up an' put the key back," Colter growled, pressing his whiskered face up against Johannes's. "An' don't git yerself caught!" Offering no further comment, he turned and melted into the darkness.

Johannes found that he was gasping for breath, his hands shaking, and he stood panting for a few moments before turning back to the armory. Carefully, he swung the door closed and started to turn the key in the lock, but he was gripped by an irresistible craving to steal some ammunition. Hurriedly, he reopened the door and lifted the cover off an open box of 0.49-caliber cartridges, shoving several handfuls into his pockets before replacing the lid and relocking the armory.

Exhilerated, he grinned with satisfaction and turned back toward Trautman's tent. It was evident that the frantic attempts to extinguish the fire on the schooner were proving successful. The flames had abated, plunging the rest of the camp into darkness once more, and a grim silence had settled over the troopers and migrants as they worked to douse the dying embers and console the distraught family.

Johannes slid into the lieutenant's tent once more and replaced the locker key. Stopping in the light from the lantern, he pulled a fistful of cartridges from his pocket and gloated over them, his indulgent delight shattered as the flap to the tent was unexpectedly yanked aside. A man wearing light blue cavalry pants stepped through the opening and Johannes's heart stopped. He gawped at the young officer, who eyed him with curiosity.

"You? Whatta yer think yer doin'?" Hanley sounded more surprised than annoyed. "I thought I seen som'ne duck in here."

Johannes stuttered, uncertain how to respond.

"What yer got in yer hand?" Now, Hanley was more agitated, assuming that Johannes had been caught stealing something from Trautman's tent. He grabbed Johannes's wrist, causing several cartridges to tumble to the ground as he opened his palm guiltily.

Hanley wagged his head in disappointment. "Cartridges! Guess I said I was gonna teach yer to shoot, but yer didn' have to go sneakin' about to git these!" He scooped the bullets out of Johannes's hand. "Yer jus' had to come an' ask."

The young lieutenant's presumed rationale for his entering Trautman's tent was a godsend, and Johannes leapt at the proffered excuse. "I . . . I im sorry." He hung his head, concealing a smirk. "I vanted to be shooting. But I hiv no bullet." He affected a dejected and apologetic air.

"Stupid kid! Could have gotten yerself in'a all kinds o' trouble." Hanley felt sorry for the lad and ushered him out of the tent. "Now, git out o' here before the lieutenant gits back. An' no more snoopin' about. We'll keep this 'tween ourselves this time, but I ain't gonna be so even-minded if I catch yer agin."

Johannes scuttled away gratefully, and Hanley was left amused at his childish innocence.

★ ★ ★ ★ ★

Stone joined the wagon train when it left Laramie, keeping a low profile as the emigrants and Gresham's company proceeded slowly along the trail to Platte Bridge Station. Colter had introduced him to each of the hired guns, making it abundantly clear that Stone would be assuming leadership in his absence, and had delighted in informing the bogus prospectors of the prowess that Winthrop's emissary displayed with his pistol. But the warning was unnecessary, since Stone's brooding demeanor left none of the men doubting that he was capable of administering discipline if required.

Gresham was concerned, but not surprised, when Colter disappeared without a word. Nobody had seen him leave with Moylan, but that did not prove anything, and he was confident that Colter would join the young captain's squad further along the trail. He was tempted to send Trautman in pursuit, to confirm his suspicions, but in the event, he judged that Trautman's services would be better utilized organizing the wagon train and helping to encourage everyone to set forth once more, many families being reluctant to return to the hardships of the trail, having become acclimatized to the comforts provided by the fort.

Trautman identified the man who took Colter's place on the prospectors' wagon as Tobias Stone, and Gresham was intrigued by his unexpected presence. He managed one brief conversation with Stone, but the man was evasive about his origin and intentions and was elusive when Gresham tried to locate him a second time.

Certainly, Stone was not of the same mold as the other prospectors. He was articulate and, despite his trail-worn clothing, he had the air of a city-dweller rather than a man of the land, his hands being strong but not calloused from hard manual toil. Gresham was perplexed by his presence and concluded that his arrival being concurrent with Colter's disappearance was no coincidence.

Stone perceived Gresham's interest in him and knew that the intelligent captain was too experienced to overlook the fact that he had replaced Colter on the prospectors' wagon. He also noticed Gresham studying his hands as they exchanged a few words, and it was apparent that the soldier's suspicions were aroused. Concluding that it would be in his interest to maintain a low profile until the wagons passed beyond Platte Bridge Station, he ensured a prudent separation between himself and the captain by day and kept clear of the prospectors' wagon during the evening.

It took five days for the wagon train to reach the fort, the migrants only pausing to carve their names into the granite face of Independence Rock, prior to diverting from the Oregon Trail to turn northeast. Inscribing one's mark on the huge two-thousand-foot-long rock was a tradition for the pilgrims, and some families were courageous enough to climb up and engrave their record on its upper surface, a hundred feet above the plains where the lazy Sweetwater River snaked alongside the trail.

Reaching Independence Rock two weeks ahead of the usual target date of July the fourth, despite the delays the wagon train had encountered, was a great achievement. Rather than stopping for the customary celebrations, the travelers decided to carry on at pace, resting for only a single day when they reached Platte Bridge.

Once at the fort, Gresham pored over a rudimentary set of maps with the wagonmaster, the documents having originally been formulated by Jim Bridger when he had first broken the trail, and helped him to develop a strategy for tackling the remaining challenges that the wagon train would face. There would be tough climbs and steep descents as the schooners traversed the Bridger Mountains, and deep river crossings of the Bighorn and Shoshone rivers as they traveled further north.

Beyond the Bridgers they would benefit from better grazing for the cattle and a plentiful supply of game, mitigating some elements of the hardship of the trail. But they could expect to encounter bears, which would be attracted by the smell of cooking, and Gresham discussed the precautions that families would have to take to protect themselves from attack.

The planning lasted for several hours, and when both men were content that every aspect of risk had been considered, Gresham's final duty was to allocate a scout to assist the captain of the wagon train to navigate the balance of the trail.

The commanding officer at Platte Bridge Station welcomed Gresham enthusiastically, delighted to be relieved of his post, and he confirmed that Moylan's squad had passed through the fort two days previously, traveling fast. To Gresham's consternation, he verified that Colter and an Indian had accompanied the cavalry troop, although he had not spoken to the mountain man because the troop had stopped only to water their horses and replenish supplies. Additionally, he informed Gresham that Colter had been heard issuing the instruction to mount up and move out, and that he had concluded that the young captain was not the man pushing the pace.

The news reignited Gresham's fears, so that once again he was tortured by the mystery of Moylan's mission to Virginia City and Colter's dubious involvement. A prickle of alarm ran down his spine as he mused the possibilities, intuitively sensing an impending catastrophe. But, though he turned the dilemma in his mind constantly, he could not assemble the pieces of the puzzle to form an explanation that compelled him to action. Remaining frustrated, he bade farewell to the emigrants and turned his attention to his new duties at the fort.

★ ★ ★ ★ ★

Free from Gresham's scrutiny, Stone was able to move about the wagon train unhindered and spent his time cultivating his relationship with the marshal leading the prospectors' group of wagons. The man was a seasoned rancher from Virginia who had worked cattle and oxen all his life and had traveled the Oregon Trail on his own previously. He was familiar with the problems the migrants would encounter and was conversant with the methods used to negotiate the topographical challenges, but, on this occasion, he was traveling with his family, destined for the fertile land bordering the Yellowstone River, where the soil was rumored to be favorable for growing corn and other high-value crops.

Stone promoted himself as a novice prospector, keen to exploit every opportunity to chance his arm at discovering a previously uncharted lode of gold, and as the wagon train passed through the Bridgers, he made conspicuous detours to reconnoiter the surrounding mountains, ensuring that the marshal became accustomed to his propensity to indulge in regular speculative panning.

As the wagon train set camp under the towering red outcrop near Ten Sleep, it was no surprise to the marshal, therefore, when Stone announced that he and several other prospectors intended diverting to explore the canyon that wound into the Bighorn range to the east.

The emigrants decided to rest for a day or two since the grazing at Ten Sleep was good and the creek provided abundant water, so they watched with interest as Stone and his ten hired guns, masquerading as prospectors, prepared their wagons and wished them luck in their quest to secure their fortunes.

Stone told the marshal that he and his companions would endeavor to rejoin the wagon train in a week or so if the prospecting proved unsuccessful, and no one considered the men's departure unusual. Indeed, it was common knowledge that almost all wagon trains broke into smaller groups along the trail, for one reason or another.

Early on the day after their arrival at Ten Sleep, Stone and Colter's group of recruits departed, reaching their destination in less than two hours, where they were hailed with an unenthusiastic challenge from the sentry standing guard at the entrance to the hunters' ravine.

Stone was pleasantly gratified to find the camp largely unoccupied and to be informed that Harrison and his men had been absent for more than six weeks hunting buffalo. Additionally, he was pleased to be shown a creditable-sized pile of fleeces stacked behind the cabins, attended by an industrious group of Indians who were busy cleaning, dehairing, and softening the skins. His previous concern that Colter had done little to progress Winthrop's instructions was significantly eased by witnessing in person the seeds of the senator's plan coming to fruition.

At the heart of Winthrop's ambition was a strategy to drive the native tribes from the Great Plains. On the one hand, he encouraged militarization of the region, but simultaneously he believed that it would be impossible to defeat the Indians' spirit through force alone, instead contending that a permanent solution necessitated the destruction of their culture and way of life.

The buffalo underpinned the Indians' existence, particularly the Sioux and the other plains tribes, providing sustenance throughout the year and enabling the Indians to endure the hardships of the severe winter months.

Winthrop's strategy was to destroy the huge buffalo herds, using his influence within the Hudson Bay Fur Trading Company to establish a demand for their fleece and hides in the European markets, thereby inciting hunters to flock to the west and scythe the buffalo down in their thousands to profit from the trade.

The team that Colter had assembled, led by Harrison, represented the initiation of Winthrop's plan. The hunters' objective was to work the plains to the west of the Bighorn Mountains, an area less sensitive to the Sioux than the Powder River Basin, enabling Winthrop to procure an early supply of pelts to stimulate market interest.

His hunting operation would sell the hides to the Hudson Bay Company, and his steamers would transport them to southern markets, New York, and Boston, where they would be sold. And, once the Northern Pacific reached the plains, he intended to utilize Stevens's railroad to expedite distribution to the east coast.

Rid of the buffalo and unfettered by the Indians, the plains would be ripe for farming, enabling Winthrop to establish his general stores in the towns that developed to serve the new communities. With Stevens's pliable cooperation, a vibrant market would inevitably evolve for shipping produce and cattle across the country to satisfy the voracious appetite of the flourishing eastern cities, particularly healthy profits being anticipated from livestock transportation and abattoir services.

Winthrop intended that his commercial tentacles would exploit each lucrative opportunity, while the legislature focused on the thorny issue of reintegration of the southern states and jostled for political power, leaving him a largely unconstrained hand to extend his wealth remote from prying eyes.

Takoda watched with interest as the hunters sat around the campfire with the new arrivals, a loop of rope pulled tightly around his waist and secured to the post behind him, his ankles bound and his hands tied beneath his knees as usual. The Pawnee spoke passable English and had taught him to pick out a few of the words the hunters used, but although he could hear the white men talking, he could not understand their conversation.

It was clear, though, that the tall man who had entered camp earlier in the day was important. The other hunters deferred to him, and the man called Doyle had escorted him around the camp, showing him the buffalo hides and demonstrating the work that the Pawnee were undertaking.

The hunters Harrison had left behind were distracted from their guard duties and relished a welcome diversion from the monotony of camp life that the arrival of ten more hired guns inspired. As the evening progressed and the whiskey began to flow, the gathering became more exuberant, conversation progressively degenerating into bawdy laughter, shouting, and impromptu singing.

The Pawnee remained remote from the revelry, retreating to the privacy of their Mandans so that Takoda was left alone, watching the white men's behavior deteriorate. He could see the tall newcomer, with his unnerving gray eyes, sitting on the far side of the fire. He remained separate from his disorderly companions, declining to participate in their entertainment and responding with monosyllabic answers when the others attempted to engage him in conversation.

His attention appeared captivated by the flickering flames of the fire, as if brooding upon an absorbing thought, but occasionally he leveled his penetrating gaze directly at Takoda, the light of the fire reflecting in his dark eyes.

The intermittent attentive scrutiny was disconcerting and disruptive to Takoda's task. He had honed his fractured piece of bone into a reasonable blade, which he hoped would be sufficiently sharp to sever the ropes that bound his hands and feet and, ideally, he wanted to set to the task undisturbed. But instead he was forced to keep a surreptitious eye on the tall man as he pushed the crude blade between his wrists, using his right hand to saw its sharpened edge back and forth against the rope binding his left wrist.

Takoda decided that the distraction caused by the new arrivals would present his best opportunity to escape, the hunters' attentions being diverted and the vigilance of the camp's guards being diminished. The Pawnee were secreted in their lodges, and he was reassured to note that McCabe's habitual scrutiny had been deflected by the merriment, the white man's fire water rendering him barely capable of standing. The only person paying him any attention was the tall stranger.

The rope was strong and, although the blade was sharp, Takoda's progress in cutting through the bindings was painfully slow. However, eventually, the first strand of the twisted braid parted, and the rope slackened enough to permit greater movement, enabling the strokes of his knife to become more effective.

Alarmingly, when Takoda glanced up from his task, he noticed that the stranger was studying him. Instantly, he stopped cutting and slouched, as if in dejected frustration, casting his head down but maintaining a tense surveillance of the gray-eyed man and praying that his attention would wane. To his consternation, the stranger stood up and started to move around the fire.

Takoda's heart missed a beat, and he hurriedly placed his blade on the ground and brushed some earth over the top of it, tucking his hands up under his knees to shield the severed strands of his bindings from view.

The man approached with a languid gait, carrying something Takoda could not identify, and sipping from his mug. He had removed his jacket, and his sleeves were rolled up, revealing muscular arms. On his left hip he wore a holstered revolver, positioned so that it could be drawn across his body using his right hand, differing from the other hunters, who wore their pistol holster strapped to their thigh on the same side of their body as the hand they used to fire the weapon.

Takoda braced himself. The stranger exuded the same cold menace as Harrison, although he seemed more intelligent and considered. The consequent impression was more alarming because he combined a sense of ruthless detachment with a calculating intellect, distinct from Harrison's raw brutality.

Takoda kept his head down as the stranger stopped a few feet away and stood staring down at him, his pulse thumping in his ears and his body rigid with the anticipation of another painful assault. But nothing happened. The man simply waited and watched, sipping occasionally at his coffee, its smell pungent and earthy. The intimidating newcomer displayed no intent to return to the campfire, so eventually Takoda was compelled to succumb to his silent scrutiny and raise his head, peering up and fearing the worst.

Impassive gray eyes stared at him, their expression unfathomable, although it was evident that the stranger had been waiting for Takoda to acknowledge his presence. He held Takoda's gaze briefly, appearing satisfied, and Takoda flinched as he bent down, expecting an unprovoked blow, but the man simply placed a plate of food under his knees and left.

The platter was heaped with a large piece of meat, some beans, and a chunk of bread, and Takoda was astonished, the benevolent gesture being entirely at odds with the inhumane treatment he had predicted. He watched the stranger return and settle at the opposite side of the fire, his attentive eyes shining in the flickering light, interested to ascertain whether the food would be accepted.

The smell of fire-grilled venison was mouth-watering and Takoda needed no further invitation to tuck into the succulent meat. Bending his head between his knees so that he could feed himself, he devoured the unexpected feast, mopping up the juices with the bread and hungrily scraping the beans into his mouth.

The rich food contrasted with the lean scraps he had been provided over the previous weeks, and his stomach ached uncomfortably. Nevertheless, he wiped the plate clean with a final mouthful of bread and sighed contentedly, placing the empty plate on the ground and casting a glance at the stranger, who continued to study him. Their eyes met briefly and the man nodded imperceptibly, before bending to sip his coffee and returning his attention to the fire.

Feeling revitalized, Takoda dusted off his improvised blade and attacked his bindings with renewed vigor, so that after a few minutes the rope restraining his left wrist parted and he wriggled his hand free of the frayed loop. Then he loosened the rope around his right wrist and pulled it away from his hand.

Takoda sustained a vigilant surveillance of the hunters around the fire and stayed his frenetic sawing each time he felt someone might have cause to cast a glance in his direction, but the tall stranger was the only person to accord him any interest, and although he continued to sit and brood, he only looked toward Takoda on a couple of further occasions, his interest diminished.

Having released his hands, Takoda pulled up his knees, drawing his feet closer so that he could reach the bindings around his ankles. Once again, he set to work with the little bone knife, its blade becoming progressively less effective. But, with both hands unrestrained, he was able to grasp the rope firmly and apply more pressure, releasing the bindings around his feet and severing the loop around his waist. He was free.

The frivolity around the campfire continued unabated, the men clearly the worse for drink and the laughter becoming more raucous. Takoda sat motionless, waiting for an optimal opportunity to effect his escape undetected.

As Takoda watched, Doyle pushed himself to his feet, lurching wildly on unsteady legs, until with a riotous bellow he tripped and tumbled helplessly into the dying embers of the fire. He howled in panic and his companions stumbled to his assistance, hauling him out of the flames and patting him down in an ineffectual attempt to extinguish his smoldering clothing. Apparently frustrated at the intoxicated hunters, the tall stranger sprang from his seat and spread his coat over the writhing inebriate, smothering his burning breeches.

Everyone's attention was focused on Doyle, so Takoda took his chance. He rolled away and darted into the gloom, keeping low to the ground and stealing into the shadows. Within seconds he reached the cover of the trees on the west side of the camp and disappeared into their refuge, running north towards the head of the ravine. Behind him the sound of boisterous laughter erupted, and he picked his way swiftly in the direction of the guard post, anxious to evade the sentry and slip away before his disappearance was detected.

Stone's anger flared at the unruly debauchery of the hunters. He hauled Doyle upright by the scruff of his neck and glared at him, thrusting him toward the cabins and growling his disapproval at the other men, whose revelry ceased abruptly, the hunters falling silent and resuming their seats, muttering apprehensively.

Stone shook out his coat and inspected the scorch marks with irritation, deciding that it was time to turn in for the night. Casually, he glanced in Takoda's direction, but pulled up sharply as he noticed that the boy had disappeared. Galvanized into action, he threw down his coat, drew his gun, and dashed around the fire, his sudden urgency drawing the attention of the other men.

Despite his drunken condition, McCabe was the first of the hunters to detect Takoda's absence and he lumbered to his feet, bewildered. "Damned Injun boy's gone! Find the son o' a bitch!" he bawled, drawing his revolver and stumbling after Stone, who knelt down and inspected the severed coils of Takoda's bindings.

McCabe bent over him, swaying unsteadily. "He gone?" he enquired, stating the obvious. "Son o' a bitch," he repeated, swinging his revolver and firing indiscriminately into the darkness.

Stone reacted instantly, seizing the pistol in a brawny fist and twisting it brutally so that McCabe squealed with pain. He whipped up his own handgun and delivered a solid crack to the side of the trapper's skull, causing McCabe to collapse to his knees.

"The Indian boy's coming your way! Don't let him out of the ravine! Stand your ground!" he bawled at the sentry, launching himself along the ravine.

Takoda worked his way as close as possible to the ravine's narrow pass, anticipating the presence of a concealed sentry, but instead, negating the risk of his stumbling upon the man unexpectedly, he was grateful to find the guard standing conspicuously, facing down the trail toward the hunter's camp.

It was evident that the sentry's focus was directed at the rowdy upsurge in laughter, and Takoda hoped that he might be tempted to investigate the hilarity, since it appeared impossible to escape unobserved for as long as the man obstructed his only viable route of escape. The attempt to secure his freedom seemed depressingly hopeless, and he waited impatiently for a distraction that might draw the guard's attention.

Unexpectedly, a series of explosive gunshots erupted, and Takoda heard the thud of bullets embedding themselves in the trees a hundred paces away. Instantly, the guard started running toward the camp, his rifle held at the ready. But he had run only thirty paces before a booming voice bellowed an urgent warning, causing the sentry to stop, clearly confused and unable to understand the instructions.

Takoda took his opportunity and rushed out of the trees, running for the narrow pass that led out of the ravine. At the same moment, the guard comprehended Stone's insistent instructions and wheeled around, picking out Takoda's fleeting movement. Hesitating only momentarily, he lifted his rifle to his shoulder and fired.

Taken in haste, the shot was inaccurate, and Takoda heard a high-pitched whistle as the bullet whizzed overhead. Relieved, he ducked down and raced onward, weaving wildly to present a more challenging target. As he crested the pass, a second bullet ricocheted off the rock to his left, eliciting a shower of razor-sharp splinters that lacerated his face. Almost immediately, a third bullet plucked at the underside of the right sleeve of his tunic, and he felt the stabbing bite as it skimmed the flesh of his torso.

The elusive specter of freedom was a matter of paces away, but he ran as though his feet were immersed in mud, resigning himself to his fate and expecting the next shot to be fatal. Much to his astonishment the bullet went astray, allowing him to clear the ravine and swing to the left, where he plunged downhill across a rolling expanse of tufty grassland aiming toward a shadowed cleft in the plain. The sky was thick with heavy cloud, obscuring the moon's iridescent glow, so that darkness enveloped him, and he managed to slip out of sight.

Intermittently, he glanced back, hoping that the hunters would abandon the notion of pursuit, but to his consternation the indistinct outline of half a dozen men materialized at the entrance to the ravine, pausing briefly as they searched the murky landscape before fanning out and advancing across the plain.

A wave of trepidation drove Takoda on, his feet stumbling on the uneven ground, causing him to stagger and fall. But he picked himself up and plunged ahead, reeling as his balance and sense of perspective became unusually debilitated. Without warning, a dark void opened at his feet, and he scrambled desperately to halt his flight as he slid helplessly over the upper edge of a deep gully.

Takoda's momentum threw him into the chasm and he plunged a dozen feet, landing in an ungainly sprawl among a collection of rugged rocks. The impact dislocated two fingers on his left hand, cracked one of his knees against a jagged stone, and twisted his right foot, stretching his tendons so savagely that he felt they might snap.

The pain was overwhelming and he lay immobile for a moment, breathing heavily before gingerly attempting to push himself upright. His dislocated fingers projected at a gruesomely distorted angle and, impulsively, he snapped them back into position, the flood of relief preceded by a knife-like stab of agony.

His knee throbbed and his right ankle struggled to support his weight, but he knew that he had to keep moving, so he shuffled close to the vertical wall of the gully and hobbled along, moving north until he was thwarted by a thick stand of sagebrush that blocked his path.

The woody clumps of sage stood as high as his shoulders, impeding his progress, but the dense foliage provided cover in which to hide from the pursuing men. Hurriedly, he forced his way under the brush and wriggled twenty paces into its welcome shelter. His nerves strung to breaking point, he froze.

A footstep scuffed the ground directly above where he lay, and he rolled cautiously onto his side, twisting his neck to look up through the thick vegetation. Dark ghostly clouds hurried across a threatening sky, heavy with menace, accentuating the sense of vulnerability of his position and framing the vertical walls of the gorge so that he felt entombed.

Struggling to adjust his vision to the poor light, he detected the hazy outline of one of the hunters as he leaned out and peered down into the gully. It was the tall stranger. Takoda awaited the inevitability of his discovery, as the man systematically scanned the stand of sagebrush and held his breath as the stranger looked directly at him. He remained motionless, closing his eyes to prevent any reflection of light that might give away his presence. His heart pounded.

A shout rang out, and Takoda convulsed with a flutter of fear. There was the sound of running feet as the hunters converged on the man who had cried out. But the urgent flurry of activity was further down the gully. More shouting ensued and two shots were fired, followed by guffaws of excited talking. Tentatively, Takoda opened his eyes and sighed with relief as the tall man turned slowly and walked away.

Stone found the men cheering on two of the hunters as they climbed down into the gully, convinced that they had successfully dispatched the Indian. Once at the foot of the gorge they stumbled around searching for their quarry, encouraged enthusiastically by their comrades, but their excitement was short-lived. One of the hunters tripped over the victim of his murderous work, a white-tailed deer, which had fled down the gully, alarmed by the presence of the hunters as they searched for Takoda.

There were hoots of laughter and ridicule as the two humiliated hunters returned to join their companions, but Stone was unamused. He berated them for their foolishness and hustled them away toward the camp, reluctantly deciding to abandon the notion of a pursuit in the dark.

Takoda remained hidden for several hours, until the clouds cleared and the silver luminescence of the moon cast enough light for him to see his way. Shuffling uncomfortably, he retreated from his hiding place, checking carefully to ensure that none of the hunters remained, and searched for an accessible point at which to haul himself out of the gully on its western side.

Determined to travel as far from the camp as possible before daylight, Takoda's injuries hampered his pace. He hobbled awkwardly on his right foot, his ankle swollen and tender, and intermittently his left knee buckled, causing him to slump to the ground. But, of most concern, he realized that he was struggling to discern the contours and he became aware of a dull ache in his left eye.

Anxiously, he touched his cheek and found that minute fragments of rock pocked the entire left side of his face, blown off the wall of the ravine by the sentry's rifle shot. Unnerved, he probed his eyeball gingerly and discovered the tip of a fine sliver of stone, the point at which it was embedded oozing a warm trickle of sticky fluid. A stab of fear turned his stomach as he realized that the disorientation he was experiencing was the consequence of an inability to see out of his left eye.

He collapsed to his knees and sat panting, the comfort and security of his family seeming a distant and illusory memory. Racked with pain and exhausted, he succumbed to self-pity and cried, his shoulders shaking as he sobbed, releasing the fear and anguish he had endured since being captured by the trappers.

Feeling vulnerable and isolated, he cried out for his mother, calling her name in a desperate plea to be liberated from his suffering. He cried for his dead brother and for the loss of his father, convinced that his misfortune was a manifestation of the Great Spirit's retribution for the responsibility he bore for their deaths. He sat unable to move, lost in his misery, until eventually he could cry no more. His body slumped, and he fell into an exhausted and fitful sleep.

Chapter 30

July 1865, Ten Sleep, Nowood Creek

The early-morning call of a sage grouse roused Takoda from his torpor. Attempting to force his eyes open, he listened to the chirruping *kuk-kuk-kuk* as it sounded close by once more. His left eye was stuck fast, encrusted with blood, and it took a moment to focus with his right eye, so that he could watch the white-chested grouse strut past, its gait a series of erratic bursts as it halted sporadically to peck at succulent new buds of sage, parading its erect tail feathers and blowing out the two yellow throat sacks on its dark brown neck in an elaborate courtship display.

The strain of the previous evening's ordeal had drained Takoda of energy. His back ached, his injured knee was stiff and swollen, and he was dehydrated. He coughed and slid sideways so that he could stretch out his legs. His damaged ankle had turned a mottled purple and he struggled to rotate the joint, wondering whether it was broken, but the bones did not click and he hoped that the inflammation was simply the result of severe bruising.

Takoda surveyed the mountains to the east, the soft orange glow spreading across their peaks hinting at the onset of dawn, and reflected upon his grueling escape from the hunters' camp. But the sense of relief was hollow. He could not imagine that they would permit him to evade capture without at least one further attempt to apprehend him once there was sufficient light. And, with horses and good visibility, they would easily chase him down if he remained in the open ground.

Wearily, Takoda pushed himself to his feet, testing his weight on each leg to feel for the point at which its strength might fail. Then he started off at a shuffling gait, each step a challenge to his resilience, driven by the knowledge that he had no alternative. He had to keep moving.

He struggled sluggishly northward until he intersected the canyon that led to Ten Sleep, where he turned west, so that by the time the sun had risen fully, he was nearly halfway back to Nowood Creek. But he was haunted by the fear of pursuit and glanced over his shoulder nervously every few steps.

Attempting to remain concealed, Takoda hugged the southern face of the canyon, constantly conscious of the need to remain within reach of a suitable hiding place if the necessity arose. His breath came in hoarse rasps, and his body dripped with sweat as he pushed himself to the limit of his endurance, dragging his right leg uncomfortably while swinging his left leg to avoid bending his agonized knee.

Uncertain whether his motivation was fatigue or intuition, Takoda stopped, breathing heavily and drained of energy. His skin tingled ominously and a creeping sense of impending danger prompted him to hobble to the cover of a cluster of boulders nestled at the foot of the canyon, where he sat down heavily, fending off a pervasive wave of nausea.

Moments later the metallic clink of a horse's shoe confirmed once again the reliability of his instinct, alerting him to the presence of a group of men following his trail. He squeezed into the shelter of the rocks, concealing himself so that he retained a view of the canyon, and waited.

Eventually, four men on horseback appeared, the tall stranger and two hunters, with McCabe trailing to the rear. But ahead of them a Pawnee jogged along with his head cast down. He was tracking Takoda's spoor.

As Takoda peered despondently along the canyon, the Pawnee raised his head and pointed directly at the position where he was hiding among the rocks. Appearing elated at the prospect of running down their quarry, the hunters stopped and squinted in his direction before urging their mounts to continue, the Pawnee jogging at their side. Takoda felt a sense of despair and resigned himself to discovery. An experienced Indian tracker would easily pick out his trail, his clumsy gait having left prominent scuff marks in the gravel that even a child could follow. He slumped and awaited his fate, listening to the rhythmic footfall of the horses as they approached.

There was a piercing cry, followed by a volley of gunshots as a chorus of shouting erupted. Takoda felt as though he would explode with the tension and sneaked a surreptitious glance at his pursuers, but to his dismay found the hunters whipping their horses into a headlong charge, gesticulating wildly toward his refuge. Conceding defeat, he considered whether to stand up and reveal his presence in favor of being discovered cowering among the rocks, and barely managed to restrain the compulsion when it became evident that the horsemen were going to gallop straight past. Instead, he hunkered down, mystified as the hunters thundered along the trail, whooping and firing another volley of shots.

Shifting position, Takoda searched the canyon for an explanation and spotted another group of riders appearing from the opposite direction. Harrison was leading the way, plodding along in front of a train of wagons, each weighed down with hundreds of buffalo hides, piled in precarious heaps. His band of hunters looked exhausted, although they sprang upright in their saddles and returned their comrade's greeting with their own salvo of gunfire.

The tall stranger held back his horse, and pulled up parallel to Takoda's hiding place, content to wait for the hunting party to reach him.

Harrison approached with suspicion and slid a hand to the pistol at his waist, anticipating an altercation, until two of his men swung alongside and hurriedly introduced Stone. The Texan drew to a halt as he reached Winthrop's man. Although irritated at the explanation for Stone's presence, regarding any oversight of his operation as an intrusion, his hand fell away from his gun.

Offering a curt acknowledgment, Harrison responded with a reluctant handshake when Stone stretched out his arm in civil greeting, and demanded the justification for his presence in the canyon. Indifferent to the terse behavior, Stone conveyed his disappointment at the drunken conduct of Harrison's men, bemoaning their inability to ensure the secure captivity of the Indian boy.

Harrison grunted, his anger inflamed by the provocative comments, and dismissed the Indian's escape as an irrelevance, digging his spurs aggressively into his horse's flank and riding off along the canyon toward the camp rather than engage in further conversation.

Stone's posse, McCabe and the two hunters from the camp, had lost interest in chasing the Indian and were engrossed in noisy banter with their compatriots, leaving Stone to conclude that there was little merit in attempting to resume the pursuit. Resigned to the boy's escape, he scanned the canyon one final time and swung his horse around, falling in alongside Harrison's wagons.

The hunters rolled past Takoda's hiding place, a cloud of dust left hanging in their wake, and he sat stunned, waiting for them to disappear from sight, astounded at his good fortune. At last, believing that he was alone, he began to stir, only to pull up in shock as he detected a subtle movement among the settling dust.

The Pawnee tracker rose slowly from where he had been squatting and walked in a deliberate circle studying the ground, pausing after a few moments, content that he had deciphered the tracks. He stared purposefully in Takoda's direction, remaining motionless, his face impassive below his dramatic porcupine roach. Takoda was certain that he had been discovered, although he was unsure how the Pawnee would react and uncertain whether the Indian intended to kill him or simply drag him back to the camp.

To his astonishment, the Pawnee pulled a pouch from his waistband and placed it deliberately on the ground. He then studied Takoda's secluded hideaway for several minutes before clenching his fist to his chest in a gesture of solidarity and turning to jog swiftly back along the canyon.

Once the Pawnee was out of sight, Takoda emerged from his hiding place and hobbled over to the pouch, apprehensively picking it up and pulling open the drawstring to inspect its contents. Overcome with gratitude, he discovered a tight bundle of medicinal herbs and realized that the Indian had detected his injuries, leaving the herbs so that Takoda could minister to his ailments. Relieved, he tucked the bag into his tunic and turned west toward the plains, buoyed with renewed optimism.

CHAPTER 31

Leaving for the Bridger Trail

To Hans, Laramie provided a welcome break from the monotony of the journey and an opportunity to evade his family for a sustained period. The saloon never closed and offered a heady blend of alcohol, music, and flouncing petticoats to captivate his attention. He and Colter's prospector friends took up residence, joined occasionally by Hardwick whenever the little man was able to slip away from his bombastic wife.

The land agent was attracted to the young women, many of whom would readily sit on his knee and smother him with affection in return for a few dollars. But his particular interest was a dusky Cheyenne girl, whose long dark hair and seductive curves he found mesmerizing.

The young Cheyenne sat cuddled on Hardwick's knee for an hour the second evening, dangling her long tresses across his face and permitting him to explore her body with hungry hands, until, eventually, she whispered in his ear and left the bar, giving the land agent an enticing nod as she invited him to follow. Moments later, Hardwick rose and bade his drinking partners' farewell, but entertained by the obvious subterfuge Hans decided to follow discreetly.

He watched Hardwick leave the saloon. The land agent appeared agitated, peering about furtively as he made haste toward the eastern end of the Indian camp, hugging the shadows as he attempted to remain inconspicuous. Hans lingered at the doorway to the saloon for a few moments, but once confident that he could follow unobserved, he trailed Hardwick to a tipi where to his amusement the door flap was cast open and the young Cheyenne hustled the land agent inside.

Hans lurked in the darkness and waited, but Hardwick was in the tipi for so long that he began to question the reliability of his own eyesight. An hour passed before the flap was cast aside and the land agent stepped out, whereupon he indulged in a meticulous routine of stretching, hauling at his pants and tightening his belt, slicking his thin gray hair across his bald pate, and straightening his eyeglasses. Suitably coiffured, he squinted cautiously up the path at the fort, donned his jacket, and started to make his way back toward the dim lights of the saloon.

Waiting for Hardwick to approach, Hans stepped out of the shadows. "Ha! You ole dog!" he chortled as the little man stopped dead and gawped, realizing that Hans had witnessed his secret tryst. "Henrietta, she not like zis, I sink," Hans teased, enjoying Hardwick's obvious embarrassment.

"No, Hans! No!" Hardwick whimpered. "You wouldn't? Please don't tell anyone," he groveled in alarmed humiliation.

Hans wrapped a bear-like paw around his shoulder and squeezed, laughing raucously. "You hif safe secret viz me," he whispered conspiratorially. "How you like savage pussy? Make you like big bull?" He grasped Hardwick's manhood in a brawny fist and the little man winced, grinning sheepishly.

Enjoying their masculine frivolity, the two men sauntered back to the saloon, where Hardwick gulped down a large whiskey to steady his nerves before taking his leave. But each evening thereafter, Hans noticed the portly land agent sneak away to partake of the pretty young Indian's sexual favors.

★ ★ ★ ★ ★

It was several days after leaving Laramie that Johannes realized that Colter might have abandoned the wagon train. Eventually, he summoned the courage to test his assessment and rode the family's old horse along the full length of the caravan, checking every wagon to ensure that he had not overlooked the mountain man until he was satisfied that Colter was nowhere to be found.

A sense of jubilation made his head buzz with excitement. The burden of terror he had been carrying evaporated in an instant, and he felt liberated. He descended upon Mary-Jane's wagon in an ebullient mood, and she was astonished when he hauled her onto his horse and whisked her off, full of conversation, as if the morose mood of the preceding weeks had been a figment of her imagination.

Subsequently, the two love birds became inseparable, and although Carla was pleased to see them looking happy, she found herself on her own as the wagons started to descend from the Bridger Mountains parallel to Nowood Creek.

Carla was delighted to discover that her wagon was running close to a small schooner driven by Edward and Mary May, the old Quaker couple she had got to know on the railroad from New York. Carla liked the couple very much and took the opportunity to reacquaint herself, walking alongside Edward while Mary rode in the wagon, her weary legs finding the arduous exercise hard to bear.

Edward and Mary chatted to each other with a relaxed intimacy that was alien to Carla's experience of her own family, where the atmosphere was frequently brittle, with explosive outbursts of anger a regular occurrence, and caustic remarks being designed with the deliberate intent of asserting superiority or inflicting humiliation.

Hans was usually the instigator of their domestic friction, but after years of mental and physical abuse, Elena could be equally hurtful, often directing vindictive persecution at her children when impotent to exact retribution upon her husband for his persistent cruelty.

Carla recognized her mother's distress and appreciated her misery, so despite her youth, she bore the brunt of Elena's malicious behavior with a fortitude and compassion beyond her years, ignoring her mother's denigration and attempting to redirect her attention to more positive endeavors.

Her heart ached to witness the desolation in her mother's eyes, and she seethed with anger at her father's callous treatment of his wife. Nevertheless, there were frequent moments when she felt like shaking Elena and berating her for her incessantly indulgent melancholy.

She felt angry at her mother's failure to assert herself and frustrated that Elena refused to acknowledge the beauty of the plains, instead regarding their journey as an intolerable burden, her attitude rendering each day an onerous toil and relegating the prospect of a bright new future in the west to no more than a fanciful delusion.

Eventually, finding herself unable to remain immersed in an atmosphere of continual despair and with a measure of guilt, Carla decided to leave her mother trudging alongside the wagon alone, her head cast disconsolately beneath her bonnet, muttering an unintelligible commentary.

Walking with Edward and Mary was an entirely different experience. They exuded a reverent appreciation of the magnificence of the wilderness, pointing out animals and birds and discussing their different behaviors, or inspecting trees and flowers, comparing their leaf structure and color, and sharing conclusions about the terrain that benefitted each plant and allowed it to prosper.

They harbored an insatiable passion for the environment and strived to understand its mysteries in a way that captivated

Carla's imagination, prompting her to share her own observations and bask in the warm praise she received when she noticed something that had evaded Mary's or Edward's attention.

The big Quaker strode effortlessly alongside his oxen as they talked. He patted his animals affectionately, murmuring to them reassuringly and humming contentedly whenever the conversation subsided. Often Mary would sing hymns, and Edward would burst into a refrain to accompany his wife with the chorus, Mary smiling broadly at her husband's booming tenor.

The old couple warmed Carla's soul and rejuvenated her spirit, causing her to revise her assumption that the fractious life she had been exposed to as a child was representative of an inevitable norm. Edward and Mary simply enjoyed each other's company, regarding life as being enriched by the sharing of its experience.

The character of the land changed as the wagons descended the Bridger Mountains, Nowood Creek running alongside the trail, its bubbling waters clear and sparkling as it cascaded over an endless series of spectacular waterfalls. The grass was lush, and the cattle wandered contentedly, slaking their hunger on the welcome abundance of better-quality grazing.

The mountain conifers gave way to deciduous trees, which lined the creek and the foot of the surrounding hills and bluffs. In contrast to the Oregon Trail, most of the forest remained unsullied by scavenging for firewood, the Kopps' wagon train being among the first to make use of the recently forged Bridger Trail, earlier pilgrimages having traversed the Bozeman Trail, which was flatter and more direct, but had become the focus of constant skirmishes with the Sioux.

Although providing a greater abundance of grazing and timber, as Gresham had predicted, a new danger emerged along the trail. Since entering the mountains, the emigrants had encountered the first signs of bears, the trunks of trees being stripped of bark and exhibiting deep lacerations inflicted by the enormous claws of the grizzlies.

During the day, the bears remained remote from the noise of the column, but at night the smell of cooking and the lure of numerous vulnerable young calves attracted bears in droves. To combat the threat, the marshals orchestrated a schedule of defensive watches, and many families unpacked their wagons so that they could sleep off the ground. But although the men enjoyed the sport of keeping the bears at bay, the persistent threat became progressively more tedious and disruptive.

Carla, however, was entranced. She marveled at the sheer size and power of the grizzlies, watching in rapture when a large boar appeared one evening. The men shouted and fired their rifles in an ineffectual attempt to scare it away, until the bear rose on its hind legs, towering above the migrants as it snarled ferociously at its attackers before disappearing into the trees unharmed.

But a man was killed one morning, when he was charged by a sow that he shot and wounded by accident. The bear ripped him to pieces. The first swipe of its front paw tore off his head, its five-inch claws slashed open his belly, and then the enraged animal flailed the unfortunate victim's body around like a rag-doll. Subsequently, a lethal-force approach to deterring the animals was invoked, the consequence being that sentries were doubled on each watch and bears were shot on sight, progressively stimulating an indiscriminate hunting frenzy.

Carla hated the slaughter of the wonderful animals and railed against the men with their guns, but her protestation was ignored, and she was ridiculed as being too young and idealistic to understand the need to act decisively to protect the wagon train.

Distraught, she shared her anguish with Edward and Mary

and all three prayed for forgiveness, entreating god to protect the bears from the relentless slaughter. Miraculously, as if answering their supplication, the wagon train passed into different terrain, reaching the fringe of a huge prairie, its panorama stretching for a hundred miles to the horizon in the west. There, they departed the mountainous habitat of the bears, and the convoy settled into a quieter routine, plodding steadily north, until ten days after leaving Laramie they caught sight of a towering red bluff, where they made camp in its shelter.

The following morning, Carla and the Mays noticed a group of prospectors leave the wagon train and start out along a canyon to the east, their apparent zest to explore contrasting with the remaining migrants' desire to settle for a couple of days and take advantage of a well-earned rest.

On the second day, a motley band of hunters appeared out of the west, trailing a short convoy of wagons laden with huge piles of buffalo pelts. The men were grim-faced and looked weary from long days in the saddle, eyeing the travelers contemptuously as they passed.

Johannes watched with interest. There was an air about the men that caused him to tingle with adrenaline. They projected an untouchable detachment that he found alluring. A state of mind devoid by emotion, providing insulation from the ordeals that beset one's life.

Gripped by his envy of the men, Johannes studied their behavior, sensing that cultivating the ability to emulate their cool demeanor might enable him to endure the sense of inadequacy with which he wrestled constantly. But he found himself struck by their similarity to Colter, and a wave of dread swept over him, so that he was compelled to sneak away and hide until the men were out of sight.

★ ★ ★ ★ ★

The wagon train broke camp early on the third day and started to rumble north again, hugging the bank of Nowood Creek as the trail wound along in the shadow of a dense forest of spruce that stretched along the foot of a high bluff several hundred yards away on its easterly flank.

The Kopps' group of wagons found themselves posted to the rear of the pedestrian column and Carla joined the Mays, whose schooner was the last to pull out of Ten Sleep, falling in with Edward on either side of the lead oxen as she watched a bird soaring high above the tree line, gliding effortlessly in the warm thermals above the bluff.

"Oh look, Edvard. An eagle!" Carla pointed up at the dark shape, silhouetted against the bright clear sky, finessing its flight with the finger-like tips of its eight-foot wingspan.

Edward squinted against the sun and smiled. "Well spotted! It's a golden eagle. Look at the lighter color behind its head as it turns."

"Is magnificent!" She studied its graceful flight with awe. "But is lonely. Vhat a shame is not having a mate."

"It might well have a mate somewhere on the bluff over there." Edward pointed across the trees at the rugged sandstone outcrop. "It's said that golden eagles mate for life. They could be nesting, so maybe its mate's sitting on some chicks."

"Oh zat vould be vonderful. How nice zat zey stay together. I vould love to see it up close."

Edward laughed. "Not too close, I hope! They have very sharp claws and a nasty peck."

Carla laughed and continued to wander along casting intermittent glances at the eagle, which maintained station alongside.

CHAPTER 32

The hunters' camp, Ten Sleep, Nowood Creek

Returning to camp, La Brais soon heard about the young Indian's escape the preceding night, it being the highlight of conversation for the men who had remained in camp, and he was furious, holding McCabe singularly accountable. He went in search of his colleague, and although the trapper made every effort to elude detection, La Brais eventually found him skulking along the creek near the treeline.

"McCabe! Tryin' t' hide outta the way, yer rat-faced pussy."

McCabe quailed at the sound of La Brais shouting his name and stopped in his tracks, gawping. "Frank! Yer back!" he exclaimed, feigning ignorance of the hunting party's return.

"Don't gimme that shit, yer little prick!" La Brais roared as he splashed across the creek, drawing his revolver. "Had one damn job t' do. Only had t' keep that chicken shit Injun tied up, an' yer can't even do that!"

McCabe stumbled backward in terror as La Brais leapt out of the creek and confronted him. "Weren't ma fault! Boy cut 'is bindin'," he whined. "Big stranger done give 'im food. Musta give 'im a knife, I reckon."

La Brais's anger boiled over and without warning he swung his arm, pistol whipping McCabe across the cheek and sending the trapper sprawling to the ground. "You think I give a shit what yer think? Was your job t' watch th' Injun."

He holstered his gun and hauled McCabe to his feet, swinging his right fist in a vicious upper cut that struck the trapper squarely on the chin, crunching his teeth and sending a mind-numbing jolt through his neck. McCabe collapsed to his knees, blood running from his mouth and a livid welt bisecting his cheek.

"Ah'm sorry, Frank. Weren't ma fault!" he pleaded with La Brais.

The whimpering disgusted La Brais and he was gripped by a sudden urge to kill the trapper, but restrained the impulse and satisfied himself with inflicting a savage kick to McCabe's midriff, prompting him to double over and slump to his side, wheezing for breath.

"Yer useless piece o' shit. Now, yer listen t' me. We gonna go find that Injun, an' we gonna bring 'im back. Don't care if he's dead or 'live, but we gonna bring 'im back, yer hear me!" He lifted McCabe by the scruff of the neck, shook him violently, and flung him to the ground. "Now, I ain't eaten decent food in four days. I'm gonna go get me some chow, an' you gonna go git us a tracker. You be ready t' git goin' first light or I swear I'm gonna kill you, 'stead o' the Injun boy." He glowered at McCabe, spat on him, and turned to plough his way back across the creek.

The gloomy predawn light concealed the vivid bruising to McCabe's face the following morning, his left eye completely closed and his lips swollen as though he had been stung by a swarm of wasps. Speech was too painful, so he acknowledged La Brais with a curt nod.

Alongside their horses, one of the Pawnee waited patiently for the trappers to prepare themselves, the Indian bounding off on foot as soon as La Brais was mounted. They jogged purposefully out of the camp and retraced the trail to Ten Sleep canyon, where McCabe hoped they would be able to pick up the Indian boy's tracks.

★ ★ ★ ★ ★

Crouching in his hiding place in the canyon had caused Takoda's body to stiffen, and the pain from his injuries racked his body once he realized that he had evaded capture, the sustaining effect of adrenaline having subsided.

He moved slowly, anxious to abandon the main trail at the first opportunity to minimize the potential for detection. Proceeding northwest toward the mouth of the canyon, Takoda reached a heavily wooded slope that extended to the north, parallel to Nowood Creek, its dense canopy providing the welcome benefit of ample concealment along his route.

Plunging gratefully into the shade of the douglas fir, he picked up an indistinct animal trail, unaware that its rambling course passed marginally to the north of the caravan of schooners camped at Ten Sleep, the sounds and smells of the wagon train swept away by a brisk wind that whipped over the steep bluff on his right hand.

Several small creeks tumbled down the hillside flowing from springs that rose at the foot of the bluff, and Takoda stopped briefly at the first of the streams to soak his swollen joints and take a deep draught of refreshing water. Feeling moderately revived, he gingerly bathed his injured eye and was surprised to find no evidence of the sharp sliver of rock that he had felt the preceding evening, although the eye still felt sticky and he was obliged to clean it judiciously.

Once satisfied with his rudimentary care, Takoda fashioned a poultice by soaking some dried yarrow leaves taken from the pouch left by the Pawnee, which he pressed against his eye, tying it in place with a strip of cloth torn from his tunic. A hot compress would have been more effective, but the cold one was better than nothing.

The icy spring water soothed the bruising around his foot and the fingers he had dislocated, so he soaked them in the creek until they were numb, massaging the swellings gently while taking time to settle his nerves and think.

Takoda's first priority was to evade any pursuit, and he concluded that remaining concealed in the woods for as long as possible would be prudent. But he knew that the stand of forest would eventually end, compelling him to venture onto the open prairie.

Requiring food to sustain himself, it made sense to trace the rivers, which would assure a rich supply of nutritious vegetation, berries, and small animals or fish. And, since he could throw a stone with deadly accuracy, there was a good chance that he could kill a gopher or jack rabbit. His conundrum was that anyone following would expect him to remain close to water, so although the rivers presented his best source of nutrition, it was possible that they might constitute the most dangerous route. He weighed the risks but was unable to resolve the dilemma of whether to follow or avoid the river, deciding only that he would remain within the cover of the trees until he could be certain that he was not being pursued.

Proceeding slowly, the rugged trail inflicted such stress upon his damaged ankle that he was obliged to fashion a crutch from a broken branch, and by nightfall he had succeeded in traveling less than six miles from the canyon. As twilight fell, he worked his way up toward the face of the bluff, where hungry and exhausted, he curled up in the concealed shelter of a small cave and sleep swept over him within minutes.

A chorus of yips woke Takoda at dawn, and he lay listening to the coyotes as he started to stretch and rotate his joints, wincing at the discomfort. But, within the hour, he moved off to find water, gathering a handful of huckleberries as he descended the hillside. As he had done the previous day, he soaked his bruised joints before journeying north once more, feeling refreshed and optimistic, and covering the ground at a better pace than the previous day.

As he walked, the sun broke over the crest of the bluff, penetrating the canopy of the trees and casting a warm dappled light that revived his spirits and inspired him to think of home. The prospect of traversing the prairies posed no concern to him, and he was confident that he could navigate his way up the great river until he came to the Greybull, which would lead him back to his village.

The snows would have receded, and the weather presented little risk assuming that he could remain hydrated, so Takoda surmised that his principle challenges would be finding adequate food and avoiding the complication of infection in his wounds. He was adept at living off the land, so the challenge of locating food did not concern him unduly, but he wished he had spent more time studying his mother's medicine. She always had two or more alternative treatments for an injury, dependent upon the herbs and plants that she had managed to collect, but his knowledge was basic and no match for her skill.

He thought of his father and grandfather, and the memories strengthened his determination as he recalled situations where he had witnessed their indomitable spirit. He wondered whether his band was still searching for him and Howahkan and whether they had found his brother's body. He imagined his family's grief and yearned to return to his people to provide them with at least partial solace.

The notion drove Takoda resolutely onward, until, as the sun reached its zenith, he stopped to rest beside a small creek. Once again, he untied his moccasins and bathed his feet, lying back against the bank and staring up at the pockets of blue sky visible between the canopy of the tall spruce.

As he gazed contemplatively at the ponderous progress of the pristine clouds, a dark speck glided overhead, and he recognized the distinctive shape and coloration of a golden eagle, the noblest of the feathered beasts, revered by his people. His confidence surged, and he wondered whether the eagle's presence represented a propitious omen, signifying his triumph over adversity.

Immersed in his thoughts, Takoda had to wrestle his attention away from the majestic raptor to comprehend the significance of a soft nicker nearby. He tried to replay the sound in his mind, straining to listen in case it was repeated, a knot of fear twisting in his gut.

He hurriedly slipped on his moccasins and stood up, moving across to the far side of the creek. If, as he suspected, there was a horse on the trail behind him, it could only mean one thing. He was being followed. There could be no other purpose for riding along the rough track through the forest, since as he recalled, a well-established trail ran below the treeline, snaking alongside the creek all the way to the great river and affording much easier passage for any traveler.

Takoda had to hide. He had to get off the trail and find a place to conceal himself from whoever was following, since anyone on horseback would soon run him down, particularly given the impediment of his injuries. But there were no obvious hiding places and he was immediately conscious of the tracks that his stumbling gait would have left.

His first priority was to confuse his spoor. He did not want to ascend toward the bluff, primarily because the route was steep and he would undoubtedly make slow progress, but he was also concerned that he might become trapped by the sheer face of the bluff. Instead, he turned decisively downhill, stepping into the creek to avoid leaving tracks in the grass and attempting to avoid dislodging any stones that might reveal his direction of travel.

★ ★ ★ ★ ★

The Pawnee led McCabe and La Brais through the trees at a steady trot. The young Sioux's tracks were easy to follow, and the tracker paused only infrequently to ensure that he was still on the trail. Midway through the morning he diverted off the path, ascended the hillside, and returned to inform the trappers that he had found a cave where the boy had spent the night. Assured that he was on the correct trail, he turned north again and continued his pursuit.

To keep up with the Indian, the trappers were forced to duck and weave through the trees, being obliged to dismount on occasions when low branches threatened to sweep them off their mounts, but the Pawnee did not wait for them, and they had to push their horses hard to keep up with his relentless pace.

McCabe said nothing as they rode. His face throbbed and he felt no desire to converse with the big Canadian for whom he now harbored a simmering loathing. By contrast, La Brais cursed constantly, frustrated by the repeated obstructions they had to negotiate, and was on the point of abandoning the chase when the Pawnee drew up sharply, bending down to examine the ground and waiting for the trappers to catch up.

"Close. Very close," he whispered, giving La Brais a malevolent smirk.

Anticipating Takoda's imminent capture, the trappers drew their guns and peered along the path, but to the Pawnee's fury La Brais's horse shook its head and whinnied, revealing their presence. Incensed, the Indian rushed off along the trail.

The sound of the approaching horsemen carried to Takoda, inspiring him to move with greater haste. He splashed his way down the creek for four hundred paces, hoping to conceal his tracks for as far as possible, and climbed carefully onto the northerly bank, judging that it was necessary to seek the seclusion of the trees once more. His legs like lead, he scrambled into the cover of the forest.

The Pawnee burst out of the trees and leapt over the creek at the point where Takoda had been bathing his feet. Instantly, he whipped around to inspect the flattened grass on the opposite bank. He studied the ground with rigorous diligence, rose, and stretched upright to complete a full sweep of the woods, searching for his quarry like a well-trained hunting dog.

The trappers caught up, and the Pawnee pointed at the bank. "Was here. Now."

La Brais's face broke into a lop-sided grin. "Gottcha!" he murmured under his breath, peering into the forest and indicating to McCabe that they should spread out. He instructed McCabe to proceed parallel on the downhill side of the trail, electing to pursue an uphill route himself, leaving the Pawnee to carry straight on along the path. Infused with bloodlust, they crossed the creek and plunged into the trees.

The Pawnee started off uncertainly and within thirty paces stopped to track back toward the creek, scanning the path for any sign of Takoda's footprints. Discovering no trace, he returned to the creek and examined the bank on either side of the stream again. Swiftly, he ascertained that the boy had not crossed the creek and that there were no footprints visible in either direction along its bank. Immediately, he realized that Takoda had entered the creek to obscure his tracks and, after pausing to consider his options, he elected to move upstream to check for spoor.

Takoda could hear the horses crashing through the trees in their blundering pursuit, and he stopped to try and gauge how many men might be chasing him. They made no attempt to conceal their presence, their behavior characteristic of the clumsy movement of the white man, but an inconsistency nagged at Takoda's mind.

The men on horseback, making so much noise, were not trackers and he could not conceive that such men would possess the skill to follow his tracks. He felt a flutter of apprehension. There had to be a competent tracker, perhaps an Indian, in their midst. If so, an experienced warrior would have no difficulty in unraveling Takoda's deception of using the creek to obscure his footprints.

Concerned to establish whether his ruse had been discovered, he remained at the fringe of the forest, standing motionless, peering back up the hill. Initially, he detected no movement and began to relax, but a flicker of color caught his eye and the top of the comb of a Pawnee roach bobbed into view. Momentarily, the head disappeared from sight, but then the Pawnee stood upright and Takoda could see him scan the forest, his penetrating gaze scrutinizing the treeline along the length of the creek.

Takoda recognized the Indian. It was a Pawnee whom he knew regarded the Sioux as his sworn enemies. Despondent, Takoda realized that the tracker would have no pity for his plight, so he waited until the Indian ducked out of sight and launched himself anxiously into the forest, weaving urgently between the maze of trees. It would be impossible to outrun the Pawnee, but he could conceive of no alternative other than flight, so he surged through the forest as rapidly and quietly as he was able.

To Takoda's great misfortune, in his haste, he stepped on a branch concealed beneath the deep layers of fallen pine needles, the wood snapping with a loud rending crack. He froze, guessing that the sound would carry to the Pawnee, identifying his location.

Confused, he glanced around desperately. There was no path and the forest ahead offered little refuge, but he noticed that the spruce were thicker to his left, their lower branches providing a dense dark canopy over the forest floor. The trunk of each tree was more than two men's reach in circumference, festooned with haphazard stubs of broken branches that projected at irregular intervals, making them easy to climb.

Takoda hurried under the spruce, selecting a tree with particularly thick foliage, and reached to grasp one of the splintered stubs. But as he prepared to haul himself up, his foot struck a rock, and he looked down to see a large palm-sized stone lying at the foot of the tree. He hesitated, realizing that he possessed no weapon, and bent down to pick the rock up and tuck it inside his tunic. Then, he scaled the tree and hid among its spread of sharp needles.

He waited, holding his breath, his heart thumping and his pulse beating at his temple. His mouth was dry with apprehension, and he licked his lips as he carefully removed the stone from his tunic.

A stealthy footfall ignited Takoda's nerves, and his muscles ached with tension as he tried to suppress even the most insignificant movement. He could not see the ground, but he could hear the cautious approach of someone on foot. A man passed below him and crept on for a few yards before turning and retracing his steps. There was silence.

"Sioux!" a gravelly voice whispered, immediately below where Takoda was sitting.

Takoda remained motionless as the Pawnee stood listening. Despite the anticipation, he was shocked when the tracker leapt up with explosive speed, grabbing at the protruding branches as he propelled himself into the tree, until his head burst in to view. A red porcupine roach, clamped in place by an ornate scalplock, crowned a long sallow face with dark, angry eyes. The Pawnee held his knife clamped between his teeth and glared at Takoda maliciously, a sly smile creasing the corners of his mouth.

Takoda's heart missed a beat, and he withdrew spontaneously along the branch he was sitting on, but his retreat only encouraged the Pawnee to thrust himself further up the trunk of the tree, shoving himself with powerful arms. Seizing his limited opportunity to attack, Takoda lifted his stone high and swung it down with all his strength at the Pawnee.

In a split second the tracker reacted, throwing himself sideways to avoid the projectile and striking his cheek against a branch, the blow causing his knife to flick from his mouth and spin away toward the ground. Takoda's aim was good and the force of his throw would have been sufficient to split a man's skull, but maintaining accuracy within the tangle of branches was far from easy, and the stone ricocheted off the bough above the Pawnee's head, diverting its trajectory so that it skimmed past his ear and crunched into his shoulder.

The Pawnee let out a piercing yelp and his right arm flopped uselessly, but he was wild with battle fever and the injury did little to slow his progress. He lunged forward with a muscular thrust of his legs and locked his left hand around Takoda's ankle. The vise-like grip dug into the tender bruising and Takoda winced, using his right leg to aim a ferocious kick at his assailant in retaliation. But the Pawnee dodged the strike and hauled violently on Takoda's ankle so that he tumbled forward, losing his balance.

The Pawnee's face contorted menacingly and in one deft movement he lunged again, releasing Takoda's ankle and seizing him around the throat. He emitted a venomous hiss of bitter hatred, sneering as he dug his fingers into Takoda's windpipe.

His hand was like iron, and Takoda thrashed back and forth clawing at the Pawnee's arm in a desperate attempt to dislodge his grasp, but the Indian drilled his nails remorselessly into Takoda's neck, probing between the taught muscles to tear at his airway. The attack was frenzied, and Takoda knew that the

Pawnee would attempt to rip out his windpipe as soon as he secured a firm hold on his throat.

Takoda cracked his knee against the tracker's face, eliciting a trickle of blood, but the Indian refused to let go. He felt light-headed, and the strength began to ebb from his limbs. He knew that he could not struggle for much longer and that attempting to break the Pawnee's grip was futile. Invoking the only option he could envisage, he threw himself forward, bearing down with all his weight.

The Pawnee was unprepared for the change in tactics and grimaced as Takoda crashed into him, his feet scrabbling for purchase on the branches below. There was a loud crack and the Pawnee dropped sharply, Takoda's weight compounding his momentum, so that they both plummeted from the tree.

Takoda prepared himself for the painful impact, but, to his astonishment, the Pawnee came up short, the throttling grip around his throat releasing in a spasm as the Indian emitted a high-pitched shriek. Takoda crashed against the tracker's shoulders and tumbled to the forest floor.

He lay on his back recovering his breath and stared up at the Pawnee, whose body hung against the trunk of the tree, one of the sharp stubby branches protruding from an ugly rend in his chest. The Pawnee's mouth gaped in silent disbelief, but he uttered no further sound. The Indian's legs twitched as if searching to find a foothold with his heels, and he let out a single long, wheezing breath. He fell still, his eyes wide, staring sightlessly into the forest.

Takoda scrambled backward and leaned against a tree, incredulous that he had escaped the Pawnee's murderous attack, but he realized that his relief might be short-lived. He was certain that the Indian's shriek would have been heard by the horsemen, who were sure to converge on the sound.

He had heard the riders pass higher up the slope and knew

that his only avenue of escape was to descend through the trees in an attempt to reach the creek that he had followed with the trappers, envisaging that he might be able to float downstream or hide among the buffalo grass.

Galvanized by the urgency, Takoda hauled himself to his feet and stumbled downhill, weaving through the trees and sliding on the slippery layer of spruce needles. Behind him, shouting erupted, and he could hear horses pushing their way through the forest, the frenetic sound of their pursuit gathering momentum as he slithered to the bottom of the steep slope.

As he came within sight of the edge of the forest, an eerie silence fell.

"Where yer goin', Injun! We gonna come 'n git yer!" an aggressive bellow echoed through the trees.

Recognizing La Brais's voice, Takoda realized that he was being pursued by the trappers and found it strangely reassuring to know his adversaries. He surmised that the brutish trapper would be unremitting in his pursuit, and he knew that the man would inevitably attempt to kill him on sight. Disturbed at the prospect, he hurried on down toward the plain.

Chapter 33

July 1865, Powder River Basin, Dakota Territory

Colter made good time crossing into the Powder River Basin, where he turned northeast, entering the heart of the Sioux's hunting grounds. Having traversed the country many times previously, and being well aware that the presence of white men was unwelcome, he had taken the precaution of enlisting the services of a Sioux guide from Fort Laramie.

Riding in the company of the scout, he was confident that his peaceful intentions would be respected by any Sioux warriors he encountered, and his expectation was fulfilled when they met a hunting party shortly after crossing the Powder River. His guide explained that he was seeking Red Cloud to discuss important business, which resulted in a swift escort to the great chief's camp.

At first Red Cloud was unimpressed by Colter's intelligence that an armed convoy of wagons carrying a consignment of glittering rock planned to cross the Great Plains, and he was scornful of the Sioux's need to apprehend such unimportant merchandise. But he became more animated when Colter explained that the gold on the wagons would be used by the Great Father in the east to fund the cost of sending many thousands of soldiers to occupy the Powder River Basin.

This implication fired Red Cloud's interest, but he remained cynical of Colter's motives and was concerned at the potential of being lured into a trap orchestrated by the mountain man and his cavalry friends. Colter scoffed at the insinuation, strongly refuting the accusation that he harbored any loyalty to the United States army, and told Red Cloud that he would only provide information about the route and timing of the gold wagons if he was given one-third share in the bounty they secured. His apparent avarice reassured Red Cloud, although he remained skeptical and required Colter to remain in the Sioux village whilst the tribal elders discussed the matter.

The deliberations took several days, but eventually the authenticity of the intelligence was accepted as reliable and significant, and Red Cloud confirmed that he would lead a war party to intercept the wagon train, on the condition that Colter participated in the sortie, the chief informing Colter dispassionately that he would be killed immediately if the warriors encountered any indication of a deception.

Moylan was highly relieved when Colter unexpectedly took his leave of the small troop of cavalry. He felt that the mountain man had usurped his authority, dismissing his rank as inconsequential and readily countermanding his orders. He could tell that the experienced sergeant and corporal detailed to accompany him were less than impressed at his leadership.

Once Colter departed, he ordered the corporal to take point and informed the sergeant that he would undertake an inspection of the men at dawn the following day. The sergeant rolled his eyes at the pretentious pup, although he kept his own counsel, and gave the men notice that they would be expected to parade in the morning.

Each day Moylan conceived of some activity that would allow him to assert his authority, and by the time the troop reached Virginia City, the whole squad were infuriated by his puerile behavior. Despite Moylan's petulence, Sergeant Ames persuaded the troopers to tolerate the young captain, assuring them that they would be reunited with their unit upon their return to Laramie in a few short weeks.

As instructed, Moylan went to the telegraph office shortly after the troop arrived, where he received instructions to proceed to Elling State Bank to meet with Mr. Henry Elling, who would provide him with a consignment that he would be required to escort back to Fort Laramie, the orders being issued by Major Kearny at Fort Leavenworth.

Moylan found Elling in his office at the bank and was greeted by a stout middle-aged man with an officious bearing, a thin flop of hair combed over the pink dome of his scalp, and small round eyeglasses lending him a maturity beyond his years.

Compounding Moylan's fragile sense of inferiority, Elling failed to extend the slightest cordiality and was brusque in his dealings. He assembled a small mountain of paperwork for Moylan to sign, each document ambiguous about the nature of his consignment, and when the Captain enquired, he was simply informed that the shipment contained valuable government property that had been placed in the charge of the bank.

Filing his papers, Elling dismissed Moylan, instructing him to attend the rear entrance of the bank at eight o'clock the following morning, where the goods would be transferred to his custody.

During Moylan's meeting with Elling, Ames made a brief trip to the telegraph office and sent a message to Colonel Sibley. He confirmed the troop's arrival in Virginia City and informed Sibley that it seemed likely that they would be entrusted with a consignment dispatched from Elling State Bank, but made it clear that he was unaware of the nature of the items to be transported.

Later in the day, he checked whether he had been sent a response, but found only an acknowledgment from the colonel, with a request that he should send particulars of the shipment in the event that he was able to establish its content. Unfortunately, as it transpired, the squad's timetable for departure left no opportunity for further communication.

The troopers were unimpressed with the enforced pace of the turnaround, since the Virginia City saloons were bustling with life and overflowing with young girls proffering their services, which was more than could be said for the attractions of Laramie. On the other hand, they were keen to return to their units, so they indulged briefly but enthusiastically in the town's decadent delights, leaving Ames to placate Moylan about their unauthorised absence when he emerged from the bank.

The next morning, the mood was somber and the troopers were grim-faced, Moylan having tracked them down in one of the whorehouses the previous evening and castigated them for their truancy. Nevertheless, they worked fast to load fifteen crates from the bank's strong room onto two wagons provided by Elling.

The captain inspected each crate as it was stowed. He was mollified to note that they all displayed a stamp with the legend "Winchester rifles. U.S. Government property," a description reflected on the final manifest papers issued by Elling, although the significance of a linen band and wax seal applied to each of the boxes eluded him. He was unaware that the unobtrusive binding signified verification by the resident representative of the Federal Mint, whose responsibilities involved oversight of the quality of gold deposited at the bank, and authentication of the weight of gold prepared for shipment.

Moylan instructed Ames to cover the crates with tarpaulins and strap them down, then he signed the dispatch note and mounted up. The preceding afternoon, he had briefed Ames on the route that he intended using for the return to Laramie, the directions having been communicated to him in confidence by Colter, and the sergeant had organized reprovisioning of the troop, so within half an hour they had loaded up and were on the trail.

Gresham hit Platte Bridge Station like a whirlwind, inspecting every part of the facility and riding out with Trautman to reconnoiter the surrounding area to assess the strategic strengths and weaknesses of the fort's location.

His orders were to establish a strengthened military post to be renamed Fort Caspar, offering protection to the people and property of the Pacific Telegraph and the Overland Mail Company, and providing defense of the recently built Guinard Bridge, which enabled ease of passage across the river to the many migrants who passed through the region.

Gresham was unimpressed with the defenses afforded by the tall wooden palisade, and within the day he had detachments of the troop digging rifle pits and building an embrasure that faced the most exposed aspect of the fort to the north.

Watch details were doubled, and he set about establishing contact with local bands of the Cheyenne and Lakota tribes, intent upon ensuring safe passage for emigrants and the numerous trains of supply wagons.

It was three weeks before Gresham was content with the organization and defenses of the fort and had satisfactorily conducted drills with his troop, acquainting them with the maneuvers and tactics he would expect them to employ in the event of hostilities. It was not until the third Monday that he managed to reflect upon the performance of his troopers with Trautman and discuss the improvements effected to his fort's frail defenses.

"You've done a good job with the men, Isaac. But it's a miracle this place hasn't been overrun before now."

"Yup, Hanley's been a rock. He's a good lad, an' the men respect him. They've put some sweat into gettin' the fort into shape," replied Trautman.

"Hmm. Maybe we'll need to organize a bit of recreation so the boys can let off some steam before we start to make our presence felt. I intend beginning routine patrols next week. We have to be visible, confident, and authoritative. I don't want the local tribes to see us as hiding behind the palisade."

"Shame Moylan ain't around. Be useful to rotate patrol teams to keep 'em fresh, and I reckon Hanley's gonna bust a gut less we give him a tug on his reins."

Gresham laughed. "Don't underestimate the lad's stamina. Anyway, I'm not sure I miss having Moylan in the troop, although I'd love to know what he's up to."

"Yeah. Can't make no sense of it. Take a king's ransom in gold to drag my backside up to Virginia City. Was in California in '49, and I seen those minin' towns for myself." Trautman reflected. "Every good-for-nothin' degenerate hauled on into town to shoot the place up. Never seen so many painted ladies. Whorehouses were overflowin' an' saloons never closed. Seen men shot for spillin' your grog, or 'cos someone didn't like the way you looked. Was anarchy. Bank must 'ave been raided five times while I was there. Marshal an' his men chased one gang for a week after they shot up the town, an' got clear away with near twenty thousand dollars in gold."

Gresham sipped his whiskey as he listened to Trautman. As a boy, the lieutenant had traveled all over the country with his father, who had been an engineer for the telegraph company. His mother had died in childbirth and his father had taken the young Isaac with him until the boy decided that he wanted to join the army.

"You got to all the best places with your old man," Gresham reflected. "Could have ended up as a prospector if your pa had been inclined."

"Not for me! Scratchin' 'round in the dirt for a livin'. Besides, ain't many people get rich, and those who do often steal it from the folk as do all the hard work. It's a dangerous business simply gettin' your gold to the bank. Not for the faint-hearted," Trautman wagged his finger.

Gresham grunted and swilled back the rest of his whiskey. "I imagine so."

He peered into the bottom of his glass, his mind turning over Trautman's account of life in the goldfields. They did not sound like the sort of place to send an arrogant and impulsive young man, and he worried again about Murray's motive in dispatching Moylan to Virginia City. The mission troubled him excessively, and Trautman's description had done nothing to allay his unease. But something the lieutenant said struck a chord. The gold.

"What happens to the gold that's deposited in the bank, Isaac?" Gresham's mind began to assemble the pieces of the puzzle.

"Not sure really. No idea what they did before the railroad hit town, but now word is they ship it out on a military rail car."

Gresham frowned. "I wonder." He stood up and walked to his desk so that he could examine his maps.

"What you thinkin'?" Trautman followed him.

Gresham spread a map of the northern plains across his desk. "Which way would they transport gold from Virginia City?" he pondered.

Trautman looked over his shoulder. "I'd expect 'em to come east. Federal mint's in Pennsylvania, but I read Congress's gone an' approved a new bullion mint down in Denver, so could make for either of those, I guess."

"You're a font of knowledge, Isaac," Gresham raised his eyebrows as he scanned the maps. "The most direct route to Pennsylvania would be to cross the northern plains to Fort

Union, where the Yellowstone joins the Missouri, continuing on to Fort Abercrombie in Dakota Territory. But the railroad isn't breaking ground across the plains yet, so they'd have to run a wagon train pretty much all the way to Minneapolis. Not a good prospect."

He moved his hand down the map and grunted. "Looks easier to come down to Laramie and on to the Kansas railhead. That's the most direct route to Denver too. The trail down through Idaho Territory is rough going, and the journey would take at least two weeks longer."

"You think Moylan's been sent to escort a gold shipment?" Trautman looked dubious.

Gresham pondered the thought. "I can't see why else a detachment of troopers would have been sent up to a gold-mining town on a short-term mission. I've heard talk of gold trains that the military move about in secrecy, but I've not heard of them coming through the plains."

Trautman looked skeptical. "A fresh-faced buck like Moylan? Seems way outta his league."

"I don't know, but the more I think about it, the more it worries me."

"You sure he ain't jus' gonna be escortin' some important folks?" Trautman looked doubtful.

"There are troopers based at Fort Benton who could easily run escort down to Laramie. No, it's more than that."

"Well, if he's gonna haul a wagon load o' gold, chances are he's gonna have to come through the Powder River Basin, so his troopers better be on their toes. Red Cloud's bin kickin' up all kinds o' trouble out there." Trautman gawped at Gresham as he realized the significance of his assessment.

Gresham nodded his head. "That's my guess. I think he's being set up. He's got no experience of fighting Indians."

"But why in tarnation would Murray go an' do a thing like that?"

"I don't know, but it's the only rationale that makes any sense to me. Why send a totally inexperienced man to Virginia City on an urgent secret assignment? It's got to be a setup. Maybe they're using him as bait to draw out Red Cloud?"

"Surely Sibley's gotta know if there's some kinda scheme to lure Red Cloud into a trap?" Trautman pawed the map as if looking for an answer.

Gresham wagged his head in frustration. "That's what I'd have thought. He's the senior commander in the field, but I think he genuinely didn't know what Murray wanted with Moylan, and I trust him. He's got no love for the general."

There seemed no logic to any of the permutations surrounding Moylan's mission, but Gresham sensed an uncomfortable premonition of impending disaster. He was unable to put his finger on the explanation with absolute certainty, but his instinct had served him well in similar situations in the past, and he had learned to trust his feelings and act upon them.

"I'm going to meet them," he declared with finality.

"What? You gotta be mad! Murray'll court-martial you!" Trautman was dumbfounded by the decision, but he could tell from Gresham's expression that he would not be dissuaded.

"I need you to take command here, Isaac. I'll take twenty troopers with me. If you get any contact from Murray or Sibley, you'll have to inform them that I'm on patrol." Gresham brooded over the map.

"John, don't do this!" Trautman implored. "You don't know what kinda crap you're gettin' into."

Gresham glared at Trautman, the set of his chin betraying his intransigence. "You have your orders, Isaac. Now, would you kindly go and brief Sergeant Jeffries. I'll want two squads ready to leave at first light." He dismissed Trautman without permitting further comment, and the lieutenant was left with no option other than to brief Jeffries and select the troopers Gresham had requested.

At dawn, Gresham led his men out of the fort, wheeling away toward the southern foothills of the Bridger Mountains. His plan was to cut around to the south of the Bighorns and join the Bozeman Trail at the southern end of the Powder River Basin, having assessed this to be the fastest route.

It would take him four days to reach Fort Reno, a small trading station where his squad could reprovision before moving north. He had no idea how long Moylan would remain in Virginia City, but he hoped that it would be long enough to provide the chance of intercepting the young officer's troop before they entered Sioux country.

Chapter 34

North of Ten Sleep, Nowood Creek

"Did you hear zat? I have heard somevon scream. I im sure." An eerie shriek emanating from the forest made Carla stop in her tracks and call to Edward, pleading for him to listen.

The Quaker turned toward the wooded hillside, shielding his eyes so that he could scan the treeline. "I'm not sure I heard anything, my dear," he said. "Are you sure it wasn't the call of a bird? Some of them can make quite a screeching noise."

"No, I im sure it vas a scream." She stood listening for a few minutes as the wagon rolled by, but the sound was not repeated. She was about to move off again when a chorus of yelling erupted, the tone angry and hateful.

"Edvard! Did you hear zat?" she called.

On this occasion Edward heard the bellowing and pulled his oxen to a halt, retracing his steps to join Carla at the rear of the schooner.

"Vhat vas it, Edvard?" she whispered.

"I don't know," he replied quietly. "But, whoever it is, doesn't sound friendly." He strode briskly to the schooner and retrieved a long-barreled musket. The old gun was a relic from the early part of the century, and he stood at the back of the wagon loading it hurriedly with powder and ball, taking care to pack the charge in place with wadding and tamp it down firmly. Lifting the gun level, he poured a small amount of powder onto the flash-pan and returned to join Carla.

The young Indian broke the cover of the trees about a hundred paces to the south of where Edward and Carla were standing and about quarter of a mile distant. It was clear that he was carrying an injury that hampered his gait considerably. He lurched as he ran, stumbling over the uneven ground and picking himself up each time he tripped, driving on with blind determination. His head was cast down, although he threw frequent hurried glances over his shoulder.

He staggered four hundred yards before the first horseman emerged from the fringe of the forest, and Carla saw the rider pull up and reach to draw a long rifle from its scabbard at the side of his saddle. The man trotted a few paces onto the plain and stopped, watching the Indian as he continued to run. Carla looked on in disbelief as he raised his rifle, fumbling to place a percussion cap, and took aim.

Focusing on escape and pursuit respectively, neither the Indian nor the horseman noticed the distant retreating caravan of schooners or the single wagon that remained stationary at the rear of the column. Instead, the horseman took aim and fired, a huge resounding report echoing off the high bluff above the spruce forest. The Indian's flight faltered and he toppled forward, falling facedown.

Carla screamed and ran towards him, causing the man on the horse to notice the caravan of wagons for the first time. Edward charged after Carla as fast as his legs would carry him, concerned that the impetuous young girl's interference might render her the gunman's next victim, since it was patently evident that he was not averse to committing murder in cold blood.

McCabe heard the gunshot a few moments before he reached open ground and burst out of the trees to see La Brais lower his rifle. He took in the scene instantly and saw the young girl and the old man converging on the Indian.

"Leave 'im be! Get outta here!" he screamed at La Brais, but to his astonishment the Canadian turned his horse and started walking slowly toward the Indian boy.

Carla ran as fast as her legs would carry her. She was uncertain whether the Indian was dead, but saw the gunman set off toward the young man's prone figure and was determined to reach him first, oblivious to her own safety. Racing across the uneven ground, she dived down to shield the young Indian as La Brais pulled his horse up alongside.

"Git out the way, girl!" La Brais snarled.

"No! Go avay! Leave him alone!" Carla screamed, distraught.

La Brais's horse stamped its feet impatiently as he studied the young girl, valiantly attempting to protect the Indian with her own body. "Yer can stay there an' die wi' 'im if yer wan'. Jus' same t' me," he growled, expecting to frighten her into moving aside. But the girl remained, resolutely defending the boy. Undeterred by her bravery, he raised his rifle and placed a fresh percussion cap on the firing nipple.

"You do that and you're a dead man." Edward stood twenty yards away, his musket leveled at La Brais's chest. "I'm no killer, but so help me god if you harm that girl, it'll be the last thing you do." His voice was steady and authoritative, and La Brais turned to see the stoic-faced migrant glaring at him over the barrel of a musket.

"You sure yer wanna do that, ole man?" La Brais swiveled his rifle and pointed it at Edward.

But the stand-off was interrupted as McCabe galloped up and swept in between his fellow trapper and the two young people sprawled on the ground. "Frank! Get outta here!" he hissed. "Look!" He pointed over Edward's shoulder at a growing mass of people who were striding toward them, led by a small woman wearing a black dress and a white bonnet.

"Let's get out o' here," he whispered again. "C'mon!"

La Brais eyed the crowd approaching from the wagon train. He had no desire to take on a mob and the Indian looked dead anyway, so he smirked at Edward and shot him a crooked smile.

"Your lucky day, grandpa," he scoffed, reholstering his rifle and wheeling his horse to lope away, heading for Ten Sleep and leaving McCabe trailing.

Edward brought the wagon around, pulling it up alongside Carla as she sat cradling the Indian's head. He was still breathing, but had an ugly gash above his ear where La Brais's bullet had clipped him, its searing velocity having knocked him unconscious.

Edward managed to clear a small space in the back of the schooner and, with the help of another family, lifted the Indian onto a nest of blankets, leaving Carla to climb up and sit beside him. She was appalled at his condition, noticing that his tunic was torn and bloodstained and that his ripped breeches exposed livid yellow and purple bruising to one knee. One ankle was equally swollen, and after she had felt the heat in each of the joints, she was left wondering how the young Indian had been able to run at all.

Carla's greatest concern was the patch tied across his eye, and she had to summon all her courage to remove the binding, since the lacerations on his cheek suggested that a truly horrific injury might be concealed beneath the bandage.

In the event, when Carla succeeded in unwrapping the tattered material, she was disconcerted at how moved she was by the Indian's appearance. His eye was closed and swollen, but the shape of his face became clear, revealing a strong handsome young man with a full mouth that possessed an endearing sense of mischief, implying a contented harmony at odds with his condition. She thought his face was kind and inadvertently found herself stroking his brow.

Mary watched the girl's compassion with a wistful smile,

until Carla detected her gaze and snapped her hand away, her face flushing with embarrassment. "He is zo young," she stuttered.

"Yes," said Mary. "Still a boy, really. But handsome, don't you think?" she giggled at the light provocation.

Carla's mouth dropped open and her cheeks blushed a bright pink as she fought to find a suitable response, only managing an unintelligible mumble. Mary laughed. "Well, I think he's going to need plenty of good care. I don't suppose you'd be able to help me look after him?"

Carla grinned broadly and placed her hand on Takoda's shoulder, keeping her eyes averted from Mary. "I sink I vould like zat," she purred. "I vill have to go unt tell mother, zough." She gave Takoda a lingering stare, climbed to the back of the schooner, and jumped down to run off to her family's wagon.

The Indian's presence attracted much attention from the other travelers. Within hours, news had spread that a savage was in their midst, and Carla spent much of her time trying to prevent curious onlookers from prodding her charge, whom they regarded as more of an exhibit than a human being.

Many of the children kept a respectful distance, intrigued to discover whether the Indian was dangerous, a bizarre response since there had been many natives camped in Fort Laramie. But an Indian discovered in the wilderness of the plains was viewed entirely differently to those the migrants had encountered along previous sections of the trail.

Carla's mother was incensed that she wished to associate herself with the Indian and, following a furious argument, Elena banished her from the Kopp wagon, explaining that if she chose to minister to the savage, she would never be permitted to return home. Carla was undeterred by the rebuke, and although she fumed at her mother's lack of compassion, she felt elated at the prospect of spending more time with the Quakers and the mysterious young man.

Takoda regained consciousness shortly before the wagon train stopped for nooning, the migrants' midday break. His eyelids flickered and his limbs twitched while he fought to regain his senses. His undamaged eye blinked open and he jerked violently, shocked at the sight of Carla's concerned face scrutinizing him from within a matter of inches.

Startled, he scrambled to escape from the unexpected apparition, causing Carla to shoot backward, alarmed at his obvious distress. "Is all right! You safe. Don' be frighten, pliz," she squealed in broken English.

Takoda pressed himself against the side of the wagon, breathlessly attempting to comprehend his surroundings while Carla fumbled for words of encouragement, his confusion blatantly apparent.

"I im Carla," she smiled, pointing at herself as Takoda continued to look bewildered. "You is hurt unt I im being your nurse." She smiled again and laid her hand on Takoda's wrist, causing him to flinch and whip his arm away.

Dismayed, she recoiled, but gathered herself for another attempt. "I im going to love after you," she stated firmly, immediately mortified at her inadvertent error and flushing a bright red. "I mean, I im help you get better." She frowned seriously in an attempt to compose herself. "Now, come. Lie down, pliz."

She adopted a business-like tone and fluffed up a blanket to coax Takoda away from the side of the wagon, progressively easing him back onto his bed. "There. Is better, no?"

She fussed around him as the schooner rumbled along, and Takoda began to realize that she meant him no harm. He eyed her curiously as she busied herself, until, to her slight embarrassment, he reached up and touched one of the long tresses of her golden hair, the honey color glinting in the morning light and sparkling with a kaleidoscope of different shades that he found mesmerizing.

Carla's hair reflected the colors of the sun, unlike the raven locks of the women in his tribe, and she sat motionless as he ran his fingers through her lustrous mane, feeling awkward at the uninvited tenderness. The absorbing caress seemed to soothe Takoda's anxiety and she was relieved to see him relax.

Interrupting their intimacy, the wagon rolled to a jolting halt and the Mays appeared, the Quakers being delighted to discover that Takoda had recovered consciousness, although they were obliged to withdraw when their presence caused the young Indian to scramble to the back of the wagon in panic.

Mary decided that providing some good wholesome food would be the best means of settling the Indian's nerves, so, as Edward went to fetch fresh water, she set about preparing a meal of beans and bacon to accompany the bread she had cooked in her Dutch oven before the wagon train had set off earlier that morning.

Takoda accepted the water proffered by Edward and drank thirstily, but he was skeptical of Mary's food until Carla intervened, picking up a slice of bacon in a chunk of bread and taking a bite herself, comically exaggerating her appreciation of the flavor.

"Mmm. See. Is delicious!" She pouted idiotically, rolling her eyes as she chewed, until Takoda flashed a weak grin and reluctantly conceded to sample some of the unfamiliar fare.

Before breaking camp the doctor visited and, following insistent reassurance, Takoda permitted the physician to inspect his injuries, although he refused to allow anyone to touch his damaged eye. Carla was presented with a small bottle of carbolic acid, which the physician instructed her to use to clean Takoda's wounds, explaining that the solution would help to prevent secondary infection, although he cautioned that it should be applied sparingly because of its caustic property.

Carla took her nursing duties seriously and before long she persuaded Takoda to grudgingly accept her ministrations, although he remained reluctant to let her touch his eye. She used a clean cloth soaked in warm water to remove the blood and dirt from his limbs and eventually managed to encourage him to remove his tunic, which she replaced with one of Edward's voluminous shirts, having washed down his torso first.

Takoda watched her with quiet fascination. She worked slowly and purposefully, careful to avoid causing him pain, and her hands were cool and gentle as she tended his battered body, using strips of linen soaked in warm water drawn from the creek and boiled by Mary to bandage his bruised joints.

Carla talked incessantly, a quiet but happy chirruping like the sound a hen might use to rally its chicks, and although the words meant little to Takoda, he found the chatter soothing and appealing, encouraging him to relax and sleep once the schooners started along the trail again after their noon break.

Takoda was able to sit up by the time the wagon train stopped to make camp, and with Edward's assistance, he disembarked from the schooner to sit alongside the fire, watching with interest as they prepared their evening meal.

The rest of the families in Edward's group maintained a healthy separation, conversing in hushed tones and casting apprehensive glances at the Quakers' schooner. Johannes provided the most extreme reaction, the overnight stop allowing him to vent his rage at the Indian's presence as he bawled abuse at Carla and swept Mary-Jane away on his horse in disgust.

Unmoved by the acrimony, Takoda devoured a hearty meal and willingly complied when Carla hustled him back to bed after he had eaten. For the first time in many weeks he felt safe, and he allowed himself the luxury of submitting to the care of strangers, relieved to be able to rest his weary body.

By morning, the migrants' consternation had boiled over, and a delegation of men arrived at Edward's schooner to express their discontent at the Indian living in their midst. Brusquely, they explained that there had been much discussion around the campfires, asserting that many people were concerned for their safety and the safety of their families. Edward was told in no uncertain terms that he would have to leave the Indian behind or leave the wagon train.

Incensed, Mary stepped to the fore in response. In strident tones, she lectured the men about their ungodly lack of humanity, representing Takoda's rescue as analogous to the parable of the Good Samaritan and calling upon them to exhibit compassion for a young man who needed their love and support, not their prejudice and bigotry.

Her criticism was withering, and the protesters looked so sheepish at her uncompromising rebuttal that the captain of the wagon train was eventually obliged to intervene and broker an uneasy compromise. The settlement required that Edward's schooner stay at the rear of the caravan and that he should camp separately in return for the boy being permitted to remain. The solution did little to placate the most fearful, who threatened to shoot Takoda on sight if he ventured close to their wagons, but it was an acceptable accommodation for Edward and Mary.

Takoda was eating breakfast with Carla and the Quakers when the delegation appeared, and he guessed that he was the cause of the aggressive dispute that followed, but he was astonished at the fervor of the couple's defense and the zeal with which Mary chastened the men. The old man was steadfast and the old woman showed a courage that warmed Takoda's heart. They were good people.

After the complainants had departed, Takoda caught Carla's

eye as she sat finishing her meal. "Takoda," he said, prodding his chest.

Carla misinterpreted his meaning, assuming that he was still hungry, and offered him some food from her plate, but Takoda shook his head and tried again. "Takoda." His expression expectant, he pointed at Carla.

Edward chuckled. "I think he's telling you his name. He wants to know yours."

Carla was shocked. Of course, it was so obvious. She did not even know his name. She gawped at him and, realizing that she now understood, he repeated himself. "Takoda." He patted his torso.

Carla laughed, bouncing on her stool, and mimicked what he had said. "Takoda. Ya, Takoda. Is zat your name?"

He nodded emphatically and pointed at her.

"Oh! Yes. I im Carla. My name is Carla." She emphasized each letter as she pronounced her name.

"Carla." Takoda replied, nodding with satisfaction as he turned to Edward and Mary.

"Edward," the old man said slowly.

"Eddar?" Takoda questioned.

"That's good enough for me," said Edward, beaming.

"And Mary," his wife piped enthusiastically.

"Marry," repeated Takoda, giving the names serious consideration. "Eddar, Takoda, Marry, Carla," he pointed to each of them in turn.

Mary burst out laughing. "He said Takoda marry Carla. What do you think of that, Carla? He's a bit forward, isn't he?"

Carla's cheeks flushed and she fumbled with her cutlery as the old couple chortled with amusement, Takoda enjoying their obvious delight but having no idea that he had prompted the hilarity.

Takoda's health improved steadily, and with persistent coaxing he even permitted the doctor to examine his injured eye, the physician's conclusion being that Carla had done a fine job of keeping it clean, but that the damage was such that his sight would never recover. Takoda understood the implication of the doctor's clumsy attempt to articulate the prognosis; nevertheless he still harbored the hope that the loss of sight in his eye would prove to be a temporary condition.

As the mobility of his joints improved, he was able to lower himself from the back of the schooner and hobble along the trail for short periods, working off the stiffness in his ankle and strengthening his knee. Carla walked with him, and they entertained themselves exchanging the names of plants and animals in their respective languages.

By the time they reached the Bighorn River, their vocabulary of nouns was extensive and they were beginning to string together short sentences. Both had keen inquisitive minds and they learned fast, each enjoying the competitiveness of attempting to remember more words than the other and appreciating the intimacy of connection afforded by a shared foreign language.

They savored the enormity of the Great Plains as they traveled, its undulating carpet gradually revealed, stretching to the horizon far to the north and west, the succulent green shoots of spring already beginning to give way to the scorched corn yellow inflicted by the intense heat of the unrelenting summer sun.

Progressively, Carla noticed that Takoda began to fall silent, a melancholy settling upon him despite her best efforts to raise his spirits, singing songs and enthusiastically pointing out unusual flowers as they walked. Occasionally, she caught him staring thoughtfully to the west, and she began to suspect that he might be thinking of home.

One evening while camped alongside the river, she huddled close to Takoda as he stood gazing out across the plain. She pointed out into the darkness. "Is your home out zere?" she asked quietly.

The sentence was confusing, but Takoda understood the thrust of her question. "Tiwahe," he responded pensively, using the Lakota word for "family."

"Do you have a brozer or sister?" Carla enquired. "Johannes ciye," she elaborated, meaning that her older brother was Johannes.

Carla had pointed out Johannes, and Takoda had taught her the Lakota word for her sibling, so he understood the gist of her pigeon language. His thoughts drifted back to Howahkan, and he replayed the grotesque sight of his brother being thrown from the edge of the cliff and falling into the void. He closed his eyes and flinched at the memory, wagging his head mournfully.

"No. No ciye." He turned and walked away, his brother's death wrenching at his conscience. He felt responsible. Howahkan had been trying to alleviate his indulgent depression by taking him to their father's grave, and now, because of his childish self-pity, his brother was dead. He was overwhelmed by a sudden sense of shame, and imagined the penetrating inquisition he would receive from his grandfather when he returned home. His clumsiness had killed his father, and his self-absorbed dejection had killed his brother. A flood of guilt provoked an intense taste of bile in his throat, and he thought he might vomit. He wondered whether it would be better for his family if they thought that he had perished too. After so many months away, perhaps his return would only serve to stir up painful emotions and raise insoluble questions about Howahkan's fate.

Takoda tried to imagine how he might explain what had happened to his mother and the Itancan. And, in retrospect, having turned and run for his life after Howahkan had been shot, it seemed evident that his courage had deserted him and that he had fled out of cowardice. Such behavior would surely bring disgrace upon his family.

Carla studied his reaction to her question with concern. She had expected that talking about his family would have been a source of joy, but the effect had prompted the antithesis, and she wondered whether his relatives were all dead. It dawned on her that perhaps he was alone, and a rush of sympathy made her want to hug him, but he walked away, the distant look in his eyes making her feel that she would be intruding in his private thoughts.

Takoda climbed into the schooner and settled into the blankets, which provided a welcome element of comfort and privacy. The more he thought about it, the more he considered it inappropriate to return to his people. He felt empty and alienated, unable to conceive what would become of him.

Permitting Takoda some solitude, Carla went to sit beside the campfire with Edward and Mary, and they offered her a steaming mug of hot milk to warm herself against the cool evening breeze.

"I sink Takoda is all alone," she mused to Mary. "I don't sink he has family to go home to."

Mary snuggled close to Carla. "Now, why would you think that?" she replied.

"I ask him if he has any brozers or sisters, unt he said no. Zen, he vent very quiet unt sad. I sink maybe zey die. He is look so lonely unt lost, unt he is gone to bed sad."

"Maybe he's missing his family," Mary ventured.

Carla wagged her head. "No. I don't sink so. I sink he vould be happy to sink about his family, but he vasn't. I thought he vas going to cry."

Edward leaned across and patted her knee, sympathetic to her concern. "Well, there's no hurry for him to leave. He can stay with us until he's ready." He beamed reassuringly, and

Carla was once again touched by the benevolent spirit of the old couple.

"Vhat vill happen to him?" she asked.

Edward sipped his coffee thoughtfully. "Time will tell. God has a plan for all his children, but for now we've been called upon to give him a little of our help, and that's exactly what we'll do." Mary smiled and rested her hand affectionately on his knee.

When the wagon train reached the fork of the Greybull and the Bighorn rivers, Takoda continued to walk with Edward and Mary's wagon. He snatched a few wistful glances toward the mountains in the west and his mood was disconsolate, but he had made up his mind that he could not return to his band.

He started to help with the daily chores as the migrants continued to move north, he gathered firewood, hunted for food, and took his turn at looking after the unusual cattle that drew the schooner. He had no inkling where his new life might lead, or what his future might hold.

Chapter 35

Late July 1865, Powder River Basin, Dakota Territory

The wagons rocked unsteadily along the trail, the cargo of crates creaking as they were thrown around by the uncompromising ground, now dried rock hard by the baking summer heat. Moylan's troop crossed the Bighorn River and cut south along the Bozeman Trail to the east of the Bighorn Mountains, traversing wide stretches of rolling plains.

There were few significant landmarks along the trail to differentiate one day from another, and they encountered no sign of Indians, so the squad's initial brittle concern about broaching the northern hunting grounds of the Sioux descended into dangerous lethargy.

They camped at the Powder River crossing, where their horses gorged themselves on the plentiful supply of cool water, the prairie trail having been dry and arid for several days previously, and the troopers relaxed and bathed their weary limbs.

Sergeant Ames took point as they broke camp the following morning, the trail set in the lee of the first significant escarpment they had encountered for some fifty miles, its dramatic ridge intersected by deep clefts, all framed by rugged pillars of fractured sandstone and carpeted with swards of prairie grass that poured down the hillside like smooth tawny-colored lava flows.

Ames scanned the ridgeline apprehensively, conscious that its elevated topography provided an ideal position from which to launch an ambush. He had trekked across enough Indian territory in his long military career to recognize the circumstances in which one should exercise prudence, and the craggy overlooks at the top of the bluff left him feeling uneasy.

He cast a glance at the young captain, who was plodding along with an indifference that betrayed his nescience of the risk, so despite his antipathy toward the young man, he dropped back to speak to him.

"Bad Indian country, sir," he nodded toward the escarpment to his left.

Moylan squinted at the bluff, shading his eyes from the sun. "Nonsense, we haven't seen so much as a smoke signal since we left Virginia City," he grumbled, dismissing Ames's concern with a disinterested shrug.

"Nevertheless, we oughtta keep the men alert, sir. We're haulin' through the heart o' Sioux territory now. Oughtta get the boys to check their weapons an' ammunition, to keep 'em on their toes." Ames ignored Moylan's contemptuous attitude, acutely aware that his own safety depended on the squad's vigilance.

Moylan's irritation was piqued by Ames's attitude. He was exasperated that the veteran seemed determined to treat him as though he was incompetent. "You'll be seeing ghosts next, Sergeant. Your duty's to take point. I'll worry about the men. Now, if you don't mind, perhaps you'd resume your position." He glowered at Ames, his face set in a truculent grimace.

"As you wish, Captain. But I'm gonna swing by Corporal Smith," he responded, only returning to his post at the front of the small convoy once he had jogged back and discussed the readiness of the squad with the corporal, leaving Moylan seething at his impertinence.

The escarpment ran parallel on their eastern flank for the next few hours, until its promontory gradually started to descend toward the plain, the sandstone boulders lining its summit still providing ample concealment for a potential enemy.

Ames maintained a vigilant scrutiny. He swept the top of the hill for the hundredth time, searching for the slightest movement, but detected nothing of concern, so was flabbergasted when he turned back to the trail to be greeted by the distant outline of four mounted Indians approaching. They were half a mile away and appeared to have materialized out of thin air.

He pulled up sharply and hailed Moylan. "Four Sioux warriors up ahead, Captain!"

Moylan snapped upright, a rush of adrenaline energizing his attention. Indians. Real "wild" Indians. Warriors, unlike the indolent traders at Fort Laramie. The natives he had seen previously had been innocuous beggars, but on the plains, the Indians lived off the land, pursuing the basic tribal existence of nomadic savages. He experienced a sudden thrill of excitement and hurried to join the sergeant, leaving the wagons to roll up behind him, where they drew to a standstill and the troopers fanned out to observe the Indians, who continued to advance steadily.

The warriors were bare-chested, their bodies and faces decorated with painted shapes and lines. Feathers were woven into their hair and braids were wrapped around their upper arms, decorated with thongs of colorful material. Each man carried a rifle and had a bow strung across his back, and they rode purposefully, their faces set and grim.

Moylan issued orders for his men to draw their weapons and waited to see what the Indians would do, but three hundred paces distant the warriors stopped and sat silently staring at the cavalrymen. Moylan's heart raced with anticipation and he yearned for the justification to attack the Indians, his revolver held at the ready and his hand quivering with excitement.

"What are they doing?" he enquired impatiently.

"Don't know, sir. Lookin' I guess, but we didn't oughtta do anythin' that'll get 'em all worked up." Ames replied, keeping a steady eye trained on the warriors.

The stand-off lasted interminably, and Moylan fully expected that the warriors would turn away, intimidated by the superior strength of his escort unit. But he was mistaken. With a sudden explosive cry, one of the warriors thrust his rifle above his head and screamed a blood-curdling challenge. Immediately, all four Indians charged, their ponies arcing out to the soldiers' left flank as they brought their rifles to bear and launched a dramatic attack.

Moylan hurriedly returned fire, shocked at the unprovoked assault, and ordered his men to do likewise. But the shots were futile. The Indians swept past maintaining a two-hundred-yard separation before circling around and returning at speed, whooping wildly as they discharged a further salvo of erratic shots.

The troopers milled about on their horses, attempting to obtain an effective arc of fire, Ames bellowing at them to lower their rifles, the experienced sergeant recognizing the warriors' behavior as no more than mischievous provocation. But, although desperate for his men to conserve their ammunition and form an orderly defensive line, he struggled to make himself heard in the melee.

"Cease fire! Dismount!" Ames screamed. "Cease fire!" He jumped off his horse and ran toward the wagons to subdue his troopers' overzealous response.

The warriors rallied and advanced again, most of their bullets whistling overhead harmlessly, although an occasional shot struck one of the wagons, producing an eruption of splinters. As the warriors swooped past for the second time, they dropped their rifles to their laps and Moylan sensed that they had expended their ammunition. He was overwhelmed with excitement and bristled with conceit at thwarting the warriors' fruitless aggression.

"Charge!" he screamed, turning to the troopers behind him. "Follow me! After them!" He waved his pistol and dug his heels into his mount, launching off in pursuit.

The troopers exchanged uncertain glances as their captain rushed after the Indians. Infused with battle fever, however, they spun around and tore after him, Ames frantically attempting to halt their flight.

Smith noticed Ames hauling one of the troopers to a standstill and pulled up his horse, yelling at the rest of the men to stop. But the chase was on, and he only managed to restrain three troopers, the rest charging after Moylan, howling their own war cries.

The warriors returned in the direction from which they had first appeared, and Moylan sped after them, gripped by a heady lust for blood. He gritted his teeth, leaning into the wind as he whipped his horse into a flat-out gallop, focused on catching the Indians and determined to teach them that they could not attack a cavalry unit with impunity. He would run them down and kill the lot of them.

The troopers thundered after their captain, sending up plumes of dust and chasing the Indians as they edged toward the tapering end of the ridge of the escarpment, their pace slowing as they ascended the rising ground.

Moylan sensed that the warriors' ponies were tiring and smirked at the prospect of overhauling them. The Indians' mustangs were no match for his cavalry horse. He holstered his pistol and drew his Springfield rifle in readiness. He would be the first to take one of them down.

The Indians slowed to a stop and, to Moylan's bewilderment, turned to meet his charge. They sat immobile, their weapons held across the withers of their ponies, and Moylan seized his chance. He pulled his mount to a halt and brought his rifle to his shoulder.

Primed to fire, he froze.

The ridge behind the four Indians started to move. A wavering line of heads appeared, stretching for hundreds of yards along the crest of the hill in either direction. Mesmerized, he lowered his gun and watched in horror as the heads morphed into bodies, and the bodies emerged over the horizon as mounted warriors.

A tide of Sioux strode forward. Hundreds of men, each decorated with war paint and mounted on a sturdy pony. Moylan's jaw dropped. It was an ambush. He had been lured straight into a trap. Stunned, he tugged at his horse's reins, yanking them so sharply that the animal reared up and snorted. His troopers converged behind him, wrestling to turn their mounts and screaming at each other to run for their lives.

Uttering a single synchronized war cry, the warriors swept over the ridge and flooded after the cavalrymen.

Ames watched in disbelief as the troopers reappeared, their panic plainly evident as a sea of Indians swarmed around the promontory of the escarpment in hot pursuit, the hopeless futility of their plight striking him like a thunderbolt.

Smith stood at his side, and his breath exploded in disbelief. "My god. It's the whole damned Sioux nation! We're all dead!"

Ames shared his dismay and, despite his battle-hardened experience, stood in shocked paralysis. "In the wagons!" he screamed, shaking himself from his torpor. "Stack the crates to give yerselves cover. Looks like we're gonna make some use o' those goddamned Winchesters!"

The men gawped, stupefied, until Ames shoved them toward the wagons, spurring the troopers to action. Smith and one of the privates leapt onto the first wagon and Ames and the other two men scrambled into the second.

Ames smashed the butt of his rifle against the side of one of the crates and broke its seal, swiftly levering off the lid and pulling urgently at the packing material to reveal the weapons. He stopped, shocked. There were no rifles. Incredulous, he fumbled in the crate, drawing his knife to slice open the hessian sacks it contained and scooping out a handful of the contents, worthless tan-gray gravelly stone.

"No guns! Rocks! It's full of bloody rocks!" He was astounded. They were all going to die for a few cases of worthless stone. The deception was complete. Not only had the Sioux lured them into an ambush, but the United States army had misled them too, sending them on a fool's errand to transport meaningless cargo.

He shoved the crate in disgust. "Gather all the ammunition you can, boys!" he shouted. "Let's take some of these sons o' bitches with us!"

Smith and the troopers worked feverishly to arrange the crates into a crude circular fortification, leaving arrow-slits between each box to provide protected positions from which to mount their final stand.

Crouching behind his defenses, Ames stole a glance at the rest of the squad, who were hurtling toward the wagons in full retreat, but to his despair he saw that they were already overrun on both flanks. They would not make it back in time. Dismayed, he turned away from the inevitable slaughter and scanned the ridge to his left. His heart stopped. Another wave of Sioux materialized from one of the clefts in the escarpment and began pouring down the slope.

"On the left, Ben! Keep your heads down, boys. Make every shot count!" Ames bawled at Smith to alert him to the additional onslaught.

★ ★ ★ ★ ★

Moylan rode in a state of numb shock. He could not comprehend his situation. His father had been a decorated hero, and he had been convinced that it was his destiny to emulate the tradition. He had been so certain that he had never doubted his rise to the lofty heights of military rank, but now the haunting certainty of death ensnared him, like a heavy burden weighing down his headlong rush to escape.

The pursuing Indians descended on him like a storm. The rumble of a thousand charging hooves snatched at his heels, and on either flank he could see warriors beginning to overhaul his weary horse.

With trancelike leaden movements, he slewed his rifle to the right and fired indiscriminately. One of the Indians fell from his horse and Moylan realized that his troopers were shooting too, wild desperate shots, as ineffectual as attempting to swat a swarm of flies.

But, as Moylan fired to the right, the warriors on his left swung in close. They flexed their bows, and with a sickening wrench he felt the first arrow thud into his left side. The arrow entered below his armpit, and the crooked barb of its head burst through his chest, ejecting a spray of blood that covered his jacket and splattered across his face.

Moylan wheeled around in shock to find two warriors galloping alongside him, their faces masked with concentration. They rode without the need to hold their reins, balancing easily and rocking in unison with the movement of their mount, their deadly bows drawn at full stretch with arrows knocked to the string.

He swung his rifle mechanically to confront them, but the action was futile. Before he could take aim, both arrows were loosed. His gun discharged harmlessly at the ground and fell from his limp hand.

An arrow caught Moylan square in the chest, the power of its flight driving the tip through his body and out of his back, and the second pierced his shoulder like a knife skewering an apple. Immediately, his horse felt the loss of impetus and began to slow, Moylan swaying listlessly in the saddle.

Oblivious to their commanding officer's demise, the rest of the troopers continued to flee, emptying their rifles of ammunition, while the Sioux warriors picked them off with devastating efficiency. Within minutes, every man lay felled, numerous feather-flighted arrows impaled in their bodies, their riderless horses dispersed across the plain.

The Indians circled with ruthless menace as Moylan slumped from his horse. The shaft protruding from his back snapped as he crashed to earth, and the arrow skewering his shoulder pinned him to the ground, its barbed tip embedded in the soil.

Moylan blinked at the bright sun overhead, disoriented. Nothing made any sense. He felt no pain. His body was numb, paralyzed by an insistent draining lethargy. The warriors surrounded him, but he could hear no sound. He could see their mouths moving and feel the vibration of their ponies' footfall, but his ears were dead.

As if responding to a regimented order, the warriors parted. At the periphery of his vision, Moylan detected the presence of a man studying him. The face was implacable. A long prominent nose, eyes that were dark and serious, and a mouth that turned down at the corners, as if saddened by the world he observed.

The image swam in and out of focus, and he presumed that the Indian must be the leader of the war party. The man gazed down dispassionately but said nothing, until a second person drew alongside. The men exchanged brief words, and the Indian moved away.

Moylan's incredulity made him gasp, and he tried to lift his head and scream at the duplicity, but he remained firmly pinned to the ground and no sound passed his lips. The bear-like form of Colter stared down at him, his heavily whiskered face phlegmatic.

Colter studied the young cavalry officer. He had found the boy a real pain in the backside, but now he almost felt sorry for him. "Looks like you was in the wrong place at th' wrong time, son." He spat a glob of spittle to the ground and regarded Moylan as if expecting some form of response, but the young man's eyes were glazed and distant.

The bearded face wavered, and Moylan tried to recall its significance, but he was unable to think. Everything was confused. A shroud of darkness enveloped his vision as an amorphous shape bent down, blocking out the sun, and he felt a sudden yank on the top of his head, followed by a searing pain. All fell dark. The final spark of life drained from him.

Ames and his men hunkered down behind their crates, and the sergeant ordered his troopers to hold their fire until the Sioux warriors were less than thirty yards away. The first volley of shots took down five Indians, and the second felled another four. Arrows thudded into the crates harmlessly, the men insulated by the tightly packed cargo, as the wave of warriors swept past the wagons to reform and charge again.

Ames and his men took aim once more and exacted a deadly toll, their bullets tearing through the wave of warriors, but the Sioux were not to be intimidated and encircled the troopers, one group of braves drawing the soldiers' fire while another party swung in close and jumped onto the wagons, their knives drawn ready to engage in hand-to-hand combat.

Despite Ames's disciplined efforts, he and his men were hopelessly overwhelmed by the tide of warriors, and within minutes they were condemned to stand and grapple with their assailants. Smith was the first to succumb as he tried to ward off two warriors and was unable to prevent the thrust of a knife, which lunged into his belly and ripped his abdomen open like a gutted fish. He slumped to the bed of the wagon grasping a handful of bloody entrails, before suffering a final deadly stab to the chest.

The other troopers were picked off one by one, until Ames was the only cavalryman left standing. His ammunition spent, he had fought wave after wave of Sioux, leaving a trail of bodies in his wake, but now he stood with his back to the wagon, staggering from side to side, an arrow protruding from his left shoulder and a second embedded in his right thigh. He snarled contemptuously at a brawny Indian that stalked him, both men's faces contorted with intractable determination, a gathering of warriors looking on, howling encouragement at their comrade.

Ames held a knife in his right hand and flourished it aggressively. "Come on y' ugly bastard!" he roared. "Yer want a piece of me, you'll have to come and git it!"

The Indian circled him patiently, forcing him to turn away from the wagon and place his weight on his injured leg, so that a stab of pain shot through his thigh and he stumbled slightly. It was the lapse the warrior had been waiting for, and he sprang, crashing into Ames's left side and stabbing down with his own wicked blade.

Ames reeled and twisted away, slashing his knife upward and skimming the Indian's chest to draw first blood. But the warrior appeared impervious to the laceration, and with sublime agility he swiftly checked his charge and drove into Ames again, seizing the cavalryman's right wrist in an iron grip, preventing him from bringing his knife to bear again. With his free hand, he stabbed his hunting knife at Ames's chest, and the two men were sent tumbling backward.

Ames crashed onto his back and the warrior leapt on top of him, forcing the sergeant's knife to the side and wrestling to press his own hunting knife down across Ames's throat. Possessed of the wild strength of desperate self-preservation, the sergeant kicked and bucked, thrashing his body back and forth in an attempt to dislodge his assailant, but the Indian was strong and used his weight to counter Ames's efforts to elude his attack.

Forced to adopt a different strategy, Ames marshaled his strength and threw himself to the left, whipping his right hand in toward his body to unbalance the Indian and freeing his knife so that he could thrust it viciously upward.

The tactic almost worked and the warrior lurched unsteadily, but anticipated the blow and twisted to his right with the speed of a striking rattlesnake, driving his elbow into the arrow protruding from Ames's shoulder. The pain was excruciating and drained his endurance in an instant. His right hand flailed uselessly and his knife strayed from its target, the blade spinning out of his fingers.

Sensing Ames's impotence, the Indian pounced, thrusting a knee brutally into the sergeant's stomach and plunging the hunting knife down horizontally across his neck with both hands. The razor-sharp blade glided through the flesh, severing Ames's spinal column as though slicing through butter. The air in his lungs discharged through his bisected windpipe with a lingering hiss, and he fell still.

Gresham and his troopers rode hard, covering nearly thirty miles each day, setting camp after dusk, and departing again before dawn the following morning. At Fort Reno they remained only long enough to obtain the bare minimum of supplies and struck out again within the hour.

As they rode, Gresham talked to each of his men in turn, preparing them for the possibility of encountering hostility and rehearsing battle drills, until he was confident that they would respond as he required in the event that they were forced to fight.

Each evening he made the troopers strip down and clean their weapons, encouraging competition to determine which man could dismantle and rebuild his rifle the fastest, the winner being allocated an extra ration of food and a nip of whiskey.

Mile after mile of uninterrupted rolling plain faded in their wake, and they drove on deep into the Powder River Basin. The baking sun was unforgiving, and the troopers' throats were parched dry by the stifling heat and the cloying dust, requiring them to divert from the trail on several occasions to ensure that their horses were properly watered and their canteens replenished.

They moved at a speed that rendered the deployment of a scout superfluous, and, as a result, Gresham detected a strange series of heaps on the horizon almost simultaneously with the trooper running point.

"Weapons to the ready!" Gresham commanded. "Come around to double echelons." Immediately, the men reformed with mechanical precision from a two-abreast column into a double diagonal row, drawing their Springfields and advancing with their rifles in hand.

The morning sun glinted off the wavering yellow grass of the plains and a shimmering opaque heat haze caused the curious anomaly of scattered mounds to distort into amorphous shapes, their form remaining unclear. Approaching rapidly, the troopers could distinguish movement, each pile rising and falling back to earth with an irregular pulsing tempo.

Gresham strained to make sense of the shapes, steeling himself for combat as the troops descended a small gully and climbed steadily up the slope on the far side, parallel to the tapering promontory of an imposing bluff on their right flank.

The horses' hooves pounded rhythmically as they crested the

gully, and the expanse of the Powder River Basin opened before them. Rolling plains of tall swaying grass flowed away to the horizon, and the true nature of the obscure forms the men had been wrestling to distinguish was revealed with devastating clarity.

A flurry of huge black ravens jostled and leapt in the air, fighting over the prostrate corpses of dead cavalrymen strewn across the trail ahead. Their navy and light blue uniforms, powdered with dust, lent a degree of form to the bodies, which had been dragged around by coyotes so that their limbs lay at grotesquely inhuman angles.

Gresham spurred his horse on, a desolate sense of failure promoting a lead weight of despondency in his stomach. Each body was riven with countless long-shafted arrows, and the exposed flesh had been devoured by scavengers, mutilating the deceased troopers beyond recognition. He was too late.

He stopped alongside the closest corpse and dismounted, his sergeant pulling up and gasping with horror. "My god, they've been slaughtered!"

Maintaining his vigilance, Gresham instructed his men to form a defensive circle while he inspected each of the bodies, walking slowly from one to the other and turning each dead man respectfully in the hope of discerning his identity. The ravens scattered at the presence of the troopers and hopped about angrily at a safe distance, squawking with irritation at the unwelcome disturbance, as Gresham assessed the scene.

The men were largely unknown to him, being deployed from Sibley's units, but he had met Ames briefly, so he searched determinedly to identify both Moylan and the seasoned sergeant. The soldiers' bodies were spread over several hundred yards. The first group of men had clearly been cut down while in flight, and at their center Gresham eventually discovered a captain's uniform. The body was prostrate, lying on its back, and the shoulder was firmly skewered to the ground, but the face was unrecognizable, its eyes removed by the birds and the raw flesh pecked into a gruesome mince.

Gresham took a blanket from his saddlebag and laid it across the boy's body, cursing himself for failing to act upon his instinct in sufficient time to save the troopers' lives. He had known that something had been amiss with Moylan's inexplicable orders, but he had done nothing to intercede. A wretched guilt swept over him, but as he looked at the boy's disfigured body and considered Murray's involvement in his demise, the guilt turned to anger, a simmering fury that would not be extinguished until justice was served upon those responsible.

Having confirmed that there were no survivors, Gresham's squad made their way to the second group of bodies, five men bundled together in a deliberately assembled pile, although one man lay slightly separate, his body decapitated. Gresham recognized the brawny stature of Ames, and the sight stoked his anger once more. He had been a good man who had been betrayed by his own command.

Gresham's impulse was to return the slain soldiers to the nearest military post, but it was impossible to conceive of a means of transporting their bodies. The horses and wagons from Moylan's escort had been captured and taken by the Sioux, and there was only sufficient space on Gresham's pack mules to carry two of the dead. Reluctantly surrendering to practicality, Gresham instructed his men to bury all of the troopers, with the exception of Moylan and Ames.

A detail was organized to dig graves, and sentries were set to maintain a vigilant watch, guarding against further attack. The troopers then set to their task with committed diligence, keen to provide their colleagues with a Christian burial despite the work being draining, with each man undertaking a shift at digging, including Gresham.

Personal possessions belonging to the deceased were removed and placed in one of the saddlebags, and in the process Gresham recovered a dispatch note folded into Moylan's jacket pocket, which itemized a consignment of Winchester rifles to be delivered to Denver. The idea of rifles being supplied from Virginia City made no sense, and he tucked the document into his pocket for safekeeping.

Having buried nineteen corpses and wrapped Ames's and Moylan's bodies in blankets, tying each securely onto a pack mule, the troopers turned toward Fort Reno with heavy hearts.

Chapter 36

Return to Fort Laramie

Upon reaching the resupply fort, Gresham sent the troop back to Platte Bridge under the command of Sergeant Jeffries, whilst he set out with single-minded purpose for Fort Laramie, trailing the pack animals with the two dead men behind him.

He paused only to water the horses and hurriedly eat enough food to sustain himself, turning over in his mind the events that had led to the massacre of Moylan and his troop, his conviction that the circumstances had been orchestrated becoming more resolute with every mile that passed.

Murray's insistence that Colter should travel with the wagon train of migrants he had chaperoned from St. Joseph remained an unexplained conundrum. Colter had no need for an escort. He knew Indian territory better than anyone and was more than capable of looking after himself. Murray had declined to explain Colter's motive, so one could only conclude that either he did not know and had been ordered to make the arrangement by others, or that he was complicit in the purpose.

There was also the mystery of Moylan's assignment to the escort from Virginia City, together with his unprecedented promotion to captain. The command had clearly been issued by Murray, since Sibley had been under no illusion that he was acting at the general's behest. Gresham was convinced that Murray was intimately involved in the decision, even though Moylan's orders had been communicated by one of the general's subordinates. He could only surmise that the latter was indicative of an attempt by Murray to distance himself from the specifics of the mission.

The more opaque factors centered around the involvement, if any, of the mysterious Mr. Stone, whose presence at Laramie had coincided with Moylan departing upon his assignment and Colter's disappearance. The fact that Stone appeared to have taken Colter's place on the prospectors' wagon seemed too coordinated to be coincidental. But Stone's intent had been ambiguous, and Gresham could fathom no reasonable explanation for his arrival and Colter's sudden departure.

The only tentative clue to the instigation of any of the circumstances surrounding Moylan and Colter's interaction appeared to be the initials *TW,* which had appeared on a telegraph sent to Colter by Murray. The operator had indicated that Colter was being directed to make contact with a lieutenant, presumably Moylan, and that TW had described the purpose as being of great importance. The fact that Murray had sent the telegraph to Colter suggested that he was aware of its intended consequence and that he was doing so at the direction of TW. Gresham had no idea to whom the initials might refer.

The consignment that Moylan had been sent to escort from Virginia City was a further enigma. Gresham had assumed it to be a cargo of gold, but the dispatch note from Elling State Bank described it as a shipment of weapons. Gresham could not imagine what conceivable explanation there might be for a bank issuing weapons to a military escort, and he concluded that the authenticity of the document seemed improbable. In which case the bank had either been duped into handling fake goods or it had been in collusion.

Irrespective of the underlying objective that connected all of the interrelated factors, Gresham was left with the abiding sense that the presence of Moylan and his troopers in the Powder

River Basin and their subsequent slaughter by the Sioux had not been accidental.

Exhausted and bedraggled, Gresham rode through the gates to the inner fort at Laramie nine days after leaving Fort Reno and careered across the parade ground firing a salvo of shots into the air as he drew up outside the administration building with his cargo of dead bodies, much to the consternation of those watching. Sibley and his orderly charged from their offices and burst onto the deck, alerted by the gunfire.

"They're all bloody dead!" Gresham growled at the startled colonel, dismounting from his sweaty horse.

"John! What in tarnation yo' doin' here?"

"Murray's killed them all, the bastard! Moylan, Ames, and the troopers." Gresham glared at Sibley aggressively, striding to meet the colonel.

"What in god's name yo' talkin' 'bout?" Sibley looked startled.

"The Sioux. They killed them all in the Powder Basin. We were too late. They were all dead." Gresham pointed at the bodies draped across the mules and hauled Sibley down the steps, untying and exposing Ames's and Moylan's corpses so that the colonel could inspect them.

Sibley gaped in disgust at the gruesome condition of the dead men and hustled Gresham away hurriedly, steering him toward the offices and barking instructions at a clerk to summon the fort surgeon to remove the bodies.

"Come and sit down, John. I don't take kindly to bein' shouted at, an' this sure ain't no conversation to be havin' out here," he admonished Gresham. "Now, ah suggest we git ou'sel' outta sight o' every goddamned man in this fort. Come on an' git inside!" He pointed toward the door and led Gresham down the corridor to his office, directing him to one of the chairs in front of his desk.

Gresham's shoulders dropped as he slumped into the seat, cradling a scalding cup of strong coffee, which Sibley's orderly delivered with consummate efficiency. Frowning with concern, the colonel sat on the edge of his desk and peered at the disheveled captain. "Yo' best gonna tell me wha' happened, John? Yo' look lahke shit."

Gresham took a long draw of his coffee and started to brief Sibley about the massacre of Moylan and his men. He reminded the Colonel of his deep concern about Murray's instructions to dispatch the young lieutenant to Virginia City and rehearsed the lack of sense in sending someone so inexperienced to undertake the task of running an escort through Indian territory.

He explained the conversation with Trautman that had led to his conclusion that Moylan might be transporting gold back to Fort Laramie, or beyond, and his concern for the boy's safety.

Sibley listened attentively and told Gresham about the telegraph he had received from Ames, which had been nondescript about the nature of the consignment, only confirming that the shipment had been dispatched from Elling State Bank.

Continuing, Gresham described his headlong dash to intercept Moylan and his squad and related the desperate scene he and his men had encountered near the Powder River crossing on the Bozeman Trail. Sibley listened with growing dismay, eventually pulling a bottle of brandy from the cabinet behind his desk and pouring two large glasses, concluding that a stiff drink was in order.

"No survivors, you say?" he enquired, as if requiring confirmation.

Gresham brooded over his brandy. "No. All dead." He paused to savor the heady aroma of the liquor and organize his thoughts, before reaching into his jacket and pulling out the dispatch note he had retrieved. "I found this in Moylan's jacket," he handed the document to Sibley. "It describes the consignment he was hauling as Winchester rifles. I think that's a fabrication. I'll lay odds it was gold. I think he was set up."

Sibley understood the assertion, but he was less convinced. "That's real dang'rous talk, John. You shouldn't oughta go throwin' around accusations lahke that 'bout Murray. He's got powerful friends, y'know."

"What do you mean?" Gresham looked quizzical.

"Think 'bout it. You don't git to be general in the United States army jus' by bein' a desk jockey. Murray ain't hardly seen no real action, and yit he's runnin' most o' th' U.S. army west o' Kansas. Someone's sure lookin' after that fella." Sibley wore a caustic expression.

"Maybe he's good at kissing ass?" Gresham scowled. "But what would he have to gain by sending a rookie into the most dangerous region of the plains, with a wagon load of gold?"

Sibley frowned as he thought about it. It would be a pretty callous act, but he could see the political impact of losing a big haul of gold and the fallout that might accrue from the ruthless murder of his men. He hardly dared think that the events could have been orchestrated.

"This'll make waves in Washin'ton. Be worse losses we' had in'a west, and 'pending on how much gold gone missin', could even make President Johnson sit up an' shit his sel'."

"Murray's not got the nerve to do something like that. He's got no backbone." Gresham was confused by the pointless waste of life. "I need to find out what's going on."

Sibley's head snapped up. "Don' stick yo' neck out, John. Yo' don' know what yo' dealing wi'." He was alarmed that Gresham would do something rash and felt the need to offer a little perspective. "Sides, might jus' give Grant the kick up the backside we need t' git enough men t' clear the Sioux offa the plains. Said yerself, ain't gonna be no half measures. Wipe 'em out or give 'em the land an' protect 'em, an' yo' kin be darned sure we ain't gonna do that!"

Gresham was not minded to start an argument with Sibley about Indian policy. Instead, he was focused on seeking answers to the ruthless sacrifice of Moylan and his troop. He jutted out his jaw in a manner that Sibley was beginning to recognize signified defiant stubbornness. "I'm not going to let this ride. These men were sent to their deaths and someone needs to be held to account for that," he murmured.

Sibley wagged his head in despair, but declined to comment. "I gotta git this on the wire t' Leavenworth. How's about we see wha' the general's gotta say afore yo' go an' do anythin' yo' might regret?"

The two men spent the next hour agreeing on the content of a telegraph to send to Kansas and formulating a formal report. When both tasks were complete, Sibley sent Gresham to Old Bedlam to get cleaned up and joined him for lunch while they awaited a reply to their communication.

But the response from Kansas proved frustratingly brief, offering little more than formal condolences, and Sibley was simply instructed to await further orders. The dismissive evasion of any meaningful comment was too much for Gresham, and he decided that he would have to go to Leavenworth to seek the truth for himself. One way or another, he would bring to account those responsible for Moylan and the troopers' deaths.

EPILOGUE

Washington, District of Columbia

News of the slaughter of Moylan and his troopers reached Winthrop through a circuitous route. Nevertheless, he was aware of the tragedy long before the President was briefed by General Grant, who compounded the grim report by informing Johnson that a little over four hundred thousand dollars in gold, destined for the new Federal Mint in Denver, had also been captured in the attack by Red Cloud.

The President was furious at the loss of both the men and their shipment, which occurred at a particularly unfortunate time, concurrent with him suffering a backlash from Congress about the proposed implementation of new Black Codes. These amendments to state statutes were being sponsored by reelected former leaders of the southern states in an effort to minimize the liberties afforded to freed men following the confederacy's defeat.

Being sympathetic to the proslavery movement in the South, Johnson was contemplating the incendiary decision of vetoing bills being hastily presented to Congress, which were designed to outlaw the Codes, and the last thing he wanted was the distraction of an emotive issue in the west.

Johnson harangued Grant for failing to effectively suppress the Indian Nations and dispatched him to implement whatever measures he deemed necessary to assert unequivocal control over the recalcitrant natives. He was instructed to divert resources to the task immediately. And, when Winthrop was summoned to the Executive Mansion, the President was still seething with frustration. He berated Winthrop for his policy failings, conveniently overlooking the senator's previous entreaties to solicit a more draconian line in the Administration's policy toward the plains tribes.

But Winthrop held his peace, savoring the success of his covert strategy as Johnson instructed him to work in concert with Grant to subdue the Indians. Grant was charged with prosecuting the military campaign, and the President transferred accountability for Indian policy on the Great Plains from the Secretary of the Interior's portfolio to Winthrop's personal supervision with immediate effect. Johnson required that he draw up a new policy framework, to be presented to Congress at the earliest opportunity, and was explicit that he had instructed Grant to provide the senator with every support necessary to achieve his policy goals.

Seizing the moment, Winthrop pointed out that Johnson had not responded to his proposals for the Northern Pacific Railroad's funding assistance and drove home the opportunity to secure the President's support, inferring that the financial obstacles for the railroad were compounded by the constant insurgency of natives in the northern plains.

The President was in no mood to entertain further infractions by the Indians, and he instructed Winthrop to wait while his assistant helped him draw up an Executive Order, clarifying the applicability of the Pacific Railroad Act to the circumstance of the Northern Pacific Railroad.

Once drafted, he advised Winthrop to place his recommendation before the Select Committee for Pacific Railroads and Telegraph, requesting that the requisite proportion of public land be allotted to the Northern Pacific. Johnson confirmed that he would give his support.

The pieces of Winthrop's strategy fell into place. Approval of land allocation for the Northern Pacific would open up the opportunity for effective financing, and progression of the railroad would serve the interest of his personal business enterprises, promoting colonization and trade across the continent. He was certain that Stevens would progressively become more malleable, keen to protect the secrecy of his duplicitous life with Mary-Anne Forrester, meaning that a little carefully applied pressure would almost certainly result in the award of construction contracts, the transfer of prime land, and discounted haulage.

The parcels of land that Winthrop expected to acquire at preferential rates would yield a good return and enable development of further retail enterprises across the west, allowing him to seize control of the major supply routes into all of the new frontier towns.

In addition, the railroad might present him with the solution to extracting his most audacious profit from the region: gold. Complicit with Henry Elling, he had succeeded in substituting Moylan's consignment of nuggets and flakes destined for the Federal Mint, and now the government assumed the vast fortune to have been lost to the Sioux.

But although the authority that Johnson had conferred upon Winthrop presented the opportunity for profitable trade, the real purpose it served was closer to his heart. It allowed relatively unfettered policy influence over the government's strategy for managing the plains tribes. He now held their future in his hands.

It was the moment Winthrop had worked to engineer for more years than he could remember, serving to exact revenge for an incident that had changed his life, an incident he continued to hold as a closely guarded secret, and the cloak of the federal goal of Manifest Destiny would ensure that no one ever discovered his true motivation.

The subterfuge that Winthrop had orchestrated in the Powder River Basin could not have been more successful, and he left the Executive Mansion elated, the sentiment causing him to reflect upon his attraction to Stevens's beguilingly beautiful mistress. He would ensure that he made her personal acquaintance.

ABOUT THE AUTHOR

Mike J. Sparrow lives in the Yorkshire Dales in England with his wife Adele, their peaceful solitude intermittently interrupted by the return from university of one of their three children. While renovating their seventeenth-century home, Mike pursued an eclectic career in business managing pubs, hotels, and restaurants, providing facilities support services to many departments of government including the police and armed forces, and leading a worldwide utilities construction business spanning Europe, the Far East, Australasia, and the United States.

A passion for sport and the outdoors has led him to participate, generally unsuccessfully, in rugby, motorcycle racing, and rock climbing. However, it was horse riding that led him and his family to Montana where they own a much-loved home at the head of Paradise Valley, a place in which Mike's interest in the culture and plight of Native Americans was kindled.

He gave up his globe-trotting job in 2013 so that he could concentrate on writing. Since that point he has spent much of his time researching the history of the American West and the American Indian tribes, with particular emphasis on the Lakota Sioux.

The employees of Five Star Publishing hope you have enjoyed this book.

Our Five Star novels explore little-known chapters from America's history, stories told from unique perspectives that will entertain a broad range of readers.

Other Five Star books are available at your local library, bookstore, all major book distributors, and directly from Five Star/Gale.

Connect with Five Star Publishing

Visit us on Facebook:
https://www.facebook.com/FiveStarCengage

Email:
FiveStar@cengage.com

For information about titles and placing orders:
(800) 223-1244
gale.orders@cengage.com

To share your comments, write to us:
Five Star Publishing
Attn: Publisher
10 Water St., Suite 310
Waterville, ME 04901

Index

A

B

C

G

H

I

J

M

N

O

P

R

S

T

U

V

W

Y

Z